Rosie Thomas was born and grew up in North Wales. She read English at Oxford and worked in publishing. Since the birth of her first child, she has written twelve novels including *Every Woman Knows a Secret*, *Other People's Marriages* and *Moon Island*. She lives with her literary agent husband and two children in North London. *Border Crossing* is her first work of non-fiction.

Border Crossing

On the Road from Peking to Paris

ROSIE THOMAS

Photographs by
Philip Bowen

WARNER BOOKS

A *Warner* Book

Published by Warner Books in 1999
First published in Great Britain by
Little, Brown and Company 1998

A CIP catalogue record for this book is
available from the British Library

ISBN 0 7515 2953 2

Typeset in New Baskerville by M Rules
Printed and bound in Great Britain by
Clays Ltd, St Ives plc

Warner Books
A Division of
Little, Brown and Company (UK)
Brettenham House
Lancaster Place
London WC2E 7EN

Many people helped us to prepare for the Peking to Paris. Foremost amongst them were Tony Barrett, Delroy 'Noddy' Burke and Geza Demeter, with the assistance of Junior and Fitz, at South Service, Stamford Bridge, London, and John Wheeler in Somerset. Without their expertise and ingenuity we could not have made it out of Beijing, let alone all the way to the Place de la Concorde.

We are also indebted to: Ianto Roberts, Mark Lucas, Mindy Lucas, Lennie Goodings, Philippa Harrison, Rosalie Macfarlane, Gail Rebuck, Simon Master, Susan Sandon, Ian Taylor, Helen Fraser, Araminta Whitley, Anthony Silverstone, Colin Bryce, Kit and Louise Chapman, Jim Livingstone, John Davis, Tony Wiggett, Nick and Jenny Evans, Graeme and Judith Robertson, Lindsay Thomas, Richard Sparks and Jenny Okun, Rik Gadsby at Virgin, Exodus Expeditions, Tony, Stephanie, Frances and Sophie Bowen, and Philippa Gimlette.

Various companies kindly provided equipment, and we recommend their products as well as valuing their support for a pair of untried rally drivers. Thanks are due to Ghost, Tim Turnbull at Aquaman UK, Derek Danks and Mandy at Britool, Stuart Galbraith at Champion Automotive Products, Colin McKinnon at Cirrus UK Ltd, Angela Clifford at Cotswold Camping and Debbie Urquhart at Timberland UK Ltd.

RT and PB, 1998

For Phil and Dan and JD, Melissa and Colin, Chris and Howard, Carolyn and David, David and Angela and Helen, Adam and Jonathan, David and Sheila, Murray and Amanda, Andrew, David and Keith, Thomas and Maria, Anton and Willemien, John and Mike, Phil, Greg and Mark and Rick, Trev and Jingers and all the other crews and officials in the 1997 Peking to Paris Motor Challenge, for their long-suffering families and friends, and for my own family in particular – Caradoc and Charlie and Flora.

Thank you all for the adventure of a lifetime.

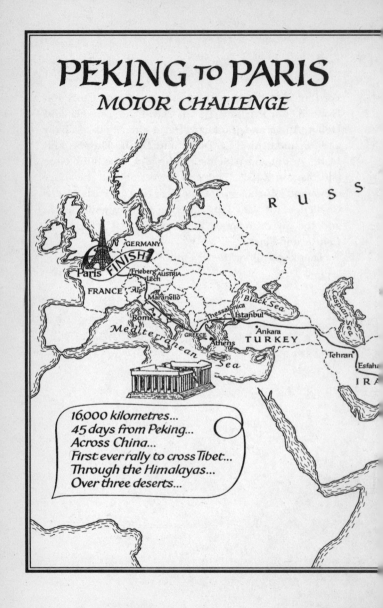

PEKING TO PARIS
MOTOR CHALLENGE

16,000 kilometres...
45 days from Peking...
Across China...
First ever rally to cross Tibet...
Through the Himalayas...
Over three deserts...

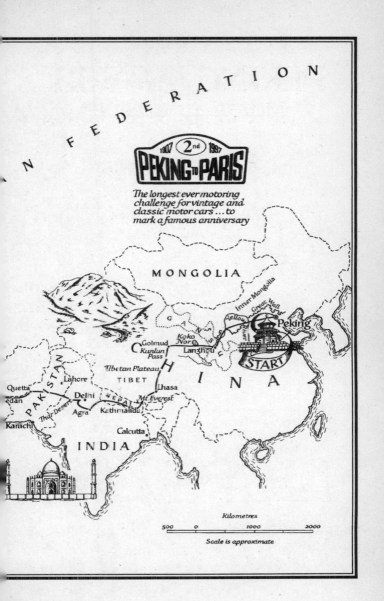

FEDERATION

AN

MONGOLIA

RUSSIAN

1907 **2nd** 1997

PEKING to PARIS

The longest ever motoring
challenge for vintage and
classic motor cars ... to
mark a famous anniversary

Inner Mongolia

Great Wall

Yellow

Peking

GANSU

Golmud
Koko
Nor
Kunlun
Pass
Lanzhou

START

CHINA

PAKISTAN

Tibetan Plateau

TIBET

Lhasa

Quetta

Lahore

Delhi

NEPAL

Mt Everest

edan

Thar Desert

Agra

Kathmandu

Karachi

Calcutta

INDIA

Kilometres

500   0   1000   2000

Scale is approximate

The Challenge

You know you want to. Just say yes. P.

The note was scribbled on a travel company's compliments slip, and it was paper-clipped to what looked like a holiday brochure.

It was 20 December 1996, the morning after my husband's fiftieth birthday. We had given a big party the night before in a favourite restaurant; there had been music and dancing and most of our friends, and much champagne had been drunk. Now the house was full of oversleeping people and piles of not yet unwrapped birthday presents and the squinty, tenderheaded aftermath of a big night. My sister Lindsay was sitting across the crumbed breakfast table watching me sifting the morning's heap of Christmas cards. I gazed at the note, and flipped through the brochure without being able to decipher what it was about.

Lindsay poured more tea. Tea is a big thing between us, it reminds us of our Welsh childhood and the distance we have put between us and it.

'What's that?'

'Um. Something about a car race. I don't know, have a look.'

She took the brochure, and the note.

'Who is this P?'

'The guide who led our group to Everest.'

'Oh, him. I see. And do you want to?'

I closed my eyes.

Later, clearer-headed, I read the brochure more carefully and gazed at one of the pictures in it.

It was a photograph of a man, shrouded in a dustcoat and a sola topi, crossing a desert landscape with a watering can in his hand. Ahead of him stood a motor car with the Italian flag hanging limp from a rod mounted to the spare wheel. It was a very old car indeed, just two grey metal boxes mounted on crude spoked wheels with the steering-wheel sprouting from the gap between the two matchboxes, a child's barely representational scribble of a car. There was another man in a sola topi in the driver's seat.

The picture dated from 1907. It was taken in the Gobi Desert and it showed Prince Scipio Borghese at the wheel of his Itala, with his mechanic and chauffeur bringing water from a well. Borghese was the eventual winner of the first – and so far only – Peking to Paris Motor Challenge.

The brochure I was now reading proposed a ninetieth anniversary commemoration of the Challenge, and offered a coloured sketch-map of the projected 1997 route. I looked at it for a long time, and then I checked the list of already-confirmed entrants and saw that the closing date for last-comers was the end of January, a little more than five weeks off. I swallowed very hard at the size of the entry fee, and then flicked back to the page with the drawing of a pagoda at one end of a red line and the Eiffel Tower at the other. The line forged across twelve countries, and bisected the Himalayas in front of Everest.

P – Phil Bowen – was right. I did want to.

Scrutineering and
Final Drivers' Briefing,
Brooklands, 8 June 1997

On quiet summer nights, the ghost drivers still race there.

The track is a ruin now, overgrown and desolate, but the people who live in the neat houses set beyond the Surrey birch trees claim that they can sometimes hear the distant roar of the phantom cars as they spin around the steep bank of the old circuit. Once or twice the police have been called out because of the noise. But when the panda cars pull up and the officers step out, the high curving walls of the race track are deserted and there is nothing to be heard except the wind in the trees.

To me, even on a late afternoon in midsummer with the sun still shining on the crimped purple petals of rhododendron flowers, even though the slabs of concrete were cracked and broken and weeds pushed up through the fissures, the sound of the racers was only just beyond hearing. Like a tinnitus buried deep inside my head, it was elusive and inescapable.

Our car looked very small, drawn up just where the concrete began to curve up from the horizontal, which was precisely as far as Alf, the guardian of the ruined track, had allowed Phil and me to drive it. It was a white Volvo, an Amazon, vintage 1968.

In a matter of weeks we would be driving it out of Beijing.

From my vantage point on a bridge spanning the track I could look down beyond the car, and the cat's cradle of shadows cast by the bridge girders, to where Phil was standing talking to Alf. The old man's neck craned forward and his grey head nodded; he was telling the Brooklands circuit stories. In my mind's eye the lean-lined cars were just as clearly visible as they flashed beside and beneath me. The drivers wore leather helmets and goggles and their faces were no more than pale crescent moons. More than a dozen of them were killed by their compulsion to loop the two-mile oval faster, and faster just one more time.

After the race-track was closed down and the war came, the site continued as an aircraft factory, for Hurricanes and Lancaster bombers and a runway was built so the finished planes could take off. One night during the Blitz the *Luftwaffe* scored a direct hit, and eighty-seven plane-makers were killed.

In the years that followed the factory became outmoded and aircraft production was moved elsewhere, and the site was turned into a motoring museum. The circuit itself was abandoned and left to crumble, cut off by the surrounding belt of trees from the populous web of suburban Surrey.

A couple of hundred yards away, on that June evening, the paddock of Brooklands Motor Museum was humming. The bar was busy and knots of people were still

gathered around the open bonnets of Bentleys and
Buicks. It was the day of the last briefing for competitors
in the Peking to Paris Motor Challenge. My co-driver Phil
Bowen and I were one of the ninety-eight teams who
would be taking part.

We thanked Alf and said goodbye. He stood aside to
watch us go, his back to the sun and his face dark under
the shadow of his raised hand.

'Wish us luck, ghosts,' I whispered.

'Help us go well,' Phil echoed, just as solemnly.

He might have laughed, but he didn't. I was pleased we
had shared this secret superstitious moment.

When we drove into the paddock that morning it felt like
the first day at a new school. Cars were rolling in – a big
silvery Bentley with sexy lines like a dolphin, another
Amazon, dark grey and more finished than ours, an old
Land Rover – all of them decorated with their red and
yellow Peking to Paris badges. More than half of the
entrants in the rally were attending. We would be driving
half-way around the world in their company, and this was
our first sight of these companions and competitors. I
must have been in a tiny minority – maybe I was actually
the only person who did so – but I looked at the people
first, the drivers and not their cars. All other eyes went
straight to the 1915 Vauxhall Prince Henry, the prepped-
up '64 Mk 1 Cortina, or the 1928 Bugatti.

I hadn't reckoned on this. It was the exotic route that
had attracted me and the challenge of the adventure
itself. The fact that it was a rally for old cars had been a
matter of insignificance.

I didn't know much even about modern cars and it hadn't occurred to me to ask myself whether I was a good driver, although I'd had a clean licence for 25 years. I packed the week's shopping into the boot of my own car without understanding or having any wish to understand what went on under the bonnet. I could park outside the kids' schools in a space a couple of inches longer than the car itself, that's all that mattered. What was the local garage for, otherwise?

Maybe if men and women adopted less of a Mars and Venus attitude to the design and function and semiotic importance of motor cars, a touch more equality and mutual respect in the matter might develop. Maybe pigs might also wing their way to Harvey Nichols in search of a witty little anorak decorated with classic car insignia. To most women a car bore ranks only a notch or two above a trainspotter with hayfever.

Accordingly I knew nothing and cared just about the same about the rare vintage and cherished classic models that were lining up in their polished glory all around me. An old car was an old car, even though it was whispered that one or two of these were worth half a million pounds. But in this company I suddenly understood that my indifference might be a disadvantage instead of proof positive of my acceptability as a human being. The very language spoken seemed to be some obscure sub-dialect of English.

– Torque down the head bolts . . .

– Need a seven-to-one compression ratio . . .

– Course, we've supplemented the stock system with 30-amp relays . . .

– Double-check the rocker-box gasket. Seen what
they've done to the Delage?

To distract myself, I took a walk around the paddock
and wondered which of all these new-to-school milling
strangers would turn out to be the equivalent of the class
bully, which the school hero or games captain, the brown-
nosing form monitor or the charming cheat destined to
grow up into a dazzling entrepreneur.

I found more than enough material to speculate upon
as I wandered between the avenues of chrome bumpers
and polished wings and sponsors' logos.

There was an English duke who looked exactly as a
duke ought to look. There was a plain madman in Rupert
Bear trousers and a pork-pie hat, several burly men whose
scarred and oil-grimed hands indicated their calling as
mechanics, women in serious earrings and *maquillage*, and
a pair of slightly younger women in matched Bermuda
shorts outfits who had already commanded the attention
of the motoring press and camera crews. The line of cars
queuing for the rally scrutineers already stretched out of
the gates.

I went back to find Phil, who had the car bonnet up
and was knowledgeably expounding on the engine modifications to a small circle of onlookers. Even Phil was
speaking the new mechano-English with acceptable flu-
ency.

'You can run on two head gaskets to help the compression ratio . . .'

I nudged him. 'Phil, look at the queue. Let's get in
line.'

He glanced back over his shoulder and raked a hand

through his hair. I'd seen this gesture before, in fact it was the first of his mannerisms that I'd noticed when we were introduced, eight months before, in a dingy hotel foyer in Kathmandu. He was vain about his hair. Even with oily hands.

'Nope. I think we should hang on a bit.'

If Phil had been my husband, I'd have argued the issue. But the whole point of our partnership in this enterprise, the fulcrum on which our mutual undertaking gently rocked, was the fact that we had no relationship outside it. We were both putting our disparate all into preparing for this bizarre rally, but we were polite to each other because we didn't know each other well enough to be otherwise. I swallowed my dissent.

Later, we went up to the museum's first-floor lecture room to sign for our entrants' documentation. The crew list gave us a start position of 82, well down the field, because of our Amazon's relative modernity, engine capacity and likely top speed. There was a high-pitched buzz of nervous conversation in the crowd, like the early stages of a cocktail party that might not quite gel, before the drink takes hold.

The driver of one of the other Amazons shouldered his way over to say hello. Daniel Orteu was preparing his own car, but he was buying his parts and spares from our ace mechanic and Amazon expert, Tony Barrett. Daniel had a pronounced dimple in his left cheek and a nice smile.

'What's your start number?' he asked.

'Eighty-two. What's yours?'

'Sixty-nine.' The dimple deepened. 'I think the girl in the rally office fancies me.'

The Rally Organiser emerged from the crush. His large frame and his lowering expression combined to give an impression of belligerence. I had met this man before, but he strode right past me and cordially shook Phil by the hand. Apparently non-car-buff women (is there such a thing as a car-buff woman?) were only visible in the shape of a well-rounded signature on a fat entrance-fee cheque. Phil raised his eyebrows at me. While he talked to RO I wandered away again. Two sides of the big lecture room were lined with wooden screens, and to the screens were pinned unfolded maps and photographs. I started at the left-hand corner and saw Beijing. From Beijing, wavering north-westwards and following the pink thread of a road, was a line of bright yellow highlighter. The line wavered across the first map and on right across the width of the next and the map after that, a defiant statement of geographical chutzpah that connected China to Paris via lakeside road and mountain pass and desert track. It ran under the Great Wall and over the Tibetan plateau. It slanted across the Himalayas and Iran and switchbacked across Europe from Turkey to Alsace. The route must have covered thirty or forty feet of map. Every inch was being closely scrutinised by drivers and navigators who peered over their bifocals and then scribbled on their own maps and in notebooks. They knelt on stiff knees to get closer to the accompanying photographs, which showed off-road sections heaped with football-sized boulders and river crossings in which water swirled up and around the car axles.

At least, I encouraged myself, just one of my battery of fears about the event was groundless. I had been anxious

that all the other crews would be young and fit and
thirtyish, like Phil, and Dan and his co-driver in the other
Amazon, and the matched pair of women. But it seemed
that a large proportion of them was actually even older
than me. There was a man in front of me who must have
been in his seventies, and there were several others who
could have lost a stone or two without suffering too much.
If following the thin yellow line turned out to be a
gruelling trip, I would probably not be the only one to
find it so. Behind me, a woman was audibly worrying
about the effects of altitude.

'Camping at 17,000 feet' she kept repeating. 'What
happens if you get altitude sickness?'

'Pour another vodka,' someone quipped.

Phil was now several feet into the maps, and instead of
marking or making notes he was videoing the route.

'I can transfer this to a VHS cassette for you, and you
can use your video recorder to look at the map markings
at home in your own time, instead –' he jerked his chin ' –
of doing it all in a rush now.'

'Good idea.'

'I've quietly filmed the underside of one or two of the
tastier-looking cars as well so Tony can have a look at what
reinforcing and waterproofing has been done to them.'

'Well done.'

While I had been wandering around staring at people
and wondering about the school sneak. Not for the first
time, I felt my complete lack of relevant practical skills.
The terms of our partnership agreement were that I
would put up the money for our entry and be the co-
driver, and Phil would be the crew leader, chief driver

and camp director, mechanic and medical aide and general all-round expert. He had some experience in the field. Before becoming a full-time Amazon mechanic and re-fitter he had earned his living as an adventure tour-leader in Nepal, Morocco and the Yemen, but he had also worked as a pearl-diver, charter-boat skipper and mountaineer. He was one of those cheerful and confident people who appear to be good at things because they always have been, so there has been no reason or opportunity for disabling self-doubt to bloom and grow.

On the other hand I am probably best at not being able to convince myself that I am particularly good at anything. I was aware that we made an ill-assorted couple, but for the sake of morale and crew solidarity I tried not to make too much of an issue of it. And it was true, I encouraged myself, that Phil had invited me to be his partner on this trip, not the other way round.

'We're a team, aren't we?' he would say cheerfully, as if that left nothing else in question.

When he had committed the entire route to film we went out again into the hazy June sunshine. It was warm in the sun but a chill wind whipped the national flags mounted on some of the cars. A French entry had 'marche ou crève' painted in a jaunty script on both front wings. The queue for the scrutineers had dwindled to a handful of cars. Phil was right, probably not for the last time. By the time we had inched the Amazon to pole position the officials were ready for a break, and much less eager to nitpick about our non-standard first-aid kit and as-yet missing fire extinguisher or anything else.

The RAC scrutineer looked briefly under the bonnet

and ticked at a list on a clipboard. A friendly film crew came by and interviewed me about our entry while the official business went on behind my back and I tried to listen in to the praise that Phil was getting for having pre-pared the car to a properly high standard for the thin yellow route ahead. We had only owned the Volvo since March, and since then Phil had worked almost full-time for Tony Barrett, under his tuition dismembering and rebuild-ing and servicing Amazons and other Volvos as they passed through the garage, as well as helping Tony's mechanics with a complete rebuild of our own rally car. He was in the process of turning himself from a novice into a compe-tent mechanic, and as the shipping deadline came closer he had been eating and almost sleeping beside the car as well as working on it. He referred to it as 'she' and talked about 'her' to the point where I wondered what went on in the garage underneath the arches by night, and whether or not his girlfriend minded about it.

The RAC man signed his form with a flourish and, unfairly, handed the little *Peking to Paris scrutineering – OK* sticker to me for the windscreen. The car was judged to be safe and roadworthy. Phil and I gave each other the double thumbs-up once his back was turned.

The next official visitor was the man from FIVA, the Fédération Internationale des Véhicules Anciens, an organisation I wouldn't have imagined needed to exist, let alone to wield the power that it evidently does. An old-car federation? Is there a clapped-out washing-machine owners' club or a Fucked Fridge Federation somewhere too, with eligibility rules and membership codes? An enthusiasts' magazine with tempting small-ads?

But I had learned that we couldn't take part in the rally at all without a FIVA Passport for our vehicle. The official checked out the bodywork and went over the engine and brake and exhaust systems, frowning in concentration and referring to the four-page questionnaire Phil and Tony had already filled in. I handed over three passport photographs of the car; full-face, plain background, no hat or false facial hair. There were no incongruous or out-of-period additions or adaptations to the Amazon for him to balk at, I knew that perfectly well, because although Tony had made enough rally pro-finish-or-die modifications to it he was too careful and too expert to have tried to get away with anything out of order. But still it was like waiting for sentence to be pronounced.

At last the man stood back.

'That will cost you thirty pounds. I can accept a cheque.'

For a confused second I wondered if this was a bribe, some kind of used-car-lot backhander that I was too naïve to know about, but this man was altogether too official and too gentlemanly to be in any way bent. He was asking me for the passport fee. We had passed. Hastily I handed over three tenners, and thanked the man from FIVA as if he had given me a present.

Phil winked. 'Nice one,' he said.

We went off for lunch in the museum cafeteria.

Brooklands Motor Museum is a fine example of one of those once real and now fully preserved Heritage Trail features of British history and culture, like the Cornish tin mines that have become Tin Mining Experiences and the focus of resigned family days out. At Brooklands there are neat thirties room sets and period paint colours, and old cars drawn up behind velvet ropes with wax-faced model drivers at the wheel all kitted out in leather helmets and driving goggles. The signwriting and chairs and tables and anaglypta in the cafeteria itself were all subduedly in period too, but the food was Standard Brit Basic. The cuke sat alone at one of the tables, behind the shield of his name badge, with only a morose-looking ham roll for company.

For the afternoon's briefing session we were back in the lecture theatre. The proceedings began with a slide show and the first image beamed up on the screen was one most of us had seen before, the watering-can-in-the-Gobi-Desert shot. The photograph had been taken by Luigi Barzini, a reporter from the *Corriere della Sera* who was also filing the story for the *Daily Telegraph* in London. He was the third crew member, with Borghese and Guizzardi the mechanic, of the Italian entry in the first Peking to Paris.

It was a heroic and absurdly risky journey, undertaken out of audacity simply because the French newspaper *Le Matin* had issued the challenge. The original proposal read: 'WILL ANYONE AGREE TO GO, THIS SUMMER, FROM PEKIN TO PARIS BY MOTOR-CAR?'

It was also a declaration that the age of the car had arrived. There were no maps for the first 5,000 miles, for much of the route there were barely any proper roads, but five drivers finally took up the newspaper's challenge. All but one of them reached Paris, but the clear winner after just sixty days on the road was Prince Borghese in the Itala, nearly three weeks ahead of his nearest competitor.

After the show the blinds went up and the audience blinked again at the map screens and their wavering yellow route. Superimposed on it now were mental images from the slide pictures of Lanzhou and Nagqu and Lhasa, Multan and Eşfahān and Tabrīz, places that we would pass through on the way to Istanbul and the gates of Europe. I thought of my childhood in the hills of Wales, when a trip to Liverpool meant a thrilling sortie through the booming artery of the Mersey tunnel and when 'abroad' was an abstract concept like trigonometry.

Back then, to see Paris was a dream of romantic impossibility; I was eighteen before I went abroad at all, and that was on a runaway trip to France with my first boyfriend. His parents were vehemently against our going anywhere alone together, and although my father was easier to deal with because he was unconcerned about what I did, the lack of support gnawed at me and made me unhappy and anxious. The adventure became an ordeal almost on the first day. Ianto was funny and diverting and quite glamorous back in Caerwys, Flintshire. Hitch-hiking around northern France, however, revealed him to be disorganised and dishevelled, as well as an irrational optimist. We had no plans and quickly ran out of money, and we ended up shoplifting food from supermarkets. I had no talent for it either, emerging with jars of apricot confiture or tinned anchovies stuffed up my jersey instead of the staples we needed.

I was glad to creep back home to Wales.

I didn't travel at all in my twenties, on any of those

druggy Marrakesh or overland to India sorties that were so popular at the end of the sixties, because I felt too poor, and not just financially. Travel was dangerous, and demanded a sense of inner strength and adjustment that I didn't possess. If I let go of my steady unglamorous job and my poky flat and set off, I might fall straight through the holes in the world and disappear altogether. There was no safety net to catch me, and so I clung to the rope of security without attempting any acrobatics.

Then, once I had met my husband, there were well-planned excursions together that turned into family holidays, and now my children were almost grown up and I was setting out on a competitive drive half-way around the world through places called Lanzhou and Quetta. I turned to glance sideways at Phil. He was sitting face-forward with his arms folded and one leg hitched over the other, apparently listening to the proceedings. A needle-prick of anxiety jabbed at me.

Who was this person, and why was I doing this or anything else in his company? I would soon turn fifty. I had a husband and two kids and a couple of novels still to write, and enough friends and some money and opportunities to do enough of the things I liked to make life interesting.

There was no real answer to either question, not yet anyway. No doubt I would find out as much and probably more than I wanted to about my travelling companion. And as for why undertake the journey at all – the closest approximation to an answer I could manage was that I just wanted to see if I could.

I held all the threads of my life in my own hands now, and if I wasn't going to travel while I was at the peak of my abilities and still had some physical capacity left, then I probably never would. Even this much was rationalising after the event. In the beginning Phil had asked me to be his partner – *just say yes* – and I had snatched at the chance of such an adventure without thinking about what it might really involve. And now I was in, for better or worse.

A small silver-haired man came to the microphone and introduced himself as Colin Francis, Clerk of the Course for the European leg. He had a soft voice with the buttery sound of the Welsh valleys in it, and he had that enviable knack of commanding attention without apparent effort.

He told us, 'This is a great motoring challenge you are embarking upon. But it is most definitely not a race. You are trying to achieve a clean sheet. That means zero penalty points. And it can be done.' He added, in a much lower voice that made us shift in our seats, 'in theory.'

'I would ask you to consider your objectives. A rally is not like a tennis match, but a game of darts. You are competing against yourselves, and the organisers, not each other. Your first task is to get to Paris. And the second is to do it with the minimum number of penalty points.

'The best way to do that is to *start* every day.'

Someone embarked on a laugh, but quickly decided against it and the sound died back into silence.

'Get your car to the start line on your start time every day. Even if you have to push it there. Don't oversleep, don't get your start time wrong, don't think you have five minutes to spare when you don't.

'And if you start every day, and keep going, you're on your way to a silver medal at least.'

At the back of the auditorium, Phil and I exchanged a look. We wanted one of those medals. But most of all I was grateful to Mr Francis for making the getting of it sound so simply and graspably just a matter of having a decent alarm clock.

The next arrival at the microphone was Rudolf Aghebagian, an Iranian ex-rally champion who was here to reassure us about driving the breadth of his country. He was a large, handsome man who looked as if he enjoyed life.

'Okay, everyone', he charmed us. 'You have no problems in Iran. You have no visa problems, you are all welcome into Iran, especially the Americans. Getting out again is maybe different.'

We all laughed obediently, *haha*. The women crew members were assured that we needed to make no major amendments to our dress. We were to cover up our arms and legs and wear a headscarf, that was all. Fears about driving to hell in a *chuddar* faded away.

After Mr Aghebagian came a succession of officials responsible for different aspects of the trip. Mike Leahy would be running the vehicle service units, Vauxhall Fronteras equipped with winch and tow-rope.

He advised that if we maintained 100 per cent concentration on the road ahead, we wouldn't be needing recovery assistance. 'Be aware of other vehicles, people waving, children at the roadside . . . when you are tired, stop for ten minutes . . . drink water, take salt tablets . . . and carry some small bribes.'

Piece of cake, I thought. No different and no more difficult than driving London to Cornwall in the traditional summer weekend sizzler tailback with a couple of whingey kids in the back, small bribes particularly.

'As for river crossings, if and when you get to a deep one, send the navigator to wade or swim across with one end of a ball of string tied around her waist. You can tie rope to the other end of the string, pull the rope over. Take off the fan belt and fix the tow-rope to drag the car across . . . Make sure your vehicle is fully waterproofed.'

Although crossing the Tamar never seemed as complicated as all that.

Mick O'Malley of Exodus, the adventure travel company who would provide camping and support facilities as far as Kathmandu, stood up to tell us about the advantages of dome tents and flexible alloy poles and using liberal quantities of anti-bacterial handwash. Mick was a dry and laconic-mannered Irishman who usually worked as a base manager in Kathmandu. Phil also worked for Exodus, as a Himalayan tour-leader, and he knew Mick of old, as well as Phil Colley, the Exodus speaker of Mandarin who would be our liaison man as far as Nepal. I thought this family connection might well come in quite handy on the road.

There were more instructions about shipping cars in containers from Felixstowe to Xingang, about insurance and medical precautions and last-minute mechanical preparations. At last we were sent streaming out into the paddock again and the flood diverged in two directions, back to the old cars or into the bar.

In the queue for a stiff drink I bumped up against the sexy-dolphin Bentley owner.

'Oh, yours is the lovely Bentley,' I inanely remarked.

The man looked at my badge, proclaiming me as Volvo.

'Yes,' he curtly agreed, and turned his back.

Phil mouthed one word. 'Wanker . . .'

We sat and had our drinks with Mick and Phil Colley and Dan and his co-driver JD, Jon Davies. Here was a nucleus of company already. Phil Colley said that he would be bringing his guitar, and I half-closed my eyes and imagined soft singing around a camp-fire under a powdery-starred sky, and maybe the scent of an exotic roll-up mingling with the camp cooking. It would be good, perhaps even better than good. Why had I doubted the sense of making such a trip?

As we drove back to London Phil and I were both quiet. I could still hear the faint tinnitus of long-gone racing cars, insistent in my head even though the engine roar of the Volvo was deafening enough. We needed sound and heat insulation, and better seats, and more waterproofing and wired exhaust joints; there was too much to do and the shipping date was less than six weeks off. Anxiety seeped back and darkened the smooth surface of pleasurable anticipation. But Phil leaned forward around the steering-wheel and patted the dusty black rexine of the dash.

'Good girl. You'll make it,' he encouraged the car.

Chapter One

Phil Bowen and I met on the road to Everest. When he sent me the challenge – *you know you want to* – I had only been back from Nepal for two months.

When I was a child, living amongst the purple-grey rounded hills that began the swell towards Snowdonia, Everest seemed both connected to me and also to be the furthest point away from where I was and what I was having to do.

There was a book about it in the glass-fronted bookcase that held the library of my village primary school. The book had a paper cover with the Union flag on it; probably it had been published after the Tenzing and Hillary conquest in 1953. I think I must have borrowed and read the book two or three times, and in the confusing and painful procession of those days, Everest came to represent a pinnacle of otherness that was both challenging and implacable, and therefore comforting. As time passed I used to think about it; not all that often, but in an occasional dreamy reverie peopled by ice-bearded and brave mountaineers. I conjured up the blinding sun on snow, and the terrible force of storms. When I grew up I kept the shape of it in the recesses of my imagination, the way the quintessential peak stood veiled in spindrift and half-masked by Lhotse and Nuptse. I read books about the various summit attempts, and kept a photograph cut from a colour supplement of the 1922 expedition led by General Bruce. It showed a group of men dressed in tweed jackets and scarves and plus fours, as if bound for a mildly rainy day out on a Scottish grouse-moor. One of them, Edward Norton, was the uncle of a friend of mine. I felt this tenuous connection as powerfully as a blood tie.

Then when I had babies and small children, Everest slipped out of my mind entirely. Reaching the end of each day was enough of a mountain to climb, and the peaks of emotional and physical involvement blocked out more distant views. It wasn't until the two of them were teenaged, and beginning the drift away into their own lives, that the landscape changed yet again. I had written eleven novels and was contemplating the twelfth. I had the uncomfortable feeling that I was sending my bucket down the well of inspiration and it was coming up half-empty, because everything I knew and understood I had already written about. I found myself confiding this to Mark Lucas, a good friend who is also my literary agent. I didn't want to start a new novel, not quite yet. A view of distant, inviting scenery had suddenly come back into sharp focus.

'So what *do* you want to do?' Mark asked me.

The words came straight out of my mouth as if somebody else was speaking them. 'Go to Everest.'

'Uh, what's stopping you?'

Immediately, I knew it was a done deal.

I booked myself on to a tour with Exodus. I chose a version of the Base Camp trek that went round in a loop via Gokyo Lakes and the Cho La pass instead of just there and back. I was warned that it was quite a tough trip.

It took about three months to arrange the details and to work up an attempt at a fitness regime. It seemed amusing if slightly unreal to go to an outdoor equipment shop and buy hiking boots, and a down-padded jacket that did nothing for the hipline, and a head torch and a penknife and numerous other accoutrements without which I had survived perfectly well until that moment.

An introduction was arranged for me to Rebecca Stephens, the first British woman to reach the top of Everest.

We met for lunch at the Chelsea Arts Club and I had to prop my chin up on my hand to stop my mouth gaping open with admiration. Rebecca had been there and stood on the top of the world, and there she was sitting across a table eating tuna salad as if the distinction counted for nothing. We talked about many things but the most crucial piece of advice she gave me was to get the best sleeping bag money could buy.

I did as I was told. The thing cost about the same as an Armani suit.

Departure day came, and in the check-in line for PIA at Heathrow I met my companions for the trip. There were three other women and a dozen men, all experienced trekkers and climbers, mostly much younger than me. The men had brutally short haircuts and looked as if they were taking a little holiday from abseiling down cliff-faces with the Marines. The women talked about their gym regimes, and previous experience of altitude. All the way out to Kathmandu I sat in a cloud of panicky foreboding. I wouldn't be able to keep up. I'd be an embarrassment and then an impediment, and there would be nothing for it but to do the decent thing and slip outside, murmuring about maybe being some time.

I first saw Phil Bowen when he appeared to give the pre-trek briefing in the Kathmandu hotel. His pale straw-blonde hair was cut in a long thick wedge that he kept raking back from his forehead as he talked. One of the women murmured beside me, *'At least he's got some hair.'* If the Marines' bristles were all lopped off and laid end to end they wouldn't have added up to an equivalent length, let alone blended to make such a glamorous gilded pallor.

After the briefing we all queued up with our individual questions and anxieties. I'd brought the wrong sort of jacket, a steamy waterproof one instead of breathable Gore-Tex. Phil prodded it.

'Don't worry. If it rains and you feel too much like boil-in-the-bag rice, you can wear mine.'

'Won't you need it yourself?'

'Nah.'

Obviously not because you're so hard, I thought uncharitably.

There was a very early morning flight up to the mountain airstrip at Lukla. The men all turned out for breakfast dressed in their mountain boots and combat pants and fleece jackets, with jingling crampons tied to their backpacks. One of them had an ice-axe as well. I wanted to sit down and put my head between my knees.

At the airport I felt even worse. The bleary departure area was packed with Japanese waiting to take sightseeing flights around Everest, but we were shepherded out on to the tarmac outside the building and waved towards a helicopter. I am a bad flier even with some avuncular Captain Tony Hetherington at the controls of a British Airways 747 bound for somewhere manageable like New York or Boston, and now I was going to have to step aboard this contraption. Asian Airlines' flight to Lukla was a decommissioned Russian Army machine, oil-slick grey in colour, with both side panels hanging open to reveal a greasy mess of machinery. Several unshaven men in cheap leather jackets were hanging around beside it, gazing into the cogwheels and muttering disconsolately in Russian. Inside the cabin were two rows of hard seats bolted to each side of the fuselage with the space between heaped high with camping equipment and our personal baggage, all of it anchored under netting. One of the leather jackets climbed in after us and handed around the in-flight catering and entertainment packages – a boiled sweet and two cottonwool balls. Two more leather jackets followed and casually yanked the door shut. These were not airport hustlers or blackmarket currency dealers – they were the *pilots*.

The engines started, more or less, after a couple of splutters. No emergency drill, no cosy reassurances about oxygen masks and removing high heels. We lifted and tilted, and the runway slanted abruptly away beneath us. Sharp little needles of draught lanced in through the holes in the fuselage. I rammed the cottonwool knobs into my ears and promised myself that if I could survive this, if I could just get my feet on the ground again without a dented grey metal coffin of ex-Russian army helicopter wrapped around me, I'd walk uphill until my legs dropped off and sing hymns of praise for the privilege. Far beneath us there were steep terraces of green and sepia farmland, and jagged snow-covered peaks ahead piercing the thin layers of cloud. I imagined how the rotors would stop, and how we would plummet downwards to torpedo into a ledge where stringy beans were effortfully growing.

An hour later, we landed at Lukla. An hour after that, having acquired a train of sherpas and porters and a dozen hair-skirted yaks, we were walking. I was duly grateful for the exoneration.

The path led beside the milk-white frothing water of the Dudh Khosi river, zigzagging over plank and rope bridges and climbing steadily. It was a two-day journey up to Namche Bazaar, the ancient Sherpa capital; at the close of the first day I spent my first-ever night under canvas and slept well and warmly swathed in the Rebecca Stephens bag. The pace of walking was bearable, almost easy. One or two people in the group had already succumbed to stomach bugs. Ang the sirdar led from the front and Phil accompanied the walking wounded at the back. At the after-dinner briefings around the mess-tent table he repeatedly warned us about the dangers of altitude beyond Namche. We must drink at least four litres of fluid every day, never any alcohol, and walk slowly and steadily, not in fast showy bursts. Any uncomfortable symptoms were to be reported to him immediately. Acute Mountain Sickness is quick to take hold, and it can kill.

I began to revise my initial unfavourable opinion of Phil. He had taken to wearing a little blue woollen beanie hat, and as his hair welded into greasy points he stopped making quite such an issue of it. He was unfailingly good-humoured and encouraging. He dealt comfortably with us and our blisters and feeble stomachs, although he wasn't exactly cloyingly sympathetic either. In the worst grip of the runs, one of the men stumbled on the edge of the brimming shit pit. He fell in, and came up mired to the elbows. There was no water anywhere. It was touch and go whether Phil would give himself an embolism laughing.

'Can you remember,' he gasped, 'how much you've *paid* to be doing this?'

Above Namche, on a crystal blue morning, we walked over a wide carpet of springy turf overlaid with gentians and turned a corner. There ahead of us, flanked by Lhotse and Nuptse and with its lower reaches modestly veiled in some translucent cloud, rose Everest. It was breathtaking and familiar at the same time, the peak like a composite of every photo image I had ever pored over, outlined sharp as a blade against the bare sky. Even the steady flow of boys' jokes that was the main refrain of the journey died away into silence. I found that my face was wet with tears.

After that, the climbing changed. It stopped being such an effort to put one foot in front of the other on the endless chest-burning ascents. Instead, I felt every step carrying me closer to a goal. My stride lengthened, and my lungs expanded as my waistline shrank. For days as we forged closer to Everest I felt invincible, and the men began to make jokes about bionic women.

But the truth was not that I had acquired some extra physical strength, nor that I was fitter than I had imagined . . . it was just that I had tapped a reservoir of self-confidence. As if the sight of Everest, at last within reach, had flipped the lid off an interior well and allowed me to drink from it. I had propelled myself here, and every fold and convolution of the territory offered a new and closer perspective. I wasn't afraid any more of not being able to make it: the shroud of fear and anxiety lifted and floated off my shoulders. Without it, I felt light and suffused with steady strength.

We passed by the string of iridescent turquoise lakes at Gokyo and scrambled over the snow and ice of the Cho La pass before dropping across the Khumbu Glacier.

The variation in the scale of the landscape was breathtaking. All around us rose a circle of saw-toothed 8,000-metre peaks, Lhotse and Nuptse, Everest and Cho Oyu and Ama Dhablam, pinnacles of silver and black against the melting sky, while at our feet in the crevices of the rocks grew tiny, perfect gardens of powdery gold and blood-red lichens. Overhead the jungle crows circled incessantly. Their call was like a low, mocking laugh – *ha ha, ha* ha – at our feeble efforts to integrate ourselves into this hostile world.

We came to the point, at a place called Lobuche at just under 5,000 metres altitude, where the various trails of the region merged and ran on up the glacier valley towards Base Camp. A brief wander around the immediate environs confirmed that Lobuche is aptly named as the capital of the Toilet Trail. We camped overnight, and the temperature dropped to –20 outside and –8 inside my tent. I had never experienced anything like that bone-penetrating Himalayan cold. To go to sleep I wore all the clothes I had brought with me, including a ski-hat, and I went down on my knees, as I had done every night of the trip, to thank Rebecca for my miraculous down sleeping bag. Signor Armani never enveloped any woman's body as luxuriously.

The day after Lobuche marked the outermost point of the trip and the objective was to climb Kalapathar, the highest point of the trek. This is a small peak, 5,545 metres high, overlooking Base Camp, the Khumbu Glacier and the Everest panorama.

We were woken at 4 a.m. by one of the porters thrusting a bowl of watery porridge through the tent-flap. Groggy with cold and lack of sleep, I promptly spilled mine into my sleeping bag. By 4.30 we were walking in the frosty, dead-black night. Dawn was a long way off. Most of the Marines were keyed up with competitive determination to be first and fastest, and they set off at a cracking pace behind Ang Sirdar. The halt and the sick were moving much more slowly, under Phil's direction. Within half an hour of crabwise progress along a steep and narrow track above a ravine, I found that I had fallen way behind the leaders, but was still a distance ahead of the hospital party. I stopped climbing to listen. There was no sound except the faint clatter of displaced pebbles rolling down into the blackness; even the jungle crows hadn't begun their day's mockery. No one was in sight or earshot. Then the trapezoid beam of my head torch suddenly shortened and thickened. It yellowed a swathe of rocks as I turned my head, before failing altogether. I was in darkness; the only glimmer of light was a lead-grey streak painted across the eastern horizon.

I took a single tentative step forward, thinking of the drop to my right. I knew that the path switchbacked ahead somewhere between boulders and chasms, but I wasn't sure now whether I had been following the right course before my torch failed. Sitting down on a rock to wait for the tail-enders to catch up therefore wasn't an option; I might sit there all day and never see anyone again.

I waited a minute and tried to decide what to do. It became clear that going on was the only choice. Slowly I began to climb again. After a while my eyes accommodated and I could just distinguish the greyish upwards turn of the path. It was very steep, seemingly much steeper than before, and I had to scramble up and over rocky obstacles. I was breathing rapidly in shallow gulps and as I moved forward in panicky surges I knew that my confidence had all blown away. I felt ill and exhausted as well as afraid. I was lost, and in the darkness I was going to blunder off this path and fall. I would break my leg, or worse, and therefore I wouldn't make it all the way to the top of Kalapathar. I would have *failed*.

The audible groan of despair and frustration had to have broken out of my own mouth – who else would be lurking amongst the rocks like a Chorus to my solitary tragedy? But still the sound of it shocked me. I had failed to estimate the extent of my grim determination to get as far as the trek went, and my buried desire to match whatever the fittest Marine might do. I was desperate to get up there. Suddenly I knew that I would *kill* to get to the top of this tourist peak that was conquered on a daily basis by bands of guffawing Aussies and children and little old ladies.

It was a moment of self-recognition like I had never known before.

I plodded onwards, thinking about it, and minute by minute the sky lightened. After another half-hour I saw, up another steep incline in the distance, the crampons tied on the backpack behind the bobbing head of the last of the Marines.

Two hours after leaving Lobuche we stumbled into Gorak Shep, the Graveyard of Crows, at the foot of Kalapathar. Beyond lay the glacial moraine and the trail to Base Camp. This was the last outpost of what passed for civilisation, in the shape of a tiny rough-stone tea house. Burned with a hot iron into the unpainted wood planks of the door were the words and figures *1. Kalapater 5,545m, 2. Everest B.C. 5,300m, 3. Goraksep 5,260m.* I sat down on a broken dry-stone wall to try to even out my ragged breathing. It was fully light now, and the snows of the peaks were washed shell-pink.

Phil was the last to arrive at the tea house enclosure, faithfully bringing up the rear of his straggling group. At the sight of him all my fears and anxieties torched into a blaze of anger. I leapt to my feet and sprang into his path, a tirade of accusations frothing out of my mouth. *This was intolerable. He was inadequate, negligent, criminal. We were ill-briefed and unprepared to undertake a hazardous journey in the dark. I might have died. Any of us might have died.*

He was lucky, luckier than he deserved as the embodiment of such
incompetence. Et cetera.

I have no idea where I got the breath from. Rage lent
me eloquence. The Marines gathered open-mouthed in a
silent semi-circle to listen.

Phil stood there and took it. At the end he said gently,
'I'm sorry you feel like that.'

Deflated, I flopped down on the wall again, trying hard
not to cry in front of everyone.

Five minutes later, he brought me a bowl of hot noodles and a Coke from the tea house. I remembered that I
hadn't eaten for twelve hours, and I was ravenous and
weak with the effort of legging it uphill over the boulders. I ate and drank, the best meal I have ever tasted.

'Go on, go for it,' he advised casually when it was time
to set off up Kalapathar in Ang's wake. It was still only
half-past seven in the morning. Phil had to stay behind
with the bravest member of the party whose chest infec-
tion finally threatened to defeat her. Her lips had turned
a frightening slate-blue.

From the peak's summit, the face of Everest seemed
close enough to reach out and touch. The ice-fall was a
terrible chaos of spilled grey ice-blocks, the South Col lay
like the palm of a cupped hand to the right of the
summit. Beneath my feet were the egg-box peaks of the
glacier and the miniature huddle of Base Camp. I stood
and gazed. It was bitterly cold, and the wind pasted my
hood across my face. Elation swelled and expanded to
the point of pain in my chest: I knew I had done something measurable. Different from writing a novel or two,
this could be quantified in metres of achievement. I was

up here, and even I would find it difficult somehow to convince myself later that I hadn't actually done it all. Even better than most of that, it was awesomely beautiful. A rainbow-shot veil of spindrift trailed from the peak, and the ice-fall glittered and dazzled with tiny points of light. None of the pictures I had seen and saved in my head did it the same justice as being there, and seeing that view for myself. For perhaps an hour I sheltered in an angle of rock and silently committed it to memory.

The return descent to Gorak Shep took less than an hour. On the way down Adrian, the biggest and noisiest and kindest of the Marines, led me to one side.

'You owe him an apology.'

Anger and fear had dissipated together. 'Yeah. All right. I know I do.'

Phil was sitting outside the tea house in the suddenly warm sunshine with his blue hat rolled down to shade his eyes. It was the middle of the day.

I said awkwardly, 'I'm sorry. I didn't mean any of that. I'm really sorry.'

For the first time, we took appraising stock of each other.

He stood up, grinning, and put his arm around me. We were so insulated by layers of Gore-Tex and down and Capilene, it was like being embraced by the Michelin man.

'Don't worry. It happens.'

A week later, Phil saw us to the airport at Kathmandu. His next group, bound for the base of Kanchenjunga, would arrive within twenty-four hours and the whole cycle would start over again. To me, longing as I was for the comforts of home and the solace of family this seemed an unendurable prospect. Yet Phil was, as usual, perfectly cheerful. He had got himself a pretty sharp new haircut in Thamel.

'Bye,' I said to him at the departure gate. I didn't imagine that we would see each other again. 'Thanks for everything. It was a great trip.' I meant it.

'Yeah, nice one.'

I was proud of what I had seen and done, but I was thoroughly relieved and happy to be home. There was work to be done on the novel in progress, and there was a half-pleasurable and half-guilt inducing sense that Caradoc and Charlie and Flora had missed me more than they were willing to admit.

Christmas was coming, and Caradoc's big birthday party.

Then Phil's note arrived. By the time I responded to his message, he had gone to lead a group on a four-wheel-drive tour of the Yemen. It was the middle of January before he came back and we could arrange to meet and discuss the idea. In the meantime my imagination had been nibbling and then gorging on the prospect. To drive across China, and into Tibet. To cross the Himalayas, via Base Camp on the Tibetan side, and wind down to Kathmandu via the hairpin bends we had overflown in the helicopter. To follow the Silk Route across Iran, and pass from Asia into Europe via the Bosphorus, before making our way to Paris via Greece and Italy and the Alpine passes of Austria . . . Sixteen thousand kilometres in all, with the challenge of a motor rally thrown in.

Good sense suggested that I should politely decline
the invitation. I didn't have the time or the money to
spare and I thought I had already used up the family
goodwill, and all the brownie points owing to me, on my
Everest trip. Very tentatively I mentioned the idea.

'You've only just come back,' Charlie pointed out,
accurately enough.

Caradoc thought about it. 'It sounds to me,' he said at
length, 'like an opportunity you can't possibly turn your
back on.'

Over-articulated gratitude sounds phony. I nodded, as
if I were still just considering the possibility. 'At least, I can
go and meet Phil and talk it over. That's not exactly com-
mitting myself to anything, is it?'

Phil telephoned me when he arrived back from the
Yemen. As we exchanged greetings I could hear him at
the other end nervously lighting a cigarette. It wasn't just
me who was unsure of what we might be about to embark
upon. We arranged to meet for dinner in a restaurant
near my house.

Phil wasn't used to driving in London, and got hopelessly lost on the way from Fulham. When he finally
erupted into the restaurant he was almost an hour late.
While I sat and waited I had veered from impatience
through anxiety to plain fury.

I pushed the table back and squared up to him. He was
looking very tidy and clean and apprehensive.

'Phil. You're asking me to drive half-way around the
world with you, and you can't even find your way to a Cal-
Ital restaurant in fucking *Hampstead*?'

Chapter Two

The winner of the original Peking to Paris *raid*, Prince Borghese's car, was the powerful but massively heavy 40-h.p. Itala. The other four cars that crossed the start line alongside it were tiny in comparison; a 15-h.p. Dutch Spyker, two 10-h.p. de Dion-Boutons from France, and a minute French Contal, a tricycle car. To drive such a distance without reliable maps, or even proper roads for much of the way, was a serious undertaking. There was no explicit thin yellow line in 1907. But to attempt the journey in the equivalent of a sewing-machine-powered Reliant Robin cobbled together from bits of Meccano was close to madness, and the Contal crew were to pay dearly for their audacity. From the outset, the contest was seen as a struggle between the big Italian car and the Spyker, lighter by 600 kg – one car that could go fast, the other that could go anywhere.

The prince was politely described by this third crew member, the *Corriere della Sera* journalist Luigi Barzini, as a great planner and strategist. Borghese was an Alpinist, a horse-breaker, a sportsman who loved obstacles because he loved victory. In preparation for the race he obtained and studied German and Russian military maps. He arranged with a Russian petrol company to have supplies of fuel deposited in advance in caches all the way across Siberia and Mongolia, and he applied to the Russo-Chinese bank for information about the tribesmen and living conditions he would encounter along the road. After he arrived in Peking, accompanied by his wife and her best friend, he reconnoitred the first three hundred miles of the route on horseback. They carried bamboo rods cut to the exact width of the Itala, and they measured every narrow point of the way to ensure that the car could pass.

Plainly Borghese was a serious-league control-freak. He was never a gambler like Pons, the Contal driver, or Godard, a charming con-artist who had talked and flattered his way behind the wheel of the Spyker. The prince always made sure he held all the cards, but his ace in the hole was Ettore Guizzardi, the devoted chauffeur and mechanic.

Tragedy had pitched Guizzardi into the Borghese household. Ten years before, a railway train had left the rails and crashed down an embankment near the prince's Roman villa. The engine driver was killed outright, and the stoker, a boy of only fifteen, was left unconscious. The prince and his staff carried the injured boy back to the villa where he was nursed. He made a good recovery, but the engine driver had been his father and by the time he was well again Ettore had lost his home and had nowhere else to go. Borghese suggested that the boy should stay on

as part of the household, and made him his chauffeur.
The boy showed a remarkable natural technical ability.
The prince sent him to train as a mechanic, and in time
he came back to take charge of all the machinery for
lighting and laundry and heating and pumping water in
the Borghese households. Ettore would relax by modify-
ing and designing and building improvements for the
prince's cars.

The journalist Barzini gave a vivid picture of his first
sight of Guizzardi.

The chauffeur was lying on his back under the Itala,
motionless, with his arms folded across his chest. He
might have been working, planning his next mechanical
adjustment, or he might even have fallen asleep. But he
was just resting and looking, letting his gaze wander from
one chunk of metal to the next, caressing the car's underbody with his eyes, like a lover admiring the curves of his
sleeping mistress.

Phil and I were clearly going to have divide these roles
between us. I am afraid of horses and suspicious of most
forms of sport, and *Alpinist* is a dated title for a member of
the week's-package-to-Méribel ski generation to aspire to,
but I thought I could handle the control-freak aspect
rather well. Developing a lovingly erotic relationship with
a camshaft would therefore, in fairness, have to be one of
Phil's responsibilities.

The first step, after we'd agreed our partnership over
the dinner in Hampstead, was to decide on which make
and model of car we wanted to enter, and then track
down, and buy, and begin preparation of a suitable

example. I learned from RO in my first nervous call to the Rally Office that most entrants were classic or historic car enthusiasts, and they were all months or even years into their meticulous 'prepping' for the big event. Phil and I were very late arrivals, and very green. We were painfully aware that we had a lot of catching up to do.

Ianto, my North Wales and France first love, was now living and working in New York – as a motor racing entrepreneur. His current project was to finance and develop a motor-racing circuit on Staten Island, with the World Trade Centre twin towers and Manhattan skyline as a backdrop. He was the only person I could think of who had any connection with cars and racing, so I telephoned and left a message on the answering machine in his Upper West Side apartment. An hour later I answered our front doorbell, and Ianto was grinning on the mat. He was in London unexpectedly, and had called by on the off-chance of finding us about to dish up dinner. I took this coincidence as a good omen.

Ianto was furiously jealous of my chance to do the rally, and also greatly encouraging. Knowing the right questions to ask he also rang the rally organisers, and took no shit from them.

'It's basically a jolly,' he said when he hung up. 'A spree, a party. Nothing like the Paris–Dakar, for example. It'll be tough enough, but you won't die.'

I felt rather put out.

'What do you mean, a jolly?' I now wanted it to be tough. A challenge. If I was going to blow the price of a small house on a mere holiday, I wouldn't choose to spend it sweating in some old car with Phil.

'I mean,' Ianto said kindly, 'that it's an adventure rally rather than a professional enthusiasts' event. It will attract some serious drivers, but it should also be within the capabilities of novices.' Like you and Phil, he refrained from adding, although he did say that he wouldn't give much for our chances in the Paris–Dakar.

It was Ianto who went out and bought copies of *Classic Car* magazine for me, and who drew up a list of possible makes for us to consider. I studied it glumly. Everyone I spoke to was suddenly an old-car expert, and everyone had a different meaningless suggestion to make. A Rover 3500? A Mark II Jag? A Mustang V8 or a Merc 220 or a Willys jeep?

The car magazines piled up. I had a stack of them on my bedside table where *Vogue* used to nestle, and the days were slipping by.

Phil was busy too. Through a friend of a friend he made contact with a man called Nick Szkiler who owned Grundy Mack, the biggest classic car dealership in the country. Nick faxed us another list of possible cars, and then we drove to Huddersfield to meet him.

It was 4 February, four days after the list of rally entrants officially closed. We had just made it. My entry fee had been banked, anyway, so I assumed we had been accepted. It was a thick, wet day, with dirty curtains of rain pasted across the M1. I was driving, and as I struggled to see through the walls of spray sent up by lorries Ianto's optimism seemed utterly misplaced. I wondered what it was really going to be like to rally-drive for 16,000 kilometres on poor roads, through extremes of heat and cold, without a fatal lapse of concentration, without making a dangerous mistake, without driving blind off some hairpin bend in the middle of nowhere and leaving my children without a mother.

That was always my worst fear, and it had been with me ever since Charlie was born. It was the black full stop at the end of every sentence of speculation. If I did *this*, and if something happened to me while I was doing it, then it would be the same for them as it had been for me.

My mother died very suddenly when I was ten. I don't remember many details about what our life was like before; it is more a fading memory of rightness, a matter of security and soft textures and good smells. Afterwards everything was wrong, mostly with me. Her loss was like being taken in the grip of an icy hand, an unpicking by destructive fingers of the person I was only just beginning to be.

Death wasn't a theory. I knew what it was like and how it could happen as fast as a light being extinguished, and if I couldn't bear the thought of my children's lives being overturned in the same way, why was I doing this trip, that was both dangerous and – unforgivably – unnecessary? I came back to the half-answer I had been giving myself all along, ever since Phil and I had first talked about the challenge. I was doing it because I wanted to see if I could, because if I didn't do it now I never would.

My knuckles turned white on the steering wheel and I was clenching my teeth so hard that my jaw ached.

In the passenger seat, Phil poured coffee from a flask, peeled oranges and leafed through car magazines. This was the longest time we had spent in each other's company since Nepal. He didn't talk too much, he was relaxed and cheerful and undemanding company, but I felt edgy and uncomfortable with him. Partly this was because of my separate but accumulating anxieties, but I was also thinking that there was an opacity about him. He was always the same, every time I saw or spoke to him, and it was making me suspicious. I wanted to see a chink, an exposure of some weakness that would acknowledge the crevasses of fear and guilt in me, but he hadn't given me even a glimpse of one yet. I was intrigued by how different we were to be exclusively involved in the same enterprise. Somehow we would have to weld ourselves into a team, and I was beginning to think that this might be as much of a challenge as crossing the Himalayas.

Grundy Mack and Nick Szkiler were a welcome lift to the spirits. The showroom was immaculate, a museum-like expanse of beautifully restored and gleaming classic cars. I fell in love at once with a sleek black Alvis TC21. I could just see us cruising the Mille Miglia route in it. In the workshop, men in white overalls were at work on more cars. Nick himself was a big, open-faced young man in a suit and tie. He took us into a conference room and gave us an hour of his time while we explained what we were doing and what we wanted.

Phil and I had agreed that our requirements from whatever car we chose were, in order of importance, strength, mechanical simplicity, easy availability of spares, power and comfort. Oh, and cost.

Noise and lack of comfort ruled out Land Rovers and jeeps. Jaguars were judged to be too unreliable. We couldn't afford a Mercedes or an Aston Martin.

Nick nodded, then went back to the list of possibilities.

Our requirements narrowed his field of choice to a 1950s
MG Magnette or a '60s Rover P6 and he happened to have
a suitable example of each in the showroom. We went to
take a look. I wanted the MG. It was two-tone green and
black, a feminine little car, suggesting leather luggage and
white heavy silk scarves. I though it looked very cool.

'What about a Volvo Amazon?' Phil persisted.

Nick shrugged. 'It would do the job. We specialise in
British cars, but we could find and prepare one for you, I
suppose.'

After the meeting Phil and I ate lunch in a pub. I felt
suddenly optimistic.

'I liked him, I thought he was really straight. What
about the MG?'

Phil was sceptical. 'He's a salesman.'

'We could buy a Volvo and get him to prep it for us. He
said he'd let you work alongside his mechanics, that
would be good, wouldn't it?'

Phil was non-committal. I guessed he didn't want to
spend weeks on end stranded in Huddersfield with only
the underside of a car for company. We drove back to
London with nothing decided.

I rang RO again, and aired Nick Szkiler's suggestions.
He roared with laughter at the idea of the MG and dis-
missed the Rover as too complicated, with tricky
suspension and no availability of spares overseas.

'I'd go for a Hillman Hunter,' he advised. 'Simple,
robust, still manufactured in Iran. You can buy spares all
across India. There's a chap at my local garage, might be
able to fix you up with one if you're quick.'

Flapping like a flag in the wind, I rang Phil with this

latest piece of intelligence.

'So he's got a Hillman he wants to sell,' Phil answered. 'Listen, I've contacted the Volvo Owners' Club. There are two Amazon specialists in London. We should go and see them.'

'I rather get the impression you want me to buy us a Volvo.'

'It's a joint decision, of course.' he responded smoothly.

I was starting to worry on a major scale. I couldn't sleep, and returning in a daze from the school run I ran into the back of a stationary car at a junction.

The radiator grille of my BMW was crumpled, the bonnet crunched up, a sorry mess that promised to eat up hundreds of pounds of my insurers' money. A momentary lapse of concentration at only 5 mph causes *this* much damage, a voice carped inside my head. What will it be like when you hit an oncoming juggernaut at sixty? The car I'd hit was undamaged, not even scratched. It was an ancient Volvo Amazon.

Two days later, on another wet morning when the streets were shiny with rain and patched with loose archipelagoes of dogshit, I went to meet Phil at a lock-up in Park Royal, west London. He was sitting in a tiny, austere and freezing cold office with a turbanned Sikh called Jeet Millchen.

Mr Millchen was a rally driver himself, as well as a Volvo mechanic. He had come eighth overall in the London–Mexico. The only decoration in his office was a colour photograph of him with the car, his turban exchanged for a race helmet.

We sat for a long time, cramped around his desk, discussing the rigorous standards to which he would prepare a rally car for us.

It wouldn't matter what the starting condition of the car might be, since it would be stripped right down to the shell and totally rebuilt. There would be a newly bored engine, a competition clutch, limited slip differential. These unintelligible phrases murmured around my ears like waves in a seashell, but Phil nodded alertly.

We would need a car that would not only stay the course – and Mr Millchen gave us to understand that in a car prepared by him this much went without saying – but one that would also be a pleasure to compete in.

This struck me as a very good point.

He himself, Mr Millchen said, had rallied his car all the way to Mexico City without having even to top up the water in the radiator.

Eventually we reached the bottom line. The cost would be a basic minimum of twenty thousand pounds, and it would be very easy to spend much more than that. This was very clearly a non-downwards negotiable figure. I tried, and Mr Millchen remained cordial but utterly steely. The job could not be done for less. What's more, Phil was welcome to come to the workshop now and again to watch the mechanics at work, but he would not be able to work hands-on under their supervision, as he was keen to do. We had both agreed that it was vital for him to learn everything possible about the car by doing it for himself. The time and the effort that this would take were going to be Phil's contribution to the enterprise, and he was very eager to make it.

'What did you think?' I asked as we mooched away again.

'Impressive. But I don't think I could work with him very easily,' Phil said.

The next morning, a twenty-page document spilled out of my fax machine. It was a complete specification from Mr Millchen, under ten separate headings like *Front suspension and gearbox; clutch and prop-shaft*, of the work that would be done on our putative Volvo. There wasn't a spelling error or a misplaced apostrophe in the entire document. I felt a strong yearning to put our fate in the hands of this perfectionist, but it was just too much money.

Another week went by. We were already half-way through February and we hadn't even found a car to support our entry, and Phil was leaving to lead a tour-group to the Yemen. We made another dismal trek to the outer reaches of London, this time to the railway arches under Stamford Brook tube station, where the other Amazon specialist had his garage.

Tony Barrett's arches were down at the far end of a narrow alleyway. I walked past various bodywork and welding operations, with their crews of speculative males in overalls and oily walls festooned with girlie calendars, towards the Volvo sign. As always in such places, it felt uncomfortable to run the gamut of the stares. When I came to the right arch there were several old Volvos in varying stages of dismantlement. There was also Phil, who had already met Tony, shrouded in his Gore-Tex jacket against the everlasting rain. Tony Barrett was standing in his tiny chaotic office cubicle, talking on the phone. This,

I later discovered, was his habitual position. He was a tall, gaunt greybeard, always dressed in a baggy grey jersey, and he had a glittering eye like the Ancient Mariner. Phone call finished, he came out and shook my hand. I was introduced to his two mechanics, Noddy and Geza, and given a tour of the shop. It couldn't have been more different from Jeet Millchen's obsessively spartan operation. It was a nether-world of part cars and car parts with not a square millimetre of empty space anywhere. Ranks of Volvo doors stood in line like buckled books on a shelf, rusted thickets of back axles grew against the walls, and there were glowering oily vats in which rocker arms and tappets blackly bathed. There were tools everywhere, and crusted tea mugs, and a thick, pervasive stench of oil and grease.

Standing exposed to the rain in the mouth of the arch, our voices regularly drowned out by the rumble of trains overhead, we began our negotiations.

Tony talked a lot. The gist of it was that he could certainly provide and prepare a competitive-level Amazon for us. He had wide rally preparation experience, and even as we spoke two cars prepared by him were running first and second in the Monte Carlo classic rally. I tried to concentrate as he breezed through the list of what he proposed to do. It sounded to be at least in the same league as Mr Millchen's specification.

'It's a beautiful car, great for the job, it'll go all the way. You'll finish in it, my love, no question of that,' he kept saying. His eyes glittered. Tony was clearly an Amazon enthusiast, in love with his cars. It was a good sign, the best, even though the man himself made the back of my neck prickle. I could pinpoint the realisation that we weren't going to be best friends at the moment when Phil asked him a question about storage space for spares and luggage.

'Well, ha ha, the lady will need somewhere to put her lipstick, won't she?'

It happened that Tony had a car, down in his garage in Somerset; an abandoned '68 Amazon that he had found in a barn on Exmoor and bought for restoration. He thought it would suit us very well. Its current crumbling condition didn't matter, because it would be entirely rebuilt. 1968 was the latest year acceptable to the rally organisers as a classic car. It all sounded very good.

After a lot more circumlocutory talk from Tony I asked the question.

How much?

He chafed his beard with a hooked forefinger, a gesture I was to come to know well.

'Er, ha ha, it's not so easy to put a figure on it, off the top of my head.'

'You must have an idea. We've had one estimate, we just need an approximate comparison.'

At last, he came out with a price. It wasn't as little as half the Millchen figure, which was what I had been hoping for but it was appreciably less than twenty grand. We told him that we'd think about it and get back to him, and we shook hands cordially all round.

Phil was off to the Yemen in the morning so we didn't have much time. I drove him to Euston in the Vauxhall Corsa courtesy car lent to me by the BMW garage while mine was having the extensive damage to its front end repaired. It was raining harder than ever and I couldn't find the demist or the rear windscreen wiper. Interior and external visibility dwindled to almost nil and I kept having to swerve and stamp on the brakes and then forgetting I wasn't driving an automatic and stalling in box junctions. It was as if I'd just passed my test, without having deserved the distinction. Phil's left foot pumped fruitlessly at the floor and I could see his fists were clenched. I kept up a flow of chat about Tony and Amazons to distract him.

'So, what do you think?'

'Um, I liked him. He really knows about Volvos.'

'Eats breathes and sleeps them.'

'I could work with him, I think. Easier than Millchen. And Noddy and Geza are good blokes.'

'Shall we go with Tony and the Amazon, then?'

'Yeah,' he said.

A decision at last.

We reached the passenger drop-off at Euston. For luck I gave Phil a chunk of turquoise that I had bought from a Tibetan street trader in Namche Bazaar. The Sherpas wear them around their necks, for protection in the mountains.

Phil seemed pleased to have it. Or maybe he was just glad to be getting out of the Corsa alive.

Things began to move. After some prompting, Tony sent me his typed specification. It was somewhat more gnomic than the Millchen version, with bald headings and bare lists of improvements and amendments as in *Transmission: rebuild gearbox/rebuild overdrive/rebuild prop-shaft/rebuild limited slip diff/new seals in back axle/replace axle bearings where necessary,/all new mountings/axle lugs strengthened/new clutch master cylinder/new slave cylinder/new clutch hydraulic hose/extended breather pipe on axle,* and so on, under a dozen more headings. In Phil's absence I was in charge, so I read the document with wrinkled forehead and pencilled in the margin whatever questions or comments seemed apposite. I was very conscious that I knew nothing, and my bewilderment expanded in direct proportion to my anxiety. I went back to see Tony again, and showed him my queries.

'Yes, my love,' he would chuckle. 'Of course the brake pressure lines will be re-routed inside the car body. For extra protection, you see. Now, if we're going to do all this we'd better get started, hadn't we? There isn't much time to spare.'

There was no argument about that, at least. I took a deep breath and wrote a cheque, less than Tony wanted and more than I had planned to hand over as a down-payment. As he tucked it swiftly into his back pocket the Ancient Mariner took on the job of building a car that would get us from Peking to Paris – a responsibility that had swelled in my mind to megalithic proportions. We shook hands on the deal.

Down in Somerset, the work got under way. The rusty shell of our as-yet unseen Amazon SRR 64F was nudged on to the ramp, and stripping back and rustproofing began. Weak points were welded, new front inner wings and panels were fitted. Tony reported regularly. The brave new shell of the car was resprayed in the original colour, pearl white. With wonderful illogicality, once I knew my fate was in Tony Barrett's hands I relaxed. I slept at night for a full eight hours, and I went back to work on my neglected novel. Months stretched ahead until August; we were in the prudent and clued-up company of entrants whose prepping was under way. I reported to RO which car we had picked.

'Not a bad choice. Although you'd have done better with the Hillman. They still make them in Iran, you know.'

Chapter Three

At the end of February I sent off another fat cheque, this time to CARS UK, the shipping company that would transport the car out to Xingang, China, in time for the start of the rally. The final date for delivery of the car to the docks was confirmed as 10 July. Now there was a real ship somewhere, with real container space booked and paid for, for a car I had never seen, let alone driven. Tony Barrett kept up a flow of telephone news, coupled with suggestions that I might let him have a couple of grand more, to be going on with. I understood, belatedly, that entering a car rally is in the same order of experience as having the builders in to do some small and perfectly defined piece of work. It always turns out to be twice as complicated as the original worst case scenario, and costs exactly half as much again as you have budgeted for, still on the basis that the original budget figure was the absolute limit of what you knew you could possibly afford.

I did some fresh worrying, this time entirely about money.

I still didn't have the fifty thousand pounds of my own to spare, which was what I now calculated our entry would cost, and even if I had done I would have been unwilling to spend it on this enterprise. I had to find a way to make the rally pay for itself or it would feel like a guilty indulgence.

I embarked on a search for sponsors. At the outset I was blithely convinced that of course Volvo themselves would want to back our entry – how could they not? Yet they declined very briskly, even to help us with spares, and so did everyone else I approached. A friend of a friend who worked in PR for Mobil Oil advised me to forget about finding backing from anyone in the motor or oil business. Applications from Peking to Paris competitors were arriving on everyone's desks at the rate of half a dozen a week, and Phil and I were novices in an unglamorous and untried car and so could hardly hope to be on anyone's list of preferred candidates. Her advice was to cast our net wider and try to make more adventurous connections. Accordingly I sent an information pack and begging letter out to everyone I could think of, from Parker Pens to Norwich Union to PizzaExpress, but without success.

In the end the near-solution came from much closer to home. I wrote a book proposal, a diary of what I thought the rally might be like, and Mark Lucas negotiated a deal with Little, Brown. The advance would just about cover my immediate outlay, and I would worry about the deficit only when there was no alternative.

At last, Phil came back from the Yemen.

'How was it?'

'It was shit. They were all Saga Holiday types.'

I suppressed the retort that this age group would include me before the end of the year.

'No one to talk to?'

'You know me. I'll talk to a dog if I have to.'

But I didn't know him, and this was feeling like more and more of a problem. Once or twice we had arranged to meet and he had either been late or blithely changed the plans at the last moment, and another time we had agreed to travel to Yorkshire in an Amazon borrowed from Tony Barrett, to the reunion of our Everest group. I thought this was a good idea because it would give us a chance to spend a few hours getting better acquainted, as well as do some practice driving. I booked myself a hotel room, not wanting to sleep on the floor in someone's house as Phil and the rest of the Marines planned to do, and made the necessary arrangements about being away from home over the weekend.

But then Phil decided, at the very last minute, that he wanted to stay in London to see Philippa, his girlfriend, who had been away for a while. Rationally, I understood that he was young, materially unattached, and therefore had the freedom to live his life on an hour-by-hour basis, whereas I was professionally busy and had family responsibilities, and had to plan my diary well in advance and stick to my plans as they were made. He had the opportunity for last-minute flexibility and I did not, and that was just one of the dozens of inevitable differences between us. But I still felt upset that he hadn't been more considerate, and the concern triggered a shock wave of anxiety about the rally itself. Before meeting any of them I convinced myself that most of the other competitors would turn out to be footloose thirty-year-olds too, and they would motor around the world in a carefree haze changing their minds twenty times a day and falling in love with each other, and I would feel ancient and out of place and lonely. What's more, I didn't care about old cars, and if I wanted to travel I had an affectionate husband and plenty of close friends in whose company to do it.

The old questions started up again. What was I doing, and why?

For a week, while I wrestled with the problem and the attendant fears, I avoided speaking to Phil. When he did reach me, he came right out with the question.

'You sound odd. What's wrong? Have I done something to upset you?'

This was disarming. I tried to explain my worries to him.

Again I could hear the scrape of him lighting a cigarette, an acknowledgement of the tension between us.

'So do you want to do the rally with someone else?'

I had thought about it. I'd come to the conclusion that Caradoc would hardly enjoy it; besides, I didn't believe it was the kind of challenge you could embark on with your partner. There was rather too much scope for marital discord. And if it wasn't to be Caradoc, I couldn't think of anyone else who had Phil's qualifications for the job. The thought of Ianto whisking up his trademark whirlpools of confusion all across China made me smile. Phil was practical, and resourceful, and I trusted him. At the bottom of myself I knew that he was the right partner for someone –

I just wanted to be more convinced that the someone was me.

'Do *you*?' I countered.

'I've been trying to think who else I could do it with. I can't come up with anyone.'

This seemed an important admission to make to each other, and given the level to which we were now committed it was bizarre that we hadn't done so before.

'Good. It's just that I find you rather inscrutable. Difficult to get to know any better,' I told him.

'I feel the same about you.'

This really surprised me.

We agreed that we'd better make more of an effort to see and to understand each other. The result was a rainy-evening walk across Hampstead Heath to eat pizza in a local restaurant. I asked him questions, and he told me about his father, and his mother and sisters, and a bit about his history. He didn't ask much in return, and I suppose this was again a reflection of the difference in our ages. Probably you don't ply your mother's generation with questions about their prehistoric love lives and druggy days back in the sixties. And maybe this gap between us and the potential to bridge it would turn out to be part of the adventure itself.

Inevitably we also discussed progress on the car.

Phil was eager to start work on it, but of course it was still down in Somerset. Tony had spoken to the rally office about seats, and distance-measuring devices, and some of the technical regulations. He had found an engine which he planned to rebore completely to take account of the 70-octane fuel we would have to run on across Asia. All

this was good. Phil agreed with me that Tony was
garrulous and difficult to pin down, but soothingly
insisted that this was for him to deal with.

'I'll look after everything to do with the car. That
includes Tony Barrett.'

'Thank you.'

We took the Tube back home from Hampstead, and
separated on cordial terms. Everything was going to be all
right.

The next assignment after the get-to-know-you pizza
dinner was to meet RO at a hotel in Paddington. Because
we had entered the list so late in the day we had missed all
the early briefings, and so RO had consented to fill us in
on background information. We were also to hand over
all the completed application forms for our Chinese visas,
and the details of the car: chassis number, all-up weight,
height, length and width, engine number and capacity,
which we had extracted from Tony with the ease of drawing unanaesthetised teeth. The Paddington arrangement
was the second attempt at a rendezvous: Phil and I drove
down all the way to Oxfordshire one Saturday morning, at
RO's suggestion, to see him at his office. Unfortunately he
forgot to come to his own meeting.

He did appear for tea and scones at the Great Western
Hotel. He turned out to be a weighty man with oddly
dense black hair and a face like a surly baby's. Phil was
supporting himself by supply-teaching at a tough school
in the East End and he arrived at the meeting looking
exhausted. It was the first time I had detected any sign of
physical vulnerability in him. He was wearing the Namche
turquoise on a thread around his neck.

RO wer t through Tony's specification.

'You're spending some money, aren't you?'

I told him about the book deal, and he pulled down the corners of his mouth dismissively.

'You'll have to sell a lot of books to earn that back.'

'We'll do our best.'

RO was evidently a man's man, like Tony Barrett. In my experience man's men don't like women who defend themselves Phil made a better impression, of course. He was always good at establishing easy, blokeish relationships. RO warmed up as he polished off the scones, and leaned across me to tell Phil indiscreet stories about some of the other entrants. There was a Land Rover enthusiast who was unhealthily obsessed with his vehicle, for instance.

'Probably sticks his dick up the exhaust every night,' RO muttered.

The duke was taking his butler as his co-driver, in a Ford Galaxy estate. On camping nights the butler would get the tent and the duke would lay out his silk sheets on a mattress in the back of the car.

I had a sudden image of all of us, disparate individuals in a hundred different cars, drawn up on a bleak plateau for the night. Trying to sleep under a cold moon. A premonition of the camaraderie touched my spine and made me shiver.

At the end of the meeting RO took our forms and details, and handed back the specification. He seemed, grudgingly, to approve of our efforts.

'You could end up in the medals,' he pronounced.

After he had lumbered away Phil and I clapped hands.

There was nothing more we could do now except hold on to our high spirits, chivvy Tony about the car, and continue our fruitless chase for sponsorship.

More time went by and more cheques were written. I worked at finishing the novel, and embarked on the promotion of that year's paperback. Down in Somerset the new engine was rebored. The roll cage was fitted inside the shell of the car and the thought of having this tough-sounding protection reassured me somewhat. I imagined the Amazon planing off some mountain bend and somersaulting through cracking saplings, our dummy-figures neatly unscathed within the branches of steel. I knew this was a cosy fantasy but I let it linger on in my mind. Eventually Phil went down to Somerset himself to work alongside John, Tony's other mechanic. He telephoned every day to give me updates about how much he was learning, sounding high on the excitement of acquiring new expertise. I tried to follow his explanations through the thickets of mechano-speak. We had new pistons, special shock absorbers and heavy-duty springs specially made in Sweden, a competition clutch. Tony said that he was building us a real contender's car, a car capable of winning. My personal antipathy to him dissolved a little. He was an enthusiast and he did love Amazons with a real passion, as Phil had understood from the beginning. It was precisely his tight focus on cars that caused his awareness of the rest of the world to be a little shaky.

One wet and windy Saturday morning in April Caradoc and I drove down to Somerset to be introduced to my car. The garage was housed in a big, red-brick building that had once been a woollen mill. Tony's part of the out-buildings was immediately identifiable by the phalanx of variously decaying Amazons drawn up outside, and by Tony himself who popped out a second later and beckoned us within, in full mad-eyed Ancient Mariner style. This second nether-world of cars and car entrails was even darker and oilier than the one under the arches at Stamford Brook. But in the middle of it all, enthroned on a ramp and looking surprisingly pristine, was our car. I had begun to be afraid that it would be as broken-down and moss-covered as some of the models outside. John came out from underneath it, ready to shake hands, proud of what he and Phil had been doing.

Caradoc and I stood on either side of it as the car was winched down to our level. It had been resprayed. The bodywork was flawless pearly white.

We opened the doors and looked inside. There was bare metal, a jungle of wiring, holes in the floor pan where the pedals would emerge. The engine lay on a bench to one side, covered by a cloth, like an organ awaiting transplant. Tony gave a commentary about what had been done and what was still to be attended to. It sounded like a lot in a very short time.

Then Phil and I slid inside and sat in our places. Without debating it, he took the driver's side and I got the navigator's.

We shifted in the old seats – the special rally ones had yet to be bought and fitted – and peered ahead through the windscreen. It was surprisingly small, and squared-off like a '50s TV screen. Even though I was in the passenger seat my feet pumped on empty air and my fist closed over the missing gear-lever. Without rear seats or any internal padding it felt as if we were sitting in a bare metal box, but this was a real vehicle at last. This glass rectangle would frame all kinds of views for us. I could imagine the thousands of miles that would roll away under the wheels.

Phil was giving his grin. I could see how pleased and excited he was. We exchanged a look, meaning 'We're going to *do* this. Good or bad, it's going to happen.'

It was a minute of pure elation. I clung eagerly to it.

Then, one afternoon in the middle of May, Tony called me at home. He said that he wanted the car in London now and he had arranged for it to come up on a truck, tomorrow. Noddy, his ace mechanic at Stamford Brook, was going to start in on the electrics, and Phil was going to work alongside him as an apprentice. It was only two months to the shipping date.

It happened that that week I was in the middle of doing roadshows with my publishers, meeting booksellers in Bristol, Birmingham and Nottingham. The paperback was about to be published and the sales push was gathering momentum. Even so, I wanted to see the Amazon again, immediately. I had begun to feel that it belonged to Phil, to Tony, even to Noddy and Geza – and was only connected to me as a source of financial anxiety. So the day after the car arrived I went to a morning meeting at the publishers and then, in my business suit, went on to the arches without warning anyone that I was coming.

In my high heels and with my briefcase in my hand I stalked past the other arches. At the far end of the alleyway I bumped into Tony. His face creased up with pleased surprise at the sight of me and he turned back to the brick mouth of the arch.

'Phil? Phil! Boss is here!'

Phil emerged in blue mechanic's overalls, his hair matted with oil, and mimed a kiss in the air so as not to smudge my incongruous silk crêpe.

'Hello.'

They were pleased I had come so soon after the car's arrival. They wanted me to admire what they had done, and to be happy with it, and this touched me. I was connected to the car, after all.

It was under the next-door arch. Its appearance had changed dramatically. Instead of just being a shiny shell it now looked like a rally car, beautiful and mean at the same time. They had raised the suspension to give improved ground-clearance and the car stood poised on tiptoe like a big animal waiting to pounce.

'It look like a scyared cyat,' Noddy grinned.

There was bold blue lettering on the rear wings, 'Peking to Paris 1997', and our two names with the Union flag on both doors. The Terratrip for calculating distances was angle-mounted on the dash in front of the navigator's seat, the four-point safety harnesses were fixed in place, and in the space where the rear seats had been was the big supplementary fuel tank. Under the bonnet everything was clean and shiny. Phil leaned over and touched the different components to show me what they were.

'Alternator, distributor, fuel filter.'

He told me that this morning he had been reconditioning our prop-shaft. He was enjoying the garage, and working with Noddy and Geza in the ambience of radio music and tannin-encrusted mugs and boob calendars. Tony had even offered to pay him some money, because he was making himself so useful.

We went around the corner to have a cup of tea together in the Turkish caff the boys used. We sat opposite each other in the floor-bolted seats, nursing the thick white mugs. Clearly there was something Phil wanted to talk to me about.

'I think I should work full-time in the garage,' he said. 'I'm learning about Amazons all day, stripping them down, solving problems. I want to be sure I know all there is to know before we go.'

I thought about all the problems he might indeed have to solve on his own, without the benefit of Noddy's patient expertise, beside the road somewhere in China or India. I admired his resolve.

'I agree with you.'

The problem was how he was going to support himself as a full-time mechanic without doing any supply teaching. Tony's contribution would go some way, not the full distance. I understood what he was asking me, and realised that he had swallowed his pride to do it, and that he was uncomfortable with this position. The ground shifted queasily as we regarded each other, apparently decked out as mechanic and madam in a city suit. Only this, of course, was a fluent misrepresentation of our real roles. From the moment when he had written his cheeky note, all the way through his insistence on a Volvo Amazon to his taking control of the mechanical preparations now, Phil had been subtly but insistently calling the shots. Ignorant about cars and adventuring I had tacitly agreed to wait and be told what to do, and where to sign, exactly as I was being told now.

It was important that Phil should learn everything possible about Amazons, and this was the route by which we would achieve it. I thought I was a powerful woman, but the lack of practical skills – even a proper understanding of what was involved – neatly reduced me to mere buying power. The realisation made me angry and, as it probably always did, the feeling showed in my face.

'How much do you need?'

He named a small sum, weekly.

'Okay,' I said stiffly. Even though I too wanted to do as much as could be done to ensure our success I felt, briefly, that I was being manipulated.

We returned immediately to one of our endless discussions of what still needed to be done, and when, and how.

Later that evening, when I was back home, Phil telephoned me.

'Are you all right? You looked so vulnerable when you left the arches, walking away on your own.'

'I'm not *vulnerable*.'

'Oh. Okay then, I'm sorry.'

The imbalance between us clearly bothered him, too.

Five days later, as I was walking back from the gym still in my workout clothes, someone shouted my name from the end of the road. I looked round and saw Phil, *in the car*, waving at me. I sprinted back down the pavement and climbed into the navigator's seat.

'Sorry. I'm really sweaty.'

'You know what? This'll flatter you. I was looking and thinking "Who's that? She looks really fit." And then it turned out to be *you*.'

'How amazing.'

'I've come to give you a test drive.'

'Move over, then.'

I took the wheel of the Amazon for the first time in the back streets of Kentish Town. The competition clutch was wickedly fierce, especially between first and second, and I stalled several times at junctions. The unassisted steering felt heavy. The steering wheel itself was the original. It was big and cumbersome, and at the same time spindly under my hands. There also seemed to be a worrying amount of travel in the clutch and brake pedals.

Phil said, 'You're doing really well. It's just that you're used to the automatic box in your BMW, and the power steering.'

I glanced sideways to check the degree of sincerity in his reassurances.

'It'll be fine. I just need to get used to driving it. I'd like to take it up to North Wales, to show my father.'

The idea had just come to me. It was a familiar road, but a sufficiently long distance for the real problems to emerge, if there were going to be any.

Phil inclined his head. 'Would you like me to come with you?'

'Thanks. But no, I'll go on my own.'

From the centre, where two straight roads intersect north-south and east-west, the village looked the same as I always remembered it. Caerwys was originally laid out as a

Roman encampment, a crossroads within a rough square of enclosing roads. The name itself is supposed to mean 'camp on the river Wys'.

The village lies in a cup of land between the Clwydian hills and the coast, under the hunched shoulder of a mountain, 'the Mountain' as we always called it, proprietarily. It's a small-scale, pretty, domestic landscape that lacks the fertile sweep of the Cheshire plain to the east or the grandeur of Snowdonia to the west. I was born there, and I lived in Caerwys until I left home at eighteen. Every contour of the hills and fields and stone walls is familiar, and so are the flat faces of the houses lining the village streets. They are plain, square houses with four windows and a door in the middle, like a child's sketch of a house. Some are stone-built, others are in the local harsh red Ruabon brick. Most of them have purply slate roofs crowned with chimneys like buckled top-hats, and even in June the milky air is residually scented with coal-smoke.

In the 1950s it was a small farming community more or less governed by the hierarchies of Chapel, Church, Women's Institute and parish council. Chester and Liverpool were distant, exotic cities, and an ambitious day's outing meant a trip to Rhyl or maybe Bettws-y-Coed. Nowadays there are plenty of commuters to Liverpool, and Manchester airport is less than an hour away by motorway, but when I was a child half of the houses didn't have indoor sanitation or even running water. The village pump stood against the wall of our house and one of my head's ingrained noises, which I can still recall with perfect clarity, is the clatter of the pump handle turning and then the rush of water into a galvanised bucket. The other is the *clink* of our front-door latch lifting and the swift following creak of the hinges. Nobody ever locked their doors in those days. People would knock and walk in, straight off the street.

'It's only me,' someone would say cosily, a body following a craning head into the room and bringing a knife-edge of cold air along with them. 'Is Pete in?'

Pete was, is, my father. He was an electrician, a gifted fixer and improviser, and the question was usually followed by a request for him to attend immediately to some failing milking machine or ancient smouldering one-bar electric fire, or even a long-case clock. Just as the cobbler's children go barefoot, so our childhood was a matter of coaxing the bare wires at the end of domestic appliance leads into the holes of a spluttering wall-socket. The missing plugs had all been appended to other people's electric irons and twin-tub washing machines.

The chafing of utter familiarity against the dislocation of long absence is experienced by every returning exile. As I drove the Amazon into Caerwys I was nine years old all over again, and also sharply conscious that in reality I would soon be fifty, that my own children were almost grown up, and that there was no stepping back into that Welsh childhood however well I knew the ochre outlines of the lichen patches on the roof opposite my old bedroom window.

Our old house stands almost in the middle of the village. It has walls four feet thick and was once the jail-house. There is a story that an underground passage links it with the court-house, two hundred yards away. My sister and brother and I loved this idea but we never found the

passage, for all the wet afternoons spent probing the
chinks in the downstairs floors with long sticks. The house
was heated with coal fires and in winter it was as cold as
Siberia any more than two feet from the brass fender. On
December and January mornings we used to wake up to
find the blooms of ice flowers inside our bedroom windows. My father and his second wife decided years ago that
the battle against the cold was too much for them and
moved to a modern bungalow at the top of the main street.

I drove up there now. The Amazon made a showy roar,
but there was no one to hear it or see it. At six o'clock on
a summer's evening the intersecting streets were deserted,
more or less as usual. I can still remember the ache, the
physical ache of childhood boredom, at the sight of those
dull streets with not even a dog stirring. No wonder I
dreamed of Everest.

My father appeared at the door as I edged the car up
the steepish slope to his up-and-over garage door. I forgot
the clutch and the Amazon promptly bucked and stalled
an inch away from his paintwork.

'Hello, darling,' he said. He was breathing hard, sucking air into his lungs with a visible effort after walking
the ten feet from his armchair.

I was more than happy to get out of the car. Even
though I had driven it flat out, notwithstanding Phil's
firm and reiterated advice to nurse it along, it had been a
four-hour journey from London. There was still no heat
or noise insulation inside the metal shell and the transmission tunnel radiated as much heat as one of Pete's
own mended one-bar fires. My head was ringing with the
amplified noise of the engine.

'Hello, Dad. How are you? You look well.'

I hugged him, trying to gauge whether he was thinner or frailer than the last time I had seen him, perhaps eighteen months before. He was already wandering around to the front of the car so I released the bonnet catch.

'What do you think?'

'Marvellous. Marvellous.'

We inspected the innards together. I listened to his wheezing chest as we bent over the engine. He was seventy-seven, approaching the age when physical infirmity is a proper concern between father and daughter, but my anxiety about him was oddly blunted. I had lived with it for too long and it had ingrown over the years, ossifying into a sad and muted resentment.

After my mother died I was always afraid that my father would die or disappear just as suddenly as she had done, but I could never tell him about my fears or ask for his reassurance. I didn't know how to begin, what shape to give the words. We didn't talk about things like that, ever. Probably no one spoke of them in Caerwys in the 1950s, and so I lived with long nights of staring into the bedroom darkness and counting my own breaths, looking for the wash of car headlights over the bedroom ceiling, waiting for him to come home from wherever he had been. Every late night I was sure that he was dead in a road accident, or murdered. I knew, in daylight at least, that my terrors were irrational and that only made them more fearsome because I couldn't explain them to myself. I thought I was mad and guilty and full of shameful secrets, and my instinct was to conceal this deviance at all costs. I tried hard to be normal, to *make* myself normal by an effort of will. I did this by pretending that nothing at all was wrong, which meant not saying much about anything to anyone in case something incriminating came spilling out.

In this way I learned not to reveal my feelings or to ask my father for anything, and by doing so I put distance and silence between us when we could have been a comfort to each other. And so I suppose, if such things are anyone's fault, the loss of love between us was mine. I must have been a very peculiar and unlovable adolescent, stiff-necked behind my careful defences. I suppose he learned not to take a very keen interest in my doings or achievements, such as they were, because I fended him off so insistently.

As I am discovering now with my own children, there is a watershed that they hurtle towards all the time that they are growing up, and then with a sudden rush they are flung over the weir into the confusion of separation, and then at last – with luck – they float on out into the calm waters as responsible adults. I suppose for most children this happens in the late teens. In my case it happened much earlier, perhaps when I was fourteen or fifteen. I knew from then on that I was in charge of my own destiny and I couldn't look to anyone else for help. My father had two other children, five and six years younger than me, and was about to acquire three stepchildren, so the diminishment of responsibility for the one older one must have been a relief.

Unfortunately, the conviction that I had to negotiate my own survival didn't make me an embryo entrepreneur or driven success machine. It just made me obsessively cautious. All through my teens and twenties I never took a single risk. Everest and everything it stood for was the exact opposite of what I craved, but in my heart I must still have hoarded the glory and the challenge of the mountain. In the meantime I clung to order and safety and routine – to the outward reassurance of domestic tidiness, clean clothes, punctuality, all as a way of regulating the threatening world. Even now, it's difficult to go to bed without polishing the kettle and emptying the bins.

As the years went by my father and I developed a formal, polite relationship more appropriate to distant acquaintances than blood relations.

With the new frankness of my generation and our let's-talk theories of human relationships I might have made it something different, I might have coaxed something different out of the pair of us, but I never did. The blood-blister of resentment thickened under my skin.

Even so I knew how much I loved him, and how inarticulately. Instead of saying anything now I showed him the steel-cased double fuel lines, running inside the car as a protection against rocks and rough roads. I pointed out the fuel tanks that would give us a daily range of more than 700 km, and the dual wiring system, and the steel underbody plates.

'Marvellous,' he repeated, his face alight with interest. He has a natural understanding of all mechanical devices, a rare affinity not inherited by one of his children. 'It's a marvellous thing you're doing.'

His pleasure in my car was a joy.

Edith his wife came out to find us, and peered in through the car windows at the bare metal.

'Did you really drive all the way up from London in this thing?'

'I'm going to drive half-way around the *world* in it.'

'Rather you than me, love.' She laughed.

Edith is merry and loyal and a good woman. My father is lucky to have her.

'Are you two ever going to come in?'

Pete closed the bonnet with obvious reluctance. We went into the house and the first of a chain of cups of tea were brewed and handed around. Through the picture-window lined with tiger begonias in polished pots, I surveyed the deserted street. In the far distance a lone child on a bicycle traced slow figures-of-eight, every movement eloquent with boredom.

'What's going on up here, then?'

They filled me in on the details of village events. Someone had put plastic-framed windows in an old stone house, someone else had fallen downstairs in an alcoholic stupor, babies had been born and an old school-friend of Pete's had died. It didn't sound very much for an interval of eighteen months, but everyone was familiar with what little news there was. Thank God for London and all big cities and traffic and restaurants, and the blessed gift of anonymity.

Later, at Pete's request, we went in the Amazon to visit some friends of his who lived half a dozen miles away. He drove us there, squeezing himself with difficulty into the space between the seat and the roll cage. Edith gamely hunched up beside the fuel tank in the rear, insisting that I'd better sit next to him to tell him what to do.

'I've been driving for more than sixty bloody years,' he

grumbled. 'Do you think I don't know what to do?'

I warned him what a pig the clutch was, but even so it took him by surprise. The car bucked and stalled, just as it did for me at the beginning. He sat hunched forward, his breathing worsening. His hands looked ribbed and old, gripping the wheel too tightly so the bifurcations in the knucklebones showed. I glanced round to see if Edith was concerned for him, but she was looking out of the window. And once we were under way Pete handled the car with ease, as just another familiar piece of machinery that would do as he directed.

The friends were politely interested in the car and the rally. We stayed for long enough to drink another cup of tea, then walked out into the soft twilight. I made to cross round to the passenger side again but Pete held the keys out to me.

'You do it,' he said abruptly.

We didn't discuss it any further, but even this oblique admission of his weariness made concern catch in my throat. I did care about him, more than I knew.

I stayed with them for two nights. Pete read the list of rally entrants I had brought for him with absorbed fascination, and we traced the route in the atlas.

'What a thing you're doing,' he kept repeating, without envy.

We drank more tea, and watched the uneventful street. On the second evening I drove them in their Ford to their favoured pub of the moment, and stuck to fizzy water so they could enjoy a few drinks together. Drink-driving is a big taboo in rural North Wales, although it wasn't always so. I remembered the roaring days when

Pete and Edith were younger than I am now, and the rivers of booze that flowed.

When it was time for me to go they came out and took photographs beside the Amazon.

'Have a good time. We'll be thinking of you with every turn of the wheels,' my father said. We embraced each other, briefly.

I wanted him to say, echoing and returning my unspoken childish plea, *don't crash, don't die, make sure you come home safely because I love you.*

He didn't, of course, but probably he thought it.

I drove the car back to Stamford Brook. There was a clunk in the transmission, most noticeable between first and second. Phil and Tony were waiting for me in the alleyway, had probably been standing there wringing their hands for the entire 48 hours of the car's absence.

'You made it,' Phil exulted.

'There's a clunk,' I said.

'Don't worry, love. Whatever you've done we'll sort it out,' Tony answered kindly.

June came and went. Phil worked all hours in the garage, and we met rarely. The car would be finished in time for shipping, but only just. The news of the other two British Amazons was relayed to us by Tony, who was supplying them with parts. Dan and JD were working hard on their car too, but had tight budget constraints. And the mechanic who was prepping the car for the matched pair of women, Jennifer Gillies and Francesca Sternberg, didn't seem to be ordering nearly enough heavy-duty spares. Tony said he thought he must be getting parts from some other source, although as he was the main UK Amazon supplier he couldn't imagine where it might be.

When I did see Phil, I thought he seemed tense. He reported that he didn't find it easy to work for Tony. I guessed that Phil was used to running tour groups and shouldering heavy amounts of responsibility, and wielding the authority that went with all of that. He didn't enjoy being treated as the garage gofer.

'Not much longer,' I consoled him. He was looking forward to taking a big group to Morocco in August, for Exodus.

One day we went up to the racecourse at Silverstone to learn some advanced driving techniques. We sat in the waiting area of the driving school amongst groups of nervily joshing young men waiting for their 'Silverstone experience', and watched the rain slanting across the windows. The Doppler effect of whizzing Formula 1 cars was just audible from the race-track.

Our instructor took Phil and me out to the shiny wet skid pan. The practice car had four fat rubber wheels on retractable legs mounted outside the regular wheels, making it look like a child's toy. Using a remote control device to lift one or more of the wheels, the instructor could simulate rear, front, or four-wheel skids, and teach us how to react to each of them. But a skid, he warned us ominously, was almost invariably the result of driver error. It was much better to drive well enough to avoid skidding in the first place.

Phil went first, and was pretty good. My turn came, and I wasn't. We spun merrily round and around which was amusing to begin with. At last, after the expenditure of much heavy instructor patience, I learned how to steer in a skid instead of just letting go of the wheel, and the importance of cadence braking. But privately I feared that if a real skid came I'd probably still panic, shut my eyes and slam my foot hard on the brake.

We moved on to emergency lane changing. The technique was to drive flat out towards a line of plastic cones until the instructor ordered a swerve, then to throw the wheel to propel the car into the next lane and to correct it sharply to continue more or less in a straight line.

My turn came. Cones flew.

Maybe I learned a little, but it was depressing to discover what a poor driver I was.

Another weekend we went back down to Somerset where a rallying friend of Tony's gave us an introduction to navigation techniques. Colin Bryce set us a series of routes to navigate at speed around the back lanes. Phil and I took it in turns to drive and map-read. I was better at this and it was much more enjoyable than being humiliated on the skid pan. The car climbed the hills and cornered like a dream.

These seemed pathetically small rehearsals against all the experienced rally enthusiasts we would meet in Beijing, but it was all we had time for.

At the last minute Tony and I fell out seriously about the provision of heat and sound insulation inside the car. He took the view that the car was the star and Phil and I would just have to get used to deafness and heat exhaustion. I insisted that the car could hardly star anywhere if no one remained in a fit state to drive it. Tony said there was nothing in the budget for insulation; he was already

seriously out of pocket on the car. I said I would pay extra.
It was not a cordial exchange.

In the end Noddy and Phil worked overnight to apply
the layers of insulating material to the bare metal. We
were glad of it later.

We assembled all our camping equipment, and the
mountain of spares. Phil compiled painstaking lists of
what was where, and locked everything into secure boxes
in the boot and rear compartments. He labelled the huge
bunches of keys with neat brown luggage labels.

On the morning of 10 July we drove our fully loaded
Amazon up to Suffolk, to the CARS UK holding point for
the docks. The only extra weight it would have to carry
out of Beijing was our personal luggage – a couple of kitbags, no more, Phil insisted. We studied the ground
clearance of the loaded car very carefully. It looked generous enough to let us sail over rocks and rough ground
and through rivers. There were front and rear steel plates
protecting the underbody from damage, and thorough
waterproofing. We assured each other that everything
that could be done had been done, and we kept our separate anxieties to ourselves.

The holding point was a barn and a farmyard. Over the
barn doors was a huge banner that read PEKING TO PARIS.
START.

Some of the other cars were being loaded, two to a
container. As we waited to wave off the Amazon, a bright
yellow 2CV with twin exhausts up the sides of the chassis
rolled into the yard. The friendly driver introduced himself as Maurizio Selci. We both thought he was a dead
ringer for Danny DeVito.

'You have rallied before?' Maurizio asked us.

We shook our heads and he grinned. 'You picked a big one to start with.'

Oh God, I thought. We are as mad as snakes to be doing this . . but luckily it's too late now to change any of it. I didn't want even to think about not going.

The Amazon was being loaded into a container with an immaculate Aston Martin DB5. We peered inside it and saw that the crew's kit was all packed in matching leather bags stamped 'Aston Martin Owners' Club'. There was that subtle scent of money in the air. Phil and I just hoped that the poor old Amazon didn't break loose in transit and damage their paint job.

Phil put the Namche turquoise in one of the side pockets. We patted the bonnet of the car, wished it a safe journey, and accepted the shipper's offer of a lift to the nearest railway station. With Maurizio, we took the train back to Liverpool Street. In a little under two months, we would be reunited in Beijing.

Chapter Four

Life should have been easy once the car was on its way to China, and for more than a month it was exactly that. In August Phil went to Morocco and we flew to Turkey for a wonderful family holiday.

I decided that I needed to gain some upper body strength in order to be able to drive such long and tiring distances without the benefit of power-assisted steering, and my trainer at the gym suggested I take up boxing. He introduced me to another gym member, John Davis, who had been a super-middleweight fighter. John was kindness itself. Twice a week we met to train: he taught me bag work and sparring, working on my punches and posture and footwork with as much attention as if I were a world champion in the making. My fitness improved dramatically, and John taught me boxers' skipping, the best calorie-burning exercise there is. I loved the discipline of trying to be a fighter. During a 2-minute round you forget everything – work, worries, the outside world. All you can think of is dodging, weaving, landing a punch, keeping your body together. On the rare occasions when John forgot *he* was only playing with me and almost let a punch of his own fly, I understood what speed really is. His right cross was faster than the flicker of a snake's tongue. I was proud of myself, and pleased with the strength and stamina I was building up.

The crisis began on a Saturday, two weeks exactly before I was due to fly out to Beijing. I came back from a week in the French Alps, where I had been writing an adventure sports story for *The Sunday Times*, to find a dozen or so messages on my answering machine. Most of them were from friends, of the 'good luck, for whenever it is you're finally off' variety, but one was from David Burlinson, the director of Exodus handling the China leg of the journey. He said that he needed to speak to me urgently about the Peking to Paris, and would I call him immediately at his office.

Which meant that I couldn't now get the news – and whatever it might be it was unlikely to be glad tidings – until Monday morning at the earliest. My immediate thought was that something terrible had happened to Phil in Morocco. He was in jail, or in hospital, or worse. Trying to decide what to do I sweated for an hour or so, and then rang Phil's mother in Dorset. We hadn't spoken before.

Mrs Bowen listened politely and then told me she had heard nothing from Exodus or directly from Phil, so the news couldn't be too serious, but would I call her if I did learn anything more? I apologised for stirring up her anxiety, but she answered calmly that with all the travelling and risk-taking Phil did, she had long ago stopped worrying about him. Except, she added, within some unacknowledged inner recess where mothers always worried no matter where their children might be or what they were doing. I agreed sombrely with that, and rang off. I managed to convince myself that Burlinson only wanted to discuss some administrative detail to do with insurance, or maybe an air ticket problem, and sat down to write about whitewater rafting.

First thing on Monday morning, I spoke to him. Oh yes, he said, it certainly was urgent. The Chinese were refusing to give me a visa.

I felt a cold stone of shock dropping into the puddle of my equanimity. Ripples of it raced through to my extremities as the implications added up. No visa, no Beijing. No Beijing, no start line, no contest, no rally at all. No money back either. After nine months preparation, all the work that Phil and I had done going for nothing, just because there was no little stamp in my passport. I thought I had considered all the possible pitfalls but even in the iciest of 4 a.m. sweats I hadn't reckoned on this one.

I was gasping and shouting into the phone.

'Why? Why not? Why me?'

Poor David Burlinson tried to explain. I had put 'author' on my visa application form. Along with a handful of other competitors and members of the film crew who had written 'photographer' or 'cameraman', I was regarded as potentially dangerous by the Chinese authorities. I might write something subversive about the People's Republic; I might already have written something in between spinning stories about women's lives. They would have to check out my professional record.

No, he didn't know how long it would take, or what the chances were.

'Do you realise,' I managed to utter, 'what a *hole* this leaves me in? Not to mention Phil Bowen?'

'I wouldn't like to be in your position,' Burlinson agreed, a little too smoothly.

I'm ashamed to recall that I slammed the phone down.

I cried for a minute, mostly out of anger and disbelief and frustration, and then picked up the phone again. I called Caradoc, who was as surprised and disbelieving as I was. How was it that neither the professional visa service handling my application, nor the rally office, had thought to mention to entrants that describing oneself as a writer might not be the best route into Beijing? RO and his chums had been out there, recceing the route and schmoozing the authorities. A visa service was a visa *service*. Didn't they know the form by now? 'Housewife' would have done fine. Company director, businesswoman, barmaid, anything.

But it was too late now. My name was on some list, somewhere in the great bureaucratic machine of China, as a putative political undesirable.

Together Caradoc and I reviewed the list of publishing bigwigs, friends of friends in the FO, fringe members of the great and good, and whoever else we might conceivably call on for help pleading my case. We divided the list between us and began calling. Simon Master, deputy chairman of Random House, and Helen Fraser, managing director of Penguin UK, my two fiction publishers, both faxed eloquent letters of support addressed to the Chinese Embassy within an hour of being asked.

Ian Taylor, international director of the Publishers Association, did the same. Each of them sensibly stressed that I wrote only commercial fiction for women, intended purely to entertain. I had never been a journalist, or a social or political commentator in any medium at any time. I was an entirely suitable person in every respect for admission into the People's Republic.

Armed with these documents, I called RO at the rally office.

Loftily he told me that he and Lord Montagu would be visiting the embassy on Wednesday afternoon to plead our case. We were all in the same boat, because the Chinese authorities were refusing to release any of the passports while there was still doubt about five individual members of the expedition. And all the Iranian visas still remained to be processed. I was on no account to do anything that might prejudice these important discussions, but I had his permission to telephone the office at the end of Wednesday afternoon to learn the result of the meeting.

I faxed my publishers' letters to him, so that he could present them in support of my case. It went against my every instinct to sit still and wait quietly with so much at stake, when I really wanted to fight my own corner with the visa section at the embassy and anyone else who might be remotely concerned, but I did it. I didn't sleep much, or eat a meal, and my preparations for departure day came to a complete halt, but I grimly waited. Ianto blew in unannounced from New York. He was in the middle of buying a motorbike design company; one evening he was CEO of the new team, the next night there had been some palace coup and he was demoted apparently to deputy teaboy. He thrived on all this; there were international calls at all hours on our line and my fax machine throbbed with his incoming messages. He had enough energy left over to want to involve himself in my troubles and offer advice, but I cut him short. He and Caradoc resorted to murmured conversations about tactics during which they shot speculative glances over their shoulders at the simmering subject. I did the ironing, cooked and washed up, and counted the hours until Wednesday.

Phil came back from Morocco at last. His handling of the crisis was impeccable. We discussed it endlessly on the telephone: we hadn't met for weeks, since before our separate summer trips abroad, and this made me feel cut off from him. But Phil was his usual even and optimistic self. If it had been he who was jeopardising our participation by some oversight or shortcoming, I would have shouted and blamed. Phil was philosophical. It was just one of those things, nobody's fault. He even apologised for suggesting the rally idea to me in the first place and so landing me in this mess. We talked about our Amazon, by now waiting in its container on the dock at Xingang for us to come and do what it had been made ready for.

'Do you want to ask someone else to drive with you, if I can't go?' I asked.

'Like who? No. It's you and me.'

If I did make it, I thought – if, if only – I would *definitely* have the right stuff for company.

Wednesday afternoon came. After counting the minutes to five o'clock I made the call to the rally office, with fingers like warm putty as I dialled the number.

But the answer was neither yes or no. RO's assistant

reported that Lord Montagu felt the meeting had gone well, and I could call RO himself on his mobile phone if I wanted the news direct.

I wanted the news direct. RO was on a train somewhere, and I had to shout to make myself heard. He told me that everyone's chances were in jeopardy, not just mine. He hadn't wanted to confuse matters by handing over my letters of support, and in any case why hadn't the letters made it clearer exactly what kind of writer I was? His tone was distinctly admonitory. The signal broke up and then collapsed altogether. I waited, but he didn't call me back.

Time crawled by until Friday morning, eight days before we were due to fly to Beijing. I should have been buying last-minute necessities and wondering how to fit everything I would need for seven weeks into one kitbag, but there seemed no point. I called the Rally Office to see if there was any more news.

'Yes, the floodgates are opening,' RO trumpeted. 'The Chinese have started to release the passports so we can get them over to the Iranian Embassy. Time is very short.'

It was indeed. Since we had submitted all our documents for the Iranian applications way back at the beginning of April, and forms for the other five visas to Visa World, the recommended professional visa service, in June, I wondered why it had become such a last minute panic.

'What about mine?' I dared to ask.

'Not yours. Yours and four others are still retained for checking by Beijing.'

'What does that mean? That they may not grant it?'

'Well, nobody's said you're not going.'

'Nobody has said I am, on the other hand.'

'That's true.'

Something snapped. I started shouting at him. I'd been making preparations for months, going to the *gym* every day, and running, and boxing, for God's sake. I'd dreamed about the rally every night. *No one* was going to keep me from the start line. I was going to get that visa whatever it cost. Maybe I should take a tent and camp on the pavement outside the Chinese Embassy until they granted it. I could ask the *Sun* along to take a picture. It was the silly season, after all.

'Romantic Rosie Going Nowhere' might fill a quarter page in the dog days at the end of August.

There was a stunned silence on the other end of the line. Then a disbelieving laugh, and some angry spluttering followed by a click. He'd hung up on me. I dialled again.

'I don't want to hear any more. That's it. Goodbye.' Click, again.

A few minutes later a fax slid out of the machine.

RO wished me to know that he was making no further attempts on my behalf to obtain a Chinese visa. He drew my attention to the official regulations – visas were the individual competitor's responsibility (oh yes? so why was I paying fees to Visa World, and why the patronising advice to sit still and shut up and leave the important negotiating to RO and Lord Montagu?). Furthermore, any competitor who put the event as a whole into disrepute or disrupted the organisation was liable to have his or her entry cancelled with no compensation. I was on final warning. And my arrogance, lack of appreciation and general ingratitude were offensive.

My breath was quite taken away. These people had only trousered a little more than thirty grand of my money in entry fees and other costs, and yet I wasn't entitled to ask questions that took up a couple of minutes of their time, or to have my panicky anxiety about not being able to take part in their rally allayed, or at least heard and understood. The fax wasn't an intemperate gesture fired off in the heat of the moment, either. Hard copy of it arrived by post the next morning, presumably in case I had been too obtuse to take the point the first time around.

The one bright spot was that I really was now responsible for achieving my own visa to enter the People's Republic of China. I telephoned the director of Visa World immediately. Mr Abrahams was everything RO had not been – he was available, lucid, and sympathetic. And at last here was someone who was ready to impart some information.

There had been a cock-up by the organisers. As experienced and well-regarded tour operators in China, Exodus Travel had been retained to make all the travel arrangements for the Chinese section. But unfortunately their experience was all in the tourist trade, not in the pre-organisation of major sporting events. They had neglected to send the visa applications for inspection and approval by the China States Sports Council, or to obtain separate authority from the Tibetan Government. Delays and confusions had multiplied, to the point that it was not until 18 August that all the passports were finally lodged at the Chinese Embassy for processing.

With these mistakes in mind and the pressure being placed on them, it was small wonder that the Chinese officials were making objections in individual cases.

I also learned that Iran visas had not yet been applied for. The rally organisers had retained an Iranian national in London to be their agent in these arrangements – but this individual had now disappeared, leaving no trace. I wondered if he was the same joky chap who had teased us at Brooklands about how it would be easy for us all to enter Iran.

Mr Abrahams told me that his company had now been asked to take on responsibility for all the Iranian visas as well. So he was withdrawing my as yet unauthorised passport from China and sending it to Iran while deliberations went on in Beijing. It was 22 August, bank holiday Friday. I was to keep my fingers crossed, with all the other entrants, that the Iranian procedures would go smoothly. He also kindly broke the rules and gave me the name and direct line number of the Head of Visa Services at the Chinese Embassy.

Mr Zhang answered his telephone at once. He was extremely courteous and took care to explain the exact situation. It was a matter of going by the book. Travellers declaring certain occupations – such as writer, journalist, photographer, et cetera – could not be granted routine visas over the counter in London. These applications had to be referred to Beijing for checking. This was not in his hands, did I understand? But he did not foresee that there would be any problem.

Of course I understood.

It was frustrating, in that Rosie Thomas novels are not

exactly ripe with political subversion, but perfectly clear and comprehensible. I would have to wait to be checked out and that was that. I mentioned the letters from senior British publishers that RO was to have presented on my behalf, and Mr Zhang sounded surprised. Of course, if I faxed them to him he would convey them to his superiors in Beijing. I did as he asked.

Bank holiday weekend came, with wind and rain, as August bank holidays traditionally do. Poor Mr Abrahams worked on processing Peking to Paris visas all the weekend, and took the trouble to ring me from his home on the Monday morning. The news sounded good. China would release the remaining visas on Tuesday or Wednesday, and in the meantime Iran had processed both mine and Phil's without any problems.

Tuesday came and went without any news, and on Wednesday afternoon I took Flora to Brent Cross to buy new school shoes and pencil case and ring binders: the traditional signal that summer is over. I had made up my mind that when I came back there would be a message from Mr Abrahams to say my visa was ready. I rushed to the answering machine but there was nothing, and when I rang him he could only tell me that the five passports were still being held at the embassy. His courier would call again in the morning, in the hope of being able to pick them up.

Despair. It now seemed certain to me that the authorities wouldn't refuse to grant the visas – they would simply go on delaying until it was too late for us to get to the start line. It was a bad night.

In the morning I waited by the telephone until Mr Abrahams rang. The news when it finally came was not good. His courier had called at the embassy yet again, but the five visas were not ready. The next morning, Friday, was the last possible chance.

'What can I do?' I groaned.

'You could try going down there yourself. They close at midday, could you make it?'

It was 11.30. 'I'm on my way.'

I drove down to Portland Place like a demon and slammed the car on to a yellow line. It was ten to, no time to search for a meter. The visa section room was a huge, high-ceilinged and slightly dingy place with two ticket-office windows at the far end, one for travel agents and groups and the other for individual travellers. Two long lines of weary-looking people threaded away from the counters.

I have the typical authority-stamped British reluctance to queue jump, but today there seemed to be no alternative. I pushed to the front of one of the lines, past disapproving frowns but no outright challenges.

'Mr Zhang, please can I see Mr Zhang? Just for a couple of minutes? He knows about me.'

The clerk blinked. I repeated myself, slowly, feeling sweat prickling under my arms. It was a humid day, with dispirited rain darkening the pavement outside.

The clerk slid off her stool and went behind a screen. Caradoc came up behind me. He had abandoned his office and leapt into a taxi to come and meet me. We were motioned to one side and told to wait. After a few minutes a door opened and a man's head popped round. He beckoned us into a side room, rather incongruously furnished with a moquette sofa and armchairs and a glass-topped coffee table laid with tourist brochures and a bowl of flowers. Mr Zhang was quite young, and humanly harassed-looking

He listened while I repeated my pleas. He took the two Rosie Thomas paperbacks I had brought, and bemusedly examined them.

'Shall I sign them for you?' I asked, idiotically going into author mode.

He asked me again exactly when I was due to fly, and shook his head sympathetically.

'Very urgent,' he agreed. 'This is small, small problem, you know. You go to China, you must behave well.'

'Mr Zhang,' I said solemnly, 'you have my word.'

His gaze moved to Caradoc.

'Your husband not going?'

'No. His work, you know. And our children.'

Thank goodness Caradoc had come with me. I was plainly an anxious and harmless wife and mother, not a subversive of any sort.

We all shook hands. I wrote down my home number for him and he promised to call me as soon as he had any news.

Whatever Mr Zhang might achieve, with only two days left it was becoming clear that I wasn't going to be on Saturday's flight. We went home again and I rang my travel agent to book myself on two later ones, including the following Thursday's – which would just about deliver me to the start line in time, with no margin for delays *en route*.

It was time to make serious alternative plans. Phil came up that afternoon and we sat down with Caradoc for a difficult meeting.

All the financial investment in the enterprise had been mine; Phil's input had been in time and expertise and so was less measurable in money terms. But if I was going to be unable to take part in the rally, I would have to think about trying to get some compensation – from my insurers or maybe the organisers (the latter seemed rather unlikely). Caradoc and I simply couldn't afford to tell Phil that it was okay, he could recruit a last-minute co-driver from the support team and take the trip as a present from us.

He considered this for a minute and then agreed. Without rancour. I found myself liking him more and more, and also trusting him.

There were other possibilities to discuss too. Maybe if the visa did belatedly come through I could take a later flight, and fly or get a car onwards to catch up with the rally somewhere across the breadth of China or Tibet. At the very worst I could fly to Kathmandu instead, and get myself to the Tibetan border to meet the cars as they crossed the Friendship Bridge into Nepal. We talked reasonably about each compromise while all the time there was a dismal hammering in my head and heart that told me if I couldn't do the entire route, and try to do it in the best time and the best way, then there wasn't really any point in doing it at all.

Maybe the visas would still come through by noon on Friday morning, which was close of business time in Beijing, the very last possible opportunity as the authorities believed I had a pre-booked and non-transferable air ticket for Saturday afternoon.

More waiting. I pushed aside the half-assembled pile of clothes and went to bed early, to try to sleep.

In the middle of the next endless morning, Caradoc called me from the office.

'Lennie Goodings just rang me from Little, Brown. Rosalie Macfarlane, their publicist, has had a brilliant idea. What about trying Ted Heath? The Chinese love him. I'm going to call Gail Rebuck at Random House to see if she can help.'

'Thank you,' I said.

A little later Gail telephoned me

'Any news?'

'Still waiting. The courier has gone back to the embassy. He's there now.'

'Look, Simon Master knows Ted Heath and he's going to give him a call and see if he can intervene with the Chinese for you.'

'Thank you,' I said again.

Minutes later, Mr Abrahams rang once more. No joy. That seemed conclusively to be that. The day was at an end in China, and now the weekend intervened. There was no chance of getting a result out of Beijing until Monday at the earliest.

Weeks before, imagining a calm and stately departure for the great adventure, I had booked myself a facial and some beauty treatments for that Friday afternoon. Now my thoughts fixed with irrational intensity on this interval of pampering. I knew I looked terrible, completely haggard and frown-faced. I wasn't going to cancel this treat, at least. I went down to the Harrods salon with my mobile phone.

I was lying in a towel on the couch, with hot wax coating my moustache, when the phone rang. Stiff-lipped as Prince Charles I answered it.

'Helleh?'

'This is Sir Edward Heath's private office at the House of Commons. Your visa is ready for collection from the Chinese Embassy.'

And there were two other messages in rapid succession. One from Gail, with the same news, and the other from Mr Zhang himself.

'Ah Ms Thomas, your passport here, no problem. Visa World collecting now.'

All five visas had been granted.

Owwwww. The wax was ripped off, with the usual eye-watering agony, but I was so happy and relieved I hardly noticed.

Maybe the delays had been unavoidable, and approval had indeed just come through from Beijing. Given the circumstances, the Chinese could hardly be blamed for the tight timing. Maybe they had been flexing their muscles in some way, and had always intended to hold out to the last second just to prove that they could. Or maybe a single word from on high had changed everything.

I still believe it was the latter. Thank you, Ted Heath.

I didn't relax until the passport was couriered around to me from Visa World. I yanked it open and there was the Chinese stamp. It didn't look much, after such a battle. Now we really were going. Phil took the view that we'd had our share of hassle. The rest of the trip would be plain sailing.

Chapter Five

After using up so much effort and energy in getting there, I shouldn't have been surprised to find that Beijing was an anti-climax.

It took precisely twenty minutes to clear customs and immigration. Bored officials in their glass cubicles waved me through without even a glance at the visa, let alone a body search or a trawl through my baggage for surveillance equipment and anti-Communist pamphlets. Phil had flown out three days earlier, and he was in the arrivals hall to meet me. He did a double-take at the sight of my luggage trolley. There were *two kitbags*, one medium-sized, one small. And a square box containing my laptop and papers.

'Sorry,' I stuttered. 'Um, couldn't fit everything into the one bag.' As it was, I had left behind two pairs of shoes I knew I couldn't manage without.

'No worries. Really. We'll find room for it all.'

We took a taxi into the city. Exactly 44 hours remained before the start of the rally. It would have to be a concentrated sightseeing programme.

With the gummy threads of jetlag beginning to drag at my facial muscles, I stared out at the view. There were all the bicycles, just like in the pictures. Millions of them flooded every intersection and billowed down the arterial roads like clouds of spiky insects. There were cars of course, dense, crawling columns of them, and bicycle rickshaws and ancient crowded buses and more modern diesel ones, and huge trucks, but the bicycle was definitely the king of the road. They had their own special lanes, while the rest of the traffic hooted at itself and crawled and belched wicked fumes into the grime-yellow air.

The buildings lining the way were mostly rectangular blocks in brutal concrete, although some of the newer ones were dressed up with awkward pediments and escarpments in a nod towards Hong Kong style. Others had pagoda roofs and pillars of twisted gilt and crimson, with scowling stone lions on guard in front of them. It was visual tedium minutely spiced with the exotic.

The Beijing Hotel stands just two minutes from Tiananmen Square. It was huge, with well over a thousand rooms, and until recently had been Government-owned and run. Apart from its size it was most reminiscent of one of those gamely modernised railway-terminus hotels in one of the larger British provincial towns – Edinburgh, maybe, or Leeds. There was the same line of blue-suited receptionists and bank of marble-lined lifts, the same smell of distant food. It was an odd sensation to have struggled so hard to be in China and to have travelled no further than the Trusthouse Forte Grand.

The blue-jacketed floor führer stationed in the

corridor outside our room handed over our key and Phil
hauled in my luggage as ostentatiously as if I was travelling
with three steamer trunks and a nest of leather hatboxes.
The room might have been anywhere in the world, but I
would have guessed at Birmingham: twin beds under
green candlewick, brown laminate cabinets setting them
chastely apart, thick net curtains, television and mini-bar.
His minimal belongings were spread on one bed, his
camera gear laid out on the low table.

We didn't look at each other, even to acknowledge that
we were disconcerted by this sudden proximity. The hotel
package we had all prepaid months ago provided a twin
room per crew, and the degree of intimacy or otherwise
between crew members was presumed to be their own
concern.

'I'll, er, leave you to freshen up,' Phil said, and went.

I lifted the net curtain and peered down at the crawling traffic five floors below. Forty-two hours until the start.

In the hotel foyer was a vast red banner, PEKING TO PARIS
1997. Also in the foyer, and milling in the lifts and restaurants and coffee shops, were rally crews. There seemed to
be hundreds of us, mostly wearing name badges and blue
rally polo shirts and busily carrying navigator's packs and
sheaves of maps. An early point of agreement between
Phil and me was that we weren't uniform or name-badge
people. Dan Orteu and JD from the other Amazon
weren't wearing any either when we met them later for a
fried noodle lunch. They had both had No. 2 bristle cuts
before coming out to China, and now looked even
younger than their real age, like a pair of Charlie's mates

or escapees from a Camden Town rave club. Nor did their
new friends Adam Hartley and Jon Turner have badges,
probably because they were charming and funny enough
to be once seen and always remembered. They were the
same age as Phil and JD and Dan. If it hadn't been for the
evidence of all the grey heads and paunches importantly
bustling past our table, my early fears about being twenty
years older and staider than all the other competitors
might have seemed to be coming true.

Adam and Jon, Phil told me, were driving Adam's 1929
4½ litre Bentley VdP le Mans. All the cars were in a secure
park at the Beijing Agricultural Museum, several miles
away. Phil had spent most of his time there, since collecting the Amazon from the docks. He knew a lot about the
different crews and vehicles, and kept pointing significant blue-shirts out to me.

'They're in the Buick. Oh, and they're in the 1934
Roller, sponsored by *The Financial Times*. The car's painted
the same pink. And there are two of the Iranians.'

'Yes?' Jetlag was fast overtaking me and I bit the inside
of my cheeks to stifle a yawn, worried that it might look as
if I was bored by the car talk. 'Shall we do some sightseeing this afternoon?' I thought I could manage the
Forbidden City before passing out.

Dan held up his hand vertically and then rotated the
flat palm through a narrow arc, a characteristic gesture
that he coupled with a dimple indent.

'Meetings,' he sighed.

Meetings was an understatement.

We spent the whole of the rest of the day assembling in
different airless places to have information handed out to

us. China went about its business beyond the hotel doors, unobserved by me. There were competitor bulletins to be read and sessions where all the uniformed red-shirted officials addressed us about their various responsibilities and invited our questions. By 9 p.m. I was falling off my chair. Through the haze of my longing for sleep the queries from the floor seemed to dip into surrealism.

'If it's freezing up on the Tibetan plateau, will the ground be too hard for us to hammer in our tent pegs?'

'Is the currency the same in Nepal as in China?'

'I have got. To go to. *Bed*,' I said to Phil, and crept away.

Up in our Birmingham bedroom I laid out my clothes for the next morning – another legacy of long ago. It always seemed too much of a risk to lie down before a new day without the suit of armour pressed and waiting. I veiled the underclothes modestly with top garments and lay down to sleep. Instantly I was wide awake. I lay for an hour staring at the ceiling until Phil tiptoed in.

'Still awake?'

'Mm.'

'Could you believe some of those questions?'

'Nn.'

He went into the bathroom to undress and perform the bedtime business. To hear a near-stranger instead of Caradoc cleaning his teeth and flushing the lavatory made me feel homesick. I glared even harder at the central light fitment. Phil came back and slid under the covers still wearing half his clothes.

'Night.'

'Night.'

In the darkness I had a short, silent and cathartic cry to the accompaniment of his even breathing. We had almost two months of this odd intimacy still to come, and I was missing everyone I had left behind.

Caradoc and I had been married for twenty-two years. We met in the lift of the publishing company where we both worked, when I was twenty-one. I was new to the company and didn't know anyone yet, and I had *War and Peace* at the top of my bag in which to immerse myself while I ate my sandwich. He glanced at the paperback and said, dismissively, 'You're reading *that*, are you?'

We went out to lunch together and we have been together, on and off, ever since.

It hasn't been a smooth progress for the entire route – how many relationships lasting that long can claim to have been? – and somewhere into the marriage we separated for almost a year. But we came back together in the end because we missed each other too much. Right from the beginning, we recognised and met a need in each other. Caradoc was given up for adoption as a baby of a year old, and was rejected by his adoptive parents when he was sixteen. After that he fended for himself, putting himself through Oxford and then hanging on to the thin security of jobs, more or less as I had done.

So almost as soon as we knew each other, Caradoc and I went about constructing the family we had both been deprived of. We didn't have an easy boy-meets-girl beginning, and ours was a partnership threateningly based on weakness, but in the end we made a strength out of it because we understood and allowed for each other's histories. And, as I lay awake in the Beijing-Birmingham bedroom listening to Phil's breathing and thinking about my husband, I believed that we had at last achieved the inevitable post-passion and also post-betrayal plateau of a durable marriage. Caradoc was now a highly successful literary agent, and I was a writer with my own reputation. Our worlds connected and gave us plenty to gossip about over dinner. We liked the same things – books, and long walks on Sundays. We considered it important to show our children that they came first, above everything else, and we were pleased to give them the emotional and material security that we had lacked. It sounded comfortable and it usually was, and I valued our life beyond measure, but maybe I was also in Beijing in order to test myself inside that comfort and to take a different perspective on the old angles of domesticity.

I probably wasn't the only competitor lying sleepless and missing home.

The first thought that came when I opened my eyes the next morning was '22 hours to the off'.

The car park at the Agricultural Museum was heavily guarded by armed police. We had to show our permits to be allowed in through the barred gates. The Volvo was parked somewhere in the middle, in a great serene phalanx of beautiful and exotic cars. I felt something like awe squeezing my throat as I walked slowly between them.

This was different to Brooklands, which had been a show-off display in an unreal setting. This was business, now. The cars all displayed their rally plates and their Chinese licence plates, and their bold black competition numbers on the door panels. They were loaded and ready to go: ropes were coiled between brackets, shovels were lashed to boot lids, headlamps and fog lights were either cross-taped or glittering with protective grilles. It made me think of Prince Borghese and the others, on the rainy morning ninety years ago, waiting for the wife of the First Secretary of the French legation to lower the flag and start them off on the absurd journey.

Nineteen hours.

The first real shiver of nervous anticipation crawled up my spine.

I looked at an exquisite bright scarlet Allard M-type coupé, and then at Prince Idris Shah's 1932 Ford Model B with its name, Humpty Dumpty, painted over the rear window. There was the Amazon belonging to the matched pair of women, Jennifer and Francesca, with their mechanic busily at work underneath it. There was the dark grey Dutch Amazon too, driven by Harm Haukes and Tonnie de Witt. Together with Bart Rietbergen and his co-driver in a 1965 PV544, Jennifer and Francesca had formed a team and named it Flying Volvos. They asked Dan and JD to join too, murmuring 'don't mention it to anyone else', but the boys had loyally decided to hang with Phil and me. In a massive burst of creativity we named ours Team Amazon.

Phil took a piece of string out of his pocket and we crept around the other three Amazons. Discreetly he used the string to measure the distance from the ground to the door sills. Even fully loaded as it was now, our car had the best clearance of the four. We sat on the dusty gravel, contemplating its underside as lovingly as Ettore Guizzardi himself.

'Can we do it?' I asked, thinking of all the way we had to go.

'Yeah. We're going to make it,' Phil answered, as he always did.

We ran a final check of the spares and our camping kit, and made some last rearrangements to even the weight distribution. Mick O'Malley gave us our competition numbers and I stuck the big black 8 and 2 on the doors. Phil was reluctant to leave but we had to go back to the Beijing Hotel to do our formal signing on as competitors. After that, I thought, it would definitely be time to see the sights.

The traffic was a steaming stationary mass. The afternoon was almost over before we were finished with the signing on, and the light was already fading from yellow to grey tinged with violet. The city looked less brash now, with the advertising posters that dominated every perspective losing some of their stridency and the night's neon signs not yet illuminated. We left the hotel and walked out together, choosing at random a street that ran at right angles from Dongchang'an. At once, a single block away from the main thoroughfare, we discovered a different Beijing from the noisy version that was galloping into consumer culture only a hundred metres away. Here there were dirty alleyways lined with bicycle repair shops, where dogs nosed in the street debris and old ladies sitting wide-legged on stools fanned themselves in open doorways. Round-faced babies smiled seraphically in the dirt.

As we lost ourselves in blind turnings between high walls we were greeted with stares of mild curiosity and then, when Phil did his energetic meet-the-people routine of smiling and shaking hands and calling 'Nihao', there were sudden beaming grins. More people edged out of shops and doorways to look at us, and little girls giggled behind their hands. The Chinese in the streets were friendly and interested. We couldn't exchange a word of conversation, let alone ask them what they thought of the world, but in that brief encounter there was none of the threat that goes with resentment.

'Tiananmen?' we asked, pivoting in a circle and shrugging to show that we were lost. Two bicyclists detached themselves from a laughing group and led us back to Dongchang'an. The square was an open space of sky away to our right.

The light was fading gently. When we reached Tiananmen we saw an awkward, flat plain fringed on three sides by blocky buildings that seemed too low for the scale of it. On the fourth side were the liver-red walls and pagoda-roofed gates of the Forbidden City. A huge, waxy-faced picture of Mao gazed impassively over the tide of tourists. Hundreds of Chinese families and couples jostled to take one another's pictures on the bridge beneath the unbending stare. Beyond, behind the walls, I could just see trees and gardens and a tantalising glimpse of the perspectives inside the City. But I knew without even suggesting it that there was now no time even for the quickest visit.

We turned back to the square and the crowds converging on the flagpole facing the portrait of Mao. A detachment of soldiers marched smartly up. Every dusk and dawn the Chinese flag is lowered and raised and the ceremony draws a great crowd of onlookers. They waited and watched with intense concentration, except for a knot of teenage girls at the fringe of the crowd who were easily distracted into blushes and giggles when Phil smiled and winked at them.

Flocks of birds on their way to roost whirled against the pearly sky, and two or three kites hovered in the windless heat. But according to the digital clock next to the flag-pole it was still some time to sunset. Phil was looking at his watch. He wanted to go back for one last communion with the car. I knew if he didn't make it, and if something went wrong in the next few days, it would be because this final check hadn't been completed. We made yet another journey by taxi through the clogged arteries of Beijing. The neon signs for Coca-Cola and cocktail bars were blinking on everywhere.

The car park at the Agricultural Museum was in dark-ness, and the police guards were reluctant to let us in. Once we had persuaded them, we worked for an hour by torchlight, tightening the last bolts and checking again that there were no leaks. It was eerie to be there in the ranks of silent cars, all of them hunkered down over their own history and waiting for the new episode that was about to be written. I drifted between them, touching the dust covers that shrouded the grandest ones, running my fingers over the chrome and tracing the drivers' names on the wings. A policeman came across and warningly shone his torch straight into my face.

As we left, at last, a truck was turning in through the gates with a car winched behind it. It was the Portuguese entry, a 1932 Ford Model B saloon that had blown a head gasket on the way in from the docks – the first major casualty of the event, although two or three other cars had also had to be towed into Beijing and one of the Aston Martins had suffered a small fire.

It was midnight before I closed my eyes in bed. My last thought of the day, like the first, was to count the handful of hours that were left.

The alarm call came at 4.30 a.m., and we were eating breakfast by five. The atmosphere in the barn-like breakfast room crackled with the static electricity of tension and excitement. It was noisy, because voices were slightly raised, and when I walked down the lines of place settings I could hear snatches of conversation, the same edgy, veiled competitive talk I had been hearing ever since I had arrived in Beijing.

The three Iranian crews were intimidatingly decked out in race overalls in team Peykan Hunter colours of blue and cream, and Paul Minassian and Paul Grogan from Marche ou Crève – the hot-looking and well fancied Peugeot 404 – were also in race overalls. For myself, in the overstuffed recesses of my kitbag I had found a pair of baggy black trousers and a sadly crumpled black T-shirt to wear. It was 6 September, the day of Princess Diana's funeral. We were a long way from home, and everything that was happening that day in London.

After breakfast there were buses to take us back to the Agricultural Museum car park for the last time. We packed into them with our luggage, and drove through the thick purple dawn. The city was very quiet, for once. There were small groups of people meditating under the trees in dusty parks, and solitary men doing t'ai-chi exercises, and gnat-like bicycles in ones and twos instead of great swarms.

By 6.30 a.m. the cars were rolling out of the park, in approximate number sequence. Lord Montagu headed the order in car number 1, the 1915 Vauxhall Prince Henry, with his long-suffering mechanic perched in the navigator's seat. There was a great noise of chugging and roaring as almost one hundred engines were fired and eagerly revved up. Our Amazon started first off and sounded sweet and even-tempered.

Phil and I had been given a nominal start time of 7.24, and even though we loaded and reloaded our hand-luggage twice over to even the weight distribution to Phil's complete satisfaction, we still had more than an hour to kill before our minute. I sat in the navigator's seat, pressing myself into the tight, black padded shell of it. The sides hugged my hips reassuringly, and we had a little Velcro-fixed inflatable cushion apiece to provide adjustable lower back support. We'd done what we could to make sure that we would be comfortable, despite Tony's lack of enthusiasm for the matter.

Sitting there, watching the vintage cars pulling away one by one at the start of their journey, I tried to imagine the road ahead, and failed altogether.

I couldn't think how Phil and I were going to cover such an immense distance in our Amazon, let alone how some of these ancient machines were going to do it. They were either desperately frail-looking, like David Arrigo's little red Allard, or seemingly as primitive as dinosaurs, like Etienne Veen's massive 1927 630K Mercedes from

Holland. Etienne and his English co-driver Robert Dean were wearing white leather motoring helmets and goggles. They gave us a gauntleted wave as they crossed the start line, car number 7.

I was sorry to see from the final start list that neither the duke, the butler nor the Ford Galaxy had made it to Beijing.

We drank coffee from our flask, and let the minutes tick by. Once the vintageants were away the classic cars began to roll. Looking down the line I could see our team-mates Dan and JD in number 69. Their Amazon was blue and white, hand-painted.

'Dulux Nightshade, in fact,' Dan had announced. 'Very attractive colour.'

The other Volvo team had had nice Flying Volvo team stickers made up for their cars, but Team Amazon somehow hadn't got around to it. We'd have to make up for it with team spirit.

Dan and JD crossed the line and disappeared beyond the crowd of spectators. The line of waiting cars steadily diminished.

The next but one ahead of us, number 80, was a chocolate-brown Mercedes 250 convertible, driven by Thomas and Maria Noor under the French and German flags. Beautiful Maria was also wearing overalls, but hers were black and figure-hugging. I saw Phil looking with interest at the gilt zips on her back pockets. Immediately in front of us was an immaculate silver-grey British DB6, driven by John Goldsmith and Murdoch Laing, and directly behind us came a red and white 1800 Austin Maxi, always referred to by Phil as 'the land crab'. (When I asked him why he said that it was because it *looked* like a crab, of course. Of course. Except that to me it just looked like a red and white car). The crew were David Wilks and Andrew Bedingham. These people would be our neighbours and companions in the dawn starts, every morning for the next forty-five days.

The Aston Martin nosed forward. And then it was our turn.

The start line was a blur of faces. The marshal at the control desk handed me a yellow spiral-bound book of time cards entitled Road Book 1, Peking–Kathmandu. The timing of the start was awry because the police were making demands that the organisers hadn't anticipated, so I didn't even notice what the minute of our departure actually was when the great moment finally arrived. The first time-control stamp was thumped unceremoniously in its place on the first time card in our road book and we were waved hastily through. There was some clapping, a forest of onlookers ahead of us with a narrow channel bisecting it, and a policeman pointing the direction we were to follow. Phil negotiated a route through the crowd and we accelerated in the wake of the DB6.

We were on our way. Another very slightly anticlimactic moment after so much anticipation. Our next stop would be the official start at the Great Wall, 75 kilometres away.

There were police everywhere, at every junction, all the way out of Beijing. Horns sounded in salute and people hung out of buses to wave us on our way. Phil pressed a road tape into the cassette player and seventies rock music – usefully acceptable to both of us – boomed out. When I peered ahead I could see the line of rally cars, strung out through the traffic, and I felt a frisson of pride at the sight. The worries about the car's durability, about money and responsibility, about Phil and me, even the visa crisis, were briefly forgotten.

We were here, we were driving out of Beijing in the early morning traffic and there were hundreds of people lining the roads to watch us. I felt a grin split my face, and when I looked at Phil I saw that he was wearing one too. We wished each other good luck.

My first job on the road was to calibrate the Terratrip. JD had explained to me how it was done. The rally computer mounted on the dash in front of the navigator's seat displayed two sets of distances. The upper one would give the total distance travelled from the day's start point, and the lower one would show the intermediates, the distances between each successive instruction in the route notes. When we were finally clear of Beijing the expressway opened up ahead. The police had cleared the outside lane for us, and suddenly the rally was surging forward in a rush of speed with police outriders at the head of the convoy. At 1-kilometre intervals along the roadside there were marker posts, and I used these to take half a dozen trip readings and averaged them out before entering the mean value into the computer's memory. The next step was to zero both readings as we passed a marker, and watch the digits flicker until we reached the next one. They both changed to a reading of 01.00 reassuringly close to the post.

So far so good. One of my little jobs in the car park had been to attach a strip of Velcro to the dash, and next I arranged my pens and kitchen timer and calculator and highlighters and specs cases within easy reach along the length of it.

'That's neat,' Phil kindly approved of this small piece of housekeeping.

I had begun to mind more acutely about my ignorance in relation to the car and its workings. Phil understood and controlled all the essential oily intricacies under the bonnet, and I fiddled about with navigator's accessories. Of course I could have gone down to Stamford Brook day after day and insisted on being taught how to recondition the prop-shaft myself – but that hadn't been our deal. Now that we were finally on the road together, I would just have to see how the deal actually worked out. I was remembering, rather belatedly, that to confine a man and a woman in a car together is one of the quickest ways of drawing up the gender battle lines.

After thinking about it some more, I decided that my sudden defensiveness was probably only related to uncertainty about whether I was going to be any use as a navigator. Phil had equipped himself to be a mechanic and now he was ensconced behind the wheel, and I was shortly going to have to demonstrate that I could handle the Terratrip and the road book with matching confidence.

Our practice day out with Colin Bryce in Somerset had been good fun but it hadn't taught us to be real rally navigators, and most of the people I had chatted with casually in the last couple of days had already importantly done classic rallies like the Monte Carlo, or the Land's End–John o'Groat's, or the Targa Espana. As Maurizio had said back in the farmyard in England, we had picked a big one for starters.

I opened the route notes and put on my specs to study them. The first instructions on the first page read:

Total	Inter	Instruction
Total	*Inter*	*Instruction*
0.00	0.00	ZERO TRIP
		Turn LEFT out of hotel; S/O at crossroads with T/L
0.60	0.60	S/O at crossroads with T/L (ad for 'LG' on right)
2.00	1.40	Under arch
2.30	0.30	Over bridge and immediately turn RIGHT on clover leaf junction joining Ring road number 2 going north
3.40	1.10	Under bridge; S/O
4.40	1.00	Chaoyangmen Qiao S/O

(. . . and so on, for the full 16,000 kilometres . . .)

Having already worked out that S/O meant straight on and T/L traffic lights, all this should have been easy except that we hadn't started from the hotel, the route we were now following bore no relation to the instructions, and I hadn't the faintest idea where in eastern China we might be. On the positive side, every other crew was in the same boat and so were the organisers. The police had changed the planned route to suit themselves, and we would be travelling in a convoy with them for at least two days. This wasn't a rally yet – just a police procession, and even I couldn't lose my way with a cop on a bike nudging up each bumper. Two days would give me plenty of time to play with the rally trip, read and re-read the route notes, unfold the marked-up maps and convince Phil that I knew what I was doing. His capabilities impressed me, and I wanted to offer him the same level of efficiency in return.

'Look,' he said.

We were pulling into the centre lane to let a big black car go by. It was a chauffeured Rolls, with Union flag pennants merrily fluttering. There were two passengers in sombre black clothes in the back: the British Ambassador and his wife, bound for the Great Wall just like us, to give the rally a proper send-off.

Out at the Great Wall there was . . . another car park.

It was still only nine in the morning, and the cars were lined up in great snaking columns, besieged by camera crews and journalists and hundreds of Chinese well-wishers, and tiny children in Peking to Paris baseball caps, and the entire staff of the Great Wall Kentucky Fried Chicken who had come out to rubberneck. There was a multi-legged Chinese dragon winding in and out of the crowds, and a Chinese band very approximately playing Strauss waltzes. And there was also the Wall itself.

I had been warned that this piece of it was tourist central; an over-restored and over-visited urban stretch which wouldn't give an impression of the magnificence of the more remote sections. The warnings were justified, particularly given the setting of fast-food restaurants and tatty souvenir shops, but even so it was a startling spectacle. The Wall was a pristine and unwavering brown brushstroke, impeccably crenellated, that switchbacked up and down the little pine-covered willow-pattern hills into the

remote blue distance, and way beyond. I took a couple of
photographs and promised myself that I would come back
when I had less on my mind.

Down at car park level no one seemed to have much
idea what the Official Start would actually consist of. The
ambassador and his lady were making their dignified
black-clad way along the files of cars. At one point I heard
some distant babbling through a microphone that might
conceivably have been speeches, but the amplification
was lousy, and the band played on. The sky had turned a
fragile pale blue, promising intense heat later in the day.
Cars began to move off from the front, but reckoning on
from this morning's tedious wait, I thought I had plenty
of time to investigate the rumoured awfulness of Chinese
public lavatories. I wandered off, and was duly convinced.
When I came back Phil and the car had disappeared.

I ran up and down for a minute like a rat in a maze,
and then heard a furious hooting behind me. They rema-
terialised and I dived into my seat.

'We had to *start*,' Phil frothed. 'What were you *doing*?'

'Peeing.'

'Now we'll have to go round again.'

'Sorry.'

Marvellous. After eight months of non-stop preparation I had actually missed the off.

Belatedly I saw that the actual start consisted of a giant
red inflatable rubber arch, easily kitsch enough to compete with the souvenir shop merchandise. We sailed
through it, apparently for the second time, to the accompaniment of applause, a trumpet fanfare and a row of
puzzled stares from the officials. We heard later that the

Chief of Police was incensed at our effrontery in starting twice over. Maybe, Phil said, we'll get a chance to *finish* twice as well.

And then we drove. The cars streamed away at their various speeds and the field was soon widely spaced, although the police did their best to push us closer together and the marshals and support crews drove up and down in their official Vauxhall Fronteras to chivvy the laggards and help out the cars who were having problems at the roadside. Industrialised eastern China featured massively hideous concrete architecture, giant heaps of coal at the roadside, and heavy traffic. All along the way were little open-fronted mechanical repair shops with forecourts heaped with dismantled machinery. The pollution was even worse than in Beijing; to wind down the window for a breath of air was to let in a gust of eye-burning filth and choking dust.

The midday heat was cruel. I sweated in my black clothes, and wished we had brought a proper supply of bottled water. The convoy rolled on, with no suggestion of a lunch stop or even a comfort break – I smiled to think how much Caradoc would have hated it. My guilt at having taken off on this great adventure and left him behind subsided a little. He was safely in London beckoning over the *sommelier* and debating the clarets, which was what he liked to do, and in turn I was trying to pinpoint exactly what it was that I liked about extreme heat, dirt and discomfort.

There was no navigating to do. For part of the way we seemed to be following the route set out in the notes, and I zeroed the intermediate trip each time we passed an instruction point. The kilometre distances from point to point seemed more or less to correspond with those in the notes, so it was safe to assume that the trips were working properly. I also checked off each instruction as we passed it, neatly striking it through in the book with a fluorescent green marker pen (keeping the pink one for Phil to use when he took over the navigation). This, I knew, was what real rally navigators did.

The properly anal ones, at any rate.

When the police route diverged from the notes once again there was nothing to do but play music and wave at the other cars as we overtook them, and then wave and smile again as they overtook us 10 kilometres further down the road.

The distance from the Great Wall to our night's stopover at Zhangjiakou was only about 160 kilometres, but it seemed much further. Ten kilometres out of the town we were pulled over into a huge queue of rally cars waiting to be refuelled. Petrol was free all the way across China, but the drawback was that it was only available at the designated filling station, which most of the cars reached at more or less the same time. The pumps worked very, very slowly.

But on this first evening we were all high on the day's progress and happy to be moving at all, even in the boring and irksome convoy. The hour or two that it took to refuel was passed in gossip, which ran up and down the queue like wildfire. Most of us had seen Lord Montagu standing arms akimbo at the roadside, in his pukka-Englishman-abroad outfit of khaki shorts and ribbed knee-socks, while poor Doug Hill the mechanic wrestled

under the open bonnet of the Vauxhall. Serious overheating was the problem, we now heard. An American
Ford Model A had dropped a valve and was unlikely to
reappear, and the Jag Mark VII and the handsome Stutz
coupé were also having trouble. Those of us who had survived the first day apparently intact exchanged our
impressions.

'Not bad,' Dan said. We bought bottles of water from
coolie-hatted women with cool boxes mounted on the
backs of their bicycles. The water looked dubious but we
were so thirsty we drank it anyway. 'How's your car going?'

Team Amazon in action.

'Seems OK.'

We pushed it closer to the pump, to save the starter
motor.

When we reached Zhangjiakou the entire town seemed
to have turned out to greet us. They watched each arrival
with amazed enthusiasm, clapping and shouting Hello!
and Welcome! as we turned into the parking lot. And as
we were coming to expect, there were dozens of police to
monitor the crowds, and us.

As soon as we were stationary Phil had the bonnet up.

'Look at this,' he said. He pulled the corners of his
mouth down towards the points of his jaw, exposing his
lower teeth. It was an expression I was to come to know,
and to dread.

'What's that?'

He was holding up a small blue cylinder about the
same shape and size as a rather unexciting mid-range firework.

'The coil. Ignition coil.'

It was oozing some treacly brown substance from the metalwork at the top. It didn't, admittedly, look very healthy.

'It's overheating,' he groaned.

'It was a very hot day.'

'I think it's where it's positioned, right on the heater there. Tony insisted it would be fine. He didn't reckon on how hot it would be out here.'

Dan and JD came over to give the benefit of their advice. Between them they decided that Phil should temporarily remount the coil bracket and leads well away from the heater, fit our spare, and monitor it very closely tomorrow. I wandered away to look at some of the other cars. A few metres away a pleasant Dutch couple, the Gulikers, were sitting in folding canvas chairs at the back of their '56 Chevy pick-up. The tail was folded down to reveal a complete and immaculately fitted kitchen, with a couple of pans merrily simmering on the gas burners. A proper meal was in preparation. The organisation of it all was a poem, a work of art. There were tupperware boxes of tea and sugar and supplies of food, symmetrically stacked, braced with shelving. It looked to be better equipped than my kitchen at home. Somehow Mrs Guliker had been allowed, possibly even encouraged, to bring a *colander*.

I expressed my admiration, and they gave me a cup of tea.

The hotel was the opening line of what was to become a very long and tedious joke. By the time we reached Iran I didn't even want to hear the punchline. The lobby was a dingy cave with a tiny shop – already sold out of bottled water – in one corner. Reception would have been better named Rejection.

At length we achieved a key, and a room to go with it, immediately off the lobby. The dark green paper was hanging in damp festoons off the wall, everything else was dark brown. In the bathroom someone had left a large deposit in the lavatory pan. I tried the handle but no water ensued. I marched straight back to Rejection. Phil Colley, our interpreter, was elsewhere – no doubt interpreting in a much bigger crisis. The boot-faced woman behind the desk stared sullenly while I tried to explain what was the matter. At last I drew a picture of a bog, tastefully omitting the turd, and crossed it out. She condescended to nod so I went back, put down the lid, ran a bath and got into it. Naturally the maintenance man came while I was lying back trying to read the weighty *Vogue* I kept hidden from Phil in my kitbag. When the time came to pull out the plug there was a subterranean gurgle and the water spouted out of a pipe in the bath side. At least it sluiced the floor somewhat.

Over what passed for dinner I met Carolyn Ward, who was driving a Land Rover Series IIA with a South African called David Tremain. The Land Rover was painted pale blue to match, Carolyn told me, the colour of her favourite evening dress.

'I have just run a bath,' she announced now, 'that I wouldn't put my *dog* in.'

Afterwards, in the velvety twilight, I sat on the outside steps of the dining-room with Phil and JD and Dan and the Bentley boys, drinking Chinese beer to offset the minimal calorie intake at dinner, and laughing too much. This was more like my imaginings. Next thing there might even be a guitar and some exotic cigarettes.

Immediately in front of us Lord Montagu's Vauxhall was parked in the middle of the hotel courtyard. It was hemmed in by an immense circle of Chinese onlookers, all of them watching his mechanic Doug Hill, who was working by the light of a ring of torches. Overheating had caused the fan to work loose, and the fan blades had smashed through the radiator. Doug was now trying to solder the radiator fins one by one.

'Poor sod,' someone said.

After several more beers it was time to go to bed – but, as it turned out, not to sleep.

'Night,' Phil said, pulling his covers over his head and falling instantly into a coma. At the same minute, out in the lobby on the other side of our door, a quartet of Chinese madwomen arrived armed with tin buckets, twenty aluminium saucepans and what sounded like a football rattle apiece. They settled to the business of throwing these at each other and seeing if they could shout loudly enough to drown the clatter. This continued without stopping until 4.30 a.m., when our alarm call came. Breakfast was the leftover cold shellfish from dinner, and some rice gruel, and then at six o'clock we were driving again.

We had a little over 500 kilometres to cover, with the police nudging us along all the way. In the morning their route changes took in some off-road sections around the back of villages, twisty and sandy tracks through fields of tall sweetcorn that made Phil frown in concentration as he drove.

'She's good,' he announced when we hit tarmac again. 'Handles well. But we could still do with improving the clearance. We might have to lose some weight.'

No problem, given a few more dinners like last night's.

In the afternoon we came to a brand-new motorway that the police had closed to all other traffic. I drove, watching the red speedo line creeping to the right. One-forty, 150, 160 kph. We ate up the kilometres, overtaking everything we saw, and I ignored Phil's left foot pressing vainly against the floor until we came very suddenly to a row of cones that marked the end of the motorway and a right-angle turn. I slammed my foot down and wrenched the wheel, feeling the chassis lurch sideways.

'Cadence!' Phil screamed.

Frantically I pumped the brake up and down and somehow we made the turn and left the cones intact, a bit of an improvement on Silverstone. Things went quiet in the car after that.

There was another two-hour wait for fuel outside West Baotou, where we would be staying the night. This was the first stop since leaving Zhangjiakou. The unmarked black-windowed four-wheel-drive vehicles had doubled up and down the field all day, keeping us together and keeping us going. I asked one of the organisers who or what was inside and he answered, 'Don't ask.' But at the same time he made a gesture as if cradling an automatic weapon across his hips. On every bend and bridge and junction, too, there had been a policeman to watch us.

In the morning I had put four bottles of mineral water and some raisins and a couple of oranges in the car, that was all, imagining that we would be able to buy food and drink at a roadside bar or café. By the time we reached the head of the queue for fuel Phil and I were both tired and dehydrated and ravenously hungry. There was no water for sale at the filling station. We pulled away from the pumps at last only to discover that we were the first car in the last police convoy to the hotel, which meant that we had to wait for every car behind us to be fuelled before we could move. Another hour at least, filthy and thirsty and exhausted, in a temperature of over ninety degrees.

I went to retrieve something from the boot, and carelessly banged the lid.

'If you slam that boot lid again I'll put you in and lock you inside.'

'Oh, fuck off.'

We stared at each other in surprise, and then sat out the rest of the wait in silence.

At last we reached the hotel. Phil yanked the bonnet up and did the face again. He raked his hair back too, a two-handed sweep, so that it stood up in a dust-thickened quiff.

'What's up?'

'Coil.'

Even though he had resited it, our spare was also oozing a drop of brown goo. Not as bad as yesterday's, but definitely not right either.

In the end Phil decided that we had just bought coils that were too cheap and unreliable. 'Only seven quid each from Halfords,' he recalled. Invoking Team Amazon, he borrowed a more robust and expensive-looking firework from Dan and fitted it, praying that it would solve the problem. It was 8 p.m. when we finally got into the hotel and in the morning, the rally bulletin-board in the lobby announced, there would be a 4.15 wake-up call. I hadn't slept at all the previous night, and I felt too tired and dispirited to eat any dinner.

On the way up to bed I met a woman I was to come to know as Jill Dangerfield, who was driving a Holden saloon with her husband Richard.

Jill asked what car I was in, and I told her.

'Oh,' she said. 'You're the people in the hot Volvo who keep overtaking us.'

Marvellous. My spirits soared. The *hot Volvo*, eh?

And in the morning we would start proper rallying. No more convoy.

Furthermore I would make myself into a good navigator, come what may, and I didn't care what Phil thought of my driving.

This was the first taste of Rally Syndrome, for me. It was possible – more than possible, almost *de rigueur* – to be in the deepest depths at one moment and in the next to be swept to the heights of exultation.

Chapter Six

Six forty-one a.m., official start time for car 82 as set out in the day's list.

It was day three of the rally, day one of proper competition, West Baotou to Yinchuan. Total distance to cover, 618 kilometres.

I felt better for some sleep and a bowl of warm rice porridge. I lined up with Maria Noor, wearing persimmon-red overalls today, and Carolyn, and Andrew Bedingham and Murdoch Laing, and a press of other navigators, all of us watching the rally clock on the marshal's table and waiting for our minute. It was barely light, and bobbing torches and car headlights heightened the atmosphere of drama. As the cars rolled away at one-minute intervals the crews still waiting patted their wings and shouted good luck! It was exciting, and also touching. A couple of tough days on the road had already welded some camaraderie out of the Beijing competitiveness.

'Car 82.' As 6.40 clicked over to 41 I presented myself to the marshal. He stamped my road book, I took it, and sprinted to the head of the line where Phil was revving the engine.

'Ready to go?'

Squeeze into the seat, buckle the harness, zero upper and lower trip – a decisive double beep. 'Ready to go.'

Now we were really doing it. The Amazon shot forward and my breath caught in my throat as I called the first instructions and distances. I was desperate not to misread the route notes and make us lose our way.

'Point nine five k, straight over at lights.'

'Okay.'

We moved fast in the light traffic down a long, tree-lined avenue, overtaking bikes and three-wheelers. As we reached the lights I crossed out the instructions as completed and zeroed the intermediate trip, *beep*. I could already see the DB6 weaving through the traffic ahead of us.

'Next one is point six five k, left at lights, shopping centre on right.'

I was trying to stop distinguishing left from right by looking down at my hands to check which one holds the pen.

'Okay,' Phil acknowledged the instruction every time so we both knew he had heard and understood it. Or 'got you', as a variation. Never 'right', Colin Bryce had warned us, because that might cause confusion.

Beep. 'Point three five, straight over lights, Bank of China on corner.'

'Okay.'

Beep. 'One point one five, turn right at junction.'

This was all right. We made it across town with the

Aston still out in front of us. If I'd made a mistake, they'd made the same one.

'Well done,' Phil said.

Beyond West Baotou town the instructions came further apart and I had time to do the maths. Two hundred and thirty-five kilometres to the first time control of the day, at a place called Xinbao. Time allowance for the distance: a generous four hours and forty-three minutes, therefore we were due at 11.24. Not a single minute earlier or later. I set the kitchen timer on the dash to tick away the hours and minutes, showing us how much time we had left to run.

'Land crab coming up behind,' Phil said. Andrew and David hammered by, giving us a wave. 'What do they think this is, a race?'

We smiled at each other. It was the signal that Phil had surfaced for the day. Ever since I had joined him in Beijing he had been cheery and upbeat, even when he was worried about the car, which made him easy to be with but also oddly impervious and difficult to fathom – as I had noticed in our early dealings back in London. But now I thought I had discovered a single crack in his cheerful armour – he wasn't good in the mornings. After the alarm call he preferred to lie under the covers in a sullen, unmoving heap while I hummed around in the bathroom. He wouldn't get up until I was dressed, packed, and departing for breakfast, and then – presumably – he did everything in a scramble because he made it to breakfast not long after me.

This arrangement also diminished the chances of my accidentally catching a glimpse of any portion of his flesh.

He was endearingly modest in his personal bearing. For my part, after boarding school and years of Miss Selfridge communal changing rooms and two babies delivered in a National Health teaching hospital with a couple of rugby teams of medical students cheering me on, I wasn't much concerned about nakedness. But I took my cue from Phil and in our bedroom I shimmied around wrapped in towels and always changed behind the closed bathroom door, and I was careful never to leave any bits of lingerie lying about to embarrass him.

'Is there any coffee?'

It's the navigator's job to make sure the driver is comfortable. After the deficiencies of the first two days I'd taken care to go out into West Baotou the previous evening to stock up. I met a friendly young man who knew some English, who had patiently guided me around the little shops in search of bottled water and cans of Coke, and fruit and biscuits. And I'd filled the flask at breakfast.

'Here.'

Phil drank it. 'Are you okay?' he asked me routinely.

'Railway crossing coming up in one k.'

'Got you.'

'Yes, thanks,' I answered, although in fact I was beginning to worry about a small problem.

'Good. How far to the control?'

I checked the upper trip for the total. We had travelled 110 kilometres already. 'Two two five. Hours of time left.'

'Let's have some music.'

I chose a tape. I had brought Radiohead and Alisha's Attic and even some of Charlie's hardcore mix tapes as part of my contribution. It turned out, though, that what

Phil liked was the Eagles, B52s and old reggae. We sang along now, *oooh, oooh, the Isreeealites*. It was a tape that Noddy had made for us. *Wake up in the morning, same thing for breakfast* . .

This is how it would be all the long way ahead, I thought happily, in the grip of Rally Syndrome once more. Phil and me and the Amazon. Bowling around the world together, winning the rally, the best team there ever could be. I forgot that I had ever felt homesick.

Everyone was going fast today. We overtook the Dangerfields, and Mick Flick in his blue and white works Mercedes 220, number 74, and then the Dangerfields overtook us again. We were coming up to a steady stream of vintageants, who had started first but moved more slowly, with longer time allowances. We swept past the Railton Straight 8, and then Adam and Jon with a fusillade of hooting and gesturing. The roads were lined with onlookers all along the way, but in the towns the crowds swelled alarmingly. In a place called Linhe there must have been hundreds of thousands of people spilling off the sidewalks and into the road. Tiny children tottered at the front and cyclists nudged their front wheels into our path. The way narrowed to less than the width of the Amazon and the police linked arms and tried to force the people back to let us through.

Hello! Welcome! English people! Speak English!

Radiant, inquisitive smiles filled the open windows. Dozens of hands pushed flowers at us, and pieces of paper to be autographed, and tried to shake our hands or grab a souvenir off the dash. It was awesome, and overwhelming, and extremely frightening. Phil kept his thumb on the horn. He was sweating and staring, dreading that the toddler just in front would be the one to break free of its mother and throw itself under our wheels.

Hello! Good car! Welcome!

There was no air. We were inching forward through a sea of bodies and clapping hands. Hands drummed on the roof and the wings. The noise was as deafening as the roar of surf, and the arms coming through the windows were tendrils of weed, pulling us down . . .

I felt tears starting up behind my sunglasses, partly out of amazed gratitude for such a welcome, partly out of raw fear. In this multitude we were going to be submerged, or we were going to run over someone. The moon-faced policemen were suddenly our allies, roughly manhandling people out of our path. We became part of a solid line of rally cars, battered by the waves of people.

It took a long time to negotiate our way out of Linhe.

A little way up the road we had to have a rest stop. Phil folded his arms across the wheel and laid his head on them. His hair was matted with sweat.

'Jesus,' he whispered.

Every town we passed through was almost the same. At the end of the day we learned that about a million people had turned out to watch us go by.

We still made the 11.24 control and each of that day's subsequent controls with plenty of time to spare. The routine was to pull off the road, joining the line of other cars, and wait for your minute to come up. It was a good time to wander up and down talking to the other crews and exchanging titbits of gossip. Lord Montagu had broken down irretrievably. His car was being towed back to Beijing for shipping home, and he had hitched a ride for himself in the Rolls Royce Phantom V. Three cars were now officially retired, and also the Jag Mark VII had a broken suspension arm, the Stutz was suffering complicated electrical problems, and Jennifer and Francesca had been pulled up by a broken shock-absorber. There were several boiling radiators. It was a punishingly hot, airless day.

I drove the next section through flat, dull country alongside the Yellow River. Sometimes the road was wide and open, but nearly always busy with streams of blue-painted wagons loaded with coal. The grass verges all along the way were grey and gritty with shed coal dust. There were farm wagons too, heavy with hay, and tricycle carts, but relatively few private cars. At other times the surface would deteriorate without warning, breaking down into unmade sections, or lapsing into vicious potholes. At the speed we were travelling, driving required constant vigilance, and lots of gear changes and braking. I became aware that Phil was unhappy.

'Change up. You should be in third by now.'

'Okay,' I would say meekly, and do as I was told.

'Too fast. You were going too fast for that bend. That was why you had to brake while you were cornering.'

'Sorry.'

In the end I was asking him, 'Brake now? Is that okay?'

'Yes. Well done.'

'Thank you.'

I might have been back in driving school, and yet I had had my licence while Phil was still in his pram. I told myself that he knew the car much better than I did, and he drove it better because he had built it and had been so possessive

about it for all those months before we left. I insisted to
myself that I didn't mind that at all.

'You see, driving the way you do isn't good for the car.
You are too heavy on the brakes and you change gear too
sharply. Everything you do should be *smooooth*.'

'The way you do it,' I snapped.

He shot a look at me, half wary and half irritable. 'If you
like. I'm just used to it. Otherwise something will break,
and we won't get to Paris.'

'Okay. I'll try, all right?'

But I was already in a position that promised trouble. I
remembered that on the walk to Everest, I had been
responsible for myself and for the effort of putting one foot
in front of the other. The determination and the ultimate
satisfaction of it had been all mine. Now, on this different
adventure I was the dependant half of a team, and we were
in a car. The classic setting for male–female discord.

My spirits sank.

It was exactly like being married, I thought. We were a
couple out on a Sunday drive, bickering about her driving – the very reason why I had decided in the first place
that Caradoc and I shouldn't make the trip together. Now
Phil had slipped effortlessly into the husband role, and to
my chagrin I was the anxious wife.

'You'll be fine. Listen, can you hear that clunk? When
you drop into low gear? It's coming from around the back
axle.'

I couldn't hear any bloody clunk. The whole noise of
the car was an atonal symphony of thumps and grinds. I
was bathed in sweat, and my problem was getting worse by
the minute.

'Yes. I've been listening to it. What d'you think it is?'

'I don't know. Could be the diff. I'll have to take a good look when we get in. *Second*. Get into second.'

Flustered, I could only find fourth. The car shuddered and rattled. As soon as I could, I pulled into the side of the road. Three rally cars immediately shot by and Phil looked anxiously after them. He was holding up the back cover of the route notes which showed a huge red OK and a thumbs-up graphic. This was required procedure, to indicate to other cars and the support crews that we weren't in trouble.

'You drive,' I said flatly.

'Oh, come on. I'm sorry, okay? You're really good, you just need a bit of practice.'

I knew I wasn't really good, so now he was definitely being patronising.

'You drive.'

I got out and made him change over. We pressed on to the next control and wearily joined the heat-shimmering column of metal waiting to check in. Even after passing some time chatting to other crews and having a car-heated can of Coke, we still had eleven minutes to go before we were due. I knew, because I was watching the timer. But Phil picked up my road book and announced that he was going to walk up to the control and get it stamped.

Blood hummed in my ears.

I wasn't going to accept that my only role was signing cheques. He was the crew leader and he could be the driver if he insisted, relegating me from co-driver to navigator, but he couldn't take the navigator's responsibilities from me as well.

I waited until he came sauntering back.

'We have to have a talk, Phil.'

I saw his smile fade, and all the pleasant lines of his face tighten into watchfulness. I understood that Phil didn't like to talk. He would prefer to duck behind a bit of banter and evade the threat of a confrontation. He got into the driver's seat and we set off on the last section of the day's drive, 165 kilometres to the overnight stop at Yinchuan.

'I was talking to Dan about the driving,' he offered. 'He says he feels just the same about his car. Protective. He doesn't like JD driving it, in case he breaks something.'

'I understand that. I'll try to be a better driver. But you can't take over everything. This is my adventure as well as yours.'

'I know. I know. I take your point, and I'm sorry.'

We touched hands, briefly, acknowledging a truce. We were out here on our own together and we needed one another. We'd had our first disagreement and we had been able to fix it, just like fixing the car, so we could drive on for another day.

At Yinchuan that night, we had a good dinner. The restaurant was a series of small rooms, each enclosing a table for ten. Considerately asking one another whether we were all right, whether this was what the other wanted, Phil and I found ourselves sitting with Prince Idris Shah and his co-driver Richard Curtis, who I now noticed bore a very strong physical resemblance to Caradoc. They had the same shiny dark boot-button eyes like an expensive teddy bear's, and close-cropped greying hair like plush fur. They were the same height and build, too, although when Richard and I started talking the resemblance diminished because Richard's voice was much lighter and his businessman's view of the world more traditional.

There were also three drily amusing American disability lawyers from car 99, a Willys jeep station wagon. They made sly cracks about RO and China and the ongoing effects of Beijing diarrhoea with such straight faces that it was hard to tell whether or not they were being deliberately funny. The remaining places were taken by David Bull from Halifax, his wife Angela Riley, and Angela's mother Helen. Helen was in her 70s; she looked frail, but turned out to be completely indomitable. Angela was a forthright Yorkshire accountant and Dave, with a rogue's smile and a line in sharp northern witticisms, was in the garage business. Looking round the circle of faces, with the lawyers and the mountain guide and the accountant and the novelist, as well as the car mechanic and the determined old lady and the Crown Prince of Malaysia, I thought it was either a pleasingly cosmopolitan gathering or the cast of a very complicated joke.

Pretty waitresses filed in with the food. They showed us what to do, with much giggling and blushing. It was a Mongolian barbecue, a big pot of simmering soup with bowls of tiny mushrooms and dumplings and slivers of lamb and fresh greens to skewer and cook in the broth. Perfect. It was a very jolly meal – chopsticks are good icebreakers and Dave Bull could have had a second career as a stand-up comedian. It was good for us to meet new people. After three long days locked in the car together Phil and I were suffering from too much close focus.

He went off on his own after dinner to work on the car.

Later he reported that the clunk was probably a loose rear shock that had been making the back axle judder. He had tightened it up. Much more worryingly, he had found that the drain plug on the side of the gearbox had worked loose. We had been hammering along at high speeds for a day and a half during which almost all of the oil had drained out of the gearbox. He borrowed a plastic siphon from Melissa Ong and topped the box up with a litre of engine oil. If it didn't leak out overnight, and if we nursed the car along to Lanzhou tomorrow, he would have a whole day to put all these worrying mechanical problems to rights.

I had my own scrap of news to relay to him. I had been nosing around the hotel lobby, trying to send a fax home, when I had overheard a conversation between RO and Thomas Noor. RO said that he and the rally mechanics had just made a tour of the car park, drawing up a list of the cars they thought would get to Paris.

'Twenty-nine,' RO announced. 'That's what we reckon. Only twenty-nine. Yours is one of them,' he assured Thomas.

Since he had slammed the phone down and threatened me during the visa crisis I had maintained a rigid policy of pretending that RO didn't exist. Not that he would have noticed. But I couldn't keep my mouth shut now. I bobbed up in front of him.

'What about us? Are we on the list?'

He turned on me, eyes bulging.

'That's an inside secret I couldn't possibly share with you.'

Phil listened to this story. His response was utterly characteristic. 'Tosser. If we're not on his list we should be.

Don't worry, we'll make it.' He lowered himself into bed, half-dressed, ready for coma mode. 'Night.'

'Night.'

I lay awake, worrying about my personal mechanical defect.

Between Yinchuan and Lanzhou the scenery changed from ugly industrial to semi-desert. We were crossing the edge of the Gobi Desert, through wide paddy fields and broad plains backed by low bluish hills. Sometimes there were wide sweeps of sand and huge dunes, with occasional brown villages of square mud-block houses reminiscent of southern Morocco. On the road we met camel trains and plodding donkeys as well as the ubiquitous blue coal wagons. In even the remotest villages, hordes of people lined the roadside to watch us go by. They had wide, flat faces with Mongolian features now. Seamed skin and bad teeth marred all the adults, but the babies and children were exquisitely beautiful. Old and young stared impassively at us at first, but as soon as we smiled their faces broke immediately into dazzling smiles of response.

After the previous day's narrow escape with the gearbox we drove more steadily, but still made all the time controls with the greatest of ease. However, after a couple of conversations with more knowing crews I learned that the present relaxed pace would soon quicken.

'Just you wait,' the Brodericks from the Anglia estate warned. Their car was called Arnie the Eco-Flow Anglia, which for a leaded-fuel 1967 car driving flat out (as Nigel Broderick always did) half-way around the world, might have seemed a slight contradiction in terms.

Even now, when we had plenty of time in hand, Phil didn't like stopping, so there was barely an interval allowed for a pee and certainly no leisurely picnic lunch. He was always mindful that we might break down in the next half-hour, and wanted to keep as much spare time in hand as possible. The only breaks we had were the compulsory waits at time controls.

Outside Lanzhou we were pulled off the road for refuelling and to wait for the police to run us in convoy into town. While Phil played frisbee on a grassy bank with JD and Dan and Simon Catt from the Mk 1 Cortina, I popped Phil's and my favourite Beautiful South tape into the player and had an impromptu aerobics session with Angela, and Adèle Cohen from the ailing Stutz.

You have to wash the car, take the kiddies to the park – don't marry her . . . we sang, as we did our twists and stretches.

The police whistles blew and the convoy suddenly shifted forward. Phil hopped into the driver's seat and turned the ignition on. Nothing. Dead as a doorknob. It wouldn't even respond to our efforts to bump start it. Doing the face thing, Phil threw up the bonnet and spotted the problem immediately. By playing the tape without running the engine, I had boiled the coil.

We were getting a bit low on coils now. He replaced the boiled one with the only slightly gooey firework he had taken out in West Baotou and the car started up immediately. We joined the end of the convoy heading for the hotel. He was quite kind to me about it.

With the prospect of a day off to come, everyone perked up that evening in Lanzhou. I had dinner with Carolyn who introduced me to her friends Howard Belim and Chris Taylor. They looked to be round about my age, even.

''68 Chevvy Camaro,' Chris and Howard said, in answer to the inevitable question. 'There aren't all that many cars that are big enough, you see.'

I did see. They were both at least six and a half feet tall.

Melissa Ong came to join us. Melissa was only in her early twenties but she was so spontaneous and affectionate that she had made friends right across all the rally age-groups. Her thick, glossy black hair was cut short like a schoolboy's at the nape of her neck with a long wedge left slanting across her eyes. Her skin was the colour of milk chocolate. Melissa was driving her own '63 Porsche 356SC coupé with her godfather, Colin Syn.

After dinner we all went out to a bar in the town. We were joined by Phil Colley and Mick O'Malley, and RO's assistant, Sarah Catt. Sarah's father and brother, John and Simon, were serious rallyists who were driving the '64 Cortina. She was a rounded, pink-complexioned blonde who reminded me of a glass dish of strawberry ice-cream. She had one of those personalities that recruitment ads for ad-agency receptionists used to describe as 'bubbly'.

Lanzhou lies in the Yellow River valley. Once the gateway to the Chinese Empire from the western approaches, it was a staging post on the route from Turkestan and Europe, and the eastern limit of the Muslim world. Now it is a big, industrial city, rapidly moving into the consumer era. The chosen bar featured karaoke, blue laser-lighting, tall and hideously uncomfortable metal stools grouped in booths, and deafening music. I thought it was more like Tokyo than Inner Mongolia.

We ordered drinks. Eagerly ricocheting between Melissa and Sarah, Phil looked as happy as a dog with two strawberry choc-ices. I sat in a corner as far away from the music as possible and talked to Chris Taylor. He was so tall that he seemed to sit with his legs hooked at least twice around his stool. We discussed the rally, and then my anxieties about the potential dangers ahead of us. Chris told me about a friend of his who had recently died, in tragic circumstances. Ever since it happened, he said, he had felt that there was nothing in life to be fearful about. There was no point in worrying about anything; life was a matter to be thankful for and relaxed about and one might as well try to be happy.

I told him that my experience was just the opposite. Tragedy made people tense and fearful, poised for the next blow because they knew with exactly what random viciousness the last one had fallen.

The expression on Chris's pleasant, rounded, faintly lugubrious face didn't change. He reminded me, I suddenly realised, of Eeyore. Eeyore with a pink sun-flush from several days driving in the open Camaro.

'Not my perception,' Chris said mildly. I envied him his optimistic disposition.

This was the first conversation I had had about anything that mattered or touched me, since reaching China. I was very grateful for it – it made me feel that I wasn't, after all, entirely adrift in a miniature universe in which nobody cared for anything but carburettors and achieving the minimum number of penalty points. It was the kind of connection I had imagined before we set out.

At last, driven out by the music, we moved on to

another bar, this one just a couple of tables outside a shop in an alleyway. As soon as we sat down a crowd of Chinese gathered, perhaps fifty or sixty of them, to stand five deep around us. They wanted to look, and talk, and they were very cheerful and friendly. 'You my friend,' they kept saying, shaking our hands. 'We all friends, all people.'

International amiability and equality was a seductive idea, here in Lanzhou, where the people all looked to be reasonably well-dressed and well-fed, and eager for the delights of karaoke and western fashions and whisky. It was less easy to imagine what life might have been like in some of the villages we had driven through today, and even more so a few miles down one of the turnings off the main roads that our police escorts kept so assiduously guarded. Translator Phil Colley told me that there are estimated to be somewhere between twenty and fifty million people in labour camps in China. Back on the road, on the way to Lanzhou, I remembered how we had driven through a cleft between two sandy hills, and had suddenly come upon a stretch of railway line. There was a work gang in action on the line, perhaps a hundred people pressed together, swinging their picks in rhythm with the overseers' whistles. It was like a scene from a film set in the American Deep South of a hundred years ago.

At midnight I left the party in the alleyway bar and walked back to the hotel. The main street was deserted, with the neon advertisements flashing their garish come-ons to nobody. It felt completely safe to be walking alone.

I spent the rest day in the hotel room, working and writing up my diaries and occasionally stopping to stare out of the twentieth-floor window. On my side of the glass was the complete familiarity of conference-hotel blandness, with table lamps and a mini-bar and padded headboards to the beds, and a marble bathroom with shower caps and a shoeshine kit, and on the other side there was the alien world of China. I could see the cocoa-brown low-rise city spreading to a ring of steep-sided mountains in the middle distance. The buildings were mostly concrete apartment blocks, six storeys high, with the occasional randomly-placed high-rise tower. Between the blocks there were a very few dusty trees, some shanty buildings, much litter and rubble and twists of rusting metal.

If I looked straight down I could see the rally cars parked in the lee of the hotel. Phil was there working on the Amazon, and most of the other cars were in various stages of dismemberment. I could see Dan and JD in their overalls, and Geoff and Jennie Dorey working on their Morris Minor, and Dave Bull's big Rover P5, and the silver DB6. We had been warned by the organisers that we were almost all seriously overloaded and were risking not making it up to Tibet and over the Himalayas. As a shining example, the two American women who were driving a Hillman Hunter (the very one RO had wanted me and Phil to buy) were quoted to us as sharing one tube of toothpaste and one toothbrush, to save weight. When they reached the mountains they were planning to jettison even those.

'Wouldn't touch 'em even with yours,' Phil and JD and Dan cruelly chortled to each other.

I went to see the rally MO at his daily clinic. It was time to do something about my own mechanical failure.

Greg Williams was an accident and trauma specialist, who was also a climber and therefore knew about mountain sickness. He had done some obs. and gyn., he assured me, but I didn't get the impression that women's medicine was exactly a major interest of his.

'Are you carrying any progesterone, Greg?' I asked. I knew they had oxygen, trauma gear, Diamox and Immodium in vast quantities, and two body bags.

He blinked at me through his round glasses, as though I had asked for frankincense or myrrh.

'No, I'm afraid not. What's the problem?'

I told him that I had been bleeding, way off schedule, ever since Beijing. In the last two days the blood loss had become worryingly heavy. Progesterone would probably slow or stop the flow.

Greg thought for a moment and then advised me to talk to the other women competitors. For reasons connected with the effects of altitude, those taking the pill had been advised to switch to the progesterone-only version. I might well be able to borrow some from one of them, and then get my own medication couriered out to Lhasa.

'Thanks. I'll try that,' I said. Greg's phone rang and he excused himself to pick it up. A torrent of heavily-accented Germanic English poured out of the earpiece. Greg listened, anxiously frowning.

'I see . . . I see . . . mmm. Oh dear . . . Come up to my clinic now and I'll take a look . . . no . . . no, I'm sorry . . . no, I can't visit you in your room . . . Yes, I know it's a personal matter. I'm a doctor . . . No, I'm running a surgery, I can't leave it to come to your room . . . No, paying me won't make any difference . . . I'm sorry . . . it isn't a question of how much money . . . No. No, I'm very sorry, I just can't do that.'

He scratched at his crew-cut and worriedly pushed his specs back to the bridge of his nose. He looked like a hedgehog.

The voice on the end of the line suddenly changed in timbre. I could hear cackles of laughter.

'Fuck you, Mark,' Greg said. 'I owe you one.'

He replaced the receiver. Mark Thake was his room-mate, a shaven-headed army paramedic who was part of the medical team.

'He got me there,' Greg said ruefully. 'Pretending to be a German with a boil on his penis.'

I thanked him for his help and went down to the car park to see what Phil was up to.

He was fairly pleased with himself. Colin Syn had been shopping and had bought us two new heavy-duty Chinese ignition coils, which were apparently much better whilst still costing much less than the Halfords ones. There was no more leaking from the gearbox, and he had had the rally mechanics over to monitor the back axle clunk. Trev and Jingers were still with him, murmuring over the car like two mother cats with a well-licked kitten. Phil introduced us and we shook hands. Trev was a robustly friendly Brummie with tattoos and a wide smile that revealed a gold tooth. Apparently the support crews all called him Dad. Jingers was much younger, antipodean, always in shorts and one of those wide-brimmed Aussie hats. I liked them instantly. Phil had wisely made firm friends with both of them.

'She's good,' Phil said happily. 'No major problems. Not like some people.'

He nodded at the scenes of carnage in the car park. There were car parts and discarded spares and bits of engine as far as the eye could see.

'All we've got to decide about is the rear protection plate.'

We had two specially-made and hugely strong steel plates protecting the underside of the car from protruding boulders and flying rocks. The only real function of the back one was to protect the lower, supplementary petrol tank. The question now was whether or not to jettison this second plate, which weighed approximately the same as me and therefore added up to quite a lot of toothbrushes, not to mention copies of *Vogue*. If the tank did get cracked we were carrying sealant, and could make sure always to have a jerrycan of fuel aboard in the unlucky event of the main tank being empty at the same time. If the worst happened and the tank got holed beyond repair, we would still have a range of almost five hundred kilometres on the main one.

Off with it, we agreed. Phil undid it and left the massive thing leaning against the fence along with the discards from other crews – spare wheels, differentials, back axles. The rally was stripping itself down, ready for the high mountains.

I went back to the room to telephone my London gynaecologist for advice. The hospital told me he was operating, but agreed to put me through to the theatres. From the other side of the world I could hear nurses' shoes squeaking on lino floors as they hurried round in search of him.

'This lady is calling from Inner Mongolia,' I heard a voice say.

When he came on the line I explained the problem. I could imagine his reassuring presence, doubly so in his theatre scrub suit. Everything would be all right now.

There was a second or two of windy transatlantic quiet, and then my doctor said, 'I think you should come home.'

'*What?*'

'Peri-menopausal bleeding can be serious. Without examining you I can't tell exactly what's causing it and if you do have a bad bleed out there, somewhere inaccessible, without proper medical cover, it could even be fatal.' This was the gist of what he told me, very gently but firmly. 'I think you should get yourself back to Beijing as quickly as possible, and then on the first flight to Heathrow.'

I blinked out at the vista of cocoa-coloured concrete and dirt-thickened air, trying to make sense of what he was saying. He was advising me to pull out of the rally and creep back home.

'I can't do that. I really can't. I want to go on.'

I couldn't let Phil down, for a start, or Tony and the boys at the garage, or any of the other people who had encouraged us and helped us to get this far. Not because of some shaming peri-menopausal bleeding I couldn't, anyway, not a mere four days into China. And of course my doctor was going to advocate the safest course – he could hardly give me a blithe go-ahead to drive a couple of days beyond helicopter rescue range and then ascend to 17,000 feet.

It was almost funny, I thought, that I had considered every possible contingency and emergency that might arise except the breakdown of my own health. I had done all that weight-training and running and boxing, and I was fitter than I had ever been in my life, and now I was being told that I was taking an unacceptable risk just by doing what I had been preparing for for more than eight months. I felt angry that this physical failure should happen now, of all times, and also stricken with a cringing sense of inevitability, that this was just my luck.

'I'm definitely going on,' I said harshly.

'Are you sure?'

'Certain,' I lied.

'You don't want to hear me say this, but your children still need you.'

'I know. I'll be okay. Will you write me a prescription for what I need and give it to my husband, so he can get the medicine couriered out to Lhasa for me?'

'Of course. I wish you weren't doing it, but good luck.'

After that I talked to Caradoc.

'What do you think I should do?'

He answered immediately. 'I don't want you to give up unless you feel you have to. I know how miserable you'll be if you have to fly home.'

He was generous. It would have been much easier for him, of course, to insist on the truth, that he and the children needed me, and that I was to take no physical risks whatsoever. But he hadn't questioned my determination to do the rally in the first place, and he went on supporting my involvement as he had done from the first mention of it. I had the doubts and the failures of confidence, and Caradoc reassured and encouraged me. If he did have a selfish consideration, it was probably preferring not to have to live with my disappointment for as long as it would take me to get over it.

'Let's talk about what we can do,' he suggested.

We went carefully through the practicalities of my situation, looking at the risks as clear-sightedly as we could. I was strong, and the bleeding might stop tomorrow. I had come this far, and it wasn't so much further to Lhasa. From Lhasa onwards I would have the medication, and once I reached Kathmandu I would be moving closer all the time to home and to civilisation.

I talked and listened, and remembered all the other serious joint decisions we had made over the years.

In the end we agreed that it was right for me to go on. Or, at least, that it would be wrong for me to give up.

The next place where we would be able to communicate with one another was Lhasa, four remote nights and five days' driving from Lanzhou. Caradoc promised once more that he would send out the progesterone and iron pills that I needed, and after that there wasn't much else to say. It was difficult to hang up and break the connection. I found myself gripping the receiver so tightly that my fingers went white, as if the force would bring him closer.

It was time for another Chinese buffet dinner. Fortified by a day's work on their cars and by brave decisions about jettisoning unnecessary weight, crews descended on the vats of unidentifiable meat and seething dishes of greens. I decided that I had better at least eat as much as I could get down, and loaded my plate with what appeared the nearest equivalents to liver and spinach. Dave Bull was stricken with traveller's gut and turned queasily away from my food mountain. He prodded at a tiny bowl of boiled rice and wondered how many minutes would elapse before he saw it again.

*

From Lanzhou to our first campsite at Koko Nor we drove 475 kilometres from another 6.41 a.m. start. The road snaked from left to right and back again across the Yellow River, and led us into Xining.

As Phil drove and I prodded the measuring beeps out of the Terratrip, I explained to him about the bleeding. I'd come to the conclusion that I'd have to tell him, in case a real emergency did overtake me, but I had been dreading the conversation. I felt embarrassed, and also ashamed of being the one to jeopardise our chances with some tiresome women's complaint.

In the end, as I should have guessed, he was perfectly matter-of-fact about it. As a mountain guide he had had to deal with enough delicate medical matters. He had even told me about the worst of them – on one long trek a woman had become so constipated that she was faced with the choice of either being flown down to hospital, or submitting to a faecal extraction. She had agreed to an extraction, and Phil had performed the operation with a spoon from the mess tent.

'I warmed it first,' he said.

He asked me if I felt ill, which I didn't. Just rather weak and insubstantial. We both knew that a sudden haemorrhage was not the only worrying possibility to be faced. A low haemoglobin count can increase the risk of high altitude cerebral or pulmonary oedema – which are potentially life-threatening conditions – and I was afraid that my blood-count was dropping by the minute. Meanwhile we would be climbing steadily, towards the highest road in the world, up and over at 17,000 feet.

Lhasa seemed very far away.

Phil didn't waste many words on sympathy or on consoling affection, but I trusted his good sense, and I felt better for having told him what was happening to me.

Xining was the last point of any kind of civilisation before Lhasa, and after we left the city behind the road began to climb steadily through a gorge towards the Tibetan plateau. Phil was looking forward to seeing all his friends amongst the Nepali sherpas and porters who had been brought over into Tibet by Exodus, to service the campsites between Lanzhou and Kathmandu, and he was happy to accept my driving for an hour or so. The road levelled out across a huge, wind-bleached yellow plain, featureless except for a few yurts and a melancholy string of black telephone poles. The sky clouded over and it began to rain. The route was as straight as an arrow, but the sudden rain made it slippery. Two or three times I had to brake to avoid an obstacle and the rear of the car warningly slithered.

We were almost at the camp when a large black pig strutted across the road. I swerved and skidded and finally missed it by a couple of inches. Phil had covered his face with his hands and looked back in disbelief when there was no thump of metal ploughing into pork.

The campsite was on a flat spit of land separated from nearby hills by a wide river. On the other side of the road lay the Koko Nor, the biggest salt lake in China, 10,000 feet above sea-level. Grey waves broke against a muddy shore-line and horizontal rain drove into the Amazon's windscreen.

'It's going to be an uncomfortable night,' Phil said happily. He loved tents and camping and all varieties of physical privation, most of which promised to be in store for us tonight.

The Exodus team had the camp fully prepared. In spite of the frozen ground latrine trenches had been dug, and enclosed with green canvas shelters. There was a row of mess tents, and a big tent where the time control had been established. We parked the Amazon and ran through the icy rain. The big white tent was a haven of warmth. I handed my book to the marshal for stamping, and saw RO slumped beside a table in a folding chair, looking as sick as a monkey. Unlike Phil and me, it seemed, he didn't go well at altitude. There were also half a dozen familiar, beaming Nepali faces. Among them were Sering and Himal, sirdars who had often worked with Phil, and Mingma and Namgel who had accompanied our Gokyo trek, and Arkle the cook, who had the most beautiful face, male or female, that I had ever seen. It was an emotional reunion, up in that cold plateau campsite. For most of the Nepalis it was their first trip out of their home territory, and they must have felt as displaced as I did. They all loved Phil, and clustered round to shake his hands.

'Namaste,' they welcomed us. 'Namaste, Mr Phil.' They put enamel mugs of hydrating hot lemon juice into our hands, just like on the trek. It was almost like coming home.

Cars were arriving in a steady stream, bumping across the rough plain. Tents were being unfurled all along the line. Phil and I put our two in a circle with Dan and JD and Melissa and Colin, and we unpacked our camp kitchen and got the gas burner going. I shook out my wonderful sleeping bag, and blessed Rebecca Stephens yet again from the bottom of my heart. Melissa produced tins of beans and frankfurters and we heated and greedily ate them. I felt happy, in spite of the rain and the cold and the medical situation. Camping was good, after the sterility of the Lanzhou conference hotel.

Local people, with the silk hair braids and yak-bone ornaments of Tibetan costume, began to collect around us. They stated impassively at our hot food, and our merrily hissing camp stoves, and our thousands of pounds' worth of duck-down and Gore-Tex clothing. Children hung about their skirts, and then put out their hands for biscuits and biros. There were no dwellings visible anywhere in the landscape. After a while it stopped raining. Dan and JD and I set off with Phil to cross the river and climb the nearest hill, with the object of walking high and sleeping lower. It makes for a more comfortable night's sleep if you can drop down even a few hundred feet from the highest altitude gained in the day. Slow and steady climbing, Phil warned me. He had tried hard to persuade Melissa to come with him, but she had only laughed.

At the top of the hill was a whitewashed *stupa*, a Buddhist shrine. Prayer flags carved a tattered arc against the pewter sky. Above were snow-covered mountains and below us, against the huge plain and the gunmetal water of the lake, the little line of bright cars and the dotted tents of their servants looked like a sci-fi fantasy.

Back in camp, I continued my pursuit of women who looked young enough to need the contraceptive pill. There weren't that many, and none of them was able to help. Melissa found a strip of her ordinary combined pills and gave it to me, just in case it might help.

'I won't be needing them,' she told me firmly, which made me worry somewhat about Phil's chances.

Arkle's dinner, served by the porters in one of the five mess tents on a strict ticket-issue and timed shift basis, was the best meal of the trip so far. Good, solid, nourishing meat stew and pasta and fried vegetables. Afterwards, Greg the medic came to find me.

'Any luck with the other women?'

'I'm afraid not.'

I must have been looking a bit pallid. He shook his head, seeming even more like a worried hedgehog.

'Lhasa's too far. We'll have to try for some progesterone for you in Golmud.'

Golmud was tomorrow night's stopping place.

'And if you really insist on going on, Rosie, I may have to ask you to sign a medical disclaimer, to make it clear that you're doing this at your own risk.'

'Of course.' I put as unconcerned a face on this as possible, but I was worried. I wasn't sure where it would put me in regard to my medical insurance, even life insurance, but I had my suspicions. Of course Greg had to cover himself against potential negligence claims, I fully understood that, but his suggestion made me feel lonely and in danger. I crawled into my tent in the darkness, and zipped up the flap. A minute later Melissa was unzipping it and crawling in beside me.

'What's up?'

I told her, and she took hold of my hand and held it.

'Should I turn back?'

'Look,' she advised, 'let's get to Golmud and see if there's any medicine for you there, and then you can decide whether to go on or not. There's nothing to be gained by turning back from here.'

She was right, and I loved her for her good sense as well as her hand when I needed some warmth.

'Come on. Don't sit here on your own, worrying. Come in the big tent and have some coffee and a fag and let's talk to some people.'

It was more excellent advice. I sat and chatted to Thomas and Maria and Mick Flick, and the dogs of anxiety stopped their yapping. Furthermore, via Sarah Catt's laptop computer and printer, the day's results were posted on one of the tent poles. The Marmon and the Stutz had now joined the list of retirements. The hot Peugeot 404, in a shock development, had been given a 6 hour 53 minute penalty because the navigator had left the road book behind at the Lanzhou hotel. A large number of other cars had also incurred time penalties including Melissa and Colin, 2 minutes, JD and Dan, 5 minutes, and Jennifer and Francesca, 17 minutes. Phil and I had cleaned the day, and were now in first place with no penalties at all. Although it had to be admitted that that was equal first, with fifty-four other cars.

Chapter Seven

We had left the frosty campsite at Koko Nor after a hearty Sherpa breakfast of hot porridge and fried eggs, the car heater was pumping out warmth, we had slept well, and we were a few minutes into our drive to Golmud, 580 kilometres further towards Tibet. I looked up from the route notes and saw a car flying towards us, headlamps blazing. A second later it flashed by, travelling very fast. It was Mick Flick in the blue Mercedes.

'Where's he going?' Phil wondered. He didn't seem to suffer from morning inertia on camping days.

Two or three minutes later we came round a right-hand bend and saw a truck upside down in the ditch at the side of the road. It was one of the ubiquitous blue transport wagons; the four wheels stuck up in the air at a rakish angle. Phil had begun a sentence about taking a photograph when we saw simultaneously that it wasn't an abandoned vehicle, the relic of a past accident. There was a little group of men clustered around it. Another was lying on the ground.

Phil wrenched the car in to the side of the road. As soon as we got out we saw how bad it was. The passengers, a group of Tibetan migrant workers, had been riding on top of the loaded truck. When it overturned some of them had been pitched into the road. The others were still underneath, trapped beneath a cultivator that had been part of the load.

'Get the first aid kit. And the crowbar and anything else you can find,' Phil shouted to me. He was already on all fours, wriggling under the superstructure of the truck. The survivors of the accident had been crying and wailing but they fell silent as soon as they saw our western faces. 'And the Stanley knife out of the tool box.'

I ran back with everything. Phil snatched the knife and over his shoulder I looked into the space beneath the truck. It had been carrying bags of flour, some of which had burst open. All I could see were terrified staring eyes, faces pasted white with flour, and seamed with tears and blood. Phil began working to cut the trapped men free. The others had sunk down on the frozen bank. They were shivering and moaning, and two or three of them were lying motionless. I wrapped one in my down jacket and took some bundles of their possessions from around the truck, looking for more clothes to cover them against the bitter cold.

Mick Flick must have been the first to arrive on the scene and he had turned right round to drive back for help. I wondered distractedly where everyone else was, from the seven rally cars travelling between Mick's and ours, one of which I knew to contain a British doctor. At least some other cars from further back in the order began pulling in now. Jill and Richard Dangerfield appeared, and Chris and Howard, and Anton Aan de Stegge and his wife from the big yellow Dutch Citroen. We did what we could. We lifted the less badly injured ones and tried to make them comfortable on flour sacks. They were so small that they seemed almost weightless, no more than loose packages of bones and skin. They were shivering violently and their teeth were chattering with shock and cold. Their bundles of belongings that we plundered for heat insulation contained just ragged clothes and a few blankets. At the heart of the heaviest bundle was an ancient dusty cassette player, obviously the prized possession.

Phil had first-aid training. When the last trapped worker had been pulled free and laid on a heap of sacks he moved round each of the injured men, checking to see what we might do.

'Head and shoulder and chest injuries,' he said. And there was one little old man who was lying very still with his legs at a strange angle to his body. He must have broken his pelvis or his back. He had bitten his lips when he fell and the plum-purple skin was gouged with deep, bleeding holes. The contents of our first aid kit, rehydration salts and Paracetamol and Immodium, looked pathetically use-less. We did have some sub-lingual morphine tables and we took them out now, wondering whether to give some to the ones who were whimpering with pain.

'Where is everyone?' I kept stupidly asking.

At home, or anywhere that any of us knew and under-stood, there would have been the blessed wail of oncoming police and ambulance sirens. In Tibet, nobody came. I could do nothing except sit and cradle the head of the old man in my lap. He was still conscious. His hair was white with flour, and his eyes held mine imploringly.

At last there was a squeal of brakes. One of the official rally Fronteras pulled up and Mark Thake jumped out with his medical bag. He pitched in at once, his face grim with concentration.

'We've got some morphine tablets. Should we give them any?' Phil asked.

'We won't give any drugs at this time,' Mark said. He kept repeating it as he worked, like a mantra against this scene of horror that he had to deal with. 'We won't give them any drugs at this time.'

The ones who were crying and wailing the loudest were all right, he told us. It was the silent ones we had to worry about.

'What about this one?' I pointed at the little old man.

'Oh, God,' Mark said and ran across to him.

A woman from one of the press crews was threading her way between the Tibetans.

'I've got some arnica,' she kept saying to Mark, over and over again. 'I've got some arnica. It's really good, shall I give them some?'

Phil and I looked up and our eyes met. An electric shock of hysterical, silent mirth flashed between us.

'If you really want to,' Mark said between clenched teeth.

Then I saw that the Chinese police had arrived. They were standing around with their hands in the pockets of their olive-drab uniforms, smart red tabs and flashes bright in the thin air, with their peaked caps pushed to the back of their heads. They were watching our efforts with mild interest.

'Why don't they do something?' I bleated to Phil.

'They will. When the Tibetans have gone they'll pinch all their stuff.'

A van with bench seats down the sides pulled up. Mark was writing with magic marker on the men's foreheads and forearms, *?fract. scapula, ?chest injury*. We made impromptu stretchers from blankets and loaded in the two men who looked to be most seriously hurt. Three of the ones who could walk folded themselves into the remaining space. Apparently there was a small clinic in the next village but one and they would be taken there for treatment. I wondered if anyone in attendance at a Tibetan village clinic would be able to read and understand Mark's black-ink messages.

Most of the other cars were beginning to drift off, the crews seeing that there was nothing more to be done. I didn't even suggest to Phil that we might go too, even though I wanted to get as far away from there as possible. I knew without asking that he wouldn't leave until the last Tibetan had been taken away.

Another truck stopped just after the van. This one was carrying a load of vegetables and we lifted or helped the remainder of the victims up on top of the knobbly sacks.

At last there was no one left at the roadside but ourselves and Mark, and the flat-eyed Chinese police. Probably Phil's prediction was quite accurate.

Mark thanked us for our help. I realised that we had been at the roadside for an hour and forty minutes.

'You won't get any time penalty,' he assured us.

We got back into the car and began driving.

'Could you believe that woman with the arnica?'

When we finished laughing Phil said into the sudden quiet, 'I'll never forget their faces.'

Neither would I. Nor the childlike frailty of their bodies, nor the poverty of their belongings.

'What do you think will happen to them?'

He shrugged. We couldn't think of an optimistic scenario to offer one another. I thought two or three of them would almost certainly die, and most of the remaining ten wouldn't be able to work for a long time. If they were breadwinners for their families it was a bleak prospect, but the worst truth was that nobody cared at all about these people. The indifference of the police had been the plainest indicator of that.

Even though we had spent so long beside the road the time allowance for the morning's drive was generous enough for us still to make it to the time control, at a place called Qinghai, with 18 minutes to spare. Mark Thake had assured us that we wouldn't be penalised but we didn't quite trust the organisers not to decide against us, and we had driven there as fast as we could go. We joined the end of a long line of rally cars waiting in a pretty, tree-lined avenue with the leaves just touched with the straw-gold of autumn. Once the challenge of getting there was over, Phil seemed to deflate. He went very pale and quiet and just sat in his seat with his face turned away. I thought he was in shock.

'You need a hot drink and some food,' I said. 'I'm

going to fix us a time allowance.'

As I walked up to the control I thought how good he had been in the emergency. I remembered how I had hung back, afraid of what I might see, and how I had sheltered behind Phil's back and waited for him to tell me what to do. I suddenly felt very proud and protective of him. I marched up to the chequered flag at the time control like a mother hen with a weak chick. The marshal on duty was a man called Mike Summerfield. I explained what had happened as he stamped my card.

'My driver's shocked. He needs a rest, and I want to cook him some hot food. Can we have a 30-minute time allowance on the next section?'

Mike shook his head regretfully. 'I understand, and I'm sure you won't be penalised, but I can't make a decision here. I can only make a representation tonight to the Clerk of the Course.'

Mark Thake appeared beside us. 'Car 82 assisted me at a serious RTA this morning. They were there for almost two hours.'

Embarrassingly, I found that I was crying. Mike Summerfield looked grimly sympathetic but he couldn't change the rules.

'Take the time, Rosie. I don't have the authority to tell you it will be all right, but I wouldn't worry about it.'

'We'll get there within the allowance, then,' I retorted stiffly. I went back to Phil and the car and lit the gas stove and cooked up one of the disgusting freeze-dried survival meals we had brought in the camp kitchen, and a big pot of noodles. The noodles made me think of the steaming bowl that Phil had brought for me, back at the Khumbu glacier near Everest Base Camp. The moment when I had really begun to like him.

Phil ate the food with his usual relish, and drank some hot coffee, and started to look much better. Dan and JD and Chris and Howard and Melissa ate with us, and we talked sombrely about the morning. As their time came up all the cars surrounding us in the order moved off, but Phil and I sat where we were until in the end ours was the only car left under the golden trees. We needed the interval of quiet.

There was another 257 km to cover before Golmud, so we couldn't sit in the afternoon sun for too long. Luckily the road that afternoon was almost empty, with long stretches of smooth tarmac occasionally alternating with little treacherous bursts of gravelly dirt. The scenery was monotonous semi-desert with inhospitable mountains crimping the horizon. Arid stretches of sandy plain were cut with dried-out river gulleys, and sprinkled with remote brown villages and herds of yak. We overtook quite a lot of rally cars on the way because Phil drove with a kind of silent, manic intent. I left him to it. We didn't need to talk – the route was so featureless that there were only twenty intermediate instructions in the whole 250 k.

When we reached Golmud we were too short of time to join the immense queue of rally cars at the official fuel stop. Phil drove me to the check-in at the Golmud Hotel and then went off on his own to fuel up. I had read somewhere that Golmud was the home of one of only three potash-producing plants in the world, the others being in Salt Lake City and on the Dead Sea, all of which places I had now visited. It wasn't quite the Seven Summits, but if

I hadn't been feeling miserable and ill I might have taken some quiet pleasure in this potash hat-trick.

I got the book stamped in the hideous hotel's hideous foyer. I was proud that we'd helped out at the accident, and stopped for a rest, and still made it to the end of the day without having to beg for any allowances from the organisers. At the time control I also learned from earlier arrivals that we were all spread out for the night between half a dozen of the town's finest hotels, and if I thought the central and best Golmud Hotel was a dump I was in for an eye-opening experience when I finally saw ours. David Burlinson of Exodus told me how to find it, and apologised in advance.

'Golmud to hell is only a local call,' he said, quoting a line from the route notes.

I found Greg, who I had hoped might come out with me to look for progesterone.

'I can't, Rosie. I've got to do the evening clinic.'

I would have to wait for Phil Colley to arrive, and perhaps Chris Taylor, who as a pharmacist would understand drug formulations, might come with us to search the town for medicine.

It was a warm, stuffy evening. I sank down on the hotel steps beside Andrew Bedingham. I felt weepy and exhausted and the images of the morning kept playing in a loop inside my head.

'Are you okay?' he asked.

'Not really.'

He gave me a cigarette and we sat and watched the cars pulling in, and the dirty, weary, irritable navigators plodding past us with their road books in hand.

'Why are we doing this? Do you have any idea?' Andrew muttered.

'No,' I had to admit.

The police were being difficult about parking and security. At last poor Phil Colley had interpreted enough of the evening's myriad problems to be able to attend to mine. With Chris Taylor, who was morose because the Camaro had picked up a three-minute penalty as a result of a navigator's error, we set off in a taxi to the People's Hospital.

It was one of the grimmest places I have ever seen. The floors were awash with what might have been sewage, the walls filthy, the tiny barred windows smeared with dirt so that the light was even dimmer than the usual Chinese dirty yellow. On our way to the outpatients' clinic we passed a side ward and peeked in. The covers on the rickety bed had been flung back and there was a person-sized lake of blood on the mattress.

In the clinic there was a small line of defeated people. A young woman with a bruised face and bandaged head looked as if she had been severely beaten up.

We were nudged to the head of the queue, to a very young and harassed woman doctor. Phil Colley explained our mission, but she seemed to have only a hazy understanding of what we were asking for. We were directed to the hospital pharmacy.

Behind a glass screen in the pharmacy were two more young women in dirty white coats. The shelves were almost bare except for a dozen brown glass bottles and some packets of bandages.

'You'll be bloody lucky,' Chris said out of the side of his mouth.

The pharmacists were unable to help or, more probably, to grasp what we needed. We were sent on again, this time to the mother and baby unit. There was another woman doctor, this one a little older but no less weary looking, attending to a mother and a tiny silent baby. No one seemed to take exception to three westerners striding in and expecting instant attention.

The doctor listened patiently. But she thought I was asking for contraception, and offered an injection of depo-provera.

There was nothing to be gained here. Empty-handed, we trailed back to the Golmud Hotel. At least I could go somewhere else – not next week, maybe not the week after that, but eventually I would be back in a civilised place where there would be reliable medical attention and all the drugs I needed. That wasn't the case for the unlucky residents of Golmud, and certainly it wasn't the case for the Tibetan workers we had given into the casual care of local drivers this morning. I wondered where my little old man with the broken pelvis might be, or even if he was still alive.

It was also time for me to make a decision. I was now bleeding in heavy, frightening bursts. There was an airport, of sorts, at Golmud. I could presumably get a flight from here back to Beijing and thence to London. On the other hand if I went on beyond air ambulance cover – even if they had such luxuries based in Golmud – and if I did have the catastrophic haemorrhage that Greg and my doctor feared I might, then I would be entirely dependent on Greg and his team for medical support. And although he had told me he carried plasma expanders and copious amounts of oxygen, the plain fact that he wanted me to sign a disclaimer indicated that the doctor didn't rate his chances of saving me if the worst happened.

I could pull out now and get home in one piece, or I could take the risk and go on.

I tried to listen in to my body, although I didn't have much practice at it – usually it functioned so efficiently that I hadn't needed to establish much of a dialogue with my internal organs. But I didn't think I had a ruptured tumour or polyp or any of the possibilities my doctor had mentioned that wouldn't respond to progesterone even if I did get hold of some. I was sure that all the bleeding was caused by a hormonal blip, just one of those things, maybe exacerbated by stress. If I could just get the pills, I would be fine.

I paced the swarming, polluted streets of Golmud, weighing up the situation. Caradoc and I had agreed that I should go on, and now I was at the point of no return before Lhasa I was still sure that we were right. I would get there, in my heart I was positive of it. I would get home safely to finish the job of bringing up my children.

I tried to find Phil or Melissa to talk this over with them, but neither of them was anywhere to be seen. Phil had disappeared. He had fuelled the car, but he wasn't either at the Golmud Hotel or at ours, when I finally found it. The place was, as David Burlinson had warned, comically dreadful. It was staffed by angry blue-suited women whose preferred task seemed to be swabbing the corridor floors with grey mops slopped in and out of enamel buckets. Their efforts resulted in a scummy tide that slowly evaporated to leave treacherous puddles and a film of grit. I paddled up and down the dim stairways but couldn't find a room that corresponded to the symbol on my key fob. The ground floor was a bleak dining area with metal furniture and more enraged blue women who were slamming enamel bowls of food on the tables. Rally crews were sitting down to eat, with Mick Flick – heir to the Mercedes multi-millions – and Dan and JD cheerfully amongst them. The food was a small helping of noodles, some sweet and sour pork balls and plenty of green salad, obviously rinsed in river water if it had been washed at all.

I thought I would give dinner a miss, and wandered back to the HQ hotel in search of Phil, and the day's order. The daily bulletin announced that after a week on the road 52 cars were still unpenalised, ours amongst them, and our start time in the morning was a civilised 9.36, which would give us plenty of opportunity to relax and enjoy the facilities at our hotel. I bumped into Greg again.

'Any luck?' he asked, in what was now becoming a traditional exchange.

'No. I'll just have to get myself to Lhasa.'

Ignoring his warning frown, I slithered rapidly away. I'd made my decision and there was no point hanging round to give Greg the chance to dissuade me. The next encounter was with John Vipond, the Clerk of the Course himself. Looking at me with deceptively sleepy eyes he asked if Phil and I needed an extra time allowance for the day. Clearly he had heard about the small scene I'd made with Mike Summerfield. No, I answered, we'd made the controls within our times anyway.

'Thank you for assisting at the accident,' he said. It was odd to be congratulated for doing what anybody with any human sympathy would have done, but it was true that – except for Mark and a small handful of other crews – the rally seemed untouched by the pathos and surprised by our involvement. The people were only Tibetans, after all. But I let it pass. Mr Vipond had plenty of other problems, one of which was now approaching.

A young man in a leather coat was crossing the foyer, moving with robotic stiffness, his face a tragic mask. This was Herman Layher, widely known as Herman the German, the driver of car number 2, an immense and primitive 1907 La France. RO was very pleased and proud to have such a fascinating old machine on the rally, and invariably mentioned it in interviews and press releases, along with Lord Montagu's Vauxhall, which was now no longer with us. Herman had been suffering a number of mechanical problems, and was clearly not happy tonight. As I eavesdropped, I learned that he was suffering from hypothermia after driving his open vehicle through the wind and rain across the plateau. It had certainly been quite chilly up there, although none of the other crews in open vintage cars had as yet succumbed to frostbite. Now, following his very belated arrival at Golmud, there was no hotel room for him.

John Vipond was soothing, 'We'll find a room. If the worst happens, Herman, you can have my bed. I'll make sure you get some sleep.'

I wandered back yet again to the other hotel. I was beginning to worry about Phil, but Dan had found him. He had been in a little hidden parking space, obliviously working on the car. He needed some time to recover from the day and this was his way of shutting out the world. He was filthy, and exhausted. With two of us on the job we managed to find a room to go with the key. We stood in the doorway, looking in, and a bubble of hysterical laughter floated between us.

There was a stone floor, two sagging beds and a torn curtain covering one third of the dirty window. There was one chair, a table, and a naked light-bulb, and nothing else whatsoever. Phil dumped the camp kitchen on the table and lit the gas burner and I got out the duty-free vodka and a jar of Marmite. It was time to eat, drink and be merry. Somehow we managed all three.

'Room service, madam,' Phil said as he handed me another bowl of noodles with a dollop of instant chow mein. Rally Syndrome had set in. Everything was suddenly very, very funny. We lay back on the rancid beds and laughed over our dinner until we cried. Next Phil decided that this was the ideal moment to tackle me about my overweight luggage and made me open up my second, very small kitbag.

'That can go, for a start, and those, and that.'

My skipping rope and my new Nikes for keep-fit purposes (no time for that anyway), and my dear old orange-back Penguin copy of *Our Mutual Friend*. My Katharine Hamnett jeans, my shower gel, my co-ordinated sets of Agnes B. vests. And *Vogue*.

'How much does *that* weigh?'

It was the September issue, fat with ads for red glossy lipstick and bejewelled watches and buttery leather coats.

'A lot.'

He tossed it on the discard pile, but I secretly retrieved it. I let a few things go, and with some shoving and squeezing I managed to press everything else into the larger bag.

'You can give all that throw-away stuff to the Nepali boys. They'll be thrilled with it.'

'Particularly *Our Mutual Friend*, of course.'

It was time to get ready for bed. I crossed the river of scummy water in the corridor to the bathroom, which consisted of a pungent squat-hole in a doorless cubicle with a urinal directly opposite. As I perched over the hole a Chinese workman came in and relieved himself. The plumbing had become disconnected, or more probably had never been connected at all, and the flow ran warmly over my feet. I squelched back to the room and told Phil about this. I hadn't heard him laugh so much since the Marine with the runs fell into the shit-pit so I went across and ineptly kicked him, shouting 'You rotten little fucker,' which made him laugh even more. I found myself helplessly giggling too.

At last we lay down in the darkness. My ears immediately filled with a scratching and popping sound, coming from underneath my bed.

'Phil? Phil! There's a rat in here. PHIL! It's a RAT, I can HEAR IT.'

'So?'

'So get UP and bloody well CATCH IT.'

Sighing, he levered himself upright. I mounted the chair and he shoved my bed aside. Beneath it, in a puddle of what I hoped was water, was an electric cable with a twisted connection. From the bare spiralling wires a little scarlet fire was merrily fizzing and sparking.

We hoisted the cable out of the puddle and draped it somewhere safer. I closed my eyes. A cocktail of physical exhaustion and laughter made a good sleeping draught. When I woke up it was bright daylight, and Phil was putting a mug of black tea beside my bed.

By nine o'clock we were sitting in the line of cars queuing up for the start. Both of us were keyed-up and happy – no one could fail to be happy at the prospect of getting out of Golmud in half an hour's time. And then I looked up and saw Greg and John Vipond striding down the line. I didn't doubt for an instant that they were looking for car 82 – Greg was going to serve his disclaimer on me, I thought, with the Clerk of the Course as his witness. Well, so be it.

'Can we have a word, Rosie?' Greg asked.

'Of course. But we're on the start in, um, a few minutes. Maybe later would be better . . .'

'I'm afraid this won't wait.' They both looked inordinately serious. Greg was holding a white envelope. He said, 'Rosie, I'm sorry. You didn't get any progesterone last night, I can't authorise you to go on.'

Not understanding properly, I said, 'It's okay, I'll sign a waiver and take the risk myself.'

John Vipond broke in, stony-faced. 'It isn't a question of that. I am sorry to tell you that we are excluding you from the rally.'

'What?'

'We can't take you any further as a competitor, not at altitude. The medical risk is too great. I'm afraid you must fly back to Beijing. You may if you wish take the option of rejoining the rally at Kathmandu as touring entrants. Phil can take a passenger and drive the car onwards to meet you there.'

Lord Montagu, maybe. He was still looking for a lift. The touring entrants were just there for the ride and the scenery. No competition, no adrenalin. I became aware of Phil, standing close beside my shoulder.

Greg held out his envelope. Inside was a letter from him, handwritten but on official rally headed paper, countersigned by the Clerk of the Course. I skimmed the paragraphs.

> *It is with great regret that, as the official doctor for the Peking to Paris Motor Challenge, I must advise you that I consider that it would be unacceptably dangerous to your own health to continue the next leg of the rally . . .*
>
> *. . . clinical condition of peri-menopausal uterine haemorrhage poses two dangers . . .*
>
> *. . . reduced tolerance to high altitude activity . . . increased risk of high-altitude cerebral or pulmonary oedema . . . medical evacuation not possible . . . large haemorrhage could easily prove fatal . . .*
>
> *I now consider it an unacceptable risk to your own health for you to continue in this event.*
>
> *Yours sincerely*

There was nothing new here. I handed the letter to Phil and heard him draw in a breath as he read it.

'If I agree to fly to Kathmandu can we rejoin from there as a sporting entry?'

'No, I'm afraid not,' John Vipond said immediately,

without a hint of a waver. I knew he meant it.

'I don't want to be relegated to tourist. We want to *win*.'

He smiled briefly. 'You aren't going to win.'

'Well then, we'll follow the field anyway. You can't stop us.'

I glanced at Phil. He looked unhappy, but he was nodding in agreement.

'We shall have to withdraw medical and mechanical support. You won't get your cards stamped at the controls, you will be outside the rally organisation.'

Phil's eyes met mine. 'Can we talk about this?'

There were now 20 minutes before our departure time. If we missed our stamp at the morning control we'd be as good as out anyway.

The Clerk nodded. 'Let us know what your decision is.' Briefly he put his arm around my shoulder and gave me a hug. 'I'm sorry, love.'

We sat in the Amazon, numbly gazing at the cars as they rolled away from the start. It was unthinkable that we wouldn't be following them when our turn came. Already it had become much more than a routine; the rally was a whole life in miniature. Phil and I were partners. I was too jealous even to think of him taking someone else and driving across the Himalayas without me.

'I want to go on,' I said. We could follow along outside the rally organisation if necessary. Phil was a mountain guide. We had our own camping and cooking supplies, we'd be self-reliant and we'd be driving across the roof of the world, which was what we had both been looking forward to for months. The rally meant only a few stamps on a few pieces of card, after all, and the possibility of a tin medal at the end of it.

Phil nodded slowly. 'But if something does happen to you up there, I won't be able to save you. I can't look after you, except to comfort you.'

I looked full at him then. He was unshaven and there were grey pouches of tiredness beneath his eyes. I knew how deeply and implicitly I had come to trust him. I took for granted his practical capabilities, and his common-sense reliability in all the details of our enterprise. But I didn't know what he felt or thought, beneath the armour of his cheerfulness. It was asking too much of him, merely as an amiable companion and not my husband nor even my lover, to bear the responsibility of taking me up into the mountains.

I finally understood what was happening. The flame of my defiance and determination died down. It was all over for us; after everything we had done we weren't competing any more, and it was my fault. I felt sick, and unable to draw breath, as if I had been thumped in the diaphragm.

'Have you asked all the women?'

I nodded miserably.

'All of them? What about her?'

He jerked his head at beautiful Maria, next but one in the line ahead of us. In fact I hadn't approached her with my muttered request. In her chic overalls with the gilt trimmings and gilt jewellery, Maria made me feel like a bag of Phil's dirty laundry.

'No.'

'Get out and ask her. *This minute.*'

I glanced at my watch, automatically, as if the time

mattered any more. Nine twenty-six. Suddenly I was running across to the Mercedes. I gabbled out my question.

Maria arched her eyebrows and then smiled at me. 'I sink I might have somesing. I take a pill to lengsen my cycle.'

'Please, please will you find it for me?'

Kindly, Thomas and Maria unpacked their black leather luggage. I watched with my heart hammering against my ribs. Inside one of the suitcases was a black leather pouch and inside that were neat sheaves of different pills, rubber-banded together with their dosage leaflets.

Maria selected a strip. 'Here you are.'

'Thank you, thank you.' I took it and ran, with Phil at my heels. There were now five minutes to our start time. Greg and the Clerk were waiting for us at the control.

'Look, progesterone.' I popped a pill out of its bubble and gobbled it down. 'Everything will be fine now.'

Greg took the pills and the leaflet. He peered through his round specs at the German formulation.

'I need to check it in BNF.' He opened a fat paperback and began leafing through the pages. The Noors' minute came up and the Mercedes shot away. One hundred and twenty seconds to go until ours.

'Quick, *quick*.' Even the Clerk of the Course was dancing with anxiety now.

Greg's face cleared and he nodded at John Vipond. 'This is the right medication. She should be all right on this to Lhasa.'

The Clerk chewed the corner of his moustache, making mental calculations. And then he nodded too.

'Right. You can go.' To the marshal on the control he said, 'Stamp their book.'

We were on the minute. The rubber stamp clapped down on TC Golmud – Out. Phil and I dived into our seats and we were away. We were laughing wildly in disbelief. To have everything snatched away from us and then handed back at such dizzy speed was completely disorientating. I struggled with the Terratrip and the route notes while Phil drove so fast that the tenements of Golmud whirled past and dropped into the distance behind us. A barren road stretched ahead, steadily and steeply climbing into the dun-coloured mountains.

'That was close,' we said, understating it.

I decided that I wouldn't tell anyone, not even Phil, that Maria's pills were two-milligram dosage and there were only fourteen of them. I knew, because my doctor in London had told me, that I needed five-milligram pills, six a day. Therefore I had just about a day's supply – and Lhasa was three days' hard driving and two remote campsites away. But I calculated that if I took a big hit of the drug now, used the rest of the pills very sparingly, and kept two in reserve for an emergency, I might succeed in tricking my body back into hormonal submission.

It wasn't fair to ask Phil to worry any more about me than he was having to do already. Greg and the rally officials very properly wouldn't let me take the risk and I had hoodwinked them very slightly by not admitting what I knew about the medicine. But by not owning up to anyone about the amount of progesterone I really needed, I reckoned I was taking all the responsibility upon myself. The gamble was mine – and after the horror

I had felt when we were briefly barred from the contest, and the ecstatic buzz when we were reinstated, I knew I wanted to go on throwing my chips down. I couldn't have gone slinking safely back to Beijing, when Maria Noor had given me the chance of Tibet.

I took out the strip of progesterone pills again and swallowed two more. When I had a minute to spare I found my diary and scribbled down the details of the situation as I understood them, in case there should be any debate later.

That morning's drive was the best we had done so far. It was a tough road, winding all the way up to the Kunlun pass at 16,000 feet, and in some places we could look up ahead and see the great side-to-side sweeps of it awesomely scarring the snow-patched mountainside. All along the way, like puffs of smoke, were the dust-trails of rally cars forging or faltering upwards. We were so happy to be there. Adrenalin was charging both of us and it made Phil drive harder and faster than ever.

We began overtaking vintageants, and some of the classics ahead of us in the start order. The road was narrow and rough, and it needed careful driving to keep enough revs and enough power in hand to be able to overtake slower cars as soon as the right moment presented itself. Some drivers were very generous and pulled over to let us pass immediately we came up behind them. Others were less considerate and we had to oscillate on their tails, looking for a place to slip through. The Amazon was going like a dream, apparently almost unaffected by the punishing altitude. I was even happy that I had jettisoned my second kitbag, to spare it some unnecessary effort. We passed Dan and JD, going very slowly with a gearbox problem. They gave us a slightly dubious thumbs-up as we went by.

This was the first time I had seen Phil really driving. I was impressed. He stuck out his lower lip in concentration, steering closer to and away again from the hideous drop at the edge of the road, working through the gears and forever fighting against a drop into crawling second, watching the way ahead and waiting for a crack to open up and let him accelerate past the car in front. Gravel spat from under our wheels. We passed the yellow Morgan, the black Mercedes 220, the two American women in the Hillman Hunter. It was breathtakingly exciting. We were shouting at each other over the howl of the engine, encouragement and imprecations. *Go go* and *Let's have him* and *Yeahhhh!*

I looked up at the white teeth of the mountain peaks against the sky. We knew we were going to make the morning's control, up on the glacier plateau beyond the pass. At this moment I might have been down at the airport in Golmud, trying to get a flight back to Beijing – but by a great stroke of luck I was here. Rally Syndrome sent me soaring into the heights of euphoria. We flew over the pass.

On the other side, winding more slowly down towards the time control, we had time to glance at each other.

'Well done, Phil.' I leaned across and kissed him on the cheek.

'Thank you. Nice one.' He gave a twitch of a smile and turned his attention back to the road.

'I don't care what John Vipond thinks of our chances. I think we're going to get a gold. I think we're going to *win*.'

'We'll do our best, eh? How do you feel?'

'Okay, thanks.'

This exchange became the ritual. Every morning, and sometimes one other time, he would ask me how I felt. And I'd answer that I was okay and keep the details to myself, partly out of embarrassment and partly out of a sense that he didn't want to hear any more unless there was something that he would have to deal with.

We pulled in to the side of the road, a few metres short of the control. We had done it with more than half an hour to spare.

That afternoon, on the way to our night's campsite at Tuotuoheyan, the bleak plateau road deteriorated from acceptable to indescribable. Most of it was unmade, and parts of it were so churned up by the succession of rally cars that it became no more than a series of greasy mud chutes. Some of these were so steep that the front end of the preceding car disappeared into them and the rear wheels were left spinning on the lip of oblivion. Rocks and boulders reared up to assault differentials and low-slung petrol tanks. The pace slowed to just a few kilometres per hour. Numerous cars were in difficulties – with suspension problems, gearbox troubles, or just bogged down in the treacherous mud. Everything was made uglier by sudden heavy rain. The four-wheel-drive crews made lots of new friends.

Our Amazon skidded and bucked through the first hour of the distance. Gouts of reddish mud flew up and splattered the windscreen and the wipers worked with a monotonous hum to clear it. We worried about our exposed rear fuel tank, but we had in any case kept it half-empty in order to save weight over the pass and we had a full upper tank waiting. Everything else seemed to be functioning well. I kept quiet and let Phil concentrate on negotiating the twists and turns.

Then we came to the edge of a particularly muddy trough that slewed into a slight dip and then rose steeply on the other side. A brisk run down into the rocky bottom with speed and plenty of revs would offer the only hope of getting up and out again. Several cars were waiting in line to make their attempt.

I got out to see what was happening, taking my camera with me. The big Australian Rolls Royce Phantom V, previously used by the Queen on stately peregrinations Down Under and now driven by Richard Matheson and Jeanne Eve, was stuck in the mud. A Land Rover was nudging up with a tow-rope and Lord Montagu, the Phantom's passenger, was standing at the top of the bank hunched against the cold like a brooding albatross.

I zipped up my down jacket and settled the hood around my ears because the wind was icy and the rain was turning to sleet. With mud sucking at my boots I slithered forward to take some photographs of the Rolls being rescued.

It took a few minutes, but the Land Rover hauled it clear. The next car through was David Arrigo in his Allard – it slewed and skidded and fountains of mud churned behind it, but he went down and up the other side with ease. He waved at me, beaming happily from under his leather helmet. The other cars followed on behind him.

I looked back to Phil, intending to signal that his way forward was clear.

But the Amazon's bonnet was up, and Phil was poking underneath it. I plodded back to see what was wrong.

'Don't know. Won't start – just completely dead.'

He was worried. A couple of cars behind us were revving their engines so I waved them past, and then stood aside to let Phil make his diagnosis. It was very cold now. Deprived of the Roller a handful of Chinese onlookers began to cluster around him, peering into the car's innards and helpfully pointing and prodding. A tide of mud crept around our ankles.

'I think it's something electrical. *Fuck* it.' He was confident about most aspects of the car, but he admitted to haziness around the electrics. He had me sitting in the car, switching the ignition on and off to order. 'Distributor, I think. I'm going to change it.'

I glanced at my watch. Two forty-five, due in at 16.56, about 104 km still to cover. It was all right, we had some time in hand.

'Okay. What can I do?'

'Just . . nothing. Sit in the car. Keep warm.'

I retreated. Phil worked in grim silence, ringed by grinning Chinese. Once or twice he sent me to find a tool or bring a part from the spares kit. The distributor changeover reached a crucial point and he asked me to find the spare rotor arm, the one that went with the second distributor. It was a little orange-brown plastic thing, I knew that much because I'd just seen it. But it was now nowhere to be found, not amongst the litter of tools nor on the ground nor in our pockets.

'It can't just disappear.'

But it had done. There could be no explanation other than it had vanished into the pocket of one of the spectators. Without it the new distributor couldn't be made to function, so it was back to the old one and an attempt to repair it. Time was going very quickly now.

I had heard a car bouncing up behind us, and now it pulled in alongside. It was one of the rally Fronteras and inside – glory be to God – were Trev and Jingers and curly-headed Richard, the second paramedic. They were back-marking the field and fixing up the stragglers as they passed them.

'What's up with you?' Trev asked, beaming golden-toothed out of the open window. I could have fallen into his arms. Two minutes later they were all heads down over the innards. It turned out that it was the coil at fault again. The new Chinese coil was overrated, and although it had worked for a couple of days, it had now burned out the points.

I looked furtively at my watch. We were going to get a time penalty.

Phil and the mechanics worked on it together, but whatever they did the car still refused to start.

'Have to give you a tow, guys,' Jingers said.

At least we'd be moving, and out of the snow and wind. The rope was fixed and we sat numbly in the Amazon. Jingers' thumb stuck out of the Frontera's window, the rope went taut and we rolled down the dip. Phil had to brake to stop us from crashing into Jingers's bumper and the car slewed dangerously as the Frontera struggled for traction on the steep slope. The rope tightened again and we were jerked upwards and over the lip of the hollow.

The road stretched across the plateau – an unending vista of mud, rock and sleet. It was going to take a long, long time to cross more than 100 kilometres of this at the end of a tow-rope.

There was no engine power and therefore no heater, and we drove with the window open so Phil could make hand signals to the Frontera. Gobs of snowy mud splattered all over us and our feet and fingers went numb. The question was no longer whether we would get a time penalty, because we were due in at 16.56 and it was already almost five o'clock, but whether we would reach the time control at the campsite within our maximum permitted lateness. Every section of the rally had a time allowed, and at the expiry of that time there was another probationary interval, usually two hours but sometimes three, during which only time penalties were incurred. Once the maximum permitted lateness had been exceeded, however, even if it was only once in the whole journey, the chance of a gold medal was gone. Today's interval, luckily, was three hours.

Phil kept asking me for the time and distance still to go. It was a hideous job to steer the car and keep the rope tight on the unmade sections. Every time we came to a tarmac stretch he would lean out and make a winding-up signal to Jingers. Faster, go faster. It was a crazy journey; sometimes our speed crept up beyond 100 kph in the wake of the flying Frontera, at others we were stationary beside the road while Trev and Jingers investigated other crews' problems. We left the Phantom V with a broken rear spring, waiting for a low-loader to bring it in, and Maurizio's 2CV also in need of a tow.

Darkness fell and the minutes flew. From being sure that we would make it within the lateness period I began to be afraid that we wouldn't. I tried to console myself, and Phil, with the reminder that this morning we would have been happy to be in this position, just rallying at all. The gold medal didn't matter. We'd still be in for a silver.

Seven-thirty came and went. It was an effort to keep staring ahead into the unrelieved darkness, we were aching from the jarring of the road and the constant jerking of the rope, and we were beyond cold and hungry. Then the Frontera flashed and hooted. I looked across the plain and saw a pinprick cluster of lights. It was the campsite. We passed through some gates into an army barracks and then bumped onwards along a rough track. There were rally cars lining up at a bowser for fuel. I stared at my watch, counting the minutes, willing Jingers just to stop so I could run for the control.

'How long?' Phil asked.

'We'll make it.'

I jumped out and ran. Sarah Catt was manning the control in the big, warm brightly-lit tent. She stamped my card 19.39. Still in for a gold, with 17 minutes to spare, but we now had a 2-hour 52-minute time penalty which would put us down into something like 60th place. At least we were here now. We'd been on the road, pitching between exultation and despair, for ten solid hours.

Grim-faced and snappy with anxiety, Phil instantly started work to diagnose what was wrong with the car. Dan and JD came to help. Somewhere during the day they had lost the kitbag containing their tent from the boot. I went to the cook tent to find Arkle, who gave me hot tea in an enamel mug to take back to Phil. Then I pitched my own tent, making a bad job of it in the snow-raked darkness. The flysheet sagged dispiritedly against the inner but I was too tired to start all over again.

The Amazon's engine suddenly coughed, caught, and roared into life. I dropped the mallet and ran over to see what was happening.

'Blown fuse,' Phil beamed. 'That was why it wouldn't start even after I changed the points.'

'So now we're fixed?'

'Now we're fixed. For tomorrow, at least.'

We put our arms around each other for comfort. I didn't want food, or even hot water. I just wanted to lie down and be safe, to get warm and stay warm, and above all to close my eyes on this interminable day.

I suggested to Phil that he might let Dan and JD have his tent, and share mine for warmth. Before long it was going to be at least fifteen degrees below.

He stepped back at once, with a look in his eyes that I hadn't seen before. It took me a minute to identify it and then I recognised fear. He was like a rabbit trapped in the headlights.

I was caked in mud, bleeding like a drive-by shooting and it was snowing in camp. We had come this far together and we had survived the last two days. And now my co-driver thought I was coming on to him.

If I hadn't been so tired and cold I would have laughed.

As it was, I just said coolly, 'Don't worry, I won't touch you.'

'You won't get any response even if you do,' Phil retorted.

I crawled inside the shaky tent and into my sleeping bag, ignoring the layers of dirt that still clung to me. After a little while Phil followed suit. We lay in the dark and talked about the time we had lost, and promised each other that we would work our way back up the order again. Even though he was two feet away, Phil still seemed to radiate warmth. I stopped shivering. The regular rhythm of his breathing was soothing and I disengaged my mind from worry about what would happen tomorrow either inside the envelope of my body or outside it. I drifted into sleep, listening to the faint kiss of rain or sleet or snow on the nylon above my head.

Phil had left his boots, the only footwear he had with him, in the porch of the tent. I had pitched it so badly askew that the flap gaped open and in the morning they were full of snow.

Chapter Eight

'How do you feel?'

'Okay, thanks.'

There was snow on the ground as well as in Phil's boots, and icy water inside the tent because the flysheet had been touching the inner. It wasn't much of a hardship to get up and immediately get back in the car. The day's programme, Tuotuoheyan camp to Nagqu, inside Tibet proper, was 433 kilometres of steady climbing over the highest road in the world.

'I hope you have a better day today,' John Vipond said kindly at the control.

In the middle of the morning we reached the top of the Tanggu La pass, at 5,180 m or nearly 17,000 feet, and the highest rally time control point ever established. The car and Phil romped along, but I didn't experience the powerful rush of physical exuberance that I had enjoyed on the walk to Everest. Instead the loss of blood was beginning to make me feel hallucinatory, incorporeal, as if I might slip sideways out of myself or catch sight of the ground through the semi-transparent smudge of my foot.

The Frontera with the chequered flag was drawn up at the side of the road, with a folding table in front of it and two well-muffled marshals. When I got out of the car to run across to them, altitude made my breath snag in my chest. They gave my road book a special stamp – 'Roof of the World'. Beyond the control we stopped again to take photographs of the stupa at the highest point. It was swathed with tattered ribbons and the brave reds and blues and yellows of prayer flags. There were undulating brown-grey hills rising on either side to white peaks in the distance, and a wide sky full of towering clouds. The thin air was sweet and pure. The narrow dirt road bisecting this remote territory looked like an irrelevance rather than our lifeline.

'You've forgotten something,' a loud voice said. It was Mike Summerfield who had drawn up behind us in one of the support cars.

Phil and I glanced anxiously at each other. Our luggage? John Vipond's birthday? Some crucial bit of rally-behaviour that would lose us points? It turned out to be the latter. We had stopped the car but hadn't left the red OK sign prominently displayed.

'I want to see that OK every time you stop.' Mike wagged his finger at me. 'You, especially.'

All the organisers must have been warned about my problem, and now they were watching me in the expectation that I might keel over at any minute. It was embarrassing, but also in a way reassuring. It meant we were still on the rally. I just hoped that they hadn't shared the details of my malfunction with RO.

'I'm fine. I love high places,' I said brightly to Mike. In fact I was very uncomfortable. Sometimes the bleeding would stop, just to trick me into relaxing, and then there would be a sudden engulfing flood. I would have to sit still and wait until I could creep away to inspect the damage in private, which wasn't easy in a bare landscape dotted with flying rally cars where a coffee-table sized rock at the side of the road was regarded as adequate shelter for personal matters. I was beginning to feel like a pariah. Soon I would have to start ringing a bell and intoning 'Unclean . . .'

It was a long, demanding day. I did that afternoon's driving, another 235 km across windswept pastureland where the only living things visible in the landscape were huge herds of yak and sheep, and our strung-out chain of muddy, battered, indomitable old cars.

We reached another camp site, this time in the crooked arm of a wide river. We made a huddle of tents with JD and Dan and Melissa and Colin, and brewed up tea and more noodles. Colin felt the cold particularly acutely, and tried to persuade me to sell him the Rebecca Stephens sleeping bag, offering me even more than I had originally paid for it. He was out of luck – I wouldn't have traded it for the Porsche itself.

Phil fondly watched Melissa swinging back from the river with washing-up water.

'Here she comes. Porsche Spice.'

He could be very funny and sometimes quite witty. He was extremely popular with everyone who came into contact with him, competitors and support crews alike, and he responded to them all with the same slightly indiscriminate and arms-length cheery banter, just as he did with me.

The only person he reacted to slightly differently was Dan. They were friendly on the surface, and probably at the most fundamental level too, but the middle level was turbulent with tricky currents. Dan had been to public school and Oxford, and he had an easy, graceful manner through which he still managed to project the impression that he was rather sensitive and interesting. Phil thought, not altogether accurately, that Dan stood for a whole series of values that were the opposite of his own. In fact their backgrounds probably weren't that different – Phil had deliberately chosen to adopt a rough-diamond persona for himself. He had *gone prole*, as Melissa put it.

Dan was a management consultant, but he had read engineering. He knew a lot about cars in general and had built his Amazon for this rally, so he had more expertise than Phil in certain areas, although Phil also knew some things that Dan didn't. They needed one another's help on most days, and Team Amazon was a team more than just in name, but there was also a noticeable and occasionally uncomfortable rivalry between them. They were very competitive with each other – I knew how much Phil minded that we had now dropped so far behind our teammates in the running order. This situation wasn't improved by the emerging fact that every single one of the eligible young women on the road, including Sarah and Melissa and the two sharp American girls from the film crew, was attracted to Dan. He made no effort to do it, and claimed total loyalty to his girlfriend back in London, but he just flickered his dimple and they came running.

JD was apparently much more straightforward. He was

ever-smiling, always laid back and good humoured and ready to joke, and just a little unvarying. He was only in his late twenties, and with his cropped hair and his earring – even though I had now spent long days getting to know him – he still seemed to me exactly like one of Charlie's mates from Camden Town or Bagley's club.

I liked watching all the social and sexual jockeying amongst the twenty- and thirty-somethings. Their constant company made me feel old, but also relieved that I was done with the chase. And they were so entertaining to be with, so funny and relaxed, that I wanted to go on being around them. Apart from raffish David Arrigo and a couple of others, I didn't make as many friends as I should have done amongst the pleasant, fiftyish Brit couples and pairs of men driving prized cars who would have made more logical companions for a middle-aged lady novelist. Our gang, with Chris and Howard and Carolyn, and Greg and the paramedics and Trev and Jingers, was already formed. It was a bit like being in with the bad lot at school: we were never going to win any form prizes (except perhaps for Adam and Jon) but we were having plenty of laughs.

At Nagqu I had dinner in the mess-tent with Adam and Jon, and Bill Ainscough from the 1929 Chrysler. I heard that Prince Idris had had an altitude-induced blackout at the wheel, and had run Humpty-Dumpty into the ditch and broken a shock-absorber. Herman the German and the La France had pulled out because Herman was ill. Numbers of other people were suffering the effects of altitude and were besieging the medics for hits of oxygen. RO was badly affected; he had got his Peugeot stuck so

deep into the mud that he had needed a tow from a
police jeep. Plenty of competitors' cars were having difficulties too, from a combination of the altitude, the
terrible roads and the 70-octane fuel. Time penalties were
building up, although a full update on the order wouldn't
be available before Lhasa. With the gas-lamps flaring and
the hot, copious food served by the Nepali camp crew,
and all this gossip and laughter, it was better than any
London dinner party.

Afterwards I took the car to join the queue for fuel
from the bowser. Tibetan families had materialised out of
the darkness to stare silently at us. Men and women alike
had their hair braided with brilliant silks and decorated
with yak-bone ornaments, and they wore yakskin coats
and boots. Tiny children with mucus-caked faces stared
from their arms or the shelter of their skirts. The families
walked impassively in and out of the lines of rare and
beautiful cars and between the latest four-season tents
stuffed with food and expensive warm clothing. From
time to time their dark faces were illuminated by the
swinging beams of passing head-torches, or the lights of a
car pulling away from refuelling.

The sky was brilliant with stars. The frosty air rang with
laughter from the mess tents, and the opulent revving of
a Bentley or a Buick. When they saw any of us looking at
them the Tibetans raised their bunched fingers and
tapped their mouths, to show us that they were hungry.

It was a painful juxtaposition. There was an impervi-
ousness about this collective dash across the world
because the blinkers of money and the demands of competition too often closed off our perspectives. It wasn't

that most of us didn't feel sympathy for the Tibetans, or recognise our own good fortune. It was just that there wasn't time. There was never time to look properly, or reflect, or to linger and learn more.

At last, we were on the home run to Lhasa. After breakfast at Nagqu I met curly Rick the paramedic making a tour of the camp.

'I'm just checking up to make sure everyone's okay this morning. How are *you*, Rosie?'

I stretched him a wide smile. 'I'm absolutely fine.'

In fact I thought I could just about make it to Lhasa and the medicine.

It was an easier day's driving than the last two. In the morning we climbed up and over another pass, the Kyogche La, at 4,900 metres, and in the afternoon we began the descent into a broad river valley. The scenery changed from the flat, windswept moonscape of the high plateau to a more fertile and intimate landscape, with cornfields and vegetable crops lining the road, and numerous little whitewashed settlements. The backdrop of high silver mountains provided a startling contrast in scale to this domestic picture. We passed a monk at the side of the road. He stood up, walked a step and then sank to his hands and knees to touch his forehead to the ground, then stood again and walked another step before prostrating himself once more. His hands were protected with pads of cloth. He was on the way to Lhasa.

Phil wouldn't stop to take any photographs of the scenery or the people that afternoon.

'I want to get you to Lhasa as quickly as possible,' he

said, and this glimpse of his concern touched me.

The day's last time control was just outside Lhasa and for the second day running we incurred no time penalties. It seemed reasonable to hope that as other crews were penalised we might have begun to creep upwards again from our present low point of sixtieth place.

Ever since I had first imagined how the rally might be, driving down from the plateau into Lhasa had been the experience that I had fixed on to be the most exotic and thrilling, the quintessence of the trip. We sat forward in our seats now, waiting for it and peering ahead for the first glimpse of the city. The first sign was a slight increase in traffic: there were a few farm wagons, bicycles, a couple of buses, even one or two private cars. The road widened and the surface improved dramatically, and the settlements came closer and closer together until they ran into one thin line. A few people gathered at the sides of the road to watch us go by, almost the first spectators we had drawn since Golmud. The road became a broad avenue, lined with trees. The verges were planted with flowers, cosmos and marigolds, the colours dimmed by a veil of dust. Whitewashed village houses gave way to the now-familiar concrete blocks of Chinese apartments, just like in Lanzhou or Golmud. In the bright sunshine it felt suddenly more as if we were entering some medium-sized eastern Mediterranean town instead of the capital of Tibet.

Then Phil leant forward. 'There it is.' He pressed his finger to the windscreen and I followed the direction he was pointing in. The Potala Palace reared up, a massive grey-white monolith against the blue sky. A second later it had disappeared again behind another dun-coloured concrete block.

The route notes brought us neatly to our destination: the Holiday Inn, Lhasa. It was modern, concrete, featureless except for a row of flagpoles lining the entrance. Sighing with relief I switched off the Terratrip and the upper and lower figures faded into blankness. Every night the zeroing beep of the trip stalked my dreams. But we were here now. All would be well.

I almost ran into the lobby and up to the reception desk. There were piles of messages and faxes waiting for arriving rally crews, but none for me. In disbelief I made the receptionist check again. Phil went to find the manager and asked him to look for my package too, but there was nothing to be found.

Fighting the fear that I was going to collapse, I went upstairs and managed to put a call through to Caradoc in London. He was even more distraught than I was. He explained that he had tried everything and everyone, including the Chinese Embassy and the Foreign Office, but it had turned out to be politically and logistically impossible to get a delivery of any kind couriered into Lhasa, even a package containing urgently needed medicines. The nearest point he could send it to was Kathmandu, and Kathmandu was five nights distant from here on the other side of the Himalayas.

I was right back to where I had been in Golmud, faced with the decision of whether to risk everything and drive on, or to head for the airport and home. This was the worst moment of the trip so far.

I went to find Phil to tell him what had happened. He

put a consoling and concerned face on it, but I knew how
tiresome all of this must be for him. I could imagine how
he must be wishing to have some robust bloke like Dan or
DJ for a partner instead of me. He must feel that he was
obliged to look after me instead of romping around with
the rest of the kids his age. I felt ashamed and inadequate
and oddly floppy, and at the same time angry with fate
and my body for playing such a cruel trick on us. Phil's
invariable advice was never to touch alcohol in high
places, but now he took me to the hotel bar for a beer and
I drank it, thinking to hell with the altitude, I couldn't feel
any worse than I did already. Our table was at the side of
a corridor down which arriving crews were heading for
their rooms and hot showers. Phil greeted them all and
the atmosphere of happy relief and anticipation was miserably at odds with the way I felt.

'Sorry,' I said ungraciously to Phil.

'Look, we'll sort something out. There must be a western doctor in Lhasa somewhere. I'll find one and get you
to see him.'

I was beginning to know him better. He was always at his
best when there was a task to be done or a problem to be
solved, and reticent when it came to emotional exchanges.
Whenever I wanted a friendly hug and some honest affectionate talk, the gap between us – whether age, or gender,
or just intuition – always seemed at its widest.

Obviously I couldn't ask Greg for help, or hint to him
that Maria's pills weren't strong enough to stop the bleeding, let alone indicate that the medicine hadn't arrived in
Lhasa after all. He and the marshals would bump me off
the rally again faster than I could say Tampax. Instead

Phil did as he said he would: from the helpful English-speaking receptionists he discovered that there was a Chinese doctor attached to the hotel, and that he was even at that moment holding his clinic in the building. Phil gave me the room number.

'Do you want me to come with you?' he asked, his face tightening up in nervous anticipation of what that might involve.

'No. I'll be fine.'

I wandered down the corridors and found the room. The door was opened by a very small man in a white coat. Inside was an ordinary bedroom, with a doctor's big black bag open in front of the dressing-table mirror. On the bed, very decoratively arranged, was a pretty girl in a tight cheongsam. I started to back out, mumbling apologies and twisting round to check the room number, but the man took my arm and indicated that I was to sit down. It was plain that he didn't speak or understand a syllable of English.

I tried to describe what was wrong, and got nowhere. I took out the strip of Maria's pills, of which there were now only two left, and showed it to him. I made what I hoped were signs plainly indicating 'give me plenty more of these and make them very, very strong medicine'. His face cleared with slightly worrying rapidity and he smiled broadly. Out of his bag he took an ordinary brown envelope, and a twist of crinkly white paper – the kind that quarter-pounds of boiled sweets were measured into in exchange for pocket money in the 1950s, ten years at least before Phil and the rest of them saw the light of day. Out of the envelope and into the paper twist the doctor counted thirty-six tiny, powdery white pills. He handed them to me, nodding encouragement. I took two of them between thumb and forefinger and popped them into my mouth with a questioning tilt of the head. The nodding speeded up.

Oh well, I thought, and swallowed. Probably not arsenic or Ecstasy. Most likely, baking powder.

The doctor drew his pad towards him and in a firm clear script wrote $90. I paid him, cash. The girl on the bed – nurse, chaperone – drew herself into a seductive S-shape as I left.

I had dinner and went to bed early. Phil and the young things headed out for a bar and then a night-club for some dancing. I spent most of the late evening fielding telephone calls from home. Phil's girlfriend Philippa was very anxious to speak to him; Tony Barrett rang for news of the car and Phil. I told him about the wrongly-sited ignition coil and the chain of disasters that had followed on from the overheating.

'Sorry about that,' he said, sounding nothing of the kind.

Caradoc called again. In some respects he and Phil were oddly similar – certainly Caradoc was also more comfortable when there was a problem, like the withheld visa, to be worried at and worked through. To be powerless was his worst case, and his inability to get my medicine into Tibet had upset him deeply. He was seriously anxious about me now, and the distance and danger and our inability to touch or help each other chafed us badly. He wanted me to come home safely, but he didn't want me to pull out of the rally. I wanted to go on at all costs, but I wanted to be with him because I felt weak and I missed him so much. It wasn't a comfortable call for either of us. When I spoke in turn to Charlie and Flora I tried to keep the stress out of my voice. Charlie told me how Arsenal were continuing their season, and Flora was full of the news that Madonna might be buying a London house from the parents of a friend of hers.

'Just think, Madonna will be swimming in the same *pool* as I swam in.'

'Mmm. Do you think she'll cut down those palm trees they planted along the drive?'

We agreed that it would be a shame if she did because they lent such a pleasantly exotic touch to Hampstead Garden Suburb.

Phil crashed into the room at 2.30.

'Mmmmhhhhhhh. Night.'

'Night.'

The bright light of the morning didn't bring a lightening of mood. Rally Syndrome had thrown a really big dip at me, and Dr Ninety-dollar's pills definitely weren't working. I ordered tea and toast from room service and sat in bed with the tray on my knees watching Phil struggling back to consciousness. When he was awake enough to prop himself up I handed him a cup of tea. He looked about as fed up as I felt. When he saw that I wasn't going to get up and make myself scarce according to custom, he rolled out of bed in his usual semi-dressed state and prepared to pull on the rest of his clothes.

I was used to living with Caradoc, who knew me so well. Ill or not, lonely or otherwise, I tried to remind myself that in Phil's eyes I was an older woman, established and successful and capable, with no reason to crave his or anyone else's affection or reassurance in a hotel bedroom in Tibet.

'Okay?'

'I'm fine. Thanks,' I sniffed. 'How are you?'

'Got a bit of a hangover, actually.'

He went into the bathroom and briskly locked the door.

It was a day off from rallying for all of us. We went sightseeing in a series of taxis, with Melissa and Carolyn and all the others, to the Potala Palace. Phil got in a different taxi from me but otherwise he was just as cheery as he always was.

The palace was an extraordinary sight. It was a series of vast grey-white blocks crowned with dark-red pagoda roofs and slotted with hundreds of tiny rectangular windows. It wasn't beautiful, but it was beyond spectacular. Its massive size, rearing on a great outcrop over the flat river basin and facing over to the ring of mountains that circled the plain, demanded that visitors tipped their heads back to take in the summit. The air was thin enough even at the base of it, and the contemplation of this further great height truly did take my breath away. From the very top, just discernible against the blue sky, we saw that the Chinese flag was now flying.

We began the long climb up the steps to the side of the palace. I very quickly felt breathless and weak-kneed. It was an effort to make each upward step, and remembering how omnipotent I had felt on the road to Everest only underlined my present feebleness. I plodded on, pretending to dawdle to admire the view when I was really forced to a standstill by exhaustion and lack of oxygen. Dan and JD and Phil waited for me under the great gates at the top, and we passed into the courtyard of the palace together. The first thing I noticed was the fringes of pleated fabric fixed like pelmets over the windows. The wind lifted them and played underneath so the effect was like endlessly rippling waves. The second was the numbers of Chinese police and soldiers there were – not apparently doing anything, except standing and watching us.

We climbed the steps and walked through the great dark-red doors. Apart from the guards there was almost no one around; a couple of Tibetans sloped unceremoniously across the courtyard and a pair of young monks in their red and saffron robes strolled past us. It couldn't have been more different from a western cathedral or palace of similar importance, flooded as they all are with sightseers and tour buses. Inside, as we drifted through the great silent warren of deserted interconnecting rooms, I felt like an invader. The light was dim, pierced with an occasional oblique shaft of light from a high window. There were pillars of gold and huge Buddhas and intricate thangka paintings on the walls. Every surface was painted in iridescent colours, viridian and magenta and saffron, crimson and sapphire and gold. The air was thick with smoke and the smell of incense.

In front of the central, hugely ornate stupa a single monk was chanting. Lounging and watching him were four Chinese guards. Remembering the flag flying at the highest point of this great edifice, I knew that it was superfluous to feel like an invader because the invasion had

already taken place. The Chinese weren't the first, either.
The British, under Colonel Francis Younghusband, had
achieved that distinction in 1904.

We climbed wooden stairs and passed through wooden
galleries to reach the palace roof. Below us was a wide,
tree-lined square, almost deserted except for a few tiny
criss-crossing cyclists. Lhasa stretched beyond it, the old
city and the Jhokang Temple compressed by blocky,
modern Chinese outskirts, and beyond that the flat river
plain was encircled by high, cold, blue-grey mountains.

Phil spent the afternoon in the hotel car-park, working
on the car on advice from Trev who showed him how to
change the needles and lean the mixture down even further to cope with the reduced air-pressure over the
Himalayas and across in front of Everest. Otherwise, Trev
said to our complete delight, everything under the
bonnet looked good. The Amazon was surrounded on all
sides by jacked-up cars – everyone was working to prepare themselves for the last demanding haul up and over
to Kathmandu. I took out a tray of food to Phil and Trev
from the hotel's Hard Yak Café – which truly would have
been better named hard tack – and left them to it. I had
asked the hotel receptionist to write 'pharmacy, please'
and 'iron tablets' and 'food shop' on slips of paper, and
armed with these I took a taxi to what I hoped would be
the Tibetan equivalent of Boots.

The driver cut through the old city. The streets were
clean and open and there wasn't a western face to be
seen. The square white buildings all had the same small-
paned windows outlined in bright paint, and the
window-sills and scrubbed steps had painted buckets and

tin cans arranged on them, planted with geraniums and cosmos and nasturtiums and even runner beans, these cottage garden plants looking familiarly innocent in their exotic setting.

My driver pulled up in front of a big neon-lit shop on the corner of a concrete block. It was definitely a pharmacy: the female assistants wore white coats and there were antiseptic-looking shelves with sliding glass doors. A course of iron tablets was no problem. A young woman glanced at the slip of paper and came back at once with an ornate package. Inside were twenty-four lurid orange vials, and even some English dosage instructions. I had run out of sanitary supplies. Imagining that I would be able to select what I needed off a shelf I hadn't asked the receptionist to write this down for me, and now I looked wildly around for something promising to point at. There was nothing at all, and the assistant was looking quizzically at me.

'Er . . .'

I indicated a pen and she gave me a scrap of paper.

'Er . . .'

I gnawed the pen for a minute and then drew a tampon. The assistant frowned and three of her colleagues fluttered across to see if they could help. Their mystified faces bent like flowers over my tampon sketch. No light dawned.

There was nothing for it but to try mime. I pointed at the drawing and acted out an insertion. Thank God I hadn't brought Phil and Dan with me.

The shop assistants reached no higher than my shoulder. I felt huge, distorted, like Alice after she had taken the growing potion. In a minute my head would hit the ceiling and my neck would bend in a loop, like in the Tenniel illustration. The tiny women blinked up at the huge westerner who was jabbing a finger at her private parts. The first one began to giggle and then the next, and then a wave of mirth engulfed the shop. I had by now drawn quite a crowd and the taxi-driver strolled in to join the party.

I grabbed the paper again and this time tried an artistic representation of a sanitary towel. It was like taking part in some surreal parlour game with incomprehensible rules. The shop was full of gasping people who were holding their sides and wiping their eyes. I was ready to run when an older woman took my arm. She choked down her mirth and led me kindly out of the shop and down the street to a dingy open-fronted kiosk. The glass counter was piled with dusty Coke tins, smeary packages of children's ankle socks and packets of 555 cigarettes. From under the counter the kiosk woman produced a squashy packet of the old-fashioned kind, with loops, the sort that I hadn't set eyes on since I was a schoolgirl. Eagerly I tucked it under my arm and gestured for a couple more packets while we were about it. The women murmured to each other in disbelief as I handed over the yuan notes. I thanked them both profusely and sank into the taxi. Boots was ticked off the list and now it was time to turn my attention to Sainsbury's. I was looking for in-car supplies to keep Phil stoked up all the way down to Kathmandu.

The 'food shop' the taxi-driver took me to turned out to be a cavernous concrete and corrugated-iron shed on the edge of the old city. Within it was a rectangle of sloping counters backed by wooden shelves, manned by sad people who sat on stools and looked as if they hadn't moved for hours on end. The food on sale consisted mostly of dusty sweets and a few packets of biscuits; on the shelves were cans of food with torn and stained labels. There was no fruit, either fresh or dried, no bread or crackers or even noodles. The only other customers were old women who shuffled along the displays of merchandise, suspiciously prodding at the sweets and biscuits.

More or less at random I picked up some biscuits and filled a tin dish with a double handful of sweets. I held them up but no one offered to take my money in exchange. So I walked to the nearest stool-sitter and pushed the goods towards him. He responded with a vicious and unmistakable negative, almost spitting with vehemence. I looked around again, and then understood. The shop was a co-operative: each of the people on stools had a tiny stall all of his own, even though the wares were identical and identically uninviting, and I had tried to pay one of them for goods from a rival, absent operator.

The poverty of the set-up was almost blinding. Some of the vendors had two tins and a small heap of sweets to sell. I wondered how much they had to pay, and to whom, for the privilege of offering their goods in this place.

Hastily I bought a random selection of sugery stuff and gave the stallholder all the yuan I had with me except for my taxi fare. He was too sad-looking even to acknowledge it.

On the way back to the Holiday Inn I stared into all the shop windows we passed, looking for a food market, but I didn't see one anywhere. How did these people eat? Where did they buy nourishing food for their children?

There must have been an answer, but I never found it. The next morning when the rally clock ticked to 8.42 exactly, car 82 was leaving yet another half-glimpsed and completely unfathomed place behind it in a pall of dust. There was no time, no energy, no curiosity left over for anything else. In the few brief minutes that did offer an opportunity for reflection, I felt ashamed that every day that we drove was a vulgar, callous display of wealth and power. But I couldn't stop. None of us could stop. The rally was all-consuming.

That day, on the road onwards from Lhasa to Xigatse, I understood why long-distance classic rallying can become addictive.

Twenty-seven cars had reached Lhasa without incurring any time penalty. According to plan and the route notes, there had been two different itineraries for the day – one for the vintage cars, and a higher, longer and more difficult one for the classics. Unfortunately a landslide had recently blocked the higher road and it was now impassable, so all the cars would have to take the lower route. The organisers decided that they would take this opportunity to make matters more interesting for us all. They divided the distance into four stages, they shortened the time allowances for each of them, and they started the classics first, so there wouldn't be a slew of fast and slow cars fighting for places on every bend.

The first stage, 68 kilometres out to Lhasa Bridge across the broad Tibet river, was uneventful. There was even time to look at the scenery, as spectacular river gorges widened out into golden cornfields interspersed with fertile yak- and sheep-grazed pastures. The second stage was harder. It was 33 km of rocky dirt-track, and we had a time allowance of 29 minutes. I had dutifully copied all the amendments for the day into road book and route notes, but I hadn't done the maths in advance – and so didn't have a minimum average speed for the stage in mind. We set out cautiously because the road was so treacherous – potholes suddenly gaped in front of us and massive rocks reared out of nowhere, and Phil was always careful to protect the car as far as possible. Then, with a nasty start, I realised how much time had elapsed and how far we still had to go.

'Faster. We'll have to go faster.'

Phil put his foot down. The potholes and rocks and blind bends whirled towards us much more threateningly and every decision became a split-second one: whether to ride on top of the bumps or to drive down into the trenches, whether to overtake a truck on this bend while we still had the power to do it or whether to play safe and wait until the road was clear, whether to accelerate and hope to achieve enough momentum to bounce over an obstacle, or whether to be prudent and brake. The front wheels would lock into a pair of ruts while the back end slid sideways, and every time we came up behind a slower car we were blinded by a thick veil of choking dust.

Phil gave it every particle of his concentration and energy, working at it so hard that I could feel the snap of each decision radiating out of him. It would be too easy to make a wrong choice and break a wheel or a half-shaft or to skid straight off at a bend and end up nose down in a ditch.

I jabbed at the trip, trying to pin-point exactly where we were over the distance, and I watched the minutes flick away on the timer, and kept computing the minimum speed we would have to keep up to bring us in under time.

We made it, on the minute. Immediately, without time to draw breath, it was time to set off again.

As soon as I added it up I saw that this stage would be even tougher. Sixty-five kilometres in 52 minutes, and the road was deteriorating all the time.

'As fast as you can,' I called out.

'Hold tight,' Phil said grimly.

We were already overtaking cars ahead of us in the order. Every time it was a plunge into grey-white swirls of dust, and we would both strain forward to catch a glimpse of the car just in front and of the truck that might always be coming the other way.

Watching the clock I kept shouting 'Faster!' and with every other breath I qualified the order with 'Be careful!'

We turned the music up so it was pounding. Phil kept his thumb hard on the horn and powered the car round the bends, wrenching the wheel from side to side. He yelled at the slower cars as we bounced behind and jockeyed for a chance to slip by.

'Eat dirt!' we howled as we roared past them.

We overtook Dan and JD, who had started 12 minutes ahead of us. I caught a glimpse of Dan's face, a crescent of anxiety, but they were still moving even if slowly.

We glanced at each other. 'Will they be okay?'

'Yes.' There was no stopping.

Once we hit the lip of a crater and all four wheels left the track.

'Shiiiiiiit!' Phil shouted. We smacked the ground with a jolt that shook our teeth and bones, but somehow the car kept running. There were still 27 km to go and only 19 minutes left; we were skidding past streams and then a waterfall, the crown of the road was studded with stones to stop cars speeding on the bends just as we were doing.

'How long?'

'Just keep going. Fast as you can.'

We were already going faster than I would have thought possible in a thirty-six-year-old car on an open dirt road where the view ahead was hardly more than a peek through a hanging pall of dust. I watched the trip and the timer, barely able to draw a breath. No one had overtaken us, no one was going any faster or harder than we were, but I still knew we couldn't make it. The question was: by how long wouldn't we make it?

'How far?'

'Ten k. Nine point eight k . . .'

Beepbeepbeepbeepbeep. It was the timer on the dash. Out of time.

'*Fuck* . . .'

Phil leaned forward, pushing his right foot harder down.

'Eight to the TC.'

At last, over the brow of a hill there was a village ahead of us. The control was there, I could see cars skidding away from it and the sun glinting off them as they accelerated sharply away. Everyone was late, everyone was pushing it.

When I ran up to the marshal, the rally clock was showing 11.29. We had a nine-minute penalty.

'Plenty of other people did worse,' I panted to Phil as I dived back into the car again and he shot away almost before the door was closed.

The last stage was all the way to Xigatse. It was much easier, only 76 km and 91 minutes to do it in, but we still gave it all we had. We were in the swing of it.

We got in with plenty of time to spare, one of the first cars to reach the Xigatse Hotel. Phil swung the car into the almost empty car park and switched off the engine. Our ears were ringing with the noise. When we looked at each other, we were still jerky with adrenalin and shaking with the demands of the road. We had completed one of the toughest days of the entire event. We had been wedged in the car together for all those hours of mutual effort, shouting and pushing forward and watching the clock and wincing at every blow to our car, until we had forgotten that we were two separate people. Now, suddenly, after the intimacy we were almost shy. We clapped hands, very slowly, and smiled.

'You were great,' I told him honestly.

Phil leaned across and gave me a kiss. 'So were you.'

I understood what rallying was all about.

The rest of the cars and the day's news filtered in. Only seven cars out of the whole field had cleaned the 29-minute section, two of the Iranian crews and the green Aston Martin among them, and three of those – including Carolyn – were in four-wheel drive machines. Dan and

JD had broken both their rear shock absorbers and had gone out into Xigatse in search of a mechanic and welding gear. Plenty of other cars were in difficulties with their suspensions, and had dropped time at two or more of the day's stages. Phil and I felt that we had good reason to be pleased with ourselves. We were still fifth out of the five Volvos competing but we had moved up to 58th place. Tomorrow would bring another hard day's driving; we thought that our Amazon had proved to be so strong over the rough roads that we could risk going flat out once again – and maybe creeping a few more places up the order.

It was a good night. I sat by Dave Bull at dinner and we talked about our lives at home and our families and what we believed in. It was one of those generous inclusive conversations about things that mattered – the first I had had since talking to Chris Taylor in Lanzhou. Dave was also very funny. He told me that his mother-in-law kept losing her false teeth. Most recently they had turned up in someone's luggage in a different car.

'They'll be found biting into some poor bugger's sandwich next,' Dave said.

Afterwards we retired to the bar, recklessly dismissing all thoughts of altitude. Everyone was buzzing with the thrills of the day, and wanting to drink and talk about it. I had a private toast to make. It was 17 September, Charlie's eighteenth birthday.

I had tried to telephone, but I couldn't get through. I knew that Caradoc was giving a party for him at our house, drinks for his godparents and close family and friends, and then Charlie and his mates were going to dinner afterwards and then out clubbing. Sitting in my chair in the Xigatse Hotel bar, half-listening to the joking and boasting about the day, I thought very hard about what it would be like at home: I imagined the conversations and speeches, and heard the laughter and congratulations, and the effort of concentration happily seemed to bring them all closer instead of emphasising the distance between us.

I remembered the day when Charlie was born.

The most vivid recollection of it was the way that every one of life's perspectives changed, immediately, irrevocably, as soon as he was handed to us. I had been warned, of course, but I had never understood how having a child is the end of considering your own needs and desires first, not just for a few years, but for ever. Once we had him, blinking and tomato-faced, I understood completely. I was awestruck. It was the biggest thing that would ever happen – bigger than bereavement, marriage, growing up, or any of life's other milestones, just to be given the responsibility and the joy of keeping this small thing safe. Even though I was running around the world on my own, risking everything with a bunch of motorists, I still felt the same, even though today he was technically an adult. The central experience, for me, was always being a mother.

The noise level was rising and the beers were going down fast.

Three more day's driving and we would be in Kathmandu. I was full of optimism. We would get there, I would get the medicine to fix my little problem, and from Kathmandu we would be running on towards home.

Chapter Nine

The scenery was astounding. On the run out of Xigatse, the road twisted like a river of dust through a fertile valley with broad banks of cultivated ground rolling away on either side of it. The mountains closing in on us were dark blue in shadow and burned ochre where the sun touched them, but in the foreground the crops grew in haphazard strips and patches that were every shade of green from sage to forest, and every brown and yellow from palest gold through cinnamon and rust to rich dark earth. I pressed my face to the passenger window, keeping only half an eye on the trip and the route notes, trying to compress the picture into compartments in my memory by naming the gradations of colour.

'How are you feeling?'

'Okay, thanks.'

Dr Ninety-dollar's pills seemed to have started working, just a little. Maybe it was only a placebo effect but it was something.

We climbed through a little pass in the hills and then

the route wound into a gorge. The gorge narrowed until we were penetrating a vee of rock, on a road that was no more than a lip of dirt twisting beside a drop that I didn't want to glance down into. The climb grew steeper.

'Morgan up ahead,' Phil said. 'He looks as if he's in trouble.'

We came up behind it and bobbed for a few hundred metres in the dust on his tail, looking for a place to slip past and losing power as our speed dropped to match theirs. At last they pulled aside. The navigator stuck his fist out of the window and angrily gestured us to go.

'They don't look too happy,' Phil grinned. He eased his foot down and we picked up enough power to struggle by.

The road climbed up and up. We were all right by the clock, but we were both worried about the demands that the ascent and the altitude were making on the car. There seemed to be a noticeable loss of power that made me wish I had jettisoned my *Vogue*. But at last, as Phil stirred his way up and down through the gears, the sky widened overhead and we crested a bleak hump of road. It was the summit of the Tsuo La pass, at 4,500 metres.

Then there was a long, steep and dusty run down to the control at Lhatse.

Last night's gossip had indicated that the next section was a crucial one – the organisers had revised the route to shake out the order again. There was now a 34 km short stage to a control sited at the top of the Gyatso Pass. At 5,220 metres this was the highest point of the road between Lhasa and Kathmandu, the watershed between Tibet and India – and 20 m higher than Everest Base Camp.

Lord Montagu and his 1915 Vauxhall Prince Henry on the start line in Beijing, September 6. Unfortunately the Vauxhall only survived for four days, but Lord Montagu hitched a series of lifts with other competitors and made it all the way to Paris.

Chinese contrasts: Pagodas and the blue wagons that clogged every highway.

Police and army personnel monitored every metre of progress across China. Wherever we stopped, there was a rush to sit behind the wheel.

Dan and me beside the Tanggu La stupa on the Roof of the World section, Tibet. This was the highest point on the rally at nearly 17,000 feet, and a stone's throw from the highest rally control point ever established.

Buddhist monks and the Potala Palace, Lhasa, for centuries the focus of Tibetan religious and cultural life. The Chinese flag flies from the summit.

Chomolungma, 'Goddess Mother of the World', is the Tibetan name for Everest. Turn left at this sign and the trail leads onwards to Base Camp. Displaying the OK sign is mandatory every time the car stops, to indicate to other crews and support teams that you are not in trouble.

A long line of rally cars snakes through Zhangmu, the Chinese frontier town, on the way into Nepal.

Car 82 negotiates the 'road' from Choksam in Tibet down to the Friendship Bridge and the Nepali frontier.

The Friendship Bridge, between Tibet and Nepal, crossed for the first time by an International motor event.

Phil in shades and the Sheikh of Araby turban with some of the Nepali camp crew.

The nightly spanner check in high camp on the Tibetan plateau.

Melissa and friend.

Jingers, Rick the paramedic and Trev (sitting down) on the morning time control at Nainital hill station, India.

Water buffalo in a roadside waterhole, somewhere in India.

In the desert, Baluchistan. The great barge-fronted wagons with their gaudy decorations bear threateningly down the centre of the road.

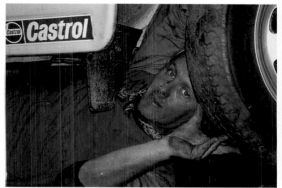

Exhausted Phil reaches the end of an all-night session in the garage, Rimini, Italy.

The Bentley Boys, Adam Hartley and Jon Turner, with Adam's 4½ litre 1928 VdP Le Mans.

Phil, Dan and JD after the shopping opportunity at legendary Maranello, birthplace of Ferrari, Italy.

Richard Curtis with Prince Idris Shah's Model B Ford on the Kandelpasse, Germany.

Rally time control with flag, Frontera, rally clock and Mick O'Malley, somewhere on the road.

We had a time allowance, once again, of 29 minutes. Anything faster than 1 km per minute, on roads like these, signalled trouble.

Our minute was 11.18. Phil went off from the start with his foot hard down. I set the timer, buckled my harness and checked that the fastening was secure.

Beep.

'One fifty, fork left. Signpost Xegar. Very bumpy road.'

'Got you.'

The car bounced and shimmied over the rocks. It was like being thrown about inside a tumble drier.

'Fork coming up now.'

'Got you.'

Beep. The sound that syncopated my dreams.

We swung round a tight bend past a little settlement. On the left was the Hillman Hunter belonging to the toothbrushless American women, stationary and slewed at an angle in the ditch. The car was surrounded by local people and an Iranian Peykan Hunter had stopped to give assistance. Barely two kilometres further along there was a huge rut in the road and dust hanging thick in the air. Phil swung the wheel to miss the rut and at the same instant we saw the Gulikers' Chevvy pick-up buried nose-down in a concrete culvert at the side of a bridge. They were both standing beside it, and there was a four-wheel drive with a tow-rope, so we swerved to keep going and bounced on over the bridge. Renger Guliker must have seen the rut and taken avoiding action and then, unsighted by the dust from the car in front, he had missed the bridge altogether and crashed into the gully beside it.

'Be careful,' I muttered to Phil. And then, seeing that we weren't achieving the necessary minimum of 65 kph I contradicted it immediately with, 'We need to go faster.'

'Hold tight then. Here we go.'

Phil looked fierce but he loved all this testosteronic display. Bare-knuckle competition made his blood sing. I could hear the tune from where I crouched in the navigator's seat. He liked it best when we skidded through some impossible gap past Mick Flick or the land crab or Thomas and Maria and accelerated into the open space in front.

Yeahhhh. Gotcha. Let's go . . .

I loved it too. It was beyond luck that he had turned out to be such a good driver.

Soon we could see the road beginning to climb into what looked like impenetrable heights. The surface was corrugated dirt; we bounced over the ridges and all the contents of the car rattled and slid. The essential cassette player was working its way loose from its mountings and Phil leaned forward to wedge it back into place. We were going up now; the air was hazy with dust and a grey-white film of it penetrated the car and settled in a thick layer over us and everything else inside. White puffs of it high up in the distance marked the progress of cars making the climb ahead of us.

'Come on, let's go for it,' Phil cajoled. 'Come on baby.'

The Amazon obliged, but slowly. Altitude sucked the power out of her. The minutes were flashing away and it was a cruel 6 km climb to the top of the pass, but I still thought we had a good chance of doing it inside our time. Seven minutes to run.

I hung on, hunched in my seat as we skidded around the bends. Up and up, as fast as it was possible to go, with the straining engine and the music drumming together and the trip flickering in front of my eyes.

Six minutes, then five.

We still weren't going fast enough, even though Phil was driving at the very limit of his own and the car's capacity. We were 3 minutes inside time when I realised we weren't going to make it. The Amazon didn't have quite enough in her and the control wasn't situated at the very summit of the pass, but a little beyond and down the other side. Even so, we were going so fast that we almost took off as we came over the top.

Beepbeepbeepbeep. Out of time again.

I shouted, 'Keep going. We're only going to be a couple of minutes adrift.'

The control appeared ahead with one car pulling away, none waiting. No one could have had any time in hand on this section.

We skidded in behind the Frontera and I leapt out and ran. Mike Summerfield was the marshal.

'Car 82, looking for 11.47.'

'It's 11.50, madam.' He stamped my card. Three-minute penalty. 'How are you today?'

'Fine. Thanks.' Or at least, I would be soon.

Phil and I were on an adrenalin high again. Gasping and laughing with the buzz of the drive we rolled past the control and parked a little further on where the Peugeot and Chris and Howard's Camaro and a couple of other cars were also pulled up. The rest of the day was decontrolled – all we had to do was proceed to Everest camp

and hand in our books on arrival so, confusingly after
the wild dash in which every minute mattered, there was
now some time for some idling.

Phil climbed out to examine our shock absorbers.
They were too hot to touch, but there were no visible
cracks or holes punched anywhere. We strolled up and
down to ease cramped legs and exchanged stories of the
day's drama with the other drivers. Paul Minassian and
Paul Grogan in the hot Peugeot had been *four* minutes
over on the section, and Chris and Howard had lost time
too. We heard that Mick Flick and several others had
taken a wrong turning down in the valley, near where we
had seen the American girls and the Gulikers, and had
dropped way back. Bart Rietbergen in Kermit, the green
Volvo PV544, had been one of the cars in equal first place
at the beginning of the day but his dynamo had fallen off
because the bolt holding it to the engine block sheared.
He had rushed to a local blacksmith to have a replacement made, but he had still lost 66 minutes.

Sarah Catt stepped out of a support car and came over
to tell us her story. She had been riding as a passenger in
RO's Peugeot this morning when he had driven into a
ditch and blown both front tyres. She had left him standing at the roadside while his co-driver battled to change
the damaged wheels, and now she was looking for a lift
onwards towards camp. We were ready to move on, and so
she squeezed in on my lap with her head bent against the
roof and her hand gripping the roll cage for balance.
Rally cars are definitely not designed for three people.
While Phil and she gossiped I turned my head and
watched the scenery through the passenger window. It

was a vast empty space of yellow-brown turf and grey peaks, without a tree or a bird or any living thing, but it was lively with vast stately cumulo-nimbus clouds drifting across the hard blue sky. The clouds drew patches of purple-grey shadow like bruises over the ground.

Fifty kilometres further on through this barren land we found John and Simon Catt, Sarah's father and brother, changing a wheel on their Cortina. They were one of only two crews to have cleaned the day – quite an achievement. We had dropped some height from the uncomfortable altitude of the pass, down to about fifteen thousand feet, and it was time to stop and cook up some hot food. Sarah hitched another lift onwards with David Burlinson, and I spread out our tarpaulin in a sheltered hollow beside the road while Phil lit the camping stove. Somewhere to our left, masked by layers of low cloud on the horizon, was Everest.

Lying on the ground warmed by the sun and wrapped up in my down jacket with the clink of tools and the comfortable hiss of gas in my ears, I almost fell asleep. I was more tired than I knew.

When I opened my eyes again there were two black shapes outlined against the sky. A pair of Tibetan children had materialised out of the landscape, there was no telling where from, and were standing staring at me. The older one was perhaps five or six, the younger one couldn't have been more than three, and they were completely alone. We exchanged greetings, *tashideli*, hello. It was unthinkable to eat in front of them, so we shared our billycan of food and gave them some muesli bars and biros. They held the trophies tight in dirty fists, and watched us all the time we were packing up again. As we drove away I looked back and they were still standing there, two tiny dots in the great windy space.

It was a long, stirring drive through the dust to the overnight stop. We passed the turning that led off the road towards the trailhead at Everest Base Camp and rolled onwards to the campsite.

It was beautiful. A huge, empty straw-gold plain miniaturised the lines of cars and tents. When we stepped out of the car, our throats thick with dust, we faced a ridge of mountains soaring in the distance, still tantalisingly veiled in cloud, with Everest hidden somewhere in the heart of it. We pitched our tent, working hard to hammer the pegs into the frost-hardened ground. The coarse turf was embedded with tiny saxifrages. Phil and I crawled underneath the car and did the evening's tightening of bolts, and checked the wheel nuts, and went through the familiar inspection routine under the bonnet. The air was so thin that putting the necessary pressure on the wheel brace to loosen and then re-tighten the nuts left me panting for breath.

All the time the light was fading and softening and then, when I looked up again from my task, the clouds had drawn back. Everest and Cho Oyu were pin-sharp against the blue. More than a hundred cars were drawn up in long ranks beneath it, with their busy outcrop of tents and trucks and striding people. It was quite a sight.

As I watched, the light seemed to drain out of the sky. The colour of the etched peak changed from silver-white to rose-pink, and then to forbidding ice-blue. Darkness fell and the moon rose against a prickle of brilliant stars.

Later, after dinner in the mess tent, the day's order was put up. No cars were now unpenalised, and the field was led by the Catts, the Brodericks, and Buckingham and Mann in their DB5, all with 2-minute penalties. Number 82 was no longer bottom Volvo. We had overtaken Jennifer and Francesca, who had been having a hard time with various mechanical failures. And we were now in 51st position.

Tomorrow was going to be another tough day, down to Choksam just above the border with Nepal. Phil was determined to give it all we'd got. The car was strong, and going well, and maybe we could claw ourselves upwards by a few more places.

I woke up very early. It was daybreak and the tent was suffused with a faint yellow glow. My first half-conscious awareness was of Everest so close at hand in the dawn light. And after that there were no thoughts of the view – only the sickening realisation that my sleeping bag was a swamp of blood. I was having a uterine haemorrhage.

Phil was a blond-crested chrysalis a foot away from me in his sleeping bag. I reached out and shook him awake.

'It's happening. Help me.'

'What do you need? The doctor?'

'No. Get some hot water and towels.' But we were camping; there were no such luxuries available. 'Just anything absorbent.'

Phil pulled on his outer clothes and scrambled out of the tent. I tried to mop up with what was at hand. It was a frightening sight. I remembered the last two of Maria's pills, and scrabbled in my washbag for them. Phil came back with a Thermos of hot water begged from the Nepali kitchen boys, a handful of his clean T-shirts, and my Lhasa sanitary supplies from the car. He pushed everything at me through the tent flap. If he was disturbed by the sight of all the gore he gave no sign of it.

'Sort yourself out,' he ordered, and withdrew his head.

I used the hot water, and made a wadding of sanitary towels and T-shirts – my own, not his. Trying to think what else I could do I pulled his half-empty kitbag across and shoved it under my hips to raise them higher than my head. I muffled myself in my down jacket and the usable half of my sleeping bag, and lay on my back to wait. I could feel the blood still welling.

Tears ran out of the corners of my eyes and trickled into my hair. I was thinking about Charlie, eighteen plus two days and at the beginning of everything in his life, and my fifteen-year-old Flora asleep in her bed in London.

I was going to die in a tent, without kissing them good-bye.

Such a waste, a stupid waste, just for the sake of a meaningless car rally.

The worst of it was the repetition, the way the implacable loop of history went round and around. My mother had left without saying goodbye and now I might leave her grandchildren in the same way when that very thing had been the biggest of all the fears I had suffered for the two of them.

On the last evening she was alive my mother had asked me to fetch something for her from upstairs and I, sulky child aged ten, had refused to do it. The last thing I said to her was *No*. Before she went out that same evening she hugged me and I said nothing in response, and I can still remember the pale green jumper she was wearing, and how narrow her shoulders seemed, and the fragility of her thin arms. We have both inherited her bony body, my sister and I. When we compare photographs now – the few creased pictures of her that we share between us – there are the same deep scoops behind the collarbones and the identical knobs of bone at the base of the throat.

I didn't want to go away and leave my sister either, my *alter ego*, who knew as exactly as I did the bad experiences that had moulded us into our awkward selves.

My mother went out to the house of some friends that night, and died there. I never knew exactly how or why, and because I was never told it became impossible to ask. We never reminisced about her and all the memories were locked up in a cupboard that was probably labelled, with the kindest intentions, 'Better not to *dwell*.'

I was sent away to a boarding school that specialised in regimes of Victorian brutality, and my father's mother came to look after my sister and brother.

Afterwards the history bundled up with my mother in the recesses of that cupboard seemed so dark that there was only one certainty – that whatever had happened to her was somehow my fault. I had said *No*, not just once but probably a million times, and so she had gone.

The determination to do the best for my own children, the importance that motherhood itself assumed for me, was an act of atonement. I *had* to do it correctly, to make their world as right for them as mine had been all wrong, and that anxiety was born with Charlie and it swelled and grew ominously and increasingly irrational until Flora was ten, the same age that I had been. Her tenth year was the darkest period of my life: fear for her submerged itself under the skin of my apparently perfectly ordered world and became depression that stalked and harried me right to the edge of reason.

Having come back from that brink was one of the reasons why I felt so strong. We had passed the point of danger, and every extra month and year I had with Flora was a bonus. She would be more all right than I had been by the same measure of days.

Now I had become so confident that I was able to take risks. I had made the trip to see my mountain after all, at almost fifty, and the hard white face of it was standing out there beyond my tent flap. I knew objectively that what I was doing was dangerous, but I had managed to equate that danger with daily risks like crossing the road – thus wrapping up fate's random viciousness in a protective coat of cliché.

The point was that I was strong enough to go adventuring, or thought I was. Entering the rally in the first place was like waving a jaunty handkerchief in the face of fate, and at Golmud and Lhasa I had kept it fluttering. But the loop of history had cunningly worked itself around again.

I thought suddenly, I won't *let* it. If I'm strong then it won't happen.

The hair behind my ears was soaked with tears, I was

reluctant to move an inch in case my innards collapsed, and I was cold. But I was less afraid now.

I wouldn't *let* it happen.

Between the firing up and revving of car engines I could hear the Nepali boys clattering pans and laughing as they prepared breakfast, and I remembered the Tibetan families walking with their hungry children between the Bentleys and Aston Martins, and the overturned truck beyond Koko Nor.

I realised the bleeding was easing a little.

Phil came back with an enamel mug of hot tea and put it into my hand. Poor Phil. He had brought a rubbish bag too, for all the bloodstained debris.

'How are you feeling?'

'I'll be okay. This didn't happen to Rebecca Stephens.'

'Or Prince Borghese. What do you want to do?'

'I want to get to Kathmandu.'

'Can you make it?'

'Yes.'

Luckily we had a luxuriously late start that morning – 9.42, still almost two hours off. I lay without moving and waited to see what my body would do, and I thought about home and all the passages and negotiations and alterations that had brought me from there to here. At last the bleeding slowed enough to allow me to get up very slowly and put on a random assemblage of clothes.

I got carefully into the navigator's seat with the route notes on my lap. Phil had done everything else. Behind me he struck the tent and bundled it into the boot, and we were prepared for the road. Two hundred and sixty-seven kilometres in the day, divided into three sections. The middle stage was another short one – 35 km up to a pass at 5,050 m, with an allowance of 30 minutes.

When our departure minute came up Phil took the book to the marshals for stamping. He ran back to the car and looked at me.

'Ready to go?'

I nodded. I was holding myself as if I were a cracked egg.

We bumped across the wide plain, and I looked back for a last glimpse of the mountain. Within a hundred metres of the start we had to cross a river. Water rose to the car's axles and the front bumper pushed out a bow-wave. Somehow, we were still rallying. We overtook car 62, Jennifer and Francesca, on the opposite bank.

The first stage was easy enough and we reached the time control with 19 minutes in hand. Phil pulled into the line of cars drawn up at the side of the road and we settled down to wait. The next thing we saw was a car coming down the hill towards us, moving very fast, with the head-lights full on.

It was unnervingly reminiscent of Mick Flick's Mercedes flying back from the accident at Koko Nor.

'Something has happened,' I said.

The car braked in front of the marshals at the control. It was another Mercedes, the black one crewed by three Germans, car number 70. One of the officials was Greg Williams and we saw him run to the Frontera and jump in to tail the Mercedes back the way it had come.

'An accident.'

We sat in silence in the line of motionless cars, waiting

for news. It was impossible not to think of everyone we knew who was ahead of us in the order, and to dread what might be happening along the road. A few minutes later the Frontera came racing past again and I caught a glimpse of Greg's hedgehog head bent inside it.

Then the second marshal walked down the line. The Mercedes had been cornering on a blind bend when a road-worker had stepped straight out in front of it. The driver had never stood a chance of avoiding him. The man was badly hurt, we were told, but not dead. Greg had taken him in the Frontera to a medical post.

The day's competition was cancelled. We were to proceed in our own time to what would have been the control point at the top of the pass, and from there down to the overnight stop at Choksam.

Phil drove slowly away.

'Will he die?'

'I suppose so. Like the truck men probably died.'

Even in depression, I had never felt the thread that connects life to whatever lies beyond it to be drawn as tight as it was that morning.

After a while we exchanged a few sentences about the ethics of rallying at full speed along these roads, using people s villages as a race track, but we didn't say much. We both knew what we felt about the plight of the Tibetans, and the uncomfortable contrast between their lives and our royal and impervious progress. The fact that we were racing, sending ripples of threat radiating out from our convoy as well as making a barefaced display of privilege, was another unpalatable truth that had hit home too late. I just knew that for all the adrenalin thrill that it generated, I wouldn't be happy to enter another international event like this one.

It was yet another blinding drive, up endless elbow bends lacing the mountainside, to the top of the pass. At the summit we found John Vipond and Mike Summerfield checking the cars through the cancelled time control, both of them looking miserable and cold. Phil stopped the car and, just to demonstrate that I could, I strolled casually back up the road to offer them a hot drink. They accepted eagerly.

Phil had gone quiet. Today's accident had affected him almost as badly as the truck disaster, and his way of dealing with distress was to close up on it. We sat in the car drinking soup and staring through the fogged windscreen at the panorama of mountains. Our temperamental differences had never seemed more apparent. My way of salving this raw day was to talk about what had happened. If Caradoc had been sitting next to me we would have gone over it again and again, until we had absorbed what it meant.

After a long time Phil admitted cautiously, 'I'm not usually with someone long enough to share my feelings.' And then, backing away from the admission, he began laughing. 'Anyway, I'm shallow.'

'I don't think so.'

Over the brow of the hill and past the time control came the Bentley Le Mans with Adam and Jon in their goggles and gauntlets. They pulled up in front and came round one to each side of the car, pushing their faces up against the windows and mugging at us. As always they made us giggle and lifted our spirits.

*

The afternoon's driving took us down through a new landscape. We left the aridity of the plateau behind and began dropping down through steep, wooded gorges stitched with white threads of waterfalls. Sometimes the cleft widened and a bridge spanned the milk-white water of a river. It grew steadily warmer too, and the sky faded behind low, damp-laden clouds. The air began to smell of moisture and woodsmoke, and I looked at the inside of the car and saw through lowland eyes the thick layers of grey dust that caked everything and penetrated our clothes and stiffened our hair. It was as though we were drifting down from the surface of the moon.

In the late afternoon we reached the hotel at Choksam. It was a cinderblock structure with lines of unlit cells like a severe penal unit in central Africa, and it made the place in Golmud look like the New York Four Seasons. The farmyard of a parking space outside was already wedged solid with cars, and with crews putting up tents rather than risk a night in the cell block.

Ever enterprising, Phil went off in search of a better option while I sat and groused with Andrew Bedingham. A couple of minutes later he came back.

'There's a little area round there. At least it's quiet.'

He drove the car up a steep ramp into a yard enclosed by what looked like rancid stables, although these turned out to be annexe rooms to the hotel that were occupied by Chinese guests who had been displaced by the rally. There was just room to park two or three cars and pitch the tents. Phil waved Dan and JD alongside us and then hovered on the look-out for Melissa and Colin.

'She'll be along in a minute,' he said happily, as he did whenever we stopped anywhere.

The Porsche rolled in a little later, with Colin blinking in owlish misery through his rimless glasses. He didn't like camping, but the rest of us were happy enough to be there. We put up the tents and brewed tea. There was even a standpipe gushing cleanish water into a drinking trough, so we could wash our hands and faces. Phil stuck his head under the flood and raked his hair into a gleaming wedge. I felt like celebrating my survival this far, so I burrowed through the layers of dust in my kitbag and triumphantly pulled out *Vogue*. We were up and over the mountains now so Phil couldn't complain too much about the excess weight I'd been smuggling. Melissa and I sat on a rock together and pored over the shining pages.

'Love those grey tweed Calvins, look.'

'Mmm. I wore flares the last time around, I'm not doing it again.'

'Boot-cut, you mean.'

'Flares to me. Oh, divine Manolos.'

Steely spike heels to strut and twirl in, a million miles from the present world of mud and dust. A quartet of black pigs rooted inquisitively at the skirts of our tents, and Dan and JD and Phil lounged on the tarpaulin and laughed at the women's fancies. It was a nice moment.

Over 'dinner' in the Choksam Hotel that night David Burlinson told me that I would have to pay a thousand pounds to the Chinese authorities for a 'special visa service fee' – the same special visa service which had made my preparations to enter the country so relaxed and enjoyable and which was of course now operating in reverse, to make it difficult for me to leave without paying for all the attention I had received. In fact, I learned that Exodus had kindly settled up on my behalf and all I had to do was take out my chequebook and reimburse them on the spot. At that moment it seemed a bargain price to pay for the privilege of getting out of China.

I crawled into the tent early that night. I was still bleeding intermittently and I wondered how much I actually had left circulating in my veins. I felt weirdly transparent and increasingly lightheaded. But tomorrow we would be in Kathmandu, with its teeming streets and grinning people. My medicine would be at the Yak and Yeti Hotel, and even if it wasn't I believed that in the haphazard hippy-scented shops of Thamel you could buy whatever you needed. Kathmandu beckoned with the crooked fingers of civilisation, and only last year it had seemed to me to be the farthest outpost of the exotic.

The darkness was full of questing pig noises.

There was no rallying the next day either, because it had been decided that the Chinese border formalities were likely to be too time-consuming to allow everyone enough leeway to drive the distance. Phil was disappointed. Bad roads, he had decided, were good for us. Everest Camp to Choksam had taken its toll even without the element of competition. Four cars would be making the journey to Kathmandu on the back of trucks, including the Chevvy pick-up and Anthony Buckingham's DB5 which had now succumbed to terminal suspension problems.

This must surely mean, Phil and I reckoned, that when the new order appeared at Kathmandu we would be up somewhere in the '40s. Back in the top half of the sporting category . . .

The drive from Choksam down to the Nepal frontier at the Friendship Bridge was the most testing yet. The rally left the night halt in a long, snaking convoy to wind down a track that was no more than a rock-strewn, mud-smeared ledge nibbled out of a series of precipices and steep forests. It was raining and the wipers dolorously arced across the windscreen. Low cloud came billowing up the gorge from the warm lands below. At one point the track passed under a waterfall – the drivers of open cars either scrambled for umbrellas or opted to accelerate and pass under it at full speed – and at another point a huge queue built up at a landslide.

Gossip about the landslide had been circulating for days. The seriousness of it had been reported in the news bulletins sent home, and even discussed on the Internet. At one point it had been stated that the road was completely blocked and the rally was therefore unlikely to make any further progress. As always in connection with the planning and organisation of the event it was difficult to winnow a few grains of truth out of the rumours, but it did seem that the collapse of the road had been a disaster that actually threatened to halt all onward progress. RO had therefore paid some unspecified (but reportedly huge) sum of money to the Chinese who were supposed to provide round-the-clock manual labour to shift the mud and rock. In fact the track was half cleared. There was now a way around the massive rockfall that was just wide enough for a car to pass, not wide enough for a truck. The drop to the side – Phil's side, luckily for me – was very steep.

Some drivers chose to negotiate the obstacle very slowly, others gamely put their foot down. When our turn came I kept my eyes closed.

'What was all that about?' Phil crowed as we swung round to the other side. 'Was that it, then?'

I opened my eyes and laughed. It was such a characteristic moment. He was a cocky little fucker precisely because he was so confident of his own practical abilities – and I had affectionately told him so on the funny night back in the Golmud Four Seasons – but he was so definitively the right stuff that you couldn't help loving him.

We bumped and slithered on down to Zhangmu, the straggling border town. The one road leading to the frontier was a long ribbon of rally cars waiting for their turn at the customs post and we joined the end of the line with Dan and JD behind us, and Melissa and Colin behind them. The unmade street, pocked with stones and sticky with mud, was lined with little open shops. Tins of food and bottles of Pepsi, packs of cigarettes and rolls of lavatory paper, were laid out on shelves with rather appealing attention to colour and form, and looped strings hanging in front of the shops were pegged with socks and dishcloths. The family washing was usually strung out too, distinguishable from the merchandise by being just slightly dirtier.

It was evidently a big day in Zhangmu, which couldn't see a great rush of border activity at other times. Faces bloomed in the open windows of the Amazon, mostly creased, brown Tibetan faces framed with loops of hair and coloured silk and turquoise or amber beads, although there were a few Chinese too. A pair of pretty young Chinese policewomen, smart as paint in short-skirted uniforms, refused to let Phil take their pictures. A woman in a pink mohair cardigan who had two words of English – *hello* and *marnie* – came by with her baby and we sat the little moppet in the driving seat and photographed her. All this time the column of cars was patrolled by hard-faced men with calculators and wads of notes in their greasy pockets.

'Shange marnie?' they muttered incessantly. 'Dollah? Rupee?'

Then a young Tibetan man struck up a conversation. He had been to school in India and had learned enough English to tell us that living in Tibet was very hard. Phil asked him about the Dalai Lama and when he might return. The man's face was immediately suffused with a soft reverence.

'Maybe some day. I hope and pray. He is my Holiness,' he whispered. 'My Holiness.'

The line of cars inched slowly forward. In fact, when we reached the frontier post, the formalities were not as tedious as we had been warned to expect. Our passports and car documents were glanced at and, in what was clearly the central transaction, US$7 was extracted as a 'non-inspection fee' for the car. A refusal would probably have resulted in all our belongings being poked through at the roadside.

A red-and-white pole lifted and we were waved through. We left Chris Taylor on the Tibetan side, lounging on a bench in the sunshine. His passport hadn't been stamped on the way into Beijing, and now he was being detained. Howard sat in the Camaro, head in hands.

'Every time, everywhere we go, it's Chris it happens to. We could be here for days.'

But in the event it was no worse than 1½ hours, with a $60 fine thrown in. Not a big price to pay for a sight of the right side of the Chinese border. Down beyond the striped pole lay 20 kilometres of the worst road in the world, no-man's land before the Nepali frontier. At one point the route turned into a fully-fledged calf-deep river that chuckled prettily over mossy rocks. There were several other streams to cross, and a bigger concentration of ruts and rocks and craters than we had had to deal with even in crossing the plateau.

At last, the bridge came into view, a span of metal girders against the sweep of the forested gorge. We had descended probably a vertical mile in height since the early morning. Down here the warm air was heavy with humidity, and pungent with the rotten-sweet smell of wet vegetation. We stripped off layers of clothes, and still felt too hot.

'Do you want to drive across the bridge?' Phil generously asked.

'Yes I do.'

We changed places and the car rattled over. Beyond was the frontier post, where smiling officials put garlands around our necks while our passports were checked, and thumb-pressed red paste tika dots on our foreheads. Rally officials in their red shirts were grinning in relief.

'Welcome to Nepal!'

'Namaste, namaste.'

This was the first car rally ever to pass through Nepal.

There was a huge banner strung across the road. The way ahead was lined with beaming faces and hands waving or clapping or pressing together in greeting. Leaving the dour monochrome officialdom of western China and arriving in Nepal was like walking from a dentist's waiting-room into a brilliant party. In the pleasure of it all I forgot how to drive. The car juddered and almost stalled.

'Clutch, clutch!' Phil shouted.

Looking back in the mirror we saw John Vipond doubling up with laughter at this little cameo of my deficiencies and Phil's response to them. An icy dart of tension immediately jabbed through the car. Phil didn't care for being laughed at, even my small attempts at teasing him had revealed that, and if my incompetence drew ridicule it was also directed towards him because we were a team.

I said nothing, judging that this was probably quite a good moment to concentrate on what I was trying to do.

The route notes had promised us that the 100 km from the border down into Kathmandu would be mostly asphalt, although broken in places. This turned out not to be the case. There were, in fact, more huge craters and potholes and head-sized rocks, very occasionally flattening out into tantalisingly short expanses of decent asphalt. At the lip of every crater it was a matter of deciding which route would be the least damaging to follow, which rock was most likely to hit the differential, what would be the optimum speed to go for.

It was the middle of the afternoon, very hot now, and we had been driving or queuing since 8 a.m. without a stop or any proper food. The road followed the Sun Khosi river, a lazy brown thread of water in which happy-looking people were bathing or scrubbing clothes, and passed through a chain of villages. In every village the people came out to greet us. They showered us with flowers and thumbed tikas on our foreheads, and they wanted to exchange greetings and shake hands as we passed by. The warmth was palpable, but after an hour of it the strain of responding began to tell on us. Smiling was making my neck ache and the sun in my eyes gave me a headache to match.

Phil must have been feeling just as tired and thirsty as I was. He was irritable, and instead of pulling his hat over his eyes and letting me learn from my own mistakes, he kept telling me to slow down or speed up or change gear. I knew he was trying to be constructive, but he was making me angry.

I began thinking peevishly that I had paid for the entire trip for both of us and I would have to work very hard to earn that outlay back. It was *my* car. If I damaged it, then that was part of the risk of having me along in the first place. If he had wanted a professional rally driver, he should have invited one to pay for the trip instead of me. Why shouldn't I enjoy my share in the adventure without being nagged and bullied? And so on. All the things that I had secretly vowed not to make into an issue between us — because it wouldn't have been fair to do so and because I knew the deal from the outset — built into a logjam in my mouth.

And now I was beginning to be afraid of the car. I didn't want to pull away from a standstill because I had lost the knack of feeling the exact point where the clutch bit. I wasn't sure where to brake, or when to change up or down. Everything I did seemed to produce a wrong response in it. A trickle of sweat crawled down the nape of my neck and my mouth was dry. My anger intensified.

We came to the edge of yet another bomb crater and Phil hissed 'slow *down*' and flapped his hands at me.

I stopped the car immediately, jamming on the brakes. I was furiously angry with him now, for the first time since the foot of Kalapathar. I got out very slowly, and walked round to the other side of the car. The sun was hot on my head and bare shoulders. I opened the door.

'You drive.'

'No, no. Come on. I'll try to shut up. I want you to drive.'

'Well, I don't. It isn't any fun for me, because you are so controlling. And if it can't be any fun, there isn't any point in doing it, *is* there?'

I slammed the door, deliberately. He was always complaining that I slammed the doors and the boot unnecessarily. I walked away to the edge of the road and lay back against a rock. It was pleasant to be out of the burning heat inside the car, and not to have the engine drumming in my head. Fifteen metres below the Sun Khosi made a wide bend enclosing a spit of sand, and there were brown-skinned people splashing in the water and sending up glittering arcs of spray. I played with the idea of walking away from Phil and the rally and scrambling down to submerge my hot shaky self in the water too. I could swim away to some pleasant village on the river bank and not have to drive another metre in this car with this companion.

After a minute I looked round and saw him sitting stiffly in his seat, staring straight ahead. Sighing, I walked round to the passenger side and waited for him to let me take his place.

'Are you ready to go on?' he asked, in a new, patient voice.

While I sat on the bank he had completely changed his persona. From unforgiving taskmaster he had turned into hired help, meekly subscribing to you're-the-boss and whatever-you-say-goes. I thought it perverse of him, and also irritating that he wouldn't admit just to being at fault once in a while.

Without answering I got into the navigator's seat and we drove the whole of the remaining 75 km down into Kathmandu in silence. Welcome committees headed by the mayor of each village stopped us as we passed and put flowers and gifts and – best of all – bottles of cold water into our arms. Phil and I smiled and smiled, and called out greetings and thanks and touched hands with everyone we could reach out to, without once looking at each other. The road improved and we spun through groves of banana palms and great clumps of red and yellow canna lilies. It was a sub-tropical confusion of growth, dizzying in its lushness after the aridity we had just left behind.

Kathmandu looked familiarly chaotic and welcoming, lying in its polluted basin enclosed by the hills. The jumble of collapsing roofs and crooked walls and tangled wires was turning from brown to grey in the evening light, and the hooting traffic closed in and swallowed us up.

The cars were to be left for the duration of the rest-stop in the huge car park of the Kathmandu Convention

Centre. As soon as we pulled in Phil threw up the bonnet and began an intent study of the engine, which was his way of being alone. I hauled my luggage over to the waiting shuttle bus and rode to the Yak and Yeti.

It is the best hotel in Kathmandu. Last year the Marines and Phil and I had gone there for a cocktail, and had looked longingly at the lush gardens and the swimming pool and the elegant dining-rooms. Now I dragged my dusty self into the air-conditioned bliss of the marble foyer and asked for my messages. The whole space was swarming with exhausted, filthy, jubilant rally crews.

We'd made it. Paris would be plain sailing from here.

I couldn't think of that yet. Please, I muttered to myself, please let it be here.

The receptionist passed a handful of faxes to me, and a square DHL package. The medicine. In my room, which had windows opening on to a little courtyard, and a bowl of fruit with a silver knife, and white bathrobes and CNN and a minibar full of western chocolate, I ate a handful of progesterone tablets and read my messages. They were full of love and congratulations.

The phone rang and it was Caradoc.

'Thank God you're there,' he said. 'Did you get it? Are you all right?'

'I've got it. I'm okay.'

I was looking at the accompanying fax from him. At the end it said, 'I love you more than I can say.' Gratitude and happiness and a sense of my own good fortune made it hard to speak for a minute.

'Are you there? Can you hear me?'

'I'm here.'

Much later, after we had finished talking, I tipped my belongings on the floor and salvaged the clean ones from the dustheap. I called Housekeeping for an iron and ironing board, and pressed my one chic outfit. I had a shower and made up my face and anointed myself with cream, and put on frivolous shoes. It was dark, and dinner-time, and there was no sign of Phil. Melissa rang and ordered me to dinner.

I was clicking across the foyer towards the dining-room when I met him coming in.

'You look lovely. Can we talk somewhere?'

We needed neutral territory, not our uncomfortably shared bedroom. We sat down on a sofa in a secluded corner of the lobby.

Phil knew Kathmandu well, he had worked there regularly for Exodus, and tonight he had been to visit some local friends. He began defiantly.

'If you want to fire me, you can. Get yourself another driver. I'll stay here, I like it.'

We stared at each other in mutual hostility. I thought it was underhand of him to try to turn the tables. He was the one who had been finding fault with me.

'Don't be so fucking ridiculous. Of course I can't fire you. You're coming with me to Paris because that's the only way we can go on competing.'

Only touring entrants were allowed to make crew changes; sporting competitors had to keep the same team all the way and Phil knew that perfectly well. He wasn't really expecting me to dump him, he was just saying it to test the water – but I played with the idea of saying all right then, he could bugger off and I'd take Lord

Montagu on board as co-driver. He had reached
Kathmandu via a series of lifts from other competitors
and was still looking for a permanent ride. This comical
notion must have thawed my icy expression a little
because Phil unbent a fraction in response.

'You see, the car is my responsibility. It's my job to get
it and you safely to Paris. You have to understand what
that means.'

Get *me* to Paris? I thought.

'So I have to look after it, and that includes the way you
drive.'

Women drivers. This banality was partly what was at issue,
and it was a shame that I hadn't been able to attack the
old cliché on behalf of my gender by driving with unri-
valled brilliance, but it was also funny enough to make me
want to laugh. It occurred to me once again that Phil and
I were going through a motoring paradigm of a marriage,
right down to every couple's petty niggles about changing
gear and folding the map in the right creases. We'd been
through the courtship and the honeymoon period, and
now we were discovering each other's flaws and powers to
irritate.

But beyond the comedy of gender clichés the violence
of Phil's reaction, so much at odds with his usual bland
good humour, had opened up a new perspective. I began
to understand that he too was less confident than he
appeared. He was probably all too aware of the windy
spaces between us. It slowly dawned on me that he felt the
differences in our age and status and purchasing power
more acutely than I had realised, and was over-asserting
his abilities with the car as a way of compensating for all

that. He was much too proud to allow anyone to see him as an adjunct, or a hired hand – even me.

Being deficient in confidence myself, I was too easily convinced by Phil's aura of general infallibility – especially in all the practical areas at which I was so inept. Our different needs and clashing temperaments guaranteed that we constantly misunderstood each other. It was an inflammatory mixture. Just like at Golmud, I had been expecting too much of him – not only to nurse the car, but also to understand my need for reassurance and encouragement.

Awkwardly, I reached for his hand. We sat there on our intimate sofa, poised between split and reconciliation, hands clasped like a parallel of a pair of quarrelling lovers. I tried to restate the terms of our bargain.

'All right, Phil. You be responsible for the car. You drive it, you service it. I'll navigate and I'll concentrate on making my notes and writing my diaries and selling features about the trip. Doing all the things that are paying for us both to be here, in other words.'

If he was going to make me feel bad, I was going to start retaliating.

He took this open reference to money without flinching.

'Fine.'

Everyone had gone to dinner.

'So, are we friends now?'

'Yeah, we're mates, aren't we?'

This wasn't quite what I had meant, but I let it go. I had a daring driver and a capable mechanic. I couldn't expect a soul-mate as well.

Around the dinner table everyone had heard about our disagreement – rally gossip travelled faster than light. Dave Bull made a grinning, fists-up gesture as I slid into my place.

'We're the best of friends now,' I said primly. It was certainly time for a new cast on the relationship.

It was a big evening. Everyone dived head-first into the drink, first in the hotel bars and then in Phil's favourite Kathmandu hang-out, Tom & Jerry's Bar. Three hours into the party I looked around and saw that the whole dingy place was heaving with drunken competitors and support crews, draping arms around each other and describing all over again the combination of rock and pot-hole that had almost done for the diff. I found a corner with Richard Curtis, Prince Idris's co-driver, because he was looking more than ever like Caradoc and alcohol enhanced this tenuous link until it seemed eye-wateringly precious. We were having a rambling conversation about which five of our possessions we would choose to have with us on a desert island. Richard's were all this Lucie Rie pot and that Persian rug; mine were photographs and my wedding ring and locks of baby hair. Another gender cliché. Chris Taylor swam up out of the throng, clearly having a good time. No one had been debating literature but he roared,

'Kafka? *Kafka?* They should put him on the National Health, mate. "Can't sleep, Mrs Jenkins? Here, read this and come back in a week."'

When the bar closed we retreated to the hotel again. I shared a bicycle rickshaw with Dan and teased him about which of the women to choose. He sighed and let his eyes close, doing the hand rotation.

'None of them. It's all *far* too complicated.'

Melissa was having a party in her extensive suite. Sarah Catt and Phil were in full flow, ordering room service and opening bottles of champagne from the maxi-bar.

'Nice bloke,' Phil was saying about one of our fellow travellers who was gay. 'Just a bit low in the leapfrog.'

I had never heard this picturesque expression before. I caught myself laughing so uproariously that I knew I had overdone the champagne and the Kathmandu draw. It was time for bed.

Phil never made it. He claimed that he and Sarah had passed out on Melissa's sofas.

Chapter Ten

We were leaving Kathmandu in 48th place.

We had only had two days' rest, but even after such a brief resumption of normal life – going shopping, wearing clean clothes, eating decent foot in civilised surroundings, and sleeping without jolting awake at hourly intervals in fear of missing the morning start – it was hard to get back in the car and zero the trip and begin all over again.

The atmosphere of the rally had changed somewhat, too. So much of everyone's energy and attention – and all the organisers' warnings – had been fixed on just getting to Kathmandu, through Tibet and over the Himalayas via those cruel, unforgettable roads, that there hadn't been much time to speculate about the distance that lay beyond. Now, studying the new book of route notes marked 'Asia and Persia', what should have been apparent all along suddenly became very obvious. The competition wasn't over. There was still a very long, very hard way to go. After the partying in the Yak and Yeti and

Tom & Jerry's Bar, there was a post-celebration atmosphere of rather weary apprehensiveness.

Some of the big-talking, more intimidating contestants
had faded a little too, beset by mechanical failures or navigational upsets, and different, more dogged characters
had begun to emerge. The most likeable of these were the
quiet couples – David and Sheila Morris in their 1956
Austin A90, Geoff and Jennie Dorey in Jennie's 1960
Morris Minor, Murray and Amanda Kayll in Murray's
Mercedes 250 SE. Murray told me that the Mercedes had
belonged to his family for years, and all his sisters had
learned to drive in it – it was pleasing to think of the faith-
ful old family runabout being rolled out of the retirement
garage and taken on this ultimate adventure.

None of these people ever made any kind of display of
themselves or their cars, or talked too loudly about how
good they were, but they were always there on the start
line, dependably ahead in the order, unflashily doing
themselves credit.

Phil did a wickedly funny imitation of Murray's mel-
lifluous burble.

'Yers, *jolly* nice chaps these Iranians, but they do drive
awfully farst.'

Like the other couples Murray didn't drive fast, and his
only declared ambition was to get his much-loved car
safely to Paris. They all thought Phil went like a maniac
too, but he was popular enough for them to tease him
gently about it. He rather enjoyed his reputation as the
wild boy racer.

We lined up for the start of the second leg at the
Kathmandu Conference Centre. The cars had been

repaired and cleaned of all the mud and dust, and most
of the crews were at least nominally rested. Phil had been
out the night before with the Exodus staff, and he looked
slightly stretched. I felt glowingly healthy by comparison
because Jon Turner had taken me out for a superb vege-
tarian thali dinner and we had enjoyed some non-car
conversation before parting for an early night, and
because my pills were working. Once I had started taking
the right medicine in sufficient quantities, the bleeding
had stopped within twenty-four hours. After all the anxiety the solution was so simple, and the relief was
immense.

Dan and JD looked grey-faced. They had met and pur-
sued a pair of Kenyan girls through an obstacle course of
whisky sours, and had only withdrawn from the chase as
dawn broke. The rear shock absorbers that had been
giving them trouble ever since Xigatse were still causing
problems – they had had to have welding work done in
Kathmandu on cracks around the lower mounting
points – but they thought they were good for the onward
journey.

The Gulikers were waiting on the line to wave us off.
They had had their Chevvy pick-up transported to a
garage and all the work to enable it to run again had
been completed, but they had received some bad news
from home. They were forced to withdraw, and were
flying out to Amsterdam that day. It was generous of them
to come and see the rest of us start.

'How are you feeling?'
I smiled opaquely at Phil. 'Never better.'

Not very surprisingly, there was still a residue of ill-feeling between us although – inevitably – it wasn't properly acknowledged. We hadn't seen all that much of each other in the two days in Kathmandu, and had spent no time at all alone.

I had begun to think that my driver didn't actually like me very much, and I was beginning to wonder about my feelings for him. At breakfast I had indicated the chair next to me and asked him – perhaps too forcefully – to sit down so we could have a talk about the day and the car's requirements. He had turned on me almost savagely.

'Don't order me around.'

I hadn't meant to. But at least he knew me well enough now to let his irritation show, instead of treating me like a client on a mountain trek.

'Okay. Let's go,' he said, and we rolled in line towards the start.

Beep. Start time 9.12. First stage, Kathmandu to Naryangat, distance 141.50 km, time allowance 2 hrs 27 mins, Phil driving. Route notes indicate steep, twisting descents, bad road surface.

Here we go again.

The way led from the Kathmandu Himalaya down a series of long, sweeping hairpin bends, and then turned west along Nepal's East–West highway. As we descended we came into thick bands of trees and sub-tropical vegetation, and the road grew busy with strolling bands of white-faced monkeys, and ribby cows with curled horns and hide so black and shiny that they looked carved from ebony, and an occasional buffalo or wandering goat.

Every village we passed through had a welcome banner

strung across the road, and all the schoolchildren were drawn up in ranks, shepherded by their teachers, to wave Red Cross flags at us. The children looked very spruce and disciplined in white shirts, the girls in uniform blue or red pleated skirts and the boys in dark trousers, all of them with lustrous dark eyes and wide smiles. Education is a serious priority in Nepal, although what opportunities exist for these children after school ends is less certain. Even so, after Tibet there was an appearance of lives being lived a grade or two above subsistence level. The sight of men smoking in convivial groups under canopies of branches and old people resting in doorways even suggested the possibility of leisure.

The Terai is the lush lowland section of Nepal. With Phil driving hard we made good progress through here on stretches of fast road, reaching the day's three time controls without difficulty – except that I was hanging out with the other crews and laughing too much on my way to the marshals with my book, took my eye off my watch, and reached the control one minute over time.

Not once but *twice*. Something was different today.

I had been a better navigator when I was ill – at least then I had been containing my anxiety by concentrating on the job. I kept this 2-minute penalty guiltily secret from Phil, thinking that my crew solidarity had better renew itself pretty soon and hoping that my lapse of concentration wouldn't lose us a place in the order that evening.

The night's stopping-place was in a broad, enclosed field at Kohalpur, our last camping of the journey. We had said goodbye to Himal and Arkle and the other Sherpas

when the Exodus camp crews left us at Kathmandu and
there was a new, unfamiliar organisation here, with different mess tents and equipment. There were lavatory tents
in striped canvas with jaunty awnings; pitched in colourful
lines they made the camp look like the Field of the Cloth
of Gold. Except that the humidity was punishing. It
drained us of energy and made every movement a sweaty
ordeal. We spread out the tarpaulin between the cars and
JD and Dan lay down, too flaccid with their hangovers to
do anything but lift cold beers to their lips. I discovered
that some of the striped tents were rigged up as bathroom
cubicles, with a plastic bucket and a jug that could be filled
from a generous tank. The arrangement was quaintly
reminiscent of the basin and ewer in an old-fashioned
Welsh washstand, and I thought of Caerwys – how far, far
away – as I sluiced myself in agreeably cold water and
poured the remainder over my head.

Darkness slowly gathered, moist and thick with layers
of heat, and luminously soft. The camp generator started
up a low hum, and lights flickered on poles across the
campsite and in the mess tent.

With the lights came the bugs.

Grasshoppers, pale pistachio-green and six inches
long, launched themselves out of the grass. When the first
one landed on my bare leg I screamed and leapt up and
Dan managed a sardonic twitch of the dimple. Dan had
worked for a long time in Africa with Operation Raleigh,
and merely helicopter-sized insects were beneath his
notice. Clearly they would have to be in the jumbo-jet
league to warrant remark. After the fifth or sixth blur of
gossamer wings and accompanying *plunk* on exposed

flesh, even I stopped doing more than half-heartedly brushing them away. Bat-sized velvet moths spun past our faces, and every lit bulb drew a fur of midges that thickened until the harsh light was diffused through a billowing veil of grey gauze, like a tactful photographer's. It was time to retreat to the mess tent, where at least the lights were widely enough spaced to leave pockets of breathable air in between them.

The scene was like an English country marquee wedding, on acid. Instead of pale pink or demure white and gold, the tent lining was sizzling tomato and green, and chrome yellow and orange and blue, with twirls of gilt ribbon for extra emphasis. There were little round tables with gilt chairs drawn up to them, but instead of women in hats and heels there were sweaty rally crews, either half-naked for the heat or swaddled against the insects. In place of the poached salmon and strawberry meringue, there were great aluminium vats of curry, and bowls of rice and daal bhat, and floppy towers of naan bread.

I was ravenous. I loaded my plate and ate, feeling my blood count rising with every searing spoonful, and letting the beads of sweat prickle on my scarlet face without bothering to mop them away. Sheila Morris muttered about the canvas screen masking scenes of indescribable squalor in the kitchen preparation area, but I didn't care. I sat next to JD, who was also eating heartily. We were joined by Nigel Challis, the Land Rover enthusiast.

'Fixed many cars today?' he asked JD, conversationally.

'Only my own.'

'Must be hard work for you, confusing, so many different cars.'

'Er, I'm a competitor too, actually.'

After the man had moved away JD scoffed, 'Just because I'm young and I've got short hair and an ear-ring, he assumes I'm a mechanic.'

I never saw JD angry, or even irritable. He only ever shrugged and smiled. Even when Dan howled at him for losing a crucial bolt in the snow at Tuotuoheyan, JD just said gently, 'Look, it's not important. I'll get you another bolt at Lhasa.'

Once dinner was over there was nothing to do but withdraw to the tents. I would have liked a drink and some talk, but Melissa had gone off to be sociable with Rick and Jingers inside the bug-impregnable Frontera and Phil had zipped himself into his, pitched within touching distance of Melissa's. Everyone else was similarly in retreat. I crawled into my own nylon capsule and fastened every mosquito flap behind me. I resisted using my head-torch – I had seen some of the spiders outside, and I didn't want to make any discoveries where I was about to lie down. I spread the Rebecca Stephens bag, for the first time without offering up thanks for its warmth, and lay down naked on top of it.

The burr of the generator swelled in volume, and the chirp and scrape of cicadas and whine of mosquitoes was as loud as a brass band. I rammed in my earplugs and lay back under a film of sweat.

Against the odds, it was one of the best nights' sleep I had on the entire journey.

In the morning, there was a porcelain-pink sunrise and a dew so heavy and silvery it looked as though there had been a rainstorm. In the cool and delicate light, before most of the rest of the camp was stirring, I felt a surge of optimism. We were about to drive into India, where I had never been and had always longed to visit; the car was going well and we were steadily climbing back up the order; Phil and I had solved our differences, superficially at least, and maybe that was enough. We had come this far, and we were going to get to Paris. I plodded through the soaked grass to the mess tent for black tea and cold rice with a balloon of exultation expanding inside my ribcage. Rally Syndrome.

The day was announced as another of the toughest of the trip. There were thirteen river crossings to be negotiated before we reached the Indian border. RO's river-crossing tip-sheet listed last-minute waterproofing techniques, in his usual admonitory style, for those who hadn't followed his preparation instructions in the first place.

'. . . Condoms over coil-leads, Plasticine or Blu-Tac in joints. A can of WD40 can make a big difference . . .'

'You will lose time if you slip the fan belt off, but you don't need a fan in water and it does spray a lot of water over the engine.'

Dan fanned himself with the instruction sheet.

'At least I'll get to use a condom for *something* on this trip.'

We all knew that almost any of the women would be happy to accommodate him, if he had made the choice. I thought Phil's laughter was touched with just an edge of resentment.

We had two time controls to reach within Nepal, a third at the frontier, and the end-of-day control in India, at a hill-station called Nainital. The road took us on through the Terai, on long, unmade dirt sections that wound through marshland and scrubby trees, and onwards through busy villages where it seemed, yet again, that the whole population had come out to look at us. Adults as well as children thrust Red Cross flags and drawings and scrawled messages in through the windows.

Wel Come en Nepal. Sir Augustine and Sangita, from the Shree Pushpanjali English Boarding School.

Wel come to nepal and I also love you, Dinesh, emblazoned with a heart pierced by an arrow.

Dhulikel Municipality: Dear participant, Peking-Perish old Timer Car Raley. We heartily welcome to you we wish all the Best for Your Travel & Your Mission. Bel Prasad Shrestha, Mayor. Ashok Byanju, Deputy Mayor.

Dear sir, this is my full adress, I do not forget you, Please write to me from time to time and I will visit your country some day.

Smiling faces and clapping, and hands beating on the Amazon's bonnet. We collected all the tributes and tried to stow them safely, and attempted to drive slowly enough to be appreciative of the welcome without indicating that we had a long way to go, and were always watching the clock.

In some of the bigger places there were dancers performing at the roadside for us. These were teenaged girls of breathtaking beauty, dressed in brilliant embroidered tunics with flowers in their hair and with bracelets of silver bells on their wrists and ankles. They stepped in perfect unison, making slow, sinuous arm and head movements, always with their eyes modestly downcast. The eastern equivalent of American high-school cheerleaders, perhaps.

The river crossings were exciting. It was a toss-up for me whether to get out and film and take photographs of the Amazon churning through the water, or to stay put instead and enjoy the experience at first hand, as well as adding my weight contribution to keeping the tyres on the riverbed.

'Slip the clutch. Keep revs up, speed down. You need lots of revs to make sure the water does not creep up the exhaust. Whatever you do, don't stall as water will be sucked up into the engine, bending valves or even con-rods.'

I read the instructions in awe and fear, but Phil knew what to do by instinct and did it perfectly. He took the car sailing across river after river, with the Nepali spectators perched midstream on rocks and balanced one-legged on stepping stones, like inquisitive storks, waving and applauding us onwards.

In the punishing lowland heat Phil had wrapped his head in a white turban, like a Moroccan herdsman. I teased him about it, but I also thought secretly that he looked absurdly handsome – a bleach-job version of Rudolph Valentino in *The Sheik*.

Our team-mates were having a less successful day. At the first river JD got out to film, and slipped on a treacherous stone. He crashed on to his back and lay hurt, immobile and incapable, while Dan drove by in a plume of water. The crews of other cars assumed he was sunbathing, and Dan waited impatiently on the opposite bank thinking he was playing silly games. At length he went back to retrieve him and they struggled on, but at the last crossing of the day their car stalled in mid-river.

They opened the doors to get out and push, and watched in dismay as river water filled the car and gently flowed out the other side. Several cars passed by, including David Arrigo and Chris and Howard, with the occupants' eyes firmly fixed straight ahead, and their wake washing even more water into the back of the Amazon. Eventually they coaxed it ashore and bailed out the water.

For long days afterwards the inside of car 69 smelt worse than an abandoned fishmonger's slab in a heatwave.

Phil and I reached the border time control without mishap, at 11.15 a.m. We passed straight through the Nepal frontier, and drove a couple of bumpy kilometres through no-man's-land to the Indian frontier. Just outside the border there was a small huddle of shacks, grubby little shops and stalls, and a steaming queue of rally cars stationary in the blinding sunshine. No onward progress was being made.

Paperwork was my responsibility, so I took the carnet documents for the car and our passports and walked forward to see what was going on. I soon discovered that what was happening was that nothing was happening. A huge mob of drivers and navigators was milling around outside three bamboo huts, inside which the Indian officials were processing their documents at the rate of about one car every 15 minutes. Sweating rally officials were trying to mediate with the immigration officers and explain the delay to crews. It turned out that RO had paid the Indians a large sum of money to ensure that we would get fast-track document processing at the border. The money had vanished, and so had any chance of getting through this bottleneck in less than 3 hours.

There was nothing for it but to attach myself to the back of the crowd outside the first hut. The procedure went like this. First of all, queue to collect embarkation cards that had been completed and handed in to Mick O'Malley at camp last night. Then join another queue to have the car import–export carnet checked and stamped, which took about ten minutes per vehicle. Then finally queue outside the third hut for passport verification. All the papers were needed by each set of officials, so there was no question of drivers and navigators dividing the job between them.

I stood in the line behind Richard Clark, from the 1948 Buick 8. He was so enraged by the tedium of this process that the veins stood out on his temples like knotted string, and I began to worry that he might have a seizure. It was very hot and there was no shade outside the huts, but it was a case of stand your ground or lose your place.

The final hut, Passport Central, was the worst ordeal of the three. As I inched towards the table in the ante-room I saw that there was one man ruling off sheets of A3 paper by hand into boxes, to make a form, triplicated with two sheets of carbon paper, on which he entered in a laborious longhand script the holder's name, date of birth, occupation, date of passport issue, place of issue, number, Indian visa number, date of entry, place and time of entry, and so on, for each of well over two hundred passports, and then checked slowly that each detail was represented to his satisfaction.

Richard Clark made some impatient noise and the man looked up from his task.

'Bureaucracy is the legacy left to us by you British,' he said coldly.

After the form had been filled, the passport holder was waved through into the inner office. Here, under a ceiling fan that wallowed in the humid air, a Mr Important sat behind a desk with a minion on either side of him.

He took my passport and frowned at it, then passed it to one of the clerks. While the senior man asked me some desultory questions about my suitability to enter India, the clerk thumbed through a greasy ledger evidently containing the details of frontier undesirables. Fantastically, the ledger entries were not in alphabetical or date order, or any other logical sequence. For each traveller every ledger entry had to be read through, from the first page to the last.

At the end, finally, the rubber stamp grudgingly descended on the passport.

We were luckier than the six Iranians, who were just behind us. They were marched off into another room for what would clearly be a long interrogation. They bore this treatment and a version of it at every border we came to except their own, with patience and great good humour.

It was now almost four o'clock. The Indian customs formalities had taken more than four and a half hours to complete.

Behind the bamboo huts was the towering face of a huge river dam, and a few metres down a bank was a crescent of gritty sand that, regarded through half-closed eyes, could almost be called a beach.

True to form, Chris and Howard had refused to queue. They were lying on the sand sunbathing, and Howard was reading a volume of A.J.P. Taylor's essays.

'Going in for a swim?' Chris enquired.

I had only intended to cool my feet, but as soon as he suggested it the idea of a swim became irresistible. I knew that Phil was lurking under the trees, chafing to get straight in the car and drive on, but I pretended not to see him. I stripped off to my underclothes and ran into the water. The current ripping away from the dam was savage, but the water looked clean and the chill of it felt like heaven.

When I waded out again, I saw that an old man, three small boys and a mangy cur had gathered to look at me. Howard peered over the top of his book.

'Hmm. When Melissa went in, she drew a crowd of about forty.'

'Thanks.'

Phil was sitting in the car by now, practically gunning the engine, with the route notes on his lap.

'Ready? There's still 150 km to go.'

'I know. I'm ready.'

We drove over the dam, and had our book stamped at the 'India In' time control. We had an allowance of 2 hours and 50 minutes to cover the distance from here up to Nainital, which I thought was generous.

I hadn't reckoned with India.

The difference from Nepal became apparent within the first few kilometres. The spectators along the roadside didn't smile or wave. They only stared.

The road was busy with crowded buses and farm carts.

We overtook pedestrians, doggedly walking between
villages under the shade of big black umbrellas, and herds
of the thinnest cattle I have ever seen. Every few hundred
metres a dead dog lay in a cloud of flies. In the fields
beyond, primitive pumping engines lifted and spouted
water into irrigation ditches.

In the first town we came to the traffic seemed impenetrable. It was a stew of tuktuks and Tata buses, trucks
and cars, and scooters sometimes carrying a whole family,
the wife in her sari perched sidesaddle behind her husband and two or three small children wedged before and
behind. Even bicycles usually carried two people, sometimes three.

'Use your horn,' we had been advised in the India drivers' briefing. Phil jammed his thumb on the button,
adding our extra note to the cacophony of hooting and
hissing and screaming brakes. It made no difference whatsoever, and it was hell for him to try to drive safely
through this careening wilderness of metal and people
and wandering livestock.

Nepal had looked poor, but there had been a grace
about it that emanated principally from the people themselves. Grace was the last characteristic that anyone would
associate with the road to Nainital, in the towns at least.
The roadsides and the shacks that lined them were vistas
of pure squalor. Men and women squatted in the dirt
amid rotting towers of rubbish, spitting and excreting,
sniffed at by starving dogs, watched by impassive children.
The noise of traffic was ceaseless, and the heat as thick as
a blanket.

We stopped for petrol, 40 litres, and were charged

seventy-nine dollars for it. I had also made the mistake of assuming that India would be cheap, or at least that a fuel pump attendant, seeing that that was exactly the value of the currency I had with me, would not immediately declare it owing to him. There was no gauge on the pump, so we had no basis for argument.

We drove on, hungry and dehydrated again. There was never time to stop, never a proper interval for food or rest anywhere on the road. It was getting dark, and the traffic was so bad I was beginning to be concerned about the time.

We came to a place called Haldwani.

'Twinned with Golmud,' David Tremain said later.

The main street was choked with thousands of people, and buses and all the rest of our traffic adversaries. It was fully dark now, but half the vehicles didn't use lights. They drove head-on into the fray, in a blare of horns, playing chicken with every oncoming driver. There was no lane discipline – there were no lanes, even. Traffic in both directions used either side of the road with complete impartiality, overtaking and undertaking and skidding around each other in the fractured darkness. Pedestrians, ancient crones to minute toddlers, adopted the same approach in crossing the street.

Phil's eyes looked as if he had been up all night on a shovel-load of speed, and his knuckles stood out of his oily fists on the wheel like white moons. He swore monotonously and justifiably.

A young man on a scooter shot out of a side turning and swooped in front of us without even a glance over his shoulder. We just missed him, but we had screamed out our fear in unison, and the narrowness of the margin left us shaking.

Then beyond Haldwani the conditions changed with disorientating rapidity. The traffic disappeared, and black night wrapped around us.

'Can't see a fucking thing,' Phil muttered as we forged onwards. 'Is this the right way?'

I had caught a glimpse of Dave and Angela in the Rover back in the chaos of Haldwani, but no other rally cars since then. The empty road and the impenetrable darkness were disconcerting, and I was finding it impossible to pick out the landmarks listed in the route notes and so to monitor the trip distances accurately enough. I peered into the featureless void.

'I think so. I'm looking for a left turn at a hairpin junction. Signpost Nainital.'

It was 12 km from there to the control, and we still had half an hour to go. Tighter than was comfortable, but we should still do it.

'Here it is,' I shouted as a bend and a left turn materialised. *Beep*.

The road began to climb. Phil swung the wheel harder as the bends grew tighter and the gradient increased. I was hunched forward, counting the kilometres and the minutes.

'Where is everyone?' Phil demanded. I had been asking myself the same question.

The road went on and on, seeming to climb ever more steeply. The minutes were running by too quickly and I knew that there should be some signs of civilisation soon, but there was nothing except the endless dark. We had already done 12 km from the left turn, so we should be there by now. I must have misread the notes, I thought, and taken a wrong turning somewhere back down the road. Which meant that we could be anywhere, nowhere near Nainital. My first major navigational cock-up.

Phil suddenly jammed on the brakes and jumped out of the car. He ran round to the front and then disappeared, but his head bobbed up again a few seconds later. He threw aside a screwed-up black handful of something and leapt back into his seat. Newly bright headlamp beams cut into the dark ahead of us.

'Forgot about the tape,' he grinned. The headlamp glass had been protected from flying stones by a thick cross of black masking tape. 'No wonder I couldn't see.'

He was driving faster and faster, up and up the terrible bends. At every one my throat tightened in the fear that he wouldn't get us round it. Suddenly, giddily high up above us, I saw a tiny powdering of lights that ought to have been somewhere in the sky but could only belong to the hill station of Nainital.

'There it is!'

A second later we skidded past a bare rock-face. Painted on the rock in dribbly white letters were the words 'Nainital 16 km'.

'*Sixteen?*' I couldn't believe it, but I knew what I must have done. I had identified the bend in the notes wrongly, and much too early, and accordingly underestimated the distance still to run. Now we had a bare 8 minutes of our allowance left.

'I'm really sorry.'

Phil was kind. 'Don't worry. At least we're on the right road. We'll get there in the end.'

The next bend was a left-hander, steep, doubling back on itself with an adverse camber. As we scrambled around it we saw a small cluster of people standing at the roadside, staring downwards over a gap in the stone wall. They were all locals, but beside them on the wall was a holdall with the Peking to Paris logo on it.

'Accident,' Phil said as he braked to a standstill. The knell that the word sounded was becoming too familiar.

The face of Anthony Jefferis, Nigel Challis' co-driver from the Land Rover, loomed towards us. He had a lump the size of a hen's egg over one eye and he looked dazed.

He called out, 'We're all right. But a major problem. Car's right over the edge. Can you let them know up there?'

It was a drop of 12 metres. Pushing against the clock, they must have taken the corner too fast and gone straight over. They were lucky to be alive. We were the first car to pass, and there was nothing we could do at the scene, so we left them with the promise that help would soon come, and pushed on towards the floating lights.

'We're not supposed to be rallying in the dark. They told us we'd never have to drive like this in the dark,' Phil kept saying.

It was bad planning and no one would ever have chosen to drive this particular road at speed at night, but on the other hand no one could have predicted the scale of the border delays.

The timer on the dash gave its dreaded beep, and I banged the button to silence it. It seemed that the climb and the brutal bends would go on for ever. Our headlights licked over another car slewed at the side of the road, and the white hands of the driver who was flagging us down.

'Please, not another one,' I whispered. It was the Greek Chevvy Bel Air, number 58. Theo Voukidis' face appeared in Phil's window.

'Got any fuel?'

They'd run out of petrol, that was all, thank God.

'No, but I'll let them know you're here. There's been an accident further down.'

Theo stood back and waved us on. Phil drove as fast as he dared on up to Nainital.

It was a busy town. We pushed forwards through the traffic and crowds of spectators, peering for the time control under the disorientating street lights. At last we found it, at the edge of a huge car park, and I ran across with the book. There was only one marshal on duty – Paul Brace, RO's driver.

'There's been an accident. Down the hill. The Land Rover.'

He looked concerned, but helpless.

'I can't leave here. There's a mass of cars still to come in. Can you go straight on up to the HQ hotel and let them know?'

He stamped my book. Ten-minute time penalty. There were other cars drawn up in the wide space beyond the control point, with crews who looked either confused or openly angry. Some of the cars were jacked up, there were knots of people muttering together. Evidently Phil and I were not the only ones who had had difficulties with the day.

The cars were to be left where they were, on police orders, Paul told us. The only way to the HQ hotel was by shuttle bus, and we would have to wait for it to return from its last circuit. It took a long time, but the wait must have seemed even longer to the two men stranded downhill beside their crashed car. At last we ran into the HQ lobby and tracked down Sarah Catt. Ever since David Burlinson and his staff had relinquished their administrative responsibilities at Kathmandu, it seemed to become harder and harder to find any of the senior organisers.

'It's all right,' Sarah reassured us. 'We know about it. Help's on the way to them.'

I checked the accommodation list. We were in another hotel – Claridges by name, probably not by nature – even further up the hill. None of the rest of our gang seemed to be billeted there. The system in operation was that, in smaller towns where there was no single hotel big enough to accommodate the entire rally, the organisers, officials, support crews and media teams were allocated rooms in the HQ establishment, which was invariably the best one. Competitors were then assigned rooms elsewhere, in descending degrees of comfort, according to the order in which they had paid for their accommodation package. Phil and I were about midway down the list, which in effect sometimes meant dossing down for the night in Bug City.

We waited for yet another shuttle bus, which eventually took us winding up steep, dark lanes to Claridges. Cold air poured in through the windows, an indication of how high we had climbed from the arid heat of the frontier. It was half-past nine. We were tired, and snappy with each other, and irritated by the slowness of the buses and the time it was taking to get where we could be clean and warm and not thirsty again.

The hotel smelled of damp, and our room featured a murky-looking double bed. Phil gave it a grimace of furious irritation but I was so cold and exhausted I just lay down and pulled the covers over my head.

I heard him moving around the room, discovering another bed on a mezzanine floor. He came and shook my ankle through the covers.

'I'm going to the bar. Are you coming?'

I didn't think I wanted to sit for an hour and talk about what had happened to someone's wheel bearings.

'No.'

'Okay then.'

I had a tepid shower, ordered a curry and some naan bread from room service. I felt gravid with loneliness. I shouldn't have come. I didn't have the necessary moral fibre. Was it only *this morning* I had been so exultant in the pink daybreak at Kohalpur? How could I have sunk so quickly into defeat and withdrawal?

Then to my surprise Phil came back, bringing two beers and the next-best palliative for my depression: rally gossip. He spooned food from the room-service tray when it arrived, and brought the plate to me in bed. I sat up to eat, greedy for curry and news, and he propped his boots on the sheet and drank beer from the bottle.

'Everyone's pissed off,' he said. 'They all say it was too dangerous, making us drive up here in the pitch dark.'

'We weren't supposed to be doing it in the dark.'

'Well, we did. Because of the border, I know, but they should have reckoned on that. There have been plenty of breakdowns and people losing time.'

'More than us?'

'Much more. We did well.'

Dan and JD had broken a rear shock absorber mounting, and would have to find a welding shop before going any further. Bart and his wife in Kermit, the green Volvo, had broken the top wishbone of one of their front wheels. They had managed somehow to chain the pieces together and limp to a garage for repairs. Jennifer and Francesca had had yet more mechanical problems. The rumour was that a number of cars hadn't even reached Nainital yet, so there would be no order published tonight. There wasn't a start time for the morning either – at least, none had reached the distant outpost of Claridges.

'We'll have to get up early and check it then.'

'I'll do that,' I said. At least I was alert in the mornings.

The view from Claridges, when the sun rose, was of a deep bowl of pine-covered hills with a silver lake set in the centre like a diamond in a ring. The air was cold and resin-scented, and a thin mist lay over the water. The story went that the resort had flourished after some British pukka sahib had had his yacht carried up the hill on the backs of coolies, and had grandly launched it on the lake. It was easy to imagine how Nainital must have been in the heyday of the Raj, when tight-laced Victorian memsahibs left their husbands to sweat down on the plains and retreated to the cool of the hill station to play cards and take tea. Today it reminded me of an Alpine ski-resort in

summer. There were even the cobweb lines of a cable car
looping the hillside.

Down at the car park the cars were leaving at one-
minute intervals, with a fine and quintessentially Indian
send-off. A loudspeaker announcement floridly boomed
the details of each car and the names of the crew, and
wished them a safe journey. A commemorative plaque
of memorable hideousness was presented to each car –
the first in what was to become a series of collectible trophies. A band loudly played, competing with the
loudspeaker, and dancers jingled and waved and leapt.
There was a long, white-clothed trestle table with a tea-
urn and pyramids of white cups and saucers, exactly as at
an English vicarage fête, and plates of triangular white-
bread sandwiches and sponge cakes. Overhead the
crystal air shimmered with sunshine against the spruce-
green hills.

I took a plate of sandwiches and cake to Phil, who had
missed breakfast. The news circulating the car park was
that because of the chaos at the border, and the lateness
of so many cars into Nainital, yesterday's timings had
been 'neutralised'. We had put in one of the best times,
and now it wouldn't count.

Phil's bed had been infested, and he was covered with
itchy little bedbug bites. Somehow, I had escaped this.

'You should have shared with me,' I teased, remembering the sheikh's turban look but feeling relieved that
the double-bed scenario had resolved itself in nothing
more penetrating than a few flea-bites.

'Yes, I probably should,' he said darkly. 'How long have
we got?'

I checked my watch. 'Seventy-five minutes.'

'I'll have to get the wheel off. There's a leak from the hub, look.'

There was indeed a sinister black patch of oil. He jacked up the car and loosened the wheel nuts while I hovered. Dan and JD came back from the welding shop where they had had their shock mountings fixed. After some consultation they decided that it wasn't brake fluid, at least; most probably the felt gasket on the wheel bearing had gone and oil was seeping out. We would have to watch it carefully and hope to make a proper investigation during the rest day in Lahore, the day after tomorrow.

Our turn came for the off. It was a short stage, 33 kilometres in 34 minutes. Down the mountain again.

Beyond the start line there was a steep ramp, and with the loudspeaker fanfare ringing in our ears we set off smartly. Only the car refused to pull away. There was no power, and we only just made it to the top of the slope without stalling. On the flat beyond, we picked up momentum with agonising slowness and Andrew and David swept briskly by in the land crab. We looked at each other, eyes dilated with horror.

'What's happening?'

'Don't know.'

Gradually the engine picked up. We climbed the hill out of Nainital, watching the red and white rear end of car 83.

'Blockage in the fuel line, maybe,' Phil said. He was sweating.

The road began to descend. I tapped the timer.

'Twenty-nine minutes. Can you speed up?'

Phil turned up the music until it pumped through the car. It was his signal that he was ready to burn rubber.

It was the first very fast downhill section we had done. There were rally cars strung out all the way down, but we met nothing coming up the other way.

'Must have closed the road for us,' Phil muttered. He pulled out on to the opposite side and, in the face of the blind bends, overtook the Morrises and the Noors, and Murray and Amanda, and David Brister and Keith Barton in their Rover 110. I closed my eyes and forced them open again. There had been no indication that this was a closed stage. I wanted to see what was coming to meet us in case I spotted it a split-second before Phil did. Our tyres and brakes screamed, and the chassis rocked. The car's various ailments were forgotten. I was terrified that we were going to overturn or spin off the road, but I was also excited beyond measure.

This was the best, the very essence of what we had come for.

Phil was reckless but I trusted him to the last degree, life or death. I knew this road wasn't really closed, but together we made a conspiracy of risk.

Go, we kept saying as we cornered on the wrong side of the road. *Go.* Somehow the wheels held the asphalt.

We saw the monkey at the same instant. It had swung down from a tree to land in the middle of the road and its black mask turned towards us with an expression of quizzical surprise. We heard its cry, a high-pitched *eeeek*, and felt the bump beneath the wheels. I looked back.

'Phil, shouldn't we . . .?'

'What do you want to do, stop and find a vet?'

'All right. Just keep going.' I was getting as brutally focused as the rest of them.

I watched the flickering dots on the timer, and called the distances and the minutes left. One set of figures rose uncomfortably against the other. Nine minutes, 11 k. Six minutes, 9 k.

Phil was inexorable. He would glimpse a car ahead of us, and at once he was pulling out to overtake. Nothing was going to stand in his way.

The timer beeped. Our 34 minutes were up, we still had 4 kilometres to go. Faster. The grassy banks and trees at the roadside became a green blur. A truck whirled towards us, we swerved to avoid it and immediately pulled out again, looking for the next car to overtake. I shivered with the fear of what we had been doing.

'There it is!'

The control was just ahead. We skidded in to the road-side, and I ran. We were stamped with a four-minute penalty.

With my heart still hammering I ran back to the car and jumped in, ready for the assault on the next stage. Beyond the control I caught a glimpse of Dan and JD standing beside their car, their faces a picture of gloom. Phil didn't stop to offer our help. I knew we should have stopped; I also knew that he couldn't, simply couldn't make himself. He was too high, too caught up, too *driven*. And so was I.

We hammered straight on, eating into the 130 kilometres that separated us from the next control, at Moradabad.

The flush and elation of high intimacy that had

coloured the hill section slowly ebbed. I rested my head against the window glass and stared out. I had misread my partner, I thought. I had had him down for an easygoing adventurer, a bland evader of responsibilities who preferred to wander instead of engaging with the world or its occupants. But that drive down from Nainital had revealed him more nakedly than any soul-baring session could have done. Phil was no team-player. He was a loner, and he was burned up by his determination to succeed to the point where, when he was aiming for something, nothing else counted. Certainly not risk, or stacked odds. I had thought I had become driven, out of a sense of deep inadequacy, into never missing a work deadline, or cooking a poor meal, or failing to reach the top of Kalapathar even if it meant crawling there on my hands and knees. But my need to succeed was no match for Phil's. We were alike in our tenacity, even though we were dissimilar in everything else. And just possibly somewhere inside, that was very well defended, he might even be as fearful as me.

After a while, he realised I had been silent for a long time.

'Have I done something to upset you?' he asked, acknowledging the different ground that had existed between us since Kathmandu.

I shook my head. 'No. I've just been thinking about some things.'

'Okay.' He fumbled in the bag of essentials that was wedged in the space between our seats, found a cigarette and lit it, and gave it to me.

'Thank you.'

We reached Moradabad. It was a terrible place, defiled with rubbish and excrement, swarming with flies, teeming with unhappy people who glued themselves to our windows and reached thin brown hands inside to pilfer our belongings. I couldn't find any corner offering enough privacy to have a pee. When I came back to the car I found that the slice of Nainital sponge cake I had wrapped in a paper napkin had turned into a brown, seething heap of ants.

Dan and JD rolled up.

'What happened?' I asked Dan.

'The welding we had done this morning lasted precisely four km down that hill. We're having to go very carefully.'

'I'm sorry we didn't stop.'

He smiled, the dimple deepening.

'I didn't mind. JD took it badly.'

I went to apologise to JD.

'Don't worry.'

It was a long, hot, congested, ugly drive onwards to Delhi. The traffic obeyed no rules. At one point Phil was overtaking a truck, and three pudgy teenage boys in a souped-up bubblegum-pink car darted between the truck and the Amazon. Metal scraped metal, and then the boys pulled in in front of us and slowed down, weaving from side to side so we couldn't overtake. All this in a seething rush of other vehicles. They slowed further, and when Phil pulled alongside to overtake they accelerated, with jeering blasts on the horn and fat-faced taunting grins.

Phil wound down the window and unleashed a torrent of four-letter words and obscene gestures.

At once the driver slammed on his brakes and swaggered out of his girly pink car, beckoning Phil out too. They were spoiled boys, overweight and unfit and Phil could easily have killed all three of them. I had to restrain him physically by grabbing hold of his sleeve and hauling him back into the car.

'*Please* don't. Please, just drive on.'

The one he whacked the hardest would certainly turn out to be the son of the local police chief or criminal don and a night in the cells wouldn't do anything to advance our place on the leader board.

'Please, Phil. I've always wanted to see Delhi. Don't deprive me of it now.'

He wound up the window in their grinning faces. He was vibrating with rage, frightening even me.

'All right. All right. Little *fuckers*.'

In the rear view mirror as we accelerated away I thought I saw three moon-faces wobble in relief.

We reached Delhi in the thick of the evening traffic. Wherever the proud Lutyens avenues and monuments were, I didn't see them.

Chapter Eleven

It was already dark when we left the car. There was going to be no sightseeing in Delhi.

The hotel bar was packed with people recounting stories of the descent from Nainital and stoking themselves up with beer because the next day we would be dry in Pakistan. Paula Broderick was telling everyone within earshot about how she and Nigel had spun right off the road in Arnie the Eco-Flow Anglia, and had still come in only 5 minutes over time. Anton Aan de Stegge, a huge bear of a man, reclined in his seat with a ham-sized fist masking half his face. He had the dryest sense of humour I had ever come across. Phil grinned happily at me across the table. He was pleased with our day's performance, and relieved that the leak from the rear hub wasn't getting any worse and we had been so wound up together in the day's competition that the threads of it were still drawn tight between us. It was good to feel that at least he and I made a team, at this minute anyway, even though our loyalty to the other half of Team Amazon hadn't been particularly impressive.

Dan and JD had nursed their car along all day, and now they had taken it to a welding shop to have the lower shock mounting fixed yet again. They weren't alone. Danny deVito was having the engine mounts of his 2CV welded – his engine had been held in place all day just by his co-driver's leather belt. Josef Feit, who drove a VW cabriolet, took over the welding gear and insisted on doing all the work himself to fix his exhaust back in place, oblivious to the uproar this caused amongst the local mechanics. His co-driver was his son, René, and in the bright scarlet race overalls they both wore they looked noticeably alike. Somewhere in Tibet they had picked up a yak's skull complete with horns, and fixed it to the front of the Volkswagen. When they came up behind us I always thought that the horns looked in the mirror like the handlebars of a Harley Davidson sprouting from the hybridising metal.

After dinner the day's order was pinned up on the rally notice board. Phil and I had been waiting and watching for it, and we pressed eagerly forward in the crowd to read the results.

We were up to 39th place. I could see Phil counting and calculating. We were still fourth Volvo out of five, but we were now only five places and 23 minutes behind Dan and JD.

First place was held by John and Simon Catt in the Cortina. Over the twenty days of the rally so far, they had only dropped three minutes. After their spin off the road the Brodericks were down to third, Chris and Howard were seventh, Murray and Amanda sixteenth and Carolyn and David Tremain eighteenth. Three of the top ten places were held by the Iranian Peykan crews. They did drive fast, but also very effectively.

'If only we hadn't had that bloody distributor failure in China,' Phil muttered. 'We'd be in the top ten as well.'

'But anyone who's had a mechanical problem will say exactly the same. The main thing is we're still on for the gold.'

We had begun to talk about what result we were aiming for. At first, we had only acknowledged that we wanted to get to Paris. Just to reach the Place de la Concorde on 18 October would be enough. Then there had been our brief flare of naked ambition at Golmud, rapidly extinguished, when we had thought of winning. Now, privately to each other, we agreed that we wanted a gold medal – and also to finish in the top twenty.

'We can do it,' Phil said. 'The car can do it, and so can we.'

The day's bulletin also announced that our morning call would be at 3 a.m. The Indians closed their border with Pakistan at 4.30 p.m., and with more than 500 km to travel to the frontier, the organisers were starting cars from 4.01 a.m., four per minute, to give us all the best possible chance of getting across in time.

It seemed I had hardly closed my eyes before having to open them again and begin another day. Delhi to Lahore.

I went to buy bottles of water and Coca-Cola from the hotel shop, to combat the dehydration that was one of the most uncomfortable side-effects of too many hot hours in the car. It was still pitch dark when I tottered outside with my bags and an armful of plastic bottles.

The Amazon had gone. It wasn't in the parking slot

where we had left it the night before, and I couldn't see it on my panicky tour of the rest of the car park. I ran back to the foyer and out again, and asked everyone I met if they had seen Phil or the car. No one had.

That's it, I thought. He's cracked, and either done a runner or gone back to hide in bed. I knew he had at least got up, at the customary last moment, because I had caught a glimpse of him at breakfast.

I ran down to the hotel gate, where cars where streaming out towards the start point. The *bastard*, I thought. If he's gone off without me . . .

In the end I bumped into a porter who had carried Phil's bags for him. He led me to a corner behind a hotel van, and there was the Amazon hidden in its shadow. Gripped by morning inertia, Phil was sitting inside fiddling with his camera.

'Sorry. I moved it again last night.'

Hot with relief and swept with a backwash of anger, I demanded 'Why?'

'Because I went for *fuel*, okay?'

The bottles began to slip out of my overladen arms.

'Help me.'

Too late. They crashed around me and burst over my feet in a series of little spouts and fountains. Still enraged, I threw the last two at him. They also burst and Phil had to spend the rest of the day sitting in trousers on a car seat that were both soaked in Coca-Cola.

A bad start to the morning.

Pre-dawn, and deserted central Delhi was dotted with rally cars trying to find their way to the start at India Gate via the gnomic instructions in the route book. In tetchy

silence we did the circuit of the Rajaji Marg roundabout
twice, neck and neck with David Brister and Keith Barton
in car 39.

We finally located the start and got away on our
minute, 4.17 a.m. We had been given an overall time
allowance of 10 hours to get ourselves over the border
and into Lahore. We drove a long way without speaking
except to exchange route information.

'Sorry,' I said humbly, at last. I held my hand out and
Phil took it

'Look,' he said. 'I'll be your whipping boy, if that's
what you want. But it's my job to get this car to Paris.' It
was becoming his mantra.

We weren't arguing about the car, of course, or Coke
bottle missiles, or bad tempers, but about the space
between us.

I sighed. 'You're nobody's whipping boy. Least of all
mine. I would just be happier if we could talk to each
other.'

'We do talk, don't we? But . . . I try to protect you from
things, as well.'

'What sort of things?'

He shifted in his sticky seat and in the end I dragged
the admission out of him as if it were some long-buried
horror. He had seen John Vipond laughing at my driving
on the Friendship Bridge. Jennifer and Francesca had
confided to him in some friendly moment that they didn't
like me. I was surprised by the latter because I had never
exchanged more than two words with either of them, but
I was much more surprised that such small things mattered to Phil. He was much more vulnerable to criticism

than I had realised – even criticism so indirect that it only related to his temporary partner.

'I couldn't care less about what they think,' I said.

He took his eyes off the road for a minute and glanced at me in disbelief.

I went on determinedly, 'I care about the people I love, and what they think of me. I care about what *you* think, because I admire you and you are important to me.'

I couldn't think of a way to be more honest. He made some non-committal response so I tried a less personal angle.

'I'm a writer, aren't I? I write about people's lives and emotions. They are my stock-in-trade.'

'Plenty of material here, then.'

Phil jerked his chin, and I couldn't tell whether it was at the road and the rally cars hopefully streaming towards Pakistan, or at the interior of car 82. But the alignment between us had changed yet again. As if we were completing some complicated dance measure, we would make a reciprocal forwards movement, to the point where we almost met, and then an unexpected twirl would send us ricocheting sideways or backwards all over again.

It was a hideous drive, north-westwards through the shrieking traffic. We passed through Ambala and Ludhiana to Amritsar, weaving dangerously in and out of the trucks and tuktuks and buses in the towns, skirting the camels and buffalo carts and teetering haywagons on the country roads. Somewhere along the way our overdrive stopped working, which left us without the benefit of a fifth gear. The brightest spot of the whole alarming journey was on the outskirts of Ludhiana when we passed what must have been a dye-works. Up on the flat roof the lengths of turban fabric had been hung out to dry. They shimmered in thick bands of every colour, palest lemon and cerise and turquoise and lavender, like a glimpse of a midsummer garden in this landscape of dirt and concrete and squalor.

We reached the Indian frontier in good time, ahead of most of the field. Those behind us were less lucky because the queues began to build up, but we cleared the Indian formalities in less than two hours. It was the same tedious procedure of waiting for obstructive officialdom, but it was made lively for us because Adam and Jon were next in the line. They hailed us with their traditional greeting.

'Ben Doone and Phil McCracken!'

'Hooray Henrys!' Phil called back.

I leaned against the long sleek nose of the Bentley. Their names were neatly white-painted on the side: Adam 'Tubby' Hartley & Jonathan 'Tubby' Turner. Naturally they were both whippet-thin.

Jon put his arm round Phil's shoulders.

'Tell me something, Phil. Do you know what they call an Irishman in a conservatory?'

'Nope.'

'Paddy O'Doors.'

'Okay. A man with a plank on his head?'

'Edward.'

'Three planks?'

'Dunno.'

'Edward Woodward.'

We were reeling with laughter. It must have been the sun. Stern, turbanned policemen scrutinised our documents.

'A nun on a washing machine?'

'Sister Matic.'

'A man with no arms and legs in a swimming pool?'

'Bob.'

'*Nah.* Clever Dick.'

'Your passport here, please.'

It was an effort to obey orders without snorting with suppressed mirth like a bunch of third-formers. We were waved on, into a last queue to have the passports laboriously checked just once more, for luck, and onwards to the Pakistan frontier. While we were waiting outside the border I pulled on the appropriate loose trousers and a long-sleeved shirt. We would have to stay covered up all the way to western Turkey.

The entry into Pakistan was a big contrast with what we had suffered in India. Efficient members of the Pakistan Motor Sports Club were waiting to expedite our passage, the officials all smiled at us, and the police officers were proud, tall and wonderfully handsome men in navy-blue frock coats with striped cravats and rows of medals on their chests. They wore printed name badges. With his mind still at Paddy O'Doors level, Phil was charmed to encounter Officer Pushdeep and Officer Hardeep.

There was a police escort for the 26 kilometres into Lahore, and we found ourselves second in line behind Adam and Jon. The police jeep took off at a funereal pace with the Bentley nosing up its behind, and after a couple of km the police driver pulled over and came around to ask Adam just how fast his car could really go.

'Try me,' Adam grinned.

We set off again. The jeep went faster and faster, the

Bentley never yielded an inch, and the Amazon surged along in their wake. At one point we were doing 110 kilometres an hour, and Adam probably still didn't have his foot hard down.

Lahore looked beautiful as we spun through it. There were canals lined with weeping willows, and wide avenues where the lamp posts were hung with red and white banners welcoming the honourable participants in the Peking–Paris Rally. We were directed through the gates of the hotel, and then out into a huge garden, to draw up in dusty lines on the immaculate grass.

To step out of the fetid car, journey-stiff and with dirt in every crease, and to absorb the afternoon sunshine and breathe in the scent of mown grass and roses, was like arriving in paradise. The green lawn was smoother than velvet underfoot. Garlands of scented crimson rose petals were draped around our necks and waiters brought silver salvers laden with beaded glasses of ruby-red iced fruit punch. I was so happy I could have lain down in the purple shade under one of the trees and spread out my arms to embrace it all. And tomorrow was a rest day. No car, no noise, no dirt, no *beep* to echo inside my skull.

The hotel was big and grand, and air-conditioned almost to dewpoint. We had a high room, looking down on the tree-tops and happily distant rally cars. There were *white fluffy robes* in the bathroom. We took long, hot showers and removed the black crescents from beneath our fingernails, then put on the bathrobes, opened the alcohol-free minibar, and lay back on one of the beds to giggle at old British sitcoms on the television. When things were good between Phil and me, they cancelled out the bad times entirely.

Before dinner I went out shopping with Melissa, and Dan and JD. That morning Jennifer and Francesca had blossomed slightly uncertainly in shalwar kameez made up in cheery Peter Jones floral prints, and Melissa and I were naturally eager to keep our end up. Down the road from the hotel we found a functional, neon-lit department store, and the assistants brought out piles of outfits for us to choose from. Every person working in the shop was a man. There were no saleswomen, and almost no women customers, and the streets outside were thronged with men.

Dan and JD selected the first garments they were shown, while Melissa and I waded through the heaps of white cotton tunics and baggy pants, rejecting this one for the wrong embroidery, that one for the wobbly neckline. They sat on a bench, waiting and watching, but after half an hour they grew impatient and incredulous.

'They are all the *same*.' Dan spread his hand, flat-palmed. 'What is the point of all this?'

We tried to explain that shopping was the point of shopping, but it cut no ice. I quickly chose an ice-blue shalwar kameez for Phil. In the end he wouldn't wear them, sticking to the customary T-shirts and Army camouflage trousers even after Dan appeared looking elegantly patrician in his pale mint-green version. Maybe he thought the look was a bit too feminine for a wild boy racer.

While I was changing for dinner there was a knock at the door, and I opened it to find a Pakistani man with a worried expression.

'Where is Murdoch Laing? Who are his friends?' he demanded.

It turned out that the man had known Murdoch since university, and he had organised a big party to welcome his old friend to Lahore. Unfortunately still dogged by mechanical breakdowns, the Aston and its crew hadn't made it to the border before it closed down for the night. His host didn't want to cancel the party, and he was looking for Murdoch's friends to celebrate with him instead. I assured him that he wouldn't find any shortage of takers.

Dinner that night was at a long, candlelit table under the trees in the scented garden, with delicious food and the best company. It was one of those evenings when nothing could go wrong. Lahore became a place of happy memory, and I thought back to it often enough in the days that followed.

Phil devoted his rest day to checking out the wheel bearings on our car, and helping Dan and JD to replace one of their front steering arms. I did some very overdue work, which wasn't too much of a hardship under a parasol beside the hotel swimming pool. Colin attended to the Porsche and its ailments, so Melissa had energy and time to spare – she hired a car and a driver and embarked on a sightseeing circuit of the Fort, the Temple of Mirrors and the Shalimar Gardens. She consoled me wisely when I bewailed my failure ever to see anything anywhere on this crazy trip.

'Just look on it as a recce,' she said. 'We can come back to all the places we like and see them properly.'

I would certainly come back to Lahore.

But at the end of the day, Phil and I did find an hour to go out on our own to the Old Bazaar. It felt good to be making this rare sightseeing expedition together – the first since the Potala Palace. The taxi-driver who took us from the hotel was four feet high and four feet round, and spoke good English. He volunteered himself as our guide, and we let him lead us into the warren of alleyways.

It was like being drawn into a moving paintbox. There were stalls selling iridescent sari lengths, and bolts of wedding fabric beaded and sequinned and reflecting darts of rainbowed light. There were wonderfully elaborate and kitsch marriage seats, wound around with metallic ribbons in purple and silver and scarlet, and men's wedding hats made of intricately pleated satin, topped with a stiff crest of paper and nodding feathers, and pinned with an egg-sized glass jewel. Kitchenware stalls shone with great copper cauldrons and kettles, and pewter-coloured pans in infinitely graded towers, and racks of forks and spoons and giant ladles. There were shoe stalls stacked with towers of white boxes, and paper merchants, and spice sellers with brown hessian sacks spilling out cumin and cardamom and cloves. The alleys were clogged with shoppers, bicyclists and strolling men, and – here at least – head-down, hurrying women in swishing saris. Wildly ornamented and glittering tuktuks cut recklessly through the crowds. There were musicians on the corners with drums and sticks of bells and little brass cymbals.

There were food vendors too. The air was thick with smoke and the smell of cooking. Men expertly fried poppadums, and stirred vats of fragrant curries. There were piles of every kind of nut, and mounds of glossy dates, and powdery sweetmeats. I wanted to try everything, but for my stomach's timid sake I didn't venture a single mouthful. I didn't need to get ill again.

Down at the far end of an alleyway at right angles to ours I suddenly saw a giant red and pink totem pole. It was Howard, all six foot six of him, in a red polo shirt. Surrounded by tiny darting people he looked like Gulliver in a sea of Lilliputians. He lifted his great hand and waved to me.

The light drained out of the sky. Looking up, I saw the colour fade from dove-grey in the distance to slate over my head. The smoky air was criss-crossed with telephone wires, with the dark blobs of roosting pigeons strung all along them, so that the sky looked like the score for some avant-garde piece of music. There were kites flying too, not kite-shaped but square, like tiny black pocket-hand-kerchiefs or tethered bats dipping against the thickening dusk.

Our round guide led us on into the antiques district and we followed him through the stalls of his friends and relatives, but it was a mechanical exercise. There was much dross, and neither Phil nor I had Howard's appetite for searching out what was not. Nobody pressed us to buy, and everyone was courteous and graceful. At last, from a bewilderingly oblique direction, we emerged from the sensory overload of the bazaar right next to our friend's parked taxi. He accepted our thanks and money with a serene smile.

Yes, he said, in answer to Phil's questions. Lahore was a very good place to live. Best in Pakistan.

Back at the hotel a bulletin had been posted. Because so many people had suffered severe delays leaving India yesterday, yet another day's times had been neutralised. There was no change in the order from Delhi.

'Every time we have a good day,' Phil muttered, 'they fucking cancel it.'

We forged on from Lahore to Multan. The overdrive still didn't work, so on long, dull stretches of road there was the tiring and monotonous sound of the engine straining. The cassette player was finally working loose from its mountings and it began to fade and then sporadically cut out. We had listened to every one of the tapes we had with us over and over – *everything's gonna be all right* – until they ran inside my head almost as insistently as the *beep*, but music was still essential.

'I'll have to fix it,' Phil vowed.

It was very hot, and a dry insistent wind sucked the moisture out of our skin and made us perpetually thirsty. The flat countryside was brown and grey, mottled with scrubby bushes and eucalyptus trees and broken up by canals and the relentless straight line of a railway. Sometimes it seemed to waver, but it was only the heat haze and a trick of tired eyes.

The few towns we passed through were dusty little clusters of single-storey shops and houses, where the people squatted at the roadside to watch us pass through. The traffic was less dense than in India, but there was the same reckless disregard for any conventions of the road. Most beautiful, but also most alarming because of their size and speed, were the great painted wagons. They had towering fronts with curved tops, and every inch of this great barque was gaudily painted with fantastic designs and stuck with mirrors and magic eyes and golden beading. The effect was like a runaway fairground roundabout bowling down the crown of the road towards you.

'They travel the Karakoram Highway,' Phil said. I imagined how stirring these great glittering monsters must look, hauling their way across territory almost as high and bleak as the way we had come over the Himalayas.

In the remote rural areas there began to be groups of children, gathered at the sides of the road in loose clothes the same colourless colours as the landscape. The first time I saw a huddle of them with their hands raised I thought they were waving and I began to wave back, but then there was a sharp rattle and a heavier clang from the side of the car. They were throwing stones at us. A few kilometres further on a handful of grit flung through the open window stung my face.

It was disturbing to be stoned, but the resentment that must have underlain it had been gnawing at our consciences ever since Tibet. Our outrage at the repeated assaults was double-edged with guilt.

We reached Multan, with a clean card, at the unusually early time of four in the afternoon.

'So probably they'll cancel the day for some reason,' we sighed pessimistically to each other.

The heat was tiring and dispiriting, but we stood up to it better than some. At one of the day's time controls I had bumped into the smaller of the toothbrushless American women. (Or maybe they had restocked their oral hygiene supplies at Lahore).

'I hate this,' she told me. 'I just *hate* it.' She looked all in. But remembering the Tibetan plateau and the temperature of −15 degrees at the Tuotuoheyan camp, I decided that for myself I would rather be too hot than too cold.

The oldest city in Pakistan, Multan was reputed to be rich in dust, beggars and burial grounds. Melissa was full of energy and always eager for the next diversion, and we had no sooner arrived in the hotel than she was mustering a fleet of taxis and persuading us all to go sightseeing. Dust and beggars were certainly in generous supply in the surrounding streets. We toured a couple of imposing mosques, which were decorated in the characteristic local cool turquoise and aquamarine tiles, and intruded on people's prayers with our video cameras and tourist stares. Some of our party were still wearing shorts, and it made me uncomfortable to see the way that eyes followed their freckled, hairy-blonde, stilt-like bare limbs. I didn't in any case like invading other people's places of worship, especially when they were the central focus of as many lives as the ones in Multan, and I was glad when our sprawling group shifted itself onwards to the bazaar.

We discovered that it was almost as lively as the one in Lahore, but there were too many of us trying to stay together and too much time was spent standing on corners asking each other where Chris and Howard had gone. I wished that I had come just with a single companion, like the night before.

In the end, we were separated and hopelessly lost in the maze of alleyways. Phil and Carolyn and I found the nearest exit and hopped into an exuberantly decorated tuktuk for a ride home. It was exactly like being in a video game. Super TukTuk Kart. Wherever three or more roads converged, half a dozen of the little machines would whirl at top speed into the middle of the junction, playing chicken until the last instant, and then somehow swerve and rattle past each other before darting on to the next intersection. We made it home to dinner with a score of 8,500 points and all our lives still intact.

With Dan and JD we chose the first restaurant we came to for dinner, and then realised too late that it was Chinese. No one wanted to eat a Chinese meal ever again, but somehow when it arrived we managed to dispose of it. For the first time the talk turned to Paris, and the Ball to celebrate our arrival there, and who each of us was hoping would be on the finish line to meet us. I knew why. Multan was the half-way point in distance and time and our perspectives had suddenly changed. Instead of looking at the rally like a great peak to be climbed, it was as if we were peering from the summit at a downhill slope. It was beginning to be conceivable that it would all end, some day, and there would be no more road and no more *beep* and Phil and I would go our separate ways again. Covertly, I watched him eating sweet and sour chicken. I knew just as much about him, I thought, as he had been prepared to let me learn. And at the beginning when I had been sharing out the Prince Borghese attributes, I had thought that I was the controlling one.

In the morning we were up early to carry out the checks on the car that we had recklessly neglected the night before. There was no more leaking from the rear wheel bearing, no leaks or cracks visible anywhere else, and apart from the overdrive and the tape deck everything appeared to be holding up well. Evidently Tony Barrett had done some sound thinking and Noddy and Geza and Phil had followed his ideas through with great thoroughness. We were optimistic again.

We left Multan in 37th place, heading westwards through Baluchistan to Quetta, almost on the border with Afghanistan. We had 622 kilometres to cover in four stages.

In the first hour of the first stage we overtook the familiar numbers ahead of us in the order. Phil was resentful about it today.

'Why are we way back here in the list when we have to overtake all these slower people every time we set off in the morning?'

'I don't know. It'll change soon.'

We made the first stage within our allowance, and waited a further half-hour for a new restart minute because the vintageants were being given more space and time to complete the difficult section ahead. Phil paced around like a bear in a cage. The time control was a dusty café in the flyblown little town of Sakh Sarawar; I made him drive a kilometre back down the road to somewhere in the scrubland where I could have a pee without an audience of forty little boys and spitting old men, and all the time he kept looking at his watch as if some malign force would send the hands spinning forward and lose us our place. It was very hot. The sun fried the tops of our heads and dried our throats.

We were still ready on our minute. We had 34 minutes to drive 45 k. *Beep.*

'This one is going to be a bitch,' Phil said.

The road was unmade, steep and potholed and blasted with oncoming traffic. The huge gaudy wagons swept down the middle of the rudimentary track, spraying stones and dust with their great tyres, and drawing in their wake cars and suicide scooters. None of them ever gave any ground. Phil had to watch the roadside each time for a place to steer into, missing the rocks and the ruts, and wrench the wheel to bring us back on course before the next act of split-second evasion was forced upon him. We skidded two-wheeled past the overloaded buses, all of which had staring faces bursting out of their windows like bunches of overripe fruit hanging on a wall. Every pothole jarred the car, every time we hit a rut we waited for the new sound under the familiar cacophony of shrieks and rattles that would tell us a part had split or cracked or broken. I hunched in my seat, half willing something to happen that would force us to slow down, half maddened by the fact that we couldn't go any faster. The timer flicked implacably. Even before we had covered half the distance it was obvious we couldn't hope to clean this section.

Phil overtook a ruck of vintageants, the yellow Morgan Plus 8, even one of the Iranian Peykans.

'How far?'

'Twenty k.'

'How long?'

'Not long enough. Just keep going.'

The beeper went and I slapped the button. No one overtook us. Every bend became a screaming rear-wheel skid. Choking dust billowed everywhere and partially blotted out the oncoming traffic.

We reached the control and I ran to the desk, 14 minutes over time. Who could possibly have gone fast enough to cover that distance, over that road, in 14 minutes less than Phil had managed?

Only a handful of drivers, surely.

The marshal on duty was motherly Betty, half of a rally-enthusiast couple who had joined the officials at Kathmandu. She was surrounded by a mass of navigators, vintage and classic, all shouting and exclaiming, and she looked hot and bothered in her cover-up clothes. I set my book in front of her and she stamped us in.

I added my voice to the clamour. 'How's everyone else doing?'

'A lot worse than you,' she sighed.

I ran back to the car. Phil had my door open, the engine revving.

'We're going up today,' I sang to him.

The next stage was longer and the road surface was better, which meant that it was more of a dirt track and less of a dry riverbed, but the time allowance was absurdly short again. Phil drove on the very edge of control all the way, whirling through the traffic and bounding over the ruts and rocks, but when we sweated up to the control at the top of the pass we were still 29 minutes down on the section allowance. John Vipond was the solitary marshal.

He checked the rally clock and stamped the book.

'Well done, Rosie,' he said kindly.

I looked down at the palm of my left hand, the one I didn't use to hold the pen or zero the trip. There were four red fingernail marks in the flesh.

'Half an hour? And Phil drove up here like a maniac . . .'

'Don't worry. They're all down today.'

We drove on. It was nearly 300 kilometres to Quetta, and we were crossing the desert now. There was no shade, no relief from the sun and the dust, certainly no chance of a rest or any proper food. We drank bottled water and ate biscuits.

In 1907, the Contal tricycle car ran out of petrol in the desert. The other four cars passed by, assuming that Pons and Foucault the crew, had stopped to allow the tiny engine to cool down before continuing. The two men waited all day without water in the burning sun, but no one came back to see what had happened to them.

The logic of our big red OK sign seemed suddenly impeccable.

At last Pons decided that they would have to walk to find help. They trudged for 20 miles without seeing a soul, drinking water from puddles along the way. At last they knew they had no option but to turn round and make their way back to the car. Thirty-six hours after that they were found, exhausted and delirious, pushing their little car towards a nomad encampment. The two men recovered but their challenge was over: they had to travel slowly back to Peking. The other four cars reached Paris, but the crews had to live with the uncomfortable knowledge that their companions had almost died in the desert.

As the heat intensified I checked our supplies of bottled water and monitored the fuel levels in our two tanks.

We passed the Dangerfields and Kermit, the green Dutch PV544. The roadside began to be dotted with broken-down rally cars. We came to Jennifer and Francesca, pulled up yet again with suspension problems. Anthony Buckingham and Simon Mann had stopped in the DB5, and Jon and Adam were there too.

'Plenty of men in attendance,' Phil muttered, but he drew up anyway to see if we could help. They needed a new spring, but our spares were the wrong size. We drove on, and came to David and Sheila Morris's Austin A90. They were being helped out by their Austineers team-mate Fred Multon, and they waved us past. We could only hope that Dan and JD were keeping going. We had passed them back in the second section, and hadn't seen them since.

The kilometres unfolded in a blur of heat-haze and sun that scorched our eyes. There was nothing to see, only grey dirt that was sometimes unrelievedly flat and sometimes scraped into random hillocks, occasional camels, little dirt-brown settlements, thorn bushes, and the sabre-toothed traffic. I was too conscious of the strain that driving in these conditions put on Phil, but I knew I couldn't have matched the speed and the concentration and the split-second decision-making that he managed, let alone kept it up hour after hour. The cassette player had finally given up altogether so he didn't even have the music to wake him up or calm him down. I concentrated on plying him with water, or snacks, or cigarettes or whatever else I thought he needed, and talked when conversation seemed welcome and kept quiet when it did not. Groups of children made as if to wave at us, and then fusillades of hostile stones rattled against the bodywork.

The sun was sinking and we were driving due west. It

was hard to keep looking ahead into the glare. We
stopped beside Harm and Tonnie in the dark grey
Amazon. They had had a blowout and were changing the
wheel, but they assured us that otherwise they were fine.
A little further on Phil drew in to the side of the road
beside a scrubby band of eucalyptus that made a narrow
ribbon of shade. He checked the car over, looking for
leaks or signs of overheating, but there was nothing unto-
ward. An ambulance truck saw us and pulled in to make
sure we were in no trouble. The friendly driver accepted
a cigarette and a small group of locals gathered to stare.
The next painted wagon also hauled to a stop, the brakes
hissing and grinding, and Phil and I took photographs of
each other standing dwarfed by the massive barque front.
We had been stationary for perhaps 10 minutes. As soon
as we were moving again I looked at the clock against the
distance we still had to travel, about 100 kilometres, and
realised we weren't going to make it within the time on
this leg either.

'Let's just get there,' I said. If I was tired Phil must
have been exhausted.

A truck was flying towards us, glued to the middle of
the road. Phil jammed his thumb on the horn.

'Pull over. Pull *over*, you arsehole . . .'

The truck didn't waver, Phil wrenched the wheel, we
swerved and bounced into a deep ditch. There was a
clang and a new, hideous noise.

'Something's happened.'

We leapt out and ran round to look at the front. Phil
kicked the nearside wheel, wiping the sweat off his face
with his sleeve.

'It's okay. Just a blowout and a bent rim. The wheel's had it, though.'

I ran to stick the OK sign in the rear window. We changed the wheel and left the damaged one in the ditch. Another 10 minutes had gone.

Dusk was creeping up behind us. Ahead was yet another rally car at the side of the road and we slowed to see who it was. It was Josef Feit and his son René, with the yak's-horn VW cabriolet, discreetly standing with their backs to the traffic. Phil hooted and Josef looked over his shoulder and gave us the thumbs-up.

The sun set, hollowing fierce black shadows out of the hills. Then, almost immediately, it was fully dark. The traffic was heavier because we were approaching Quetta, and half of the oncoming vehicles drove fast without lights. Every bend was a gamble on what might be coming the other way. It was a terrifying drive. I stopped watching the time and stared at the trip instead, willing the tenths to add up into kilometres and the kilometres to reach the day's total. It was too far for one day, under such pressure.

'They told us we wouldn't have to rally in the dark. They *told* us,' Phil said. His thumb was permanently on the horn. 'This is dangerous.' We were both thinking of the hill climb to Nainital, and the plunging Land Rover. Nigel Challis and his co-driver had had to fly home from India, their rally over.

'Don't worry about the time, let's just get there,' I repeated. We were already over our allowance. In the distance was a smear of dirty orange light. Quetta.

At last, 22 minutes over our time, we reached the hotel. The car park was full of local media crews with cameras and lights, but almost empty of rally cars. I went in with the book and saw RO standing in the middle of the lobby. He was ticking off somebody who had had the temerity to object to the day's timings.

Outside in the car park again I found that Phil had already flung himself into a flurry of mechanical adjustments. He already had the car jacked and both rear wheels off.

'Come inside and have a drink and something to eat before you do that.'

'No point in getting clean and then dirty again.'

'Phil, you are exhausted. Don't push yourself so hard.'

I was impressed by his determination, as I always was, but I was also worried about him. He seemed to have to demonstrate that he was unbreakable; I already knew his strength so I hoped it was for his own satisfaction that he forced himself to do more.

'Look, I want to make sure the car is all right before I go in. Okay?' He was perfectly equable but quite resolved.

I sighed. Now I would have to stay out here and try to help him while every fibre of me cried out for soap and water and cold drinks and hot food. I went inside for cans of Coke, and came back and sat in the dirt beside the car. Phil's feet protruded from under the body. One of the intrusive camera crews came and shone their lights in my eyes.

'What is the prize for Paris?' the reporter asked.

'Nothing. There's no prize. Or maybe a silver cup, something like that. We do it for fun.'

The man's eyes reflected my own incredulity straight back at me.

Fun, was that the definition of today?

Every two or three minutes headlamps raked along the boundary hedge and another rally car followed the beam into the parking area. Bone-weary crews stumbled out, blinking in the lights, the navigator's head rotating in search of the control desk. Harm and Tonnie's Amazon appeared and stopped next to ours. They were white-faced.

'Did you hear?'

'What?' Phil looked up from the tool-box.

'The Germans. In the VW. Totalled their car.'

I thought they had hit a ditch and maybe smashed the differential, or even blown the engine. Josef was known to drive hard and fast.

'Oh, what bad luck.'

'No, no. Dead, I think.'

The Dutch Amazon had been one of the first cars on the scene after the accident. In the dark the Feits had crashed head-on into a tour bus, and neither of them survived the impact. René was seventeen, the youngest competitor.

The news spread, and a numb silence followed it. The television crews circulated with their lights and mikes, and competitors shook their heads and turned away from them. The slow procession of arrivals continued, each one rolling into a pool of quiet.

I saw Geoff and Jennie Dorey come in, late and weary. Jennie went off with the book and Geoff rolled up his sleeves at once, like Phil, to check over the Morris Minor. A minute later Jennie was back.

She said, 'Geoff?'

He straightened up and took one look at her face. Immediately he put his arms around her and held her against him. I turned away.

It was late when the car was finally adjusted and checked out to Phil's satisfaction. He had retreated into himself as he always did when he was shocked or unhappy.

Our room at Quetta had another double bed. I was grateful. It wasn't anything to do with sex, nor did I think it would wipe out any of the night's fearful images, but there would be warmth and a measure of comfort in it, and we could offer each other the much-needed security of closeness. In the corner of the room there was a mattress on the floor and a thin, folded blanket. I took the blanket and smoothed it on top of the bed, as if I was preparing a rest with an extra layer, and then crawled under the covers to wait for Phil. We had travelled a long way together.

I woke up in the middle of the night alone in the big bed. I sat up, and saw that he was fast asleep on the mattress, fully dressed and with no covers. I put my hand out and felt the cold expanse of the sheets beyond where I had been lying. If Caradoc had been there I would have huddled myself against him and he would have shifted his position to accommodate me, the instinctive move of long familiarity. I remembered how Geoff Dorey had unthinkingly put his arms around Jennie. Only Caradoc was at home, a long way away.

I lay back again and shut my eyes, waiting for the spectres of the subconscious to steal out and surround me. I felt as lonely as the nights when I was a girl, waiting for my father to come back from wherever he had been, so I could go to sleep reassured that he was alive for another day.

I thought about the accident. I wanted to block it out, but dread of the random viciousness of fate stalked every recess inside my head. I could imagine too clearly the shockwaves that were spreading from a collision beside a desert road, and all the weight of consequences that would follow. Juxtaposed with tragedy, my own fears swelled out of reason. Today this family. Tomorrow, maybe another one. It could have been any of us today. Or any day.

I wondered if Chris Taylor was asleep, like Phil, in some identical boxy room down some adjacent corridor. Maybe his hard-won equanimity would have deflected my panic. As it was, I hunched up under the bedclothes and waited for the next day to come.

Chapter Twelve

There was no competition the next day, as a tribute to the Feits, but the rally moved inexorably onwards.

The daily information bulletin that was faxed to competitors' relatives announced that, 'Having talked to many of the competitors, the ‹organisers› decided that the event should leave Quetta this morning, and make for Iran, as scheduled.'

This may indeed have been the case, but no one spoke to Phil and me, or to anyone else we knew. At least as far as our little group was concerned, there was no proper acknowledgement of what had happened, nor any official account of the events of the night before for us to focus on, either personal or general. Neither RO nor any one of the organisers was in evidence in the morning; presumably they were busy with the police, the Pakistani authorities and the world's press. The people actually competing in their event were, as always, the last to hear anything concrete. All we had was a brief note on the information board, advising us that in view of last night's tragedy we should make for the border in our own time, and proceed from there to Zāhedān.

The German crews had planned to remain behind in Quetta for 24 hours, out of respect for their fellow nationals, but they were advised by the marshals that there would be police assistance along the road and at the border for one day only, and after that they would be on their own. Thomas and Maria and Mick Flick and the others decided that their staying in Quetta would not make any material difference to anyone and in the end they travelled on with the rest of us. Thomas and Maria had already made many of the necessary arrangements following the accident, and they had also been to see the bus driver. He was in prison, in chains. There had to be a scapegoat.

Phil and I sat sadly around the breakfast table at Quetta with Dan and JD and Melissa and Colin. Phil brought me orange juice, and a plate of bread and fruit. It was his way of demonstrating concern and affection. Nobody said much at all, but we agreed sombrely that our three cars would travel to Zāhedān in convoy, supporting each other. Dan's differential seal had gone and oil was pouring out of the diff: they would have to keep stopping to top it up until they could effect a repair.

We were the last to leave. John Vipond and Mike Summerfield were sitting at a nearby table, and John came over and quietly advised us that we shouldn't linger too long in case we were prevented from reaching the border before it closed.

The pressures were always the same, I thought, both relentless and – so it seemed now – disturbingly trivial. We were in a *rally*. That was our sole reason for being here. There was a distance to cover and if we were going to continue we would have to drive it, leaving the unacknowledged as well as the unseen and unexplored in our dusty wake.

We trailed outside with our overnight bags, into the hard sunshine, and as we drove away the blue Amazon and the Porsche tucked in behind us. Phil and I sat in silence except for the minimal exchange of route information. I looked out of the window. There were women walking with their backs to us, dressed in shalwar kameez patterned in diamond-shapes of red and orange and purple, each of them balancing two or three earthenware pots on their heads. There were clusters of straw and canvas shanties, a camel dragging a cartload of bricks, and two uniformed policemen nodding us by with a smart salute. We passed a huge brickyard with two conical brick chimneys belching out smoke and then a mosque with green minarets. The road was lined with eucalyptus trees and brown mud-block walls with children playing at the foot of them. A group of tribesmen in elaborate blue turbans shaded their eyes to look at us. There were bicycles and buses and more of the overloaded gaudy wagons, a hay-wagon almost submerged under the mass of its load, and a tethered donkey trying to reach a patch of shadow. In the ditch was the wreck of a smashed car, and in the distance a ring of sepia-coloured mountains.

I didn't have to name or enumerate any of this in an effort to fix it in my memory. I knew I would always remember it all, and the weight of sadness and guilt that dimmed the colours of the scenery. Simple grief was, as

ever, overshadowed in my mind by the spectre of responsibility as well as dread of what might come next. It was
self-absorbed as well as grotesque to imagine that any of
the events of the night before were anything to do with
me, or that I could have done anything to prevent them
even if we had stopped at the roadside when we passed
the Feits, but the association was too strong to dismantle.
If we had only pulled in, I thought, and exchanged a few
words. Even 10 seconds delay would have made the difference. The jerky videotape of imagined near-misses kept
on running in my head until I felt sick.

We left Quetta behind and entered an empty landscape. The flat, gritty ground was broken only by clumps
of pampas grass, and grey mounds of dirt that reminded
me of old Harmon's dust heaps in my abandoned *Our
Mutual Friend*.

Phil jerked his chin as he looked in the rear-view
mirror.

'Why is she driving so slowly?'

Melissa had fallen further and further behind and was
now out of sight. Phil couldn't bear the slow pace, even
today. Convoy driving went against all his instincts. He
accelerated and soon we had left Dan and JD behind us as
well as the Porsche. There was nothing except the desert
and our own separate, silent ruminations.

The drive from Multan to Quetta had taken a heavy
toll.

Bart Rietbergen broke Kermit's right-hand front wheel
in the short stage, and half an hour after he had had it
welded the left-hand one also broke. The delay meant that
he came into Quetta outside the maximum permitted

lateness, and he lost his gold medal. The Catts' Cortina dropped out of the lead with broken rear shock absorbers, the Brodericks snapped two throttle cables in their Eco-Flow Anglia – and they were among the luckier ones.

The yellow Morgan had to retire from the rally with a blown V8 engine. David Brister and Keith Barton in their Rover were almost at the control in the short stage when a Pakistani Army Land Cruiser rounded a blind bend on the wrong side of the road and smashed into their right wing. They were unhurt, but the wing was squashed into the wheel, the headlamp, indicator, sidelight, spotlight and horns were demolished, and coolant was pouring out. To any outsider it would have seemed certain that their rally was over but David and Keith, a pair of British Airways pilots with technical resources as well as plenty of initiative, were determined not to give up without a struggle. As the rally pushed onward towards Quetta they spent the afternoon removing and patching up their holed radiator and engaging a passing tractor to pull the wing clear of their wheel. By the time dusk fell they had the car's engine going and they had lashed a 10-watt sidelight to the offside. It was just possible to drive the Rover, although the tracking was badly skewed, the radiator was unpressurised and the water pump was leaking. They filled and refilled it as they drove until their reserves of water were all gone, and then a thunderstorm came and they filled the empty bottles from puddles and limped onwards to Loralai, 260 kilometres short of Quetta. The next day, while what was left of the rally made for Zāhedān, they had the damaged wing bashed back into approximate shape while they changed the water pump and found a mechanic to solder and repressurise the radiator. By the end of the second afternoon the wing was replaced, one horn was salvaged and bolted into the headlamp hole, a sidelight was fixed on the repaired wing and the bonnet was hammered until it would open and close. They chased determinedly on in the wake of the rally and finally caught up beyond Zāhedān, three days after the Army assault.

Nor were David and Keith the only ones to be suffering major setbacks that would, in the normal world, have brought their car to a final halt.

Anton Aan de Stegge hit a rock in his big Citroen and smashed the disc brakes and his differential and disappeared for two days. Murdoch Laing's Aston had developed serious steering troubles and was also a couple of days behind. An Italian Lancia was undergoing a complete gearbox rebuild, Richard Clark's Buick had a main bearing failure, and the Doreys' Morris Minor had a holed piston. It seemed that Phil and I were lucky to be still sturdily *en route* to Zāhedān. We were physically exhausted and emotionally battered and marooned in separate silence, without any music to fill the space between us, but our Amazon at least was invincible.

It was a long drive to the border, 633 km through inhospitable desert country without even a string of camels to enliven the view. The road was good for quite long stretches, and then suddenly the carriageway would be blocked by large rocks marking a sudden diversion into a rough unmade section that might last for 10 km before swinging into smooth asphalt again, presumably where more money became available. In daylight, without too much traffic in either direction, all this was boring but fairly easily negotiable. The only problem was the heat. In order to cool the engine as far as possible Phil drove with the heater and the fan going full blast. The temperature inside the car mounted to 116 degrees and I kept hearing Tony Barrett's voice rasping, 'The car's the star, love. The car's the star.'

We reached the border at four o'clock. The field was widely strung out – rally officials at the Pakistan Out checkpoint told us that we were only the 24th car to pass through, even though we had been one of the very last to leave Quetta. We drove through a dusty compound, turned left, and came to the Iranian frontier.

We were warmly greeted. Formalities were few, and quick. There was a reception committee to shake our hands and welcome us to Iran in the name of Allah, and smiling members of the Iranian Motor Federation to press gifts of flowers and cold drinks and snacks into our car. The three Iranian crews were mobbed by admirers and press. There was even a medical tent offering attention to those who were about to succumb to heat and dehydration, and for all the women a present of a shiny, silky fringed scarf in a remarkably hideous shade of brown. I accepted this poisoned chalice and meekly wound it around my head. I put on little white cotton socks that I had bought in the bazaar in Lahore, hiding my sandalled toes and ankles even though I was ready to melt in the heat. We filled up with free 90-octane fuel, accepted and gulped down more chilled cartons of grape juice, and turned towards Zāhedān. It was a short run on wide, beautifully silken, oil-money roads.

Zāhedān itself appeared to be a dusty, unremarkable collection of concrete blocks set around busy round-abouts decorated with portentously ugly modern sculptures. We found the rally headquarters hotel, which was fully occupied by officials and media crews and the rest, and were directed onwards to our allotted place in the third hotel in town. There was no parking permitted there, so we waited in the wilting sun for a shuttle bus to take us.

We found a dingy, brown-plastic-veneer, neon-lit estab-lishment on a four-lane highway which our room directly overlooked without the insulation of curtains. There were two beds, an empty but volcanically noisy old refrigerator, bare lightbulbs, and a box bathroom acrid with the Soho-alley scent of urine. After I had squatted over the hole I discovered the reason for the smell. The flush worked on an interesting reverse principle – one tug of the string and water welled up and washed the contents of the pan over the tiled floor, which then dried in the sticky heat. Phil had a scoring system for the relative luxury of hotels, called the Fluffy Towel Index. This one scored nil. There were no towels, fluffy or otherwise. Nor were there any facilities for doing laundry or changing money.

Downstairs, we discovered that we didn't really know any of the other crews who were sharing our romantic hideaway. I introduced myself to Kurt and Roswitha Dichtl, who were driving an immaculate 1950 Rolls-Royce Silver Dawn, and Andrew Snelling who was one of a three-man crew in a 1966 Wolseley. Andrew looked as if he had a permanent head-cold, but he was very friendly. The couple who were his co-drivers were having a loudly acrimonious argument in the lobby and he was happy to find a separate focus for his attention. We sat around a plastic flower arrangement, waiting for dinner and smoking because there was no other form of gratification available. I would have swapped the Rebecca Stephens sleeping bag for three ice-cold vodka martinis to be drunk in rapid succession.

Two more people arrived. They were Francis and Casper Noz, father and son, whose 1928 Ford Model A hadn't made it out of Beijing. They had been following the rally ever since in a series of *taxis*, although they had hopped on a plane to cross the Himalayas. Even though they had struck out personally both Nozes still had plenty of advice to offer the rest of us about our cars and the competition.

Dinner was barley soup, chicken and rice, and Coca-Cola. It would have been a lugubrious occasion if Phil hadn't decided to snap into tour-leader mode and jolly everyone along with some teasing banter. I was probably the only one among the company to find this intensely irritating. I abandoned the fibrous chicken and went upstairs to call home.

Caradoc had not yet received the daily fax bulletin. He hadn't heard about the deaths on the road to Quetta. I described what had happened, spilling out the words, and it was a relief to give voice to all the fears and forebodings clustered around yesterday and today, for all their irrationality and self-centredness and black roots buried in the unaccommodating past. I could hear the concern in his voice when he answered.

'Do you want to come home?'

I did, more than anything, and yet I did not. I was crawling up Kalapathar, in double-quick time. I was lonelier and more homesick than I had been since I was a small girl at boarding school, but there was absolutely no option except to carry on. At least the Zāhedān hotel from hell was more luxurious and welcoming that an English girls' school, and the food was distinctly better. I might be muffled up in long robes and a veil, but I didn't have to wear thigh-chafing divided skirts and an Aertex shirt, or lose hearty games of hockey in sub-zero temperatures, or walk around town in an ankle-length Harris tweed cloak and a grey felt po hat for the amusement of the local talent. And the bathroom might stink but I could use it to wash my hair whenever I felt like it instead of having to wait in greasy misery for Matron to supervise the fortnightly sluice. It was the British officer's prisoner-of-war defence, and it worked. Nothing would ever be as bad as public school. I felt suddenly much more cheerful.

'I can't come home before Paris,' I said.

Caradoc didn't try to persuade me to go or to stay, nor did he deprecate my wallowing guilty fears. He simply listened to them. We knew each other well, and it was the greatest comfort not to have to pretend to be brave or resourceful for his benefit. I had been living alongside strangers for what felt like a very long time, and trying to be cheerful and practical, neither of which attributes came very naturally to me. So even at this distance the give-and-take affectionate shorthand of marital intimacy was as comforting as a blanket. It was no sugary match of perfection, I knew how quickly our affection for each other could flip into irritation and then anger, but somehow the balance seemed always to tip the right way in the end.

Even though I had made a handful of valuable friends amongst the minority of sane, sensitive people on this trip, living amongst the petrol-heads and self-publicists and win-at-all-costs wankers of one sort or another who formed the rest of the company was making me appreciate my clever and cultivated husband more than I had done for years. So that was a positive gain, at least.

'Will you try to take care?' he asked.

'Yes,' I promised, for what that was worth.

The news from home was that the children were happy and busy and well. Caradoc was dutifully ironing and making shepherd's pies for the freezer. This little picture made me smile. And he told me that I had been invited to chair the judges of the next year's Betty Trask Award. This lucrative prize for unpublished first novels had been won by our friend John Lanchester a couple of years before with his blackly amusing *The Debt to Pleasure*, and I was immediately looking forward to reading and arguing the merits of a big batch of possible successors.

Out there, I thought, there still is a world where people sit in the Groucho or Soho House, gossiping over glasses of wine and sniping about one another's books and reviews and agents and publishers, eating chargrilled tuna and wasabi before stumbling out into Old Compton Street to hail a taxi to take them home. Soon, I would be readmitted into it. There would be no more carburettor conversations, no more dust or time cards, no more counting the minutes or hearing the *beep* in my dreams.

I told Caradoc that he wasn't to worry about me, or to

tell the children what had happened outside Quetta, and we said a cheerful goodnight. I ventured into the bathroom as briefly as possible, opened the bedroom window to let in some air and then hastily shut it against the traffic noise, swallowed a sleeping pill, rammed in my earplugs and went to sleep.

It was a rest day but Phil was up at six the next morning. I unstuck my eyes to peer at him. The room was full of grey, glutinous light and the renewed shriek and hydraulic hiss of traffic. Heat was already seeping through the window frame.

'Where are you going?'

'There are about eighty cars all wanting help from the Peykan mechanics. I want to be first in the queue.'

'What would you like me to do?' I asked.

'You've got your own work.'

Translated, I thought this probably meant 'Keep well out of my way.'

'Okay.'

I lay down, pulled the covers over my head and willed myself back to sleep. When I woke up again I felt completely disorientated. The noise in the room and the heat were overwhelming. Slowly I remembered where I was and what the day would probably involve and even though I hadn't had a drink for nearly a week depression took hold of me, a physical assault like the worst hangover. I crept out of bed and the smell in the bathroom grabbed me by the throat. I dragged on the long skirt, the long-sleeved shirt, the white cotton socks and swathed my head in the clammy headscarf. It kept sliding off my wiry curls and I had to secure it with a series of ravishing hairgrips. One glance in the mirror was enough to send me spiralling into the depths of Rally Syndrome. I looked like an amateur production of *Mother Courage*.

I went downstairs to breakfast, but the oilcloth-covered tables in the basement eating area – dining was too elegant a concept – were wiped bare except for a few crusty smears. There were no rally competitors to be seen anywhere. I went back up to the reception desk and found the hapless, bespectacled young man from Tehrān who had been attached to us as tour interpreter and general facilitator. He was assisted by a pair of women, moon-faced in their tight blue swathes of headgear. Under the voluminous folds they appeared to be wearing ankle-length grey gaberdine mackintoshes. I almost fainted with heat just through looking at them. All three spoke excellent English, and they answered my tetchy questions with polite regret.

Unfortunately, breakfast was over. It was ten o'clock, I must understand. Lunch would naturally be served at lunch-time. There was nobody about because most of the honoured rally competitors had taken the shuttle bus to the car compound or the HQ hotel. Unfortunately I could not do the same because the bus had now departed with the remaining rally competitors for an interesting sightseeing tour of the Zāhedān environs. The shuttle would start running again at 4 p.m.

I asked if I could change some dollars into rials at the hotel desk, so that I could buy fruit and bottled water. I learned that unfortunately this would not be possible. Looking out of the window, across the solid river of trucks and cars, I saw that there was a bank directly opposite.

Surely I would be able to change dollars there? All three shook their heads regretfully. Unfortunately I could not use that particular bank. Arrangements had been made elsewhere.

Very well, I said. Perhaps they could call a taxi to take me to the bank where the arrangements had been made, so that I could change money to buy what I needed?

Unfortunately, they sighed in unison, that would not be possible.

'Why not?'

Because it would be too dangerous.

Very well, I said. I would walk to the rally headquarters. Remembering last night's bus journey I thought it couldn't be more than a kilometre. The trio moved in unison to bar the door.

'No,' they said firmly. That would not be possible.

'Why not?'

Because it would be much too dangerous.

Light was slowly beginning to dawn. I was a virtual prisoner in this facility-free hotel. No food, no fruit, no company, no transport. With gentle courtesy, one of the mackintosh women brought me a glass of warm Coca-Cola and I trailed back to the stifling bedroom with it. I spent the morning writing notes with my earplugs in, thinking, and trying to count my blessings. I might be briefly stranded here, but at least I wasn't an Iranian woman.

At one o'clock I went ravenously downstairs again and, to my great delight, found David and Sheila Morris already at the table. Lunch was barley soup, chicken and rice and Coca-Cola. We talked about the accident, and I learned that they were as shocked as I was by the deaths of the two men, and the absence of information from the organisers, as well as the lack of a focus for our respect and sympathy. Bound up in a headscarf, Sheila's high-cheekboned face was a tense mask of unhappiness.

'I just want to go home, now,' she told me. 'The pleasure of it is all over. We didn't come to race at the speeds we had to do to Quetta. We didn't expect to drive in the dark, on those roads.'

'Neither did I. I want to go home too,' I sighed. I prodded at my unyielding chicken. 'This place doesn't help morale, either. Why do all the paid employees get to stay in the comfortable hotels while we are shoved out into the fleapits?'

David's habitually mild expression turned angry. 'I must say, this is the first business I've ever known where the customer comes last.'

It was true. I understood perfectly that the competitors were allotted rooms in the order in which they had paid their money, but I hadn't taken account of the fact that the staff and supporters took priority even over the crews at the head of the list. Phil was particularly bitter about this. He had worked on enough tours, and he knew that he always took the worst room, not the best.

I plodded back up to my cell and did some more work.

For long stretches of the journey I had felt that it was an imposition to be a writer because I had to spend so much time recording what I saw and felt instead of experiencing it directly. The veil of enforced objectivity went on cutting me off from the purest sensations. At home it was different because I was always listening in and watching out for scenes that would trigger off ideas. I sat on trains and stood in queues with my notebook in my pocket, eavesdropping for the slice of life that would set off the shiver down my back that presages a story. To be an observer rather than a participant suited me well, and I was as comfortable with that metaphorical veil as I was uncomfortable with the actual slippery, unwieldy, blinkering head-drapes forced upon us in Iran.

But the mad adventure of the rally had been quite different. I was a participant willy-nilly, and there had been so many choking feelings from delight to despair and so many sensations to be absorbed that I longed to give myself up to them completely. The demanding immediacy of it all had left me unwilling and almost unable to stockpile and analyse and discard. But this afternoon I found real solace in writing. I sat on my bed because there was nowhere else, with my spiral notebook on my knees, and wrote about Iran and Quetta and isolation and home, in a hot jumble of unconsidered words, and the sweat from my fingers made the pages ripple and blurred the blue feint lines.

At four o'clock, as if I was escaping from Alcatraz, I took the restored shuttle bus to the Tourist Hotel where Rally HQ was based. The lobby was a sea of red-shirted officials. It wasn't the New York Four Seasons any more than Golmud or Choksam had been, but at least it was air-conditioned. There was a fax waiting for me from my friend and fellow novelist Nick Evans. It was a parody of genre writing and it was about notebooks, and it made me laugh a lot. It went like this:

The lights of another town flicked past like ghosts and were gone. The road stretched ahead blindly to the black horizon.

'How much longer?' she said.

He didn't even look at her.

It was the same question she'd asked all the way, a hundred times in a hundred countries. From Lhasa to Lahore, from Pakistan to Paris, the same goddamn question. He pulled the last cigarette from the pack with his teeth and lit the match with his thumb nail. He drew the smoke deep into his lungs. It felt good.

Women he thought. They came in different shapes and sizes and colours, but in the end they were all the same. Just women.

She had her head tilted back on the seat, so he couldn't see her face. All he could see when he looked from the corner of his eye was the glow of the Amazon's dashboard on her Dolce & Gabbana T-shirt. The notebook lay spine-up over her left knee.

The notebook. Six whole weeks of notes.

Every time he moved a muscle, every time he broke wind, she'd noted it down. Sometimes it was all he could do not to grab it and throw it out the window. At night, in some godforsaken hotel room, with the floor awash with someone else's piss, he'd lain there, listening to her moaning on about Sainsbury's in her sleep to someone called Caradoc and wondering if she'd wake if he went to get it from the pocket of her jacket.

She stirred and the notebook fell from her knee among the fruit and discarded Evian bottles at her feet.

'How much longer?' she asked.

He sighed and looked at his watch.

'It's time,' he said.

'Thank God,' she said.

And she took the two slices of cucumber off her eyes and sat up.

Cucumber, he thought.

This was all very funny and apposite. I was looking forward to sharing it with Phil. Smiling, I tucked the fax safely away and went to ask a man behind a bar if I could have a cup of coffee.

'No,' he answered. Just no, that was all.

'Are you closed?'

Dave Bull leant beside me.

'They're not closed. You're a *woman*, aren't you?'

'Oh, I see. Okay, Dave. Since you have the good fortune to be a man, will you order me a cup of coffee?'

'Of course I will.'

A minute later the cup of tepid Nescafé was handed to him, and he handed it on to me. I went to sit on a lobby sofa and after a while John Vipond drifted over and sat beside me.

'How are you?'

'I'm fine,' I assured him, in case he was referring to my long-restored health. 'But I think the rally as a jolly adventure more or less ended for me at Quetta. And I know that quite a lot of people feel the same way.'

'Why is that?'

I stared. 'Because two people died.'

I told him that I thought the Multan to Quetta timings had been too severe and the overall distance too long for

one day. We should not have had to drive those treacherous
roads in the dark, under pressure, particularly after what
had happened to Nigel Challis's Land Rover on the way up
to Nainital.

John was sympathetic but also eloquently defensive of
the organisation and planning. He assured me that no
one was obliged to go for the sections as timed.
Competitors were free to drive at whatever speed they
considered to be safe for them and their cars, and it just
happened that Josef Feit had been an aggressive and
highly competitive driver.

I liked John Vipond very much, but I thought he was
wrong. It seemed to me that the mere imposition of tight
timings made people want to go for them, particularly
testosteronic young men like Phil and, presumably, the
Feits. However, there was no future in arguing the point
because I was only a novice, and John had years of motor-
sports experience. I only added that all the crews I had
spoken to since Quetta wanted there to be a brief gathering, a simple meeting somewhere at which we could all
express our respects and sympathy. I didn't try to go into
any of the business of how deeply I believed in it being
better to acknowledge a loss than to pretend it had never
occurred.

John's sleepy eyes narrowed further.

'This is rallying, Rosie. I am afraid that people do get
killed. You have to put it behind you and carry on.'

There seemed no point in discussing this any more,
either. John moved away, but after a little while he did
come back and murmur in my ear.

'I have had a couple of words with people. We'll try to

arrange something appropriate at Eṣfahān, all right?'

They never did, though. Or if they did, the invitation to participate never reached our little circle.

Chris and Howard were high up the accommodation list and were in the right hotel. They swooped across the lobby now, spruce in their chinos and clean polo shirts, announcing that they had a taxi and a driver and were off to the Zāhedān Bazaar, so why didn't I go with them?

Since this morning, I had learned that Zāhedān was indeed a dangerous place. Its position close to the border with Afghanistan as well as Baluchistan meant that there was traffic in arms and drugs and other contraband, and there was plenty of violence in the town itself. The guides at the hotel this morning had been protective rather than restrictive in not allowing me to go out and wander around alone. However, I thought I would probably be safe enough in a taxi with two giants to protect me, so I told the Camaro boys I'd love to go shopping with them.

We were on the way down the steps to the taxi when we met Phil trailing in. He was covered in oil and he looked entirely exhausted and dejected. But, meanly, all I could think was that he had been having a sociable time with the other blokes in the car pound, borrowing each other's grease guns and forging mechanical meta-friendships, while I had been stranded all day in a stifling hotel room.

'Phil, you're wearing my hat,' I snapped at him.

He was. It was a green baseball cap, with sentimental value, that I kept tucked behind the roll bar above my seat. It now had a row of oily finger marks all across the peak, and I didn't rate my chances of ever seeing it again if it remained in Phil's possession. He had lost all his own hats, and his socks and underpants, and his set of car keys. He now used my keys, and appeared to manage without smalls.

'Sorry,' he said stiffly.

'I'm going shopping with Chris and Howard,' I said, and stalked off.

It took me an hour to start feeling ashamed, but when remorse came it bit deep. I might be lonely and anxious, but it was no excuse for harshness. I resolved to try to get the negative feelings under control and to be a better partner for the rest of the trip.

The bazaar turned out to be a grubby two-floor mall, almost deserted except for a couple of soldiers with semi-automatic rifles slung at the ready. It was dark when we reached it. There wasn't a woman to be seen anywhere, not in any of the shops or seedy cafés or walking between them. The men looked at me, even though I was dressed in the height of propriety, and whistled between their teeth or muttered in low voices. We bought some provisions, but beyond that I wasn't looking for plastic shoes or gaudy gold jewellery and there was nothing else to buy. The three of us mooched along, pretending to be interested in the shop window displays, attracting uncomfortable amounts of attention from the few passers-by. Howard lingered at a collection of lampshades and domestic ornaments, delighted by the full-on kitsch of the merchandise, but Chris and I wanted to go. The atmosphere was too threatening to be comfortable. Suddenly there was a scuffle behind us.

There was a man with a gun. It looked the same as the soldiers' guns, except that this one was being waved at us. The soldiers themselves were looking on in bored passivity.

Living in Camden Town, I was well used to the daily appearance of care in the community cases. It seemed to me that this was plainly a madman with a replica weapon, or otherwise he wouldn't be allowed to brandish it in public. But Chris and Howard, resident in nice expensive rural neighbourhoods, were less sanguine.

'Run!' they shouted. And did so. I looked round. The maniac was following us, shouting incoherently. Chris and Howard were a hundred metres down the road, sprinting in the direction of the waiting taxi.

'Run, Rosie!' they yelled over their shoulders.

I was encumbered by a long skirt, little white socks and strappy sandals and a flapping veil, and two plastic carrier bags of in-car provisions for Phil. I tittupped across the street, heels clicking on the asphalt. I didn't know if the gunman was still at my back or not, but I kept moving as fast as I could. It did cross my mind that if Phil were here he wouldn't have run off ahead. He would probably have performed some SAS-style manoeuvre for wresting plastic AK47s from Zāhedān care in the communities, and said 'Nice one' as he sat on the poor creature's chest.

I reached the taxi in the wake of Chris and Howard.

'That was close,' they puffed.

'It was a replica,' I said. 'It *must* have been.'

'I wouldn't like to have taken a bet, looking down the wrong end of it,' Howard retorted as we zoomed away. Neither of them was laughing. I began to think that they might have been right, and a cold drip of retrospective terror trickled all the way down my spine.

The taxi dropped me off at the hotel from hell. Phil had already eaten with the land crab boys and Andrew Snelling. Dinner was barley soup, chicken and rice, and Coca-Cola. I realised that I didn't mind so much about having missed breakfast.

After the chaos of Multan to Quetta, a new leader board was published as at Zāhedān. There were a great many changes to the old order.

Seventy cars were still classified, plus another twelve in the touring category. Car 82 was in 22nd place, and we were now top Volvo. Harm and Tonnie were four places behind us and Dan and JD nine. After the broken wheels, poor Kermit had dropped behind even Jennifer and Francesca. Top position was now held by two characters in a Willys jeep. One of the mechanics had muttered weeks back to Phil and me that it was full of Cosworth parts.

The next day, from an 8.30 start, we set off yet again.

That morning was the first time I felt that we had come far enough and that I didn't want to rally any further, through any more endless dangerous days. I was too tired and sad. No night's sleep seemed long enough to rub out our weariness.

Waiting in the line for our minute I turned to Dan. He was generous with his expressions of physical affection: Melissa was always curling up on his lap, and now he wrapped his arms around me and rocked me backwards and forwards.

'Cheer up,' he said. I leant my head against his shoulder and sniffed. I was tired of my lachrymose self, as well.

Beep.

We had 558 km to travel, in three stages, across the Dasht-e-Lūt desert to Kermān. The desert was hot and hostile. High winds swept across it and leached the moisture out of lips and cheeks until they cracked in painful protest. There were acres of gritty scrub blistered with hummocks and scrubby thorn bushes, and then patches of sand where vast, silvery mirage lakes shimmered under the heat-drained sky. Camels stalked at the roadside. Once, we passed a dead one lying in the road with its stiff legs extended. Sometimes we saw barchan dunes. These great arcs of sand built up behind some obstacle that the wind couldn't shift, a rock or a bush, and grain by grain the mountain swelled behind it, a steep crescent enclosing the rock and a huge, perfectly graded slope facing into the wind. When the wind changed, the dune nudged round into a different alignment. The flawless architecture of wind and sand was implacable and magnificent.

Phil turned suddenly and looked at me.

'Do you want to talk about it?'

'Yes.' We had barely spoken since Quetta. I was so surprised and disarmed by the invitation that the words flooded out instantly, quite unrehearsed. I told him that I was hurt when we couldn't comfort each other on the night of the accident, and that I had minded being cut adrift at Zāhedān, and that I was sorry I had been horrible about a stupid hat when he was tired from working on our car.

Phil sighed. 'I don't particularly want to climb into bed with you, because of what will inevitably happen if I do.'

I thought a bit harder about what I really wanted. I thought it was simple affection and warmth but perhaps the distinction was becoming blurred for me too. We had been away from home for a month and I felt as if I had been living alongside Phil, in our parody of a marriage, for longer than a lifetime. He was staring angrily at the road.

'Body language says everything. I saw you with Dan this morning. You leaned towards him and smiled, and I felt like shit. I haven't seen you smile for days.'

It was my turn to sigh. It would have to be Dan that he resented, of course. In our inverted way, even though we couldn't get along smoothly together we were jealous of each other's affections. I was certainly jealous because he liked Melissa so much.

'Phil, I want reassurance and affirmation that you can't give me. I don't even know what you want, but you probably aren't getting it either. Maybe this partnership has just failed.'

'That's putting it very strongly,' he said. 'Listen, do you want to call it a day and go home? You're the boss. Sack me if you don't think I'm doing the job.'

'Of course you're doing the job,' I muttered. 'We're in 22nd place, aren't we?'

We looked at each other and Phil grinned.

'Yeah. I don't think we've failed, even if you do.'

I sneaked out my hand and stuck my fingers between his hip and the lip of the seat, and he obligingly shifted his position to make room. It was a nice, warm, unthreatening place without any suggestive associations to bother either of us. I liked to feel connected to him, and through him to the Amazon, and we drove on in restored harmony. It was a resolution of sorts.

'I wish we had some music,' I said.

Phil grinned again. 'It's a pity the best in-car entertainment is off limits.'

'We can buy a new tape deck in Eṣfahān,' I responded primly.

The day's highlight was the second time control at a place called Arg-e-Bam, the Fort of Bam. True to form, I hadn't had time to read up on the Fort in advance but I knew vaguely that it was a sight worth seeing. When we reached it rally cars were drawn up all down the side of the road and crews were climbing some brown steps that led through a small arched doorway in a high, brown, crenellated wall. Phil parked under a palm tree behind one of the official Fronteras. As we watched, two of the mechanics spilled out of the back and one of them clasped his hands around the other's throat.

'Don't fuck me off, asshole,' the aggressor spat, then released his prey and stalked off. The other one dazedly shook himself.

Phil and I raised our eyebrows at each other. The heat and the tension were getting to everyone, not just us. At least we hadn't been reduced to physical violence. Yet. I demurely arranged my veil and drapes and sunglasses and stepped out into the crucifying sun.

Beyond the archway and up some steps to a rampart an astonishing vista spread out. Bam was a huge citadel, acres of sere avenues and steps and houses and domes and squares, all made of mud and excavated from the burning sand. It was a dung and straw Pompeii, full of vanished histories, too dry and hot to be properly explored. I stood in the scrap of shade beneath the enclosing wall, looking down on the twelfth-century streets and imagining them swarming with traders and soldiers and prostitutes and merchants and donkeys and mangy dogs, and their shouts and pipe music and the smells of oil and spices and camel dung. I lingered, making up stories in my head, with Melissa sitting on the wall beside me. In a skimpy white headscarf and a tunic and baggy pants even the radiant Porsche Spice looked flattened. She said that for a reason she couldn't quite pin-point, Bam made her think not of old stories but of being taken rather roughly from behind.

We had all been away from home for a long time.

I looked down the steps to see Phil, wearing his Sheikh of Araby headdress and Oakley shades and a camera round his neck, beckoning me back to the car. We drove on through the desert to Kermān.

Yet again, we were out in the flophouse. At least we could park right at the steps this time. Phil decided that the car was due for a serious checking over, and he had it jacked up and the rear wheels off almost before they stopped turning. I went inside for cold Coca-Colas and when I came back he was stretching his lower lip downwards and showing his bottom teeth. I hadn't seen him do the face thing for weeks, and my heart sank.

He pointed. 'Look at that.'

The shiny internal ring of the left brake drum was gouged with deep, gritty grooves. I understood, when he explained, that the rivets in the brake shoes had worked proud and had scored the drum. I ran the tip of my forefinger around the damage.

'Does it matter?'

'Reduced brake power.'

'What needs to be done?'

'Change the shoes on both sides. I think we'll have to get Tony to send a new drum out to Istanbul. We'll have to nurse the brakes until then.'

'Okay.'

Dan and JD had nosed in beside us, and they had their bonnet up and a knot of drivers with mechanical interests was gathering to peer into the engine. They had been having peculiar difficulties all day – the car would only run smoothly at high speed.

I guessed that it was going to be a long evening without much opportunity for lingering over the dinner-table. I was proved absolutely right.

Dan's problem was finally diagnosed as a jammed-open carburettor, and satisfactorily fixed. Phil serviced our brakes and changed the fuel filter and doggedly worked over the rest of the car. I passed the spanners and found the grease gun and cleaned the plugs and fetched drinks and did whatever else I could to make myself useful to Team Amazon. I was very slow at the simple tasks I was given and I pondered the merits of feeling mechanically inadequate as against completely redundant if I didn't help out at all.

Swift, desert darkness fell and we continued our efforts by the light of head torches. Bats threaded overhead and beyond the hotel railings a crowd of dark-faced men and boys stood silently watching us.

When I finally gave in and headed inside, I passed Jolijn Rietbergen sitting on the steps in the cool night air. She pointed a stern finger at me.

'Bed,' she advised.

I must have looked entirely frightful. Not least because I was wearing Phil's oil-stiff khaki trousers, a beaten T-shirt, and a flowing white headdress secured with hairgrips and decorated with black fingerprints. My hands and nails looked as if I had taken up employment as a spadeless gravedigger. Actually, I was past caring. The car was fit to drive tomorrow, at least, and we would be another day closer to home.

Eight-thirty a.m., after another restless night's sleep in another comfortless room, with Phil's steady breathing and the Terratrip's monotonous note in my head.

'Ready to go?'

'Ready.'

Beep.

Six hundred and seventy-five kilometres onwards to Eşfahān, one of the most ancient cities of Iran. Three stages: 4 hours 35 minutes, 2 hours 51 minutes and 2 hours 2 minutes allowed. If we made our times we were due into Eşfahān at two minutes to six. A cool morning, with the blankness of pent-up heat waiting in the sky.

'Three point three five. Turn left at crossroad before airport gates '

'Got you.'

The traffic was heavy, mostly fast private cars and big Volvo trucks, some with UAE plates, but it was easy driving because the Iranian roads were so good. It was reassuring to bowl along knowing for certain that there were no huge potholes waiting to assault the half-shafts, and no punishing unmade sections opening their jaws around the next bend. It was easy to make the time allowances.

The first stop was Mehriz, a closed-up roadside café in the heart of nowhere. We were almost there, with more than an hour in hand, when we came up behind Jon and Adam. Jon suddenly stood up in the navigator's seat and held a mineral water bottle tilted over his head. A silver and diamond plume of water arched backwards and sprayed our windscreen.

Phil turned to me. 'Quick. Find a plastic bag.'

I rummaged in the deep litter on the floor of the car and found one.

'Fill it up.'

I tipped a bottle, and handed the white plastic bladder to him. He put his foot down and pulled level with the Bentley.

'Jon?' he called conversationally. Both the Bentley boys turned their heads to look at us. Phil lobbed the bag of water, with perfect aim. It exploded in their faces and we drove into Mehriz choking with laughter.

'You wait, Phil McCracken,' Jon threatened when he pulled in after us.

It was the beginning of the Water Wars, which later escalated into the Sanitary Bag Battles. It was to this level that Iran and its privations reduced us.

The Mehriz café had a long arched arcade down one side, providing a ribbon of shelter against the white sunlight. Dan was reclining there reading *Birdsong* next to Chris, who had Melissa propped beside him. The Dangerfields were there, and the three American disability lawyers from the red and white Willys station wagon, and Carolyn. In the middle of the featureless landscape outside I could see Lord Montagu looking helpless, with a roll of white lavatory paper in his hand. Phil was playing frisbee, oblivious to the heat, with JD and Simon Catt.

I felt a sudden throb of affection for all these people and their foibles, and their cars which had grown as familiar as the furniture of my own bedroom. We had come a long way together. Quetta and its aftermath had after all forged a new bond of companionship between us.

'Hello,' a familiar voice said. I turned round and saw Anton.

'*Anton!* I thought you were out! What happened?'

'Uh, there was only the one stone in 16,000 kilometres and I hit it. The brake disc broke off, and the differential casing, it was a terrible mess. I thought, I'm out now and I might as well go home.'

'We heard that much.'

'But 10 minutes later I was on my satellite phone ordering this part and that part, and 2 hours after my man was on a flight from Amsterdam to Karachi. He flew 15 hours and had a 10-hour wait in Karachi for a connection to Quetta. We put the car on a truck and it took 20 hours to reach Quetta. We got tired of it and got out at Loralai to take a taxi, and the guy had four flat tyres one after the other. He ran out of spares at two o'clock in the morning and had to go off for a wheel so we stopped at a mud hut, and the people there got up and let us sleep three hours in their bed.

'When we reach Quetta it was eight o'clock in the morning, and the driver had the last flat tyre 500 metres from the hotel. Everyone was checking out and I told the people, "We want to check *in*". And so we mend the car with the parts from Holland, and we drive on and now we are here.'

This certainly put our anxiety about some grooves in the brake drum into brighter perspective.

'You deserve to win now.'

Anton laughed with bearish abandon. 'I don't know about win. But it is very good to be here with all you people again. Rosie, you look lovely in this Islamic dress.'

'Now you are just being a flatterer.'

The afternoon was more desert. The emptiness, and Iran itself, seemed to drive us in on ourselves within the boiling capsule of the car. Being spread between so many hotels at night meant that there was less socialising, and even in the scattered outposts there was no lubricating alcohol to bring the diminished groups together. It seemed that I had hardly spoken more than a few words to anyone except Phil for days. My headscarf made me feel deaf and blinkered, as if my senses were actually impaired. Beyond the windows there was nothing to see. The road was dead straight and spirit-level flat and on either side there was only a colourless expanse of dirt in all directions. A sandstorm blew up and the air became thick and yellow and the sun turned to a blurred disc of metal hanging in the murk dead ahead of us. It was like driving through simmering smog.

The absence of stimuli was almost hallucinatory. I began to feel that there was no one left alive, nothing moving in the world but Phil and me and the car and the greedy wind.

'It's funny. It's quite different but it reminds me of

when I was working as a pearl diver off Western Australia.'

He was right, it was like being at sea.

He lit a cigarette. I remembered Nick Evans's fax, still in my pocket, and smiled. I was a long way from Dolce & Gabbana and I hadn't been able to pick up even half a cucumber in Zāhedān.

'We were on the boat for six weeks at a stretch. Four divers, four crew. The divers worked underwater for eight hours a day, hunting for shell. Very isolated, very intense. I think we all turned quite strange. I remember having very vivid dreams.'

'How did you find the shells?'

'You learned what to look for. Just a bump in the sand, the right shape and size.'

'Were you lonely?'

He looked at me. 'Yes, I suppose.'

He talked for quite a long time about the past. He had lived under a tree in a car park in Dorset for a whole summer and taught windsurfing off the beach. He told me about leaving home and going to Australia and moving on from there to the Virgin Islands, and a friend of his who worked flying helicopters for Branson on Necker Island.

'I had a shower in Di's bathroom,' he said.

I thought that this all sounded daring and solitary, and comfortless except for the usurping of a Princess's bathroom, and painfully devoid of ties.

I wondered why and then thought that I would probably never find out. I just knew that I liked him, whatever.

The surreal desert road arrowed westwards, and the kilometres flickered upwards on the trip. I thought that we had made a new manoeuvre in our dance, one that made us move more comfortably together. I kept my fingers tucked down the side of his seat to maintain the new connection.

'I learned to dive too, when I was a girl.' In the rural confines of North Wales.

'Yes?'

Ianto's parents had a big house on a trout lake that lay enclosed in a private bowl of pine trees. They were friends of my father's. Long ago Ianto's father had almost married my father's sister. Sam and Penny were rather rich. The house had two staircases, and a drawing-room with silk cushions, and Penny was glamorous and impeccably chic. She always made her son's girl-friend feel very young and rather grubby, which is just what I was.

Ianto belonged to the local sub-aqua club, and the members used to come on Friday evenings to dive in the glassy lake. I did my first open-water dive there, and I remember the trout suspended motionless like stuffed fish in a green tank, and the fat black eels sidewinding through the weeds on the bottom. After that there was a summer of drift dives in the spiralling bubbles of currents that ripped through the Menai Straits, and long weekends exploring the wrecks off remote beaches down the Lleyn peninsula.

I was just out of boarding school, and making the heady discovery that I wasn't an unlovable ugly duckling any longer. At least as far as men were concerned. Grabbing with two fists at this sudden huge supply of attention and potential affection, I went diving because there were so many men and the only other woman was

Ianto's sister Shan, not because I particularly enjoyed the sport itself. The truth was that I found it rather frightening. The equipment was very primitive in those days – no self-clearing regulator, no buoyancy control jacket, only cumbersome lead weights for buoyancy adjustment. The lifejacket was either inflated by mouth, or in an emergency by firing a gas canister which then had to be replaced. Masks were stiff plastic and wetsuits were leaky neoprene. Shan's and my made-to-measure one-piece suits were the first the manufacturers had ever attempted for women. They had problems with cutting the upper half.

Diving was uncomfortable, quite a lot of the time, and the waters were dark and cold. But just occasionally there were flashes of awe or elation that made the rest endurable, and anyway I knew I wouldn't have been happy sitting on the beach waiting for the boat to bring the boys ashore again.

There was a boating accident at a seaside resort. A pleasure craft struck one of the piers of a bridge and sank immediately and twelve people were drowned. Back then in North Wales there were no police divers, and the only option was to call in the local diving club to recover the bodies. We groped underwater, roped in a line, in twelve inches of visibility. Grains of sand whirled in the tidal shifts, dancing magnified beyond the screen of my mask. It was like a desert sandstorm. That was why it had come into my head, after so long. I had never seen a dead body before and my breath sucking in and out of the demand valve seemed to roar with terror in my ears.

In the end we recovered the last two people, a mother

and son. The discovery itself was sad, not terrifying at all. But I had nightmares for months afterwards. Dread of drowning made sexy, carefree diving weekends into paradoxical ordeals.

More fear. I had always been afraid of something. I had been hunched up with fear, maybe all the time since my mother died, right up until the walk to Everest. And then in sight of the mountain the weight of it had lifted off my shoulders and I had briefly walked free.

I thought yet again about Chris Taylor and the talk we had had way back in Lanzhou, and I envied all over again his perception that if the worst had already happened there was nothing else to shrink from.

I was still afraid: I was scared right now, of death by the roadside, of loss and loneliness and failure and despair. Probably that would never change.

But then, I thought, I had come on the rally for those very reasons. Taking risks and surviving them was a way of bare-knuckling dread into a corner. I could also watch other people and listen and make discoveries, because they revealed more of themselves when they were under pressure, or afraid too, and that went with the job I did. Spinning stories out of ordinary lives, and making ordinary affairs significant. The alchemy of fiction.

If I sat in my bedroom and wrapped myself in an eiderdown for protection, or tried to do the same for my children – well, then, the ceiling would probably fall down on our heads, and we wouldn't be having any fun either. Nor would I ever have any new ideas.

I glanced sidelong at Phil and he nudged against my hand.

'How far to go?'

I looked at the trip and the route notes.

'Just about 10 ks.'

The desert was slowly unclasping its grip. There were one-storey concrete buildings interspersed with mud huts, and low walls, and a glittering modern bridge in the distance.

We arrived in Eṣfahān in the same yellow light that seemed to have followed us half across the world, and as it slowly faded to grey and birds came to roost on the tangled overhead wires we were overtaken by the pleasant melancholy of evening, and of arriving late in yet another unknown place.

Chapter Thirteen

Eşfahān was good. We had another rest day.

Phil spent the morning massaging the car again. A little leak had developed from the radiator and he was busy with sealant and a spanner check. There were plenty of other people working alongside him under the shade of the trees in the garden of the Abbasi Hotel. The yellow MG had come to Eşfahān on the back of a truck, the Jaguar Mk VII had terminal problems, David Arrigo and the Allard had fallen days behind, and even Adam's Bentley Le Mans had an ailing clutch. Jon and Adam were in their overalls, working on it with the help of Robert Dean and Bill Ainscough. Beyond the railings, a great crowd of solemn men gathered to watch the foreigners and their busy dismembering of cars.

I found a helpful member of the Iranian Motor Federation, our hosts, who escorted me to the correct bank to change dollars.

Inside the bank, in the foreign exchange department, there were seething mobs of people with no notion of queuing, all of them thrusting pink forms at blank-faced cashiers. Some of the tellers, surprisingly, were attractive young women who eyed me in my oily veil and approximation of suitable dress, and giggled behind their hands while my guide explained what I wanted.

The transaction was complicated. There wasn't a computer console to be seen anywhere. The lack of technological advancement seemed extraordinary in the central bank in a major city. First a form was filled in by hand over two carbons, and then the sheets of carbon paper were removed and smoothed out for re-use. Then the forms were transferred behind the counter to another clerk, in another cubicle, who crunched the numbers using an old hand-cranked adding machine. Sweating in the press of unshaven men and sharp-elbowed black-shrouded old women, I reflected sourly that there hadn't been much of an onward march here from the abacuses and pieces of silver in the market place at Bam.

Finally the details of my transaction were referred to Mr Big behind a desk who nodded and signed and then the focus of the action returned to the first cubicle, where the currency was produced and counted out. Four hundred dollars made a wad of rials about three inches thick. I needed the cash to buy us a new cassette player.

By the time my friendly guide and I emerged at the other end of this process it was midday, the shops were closing and it was too late to find an electrical supplier. Phil and I would have to chance it on our own this afternoon. I thanked my escort and warmly shook his hand, only remembering afterwards that women aren't

supposed to put out their hands and touch strange men.
He took it very well.

In the afternoon, miraculous to tell, Phil and I went
sightseeing. There was much to see in Eşfahān, the
ancient city of Persia.

At the heart of the city was a great square, now named
for the Ayatollah Khomeini. At either end, the Shah's
polo goalposts still stood planted in the scrubby grass and
in the thick afternoon heat it was easy to hear the crack of
mallets and the furious drumming of ponies' hooves. At
one end of the square the sky was blocked by the domes
of a great mosque. We paid our entrance fee and went
inside.

It was no longer used as a place of worship, and it was
almost deserted except for wandering tourists, but it
retained an atmosphere that was both serene and spiri-
tual. It was high, and cool, and vivid with the aquamarine
and turquoise and sage and straw-gold tiles of the region.
The pierced screens covering the windows filtered the
light in intricate patterns, and under the central dome a
stone marked the place where you could stand, and clap
your hands once, and listen to the sevenfold echo that was
delivered in return.

Outside again, we threaded our way across the square
between the little boys who were playing football, and
ducked into the old bazaar. It was just reopening for the
evening and the alleyways lined with stalls were quiet
under an arched stone roof. It was the best bazaar yet.
There were things that even Phil, the king of material dis-
encumbrance, wanted to buy, and we wandered up and
down in the insulated, shadowy coolness looking at

jewellery and glass and old ceramics and inlaid work and brass and fussy Persian carpets. Afterwards, with our purchases, we climbed some spiral stairs to a tiny café with a balcony, just wide enough for a cushioned and carpeted bench, looking west over the square.

We drank black tea and ate cloying sugary pastries and watched the sun set behind the domes and minarets. Three sunburned English boys clambered out on to the balcony and sat on the carpets beside us. They ordered a hookah, and passed the mouthpiece around between them. The water bubbling in the bowl sounded exactly like a diver's breaths through a regulator and I began to think that the sun and the desert and the view had touched me to the point where everything began to sound like everything else and the loops and circuits of history and association were finally closing in to cut me off.

But then the boys began to talk loudly about a diving holiday they had had in the Red Sea.

'Always the same,' Phil muttered on the other side of me. 'Just like every group I've ever led. They never talk about where they are, only where they've been. And sex, and food. In that order.'

He had had enough of watching the light on the old stone. He didn't have the highest boredom threshold in the world, and he wanted to move on. With a last look at the turquoise domes turning to ash-grey, and the abandoned polo goals with all their melancholy associations of another age, I followed him down the twisting stairs again. We found a taxi driver to take us to the Tottenham Court Road of Eşfahān.

'Fifty dollars,' the shopkeeper in the biggest, brashest shop beamed at us.

The cassette player was gold, with gold filigree knobs. It was the very thing, and I was too taken with it even to try bargaining. I counted out the money, Phil took the machine back to the car and wired it in, and it kept us happy with tunes on the road from that day onwards.

The hotel in Eşfahān had once been a caravanserai, and after that a magnificent establishment where the Shah kept his own suite of rooms. It was run down and faded now, and although there were a hundred waiters and porters they were all surly and inefficient. But it was still good to eat dinner and laugh and talk in the huge, lamplit central garden and afterwards to retire to the arched recess at the far end to recline on cushions and pass the hookah pipe around.

Mark Thake appeared. He had just been introduced to the wife of one of the Iranian drivers. He told us that he had put out his hand to shake hers, then remembered the protocol and snatched it back. He tried to cover his embarrassment by giving her the double thumbs-up instead, and then recalling too late that that was a very rude gesture he fell back helplessly on the closed finger-and-thumb okay signal, which was the rudest of all.

He hopped about now with his hands buried in his armpits.

'Just off to have my arms cut off,' he said. Everyone hooted with laughter.

We made a lot of impervious rallyists jokes about women in Iran. I did it myself; in the car park that morning I had seen three young women in full black chuddars

peering over the wall at us. I had been smoking and giggling with JD and Phil, and striding around so that my
drapes slipped off my hair.

I waved across at them and grinned.

'Yeah, come on, girls. Come and live in the west. You
can swan around as well, laughing with men you aren't
married to and having a fag and a fun time.'

Except that it wasn't funny. Ever since we had entered
Iran, I hadn't seen one woman walking tall with her head
up and her shoulders back. They all scurried like eyes-
down mice, hunched up and with their hands at their
throats to keep their horrible wraps in place. Even little
girls of seven and eight. Nor did one of them have the
ease and grace of a nun in her habit. I couldn't see how
any of this had anything to do with religious piety or spir-
ituality, but it had plenty to do with repression.

I had struck up a conversation with one of our mack-
intoshed escorts, and tried to discover from her what their
life was like.

'Of course we women have an equal voice here in
Iran,' she insisted. 'And when we are at home, of course
we wear whatever clothes we please.'

I was only a visitor, passing through at high speed and
with no real knowledge or insight. But I thought that
there was a wistful defiance in her eyes that was sadder
than any of the truths she might have told me.

It was yet another night in another outlandish place,
only half-glimpsed. In this bedroom out of a series of bed-
rooms the brass light fitment threw a dapple of crescent
moons and stars over the cracked ceiling. I lay staring up
at it for only a little while. I was beginning to learn Phil's

trick of sleeping anywhere, whatever thoughts were running through my head.

Out of Eşfahān, we were 21st. The yellow MG YB had slipped from 14th to 45th, and we had edged up one place accordingly.

'Just one more,' we encouraged each other. 'One more will be good enough.'

RO had been overheard trumpeting to someone that as a test of driving and endurance the rally ended at Istanbul, and from there on westwards it was just a matter of mechanical continuity. There were five more testing days, in that case.

Eşfahān to Hamadān turned out not to be testing, excepting our ability to entertain ourselves sufficiently to stay awake in the car. It was a long, featureless run through country that slowly turned from desert to sparsely populated farmland. We passed through Khomein, birthplace of the Ayatollah, which was marked by huge murals of the frowning visage, and even more roundabout statuary. These decorations were a striking feature of all the towns we passed through. Sometimes they were inspirational, perhaps huge shiny-yellow warrior figures helmeted like *Star Wars* storm troopers, or abstract, in the shape of monster arrangements of blue glass shards, or representational, such as vast metal tulips painted in coarse colours. Sometimes there were stainless steel fountains, or great slabs of livid stone. All the items of roundabout art had in common overblown scale and striking ugliness.

We reached Hamadān, and another outpost hotel. We

had climbed into the hills and it was cooler here, with a clean wind blowing.

Phil was tired, for once too tired even to work on the car. He abandoned it, ate dinner, and went straight to bed. I worried about him for a little while, and then left him alone. I agreed to go with them when Dan and JD suggested a stroll around the town. Hamadān is a quiet university city. There was no apparent threat even in the dark and silent unpaved streets away from the main thoroughfare.

As we left the gates of the hotel I realised it was cold, and I needed a sweater. I called to Dan and JD that I would catch them up, and doubled back. They were perhaps a hundred and fifty metres ahead of me when I re-emerged into the empty street. I hurried after them, pulling my sweater over my head at the same time.

The man materialised from behind a little kiosk selling magazines and coffee. He was middle-aged, middle-sized, bearded, unremarkable. He walked briskly and purposefully straight towards me, and as he pushed by his shoulder struck mine. I was still tangled up in knitwear, and moving too slowly to avoid him. I was caught off balance, and as I spun back to face the hotel again he shoved his hand up between my legs, high and hard, and pinched. I was wearing loose trousers and it was only a momentary connection, far from the worst sexual assault I had suffered in my life, although I would hate it to have happened to my daughter. But there was a level of cheap and sneering lust combined with such dismissive arrogance in the gesture that it made anger choke off my breath. He was already melting into the shadows under the trees, but I wanted to run after him and smack the back of my hand across his bearded maw until the blood ran and his teeth broke. I clenched and unclenched my fists, panting, staring into the darkness. The man had gone.

This was what happened, Prohibition-like, when you forced your women into submission and denial. Sex just bobbed up elsewhere as lechery and violence and sexual degradation. And it was men and the prevailing culture that were degraded by the momentary collision, not me or any other woman on earth.

I pulled my clothes tighter around me and marched on after Dan and JD. We had a pleasant walk around the town, although there was no café or public meeting place to make a focal point of it. The other people in the streets were nearly all studious-looking young men, books under their arms, with not a single young woman student amongst them. Of course there was not.

We had received nothing but courtesy and kindness from our hosts, and friendly warmth from almost all the individuals we had come into contact with, but I wouldn't be sorry to leave Iran behind. One more day, Hamadān to Tabriz, and then home free into Turkey.

Over breakfast at Hamadān we heard from Mohsen Eijadi, one of the Iranian drivers, that there was a short, tough second stage in the day's route. Gossip about the details was already spreading and at the start line there was a definite change in the atmosphere. The long, wearisome days of featureless desert driving had sapped everyone and had produced very few changes in the order. Now people were briskly checking their watches against the rally clock and frowning intently over the route notes.

'Here's a chance for us,' Phil said. A night's sleep had done him good. He was fully revved up, flexing his fingers on the wheel as we waited for our minute at the end of the day's first stage.

A man nicknamed Too-Tall Don, a huge American journalist in a somewhat unlucky Packard, loomed up at the Amazon's window.

'Got an e-mail for you, Rosie.' The paper fluttered in the wind. 'From Beverly Hills.'

My old friend Richard Sparks was sending me love and good luck via Don's website e-mail address.

I read the message hungrily and then stared ahead through the flyspotted windscreen at the dusty road, and the tattered and unshaven crews with their broken cars. David Brister's Rover looked as if it had come through hell-fire.

Oh God, I yearned. *Beverly Hills.*

Time to go again. *Beep.*

One hundred and two km, one hour seventeen minutes.

Phil had worked out a strategy; we'd drive the flat section full out and maybe win ourselves a few minutes in hand for when we came to the 28 km hairpin-climb at the end of the stage. He went off from the start like a bullet, left hand reaching out to turn up the volume on the tape player.

'Okay, yeahhhh . . .'

It was the first adrenalin buzz we'd had for days.

The trip flickered busily and I called the distances, just

like back in Tibet. How far behind us, how long ago.

The road surface was impeccable, and there was almost no traffic. We realised even before we reached the hill climb that we were going to clean the section with ease and so, therefore, was almost everyone else.

'Fuck it,' Phil said resignedly.

The time control came into sight, and we were 25 minutes inside our time. It was a pretty little whitewashed stone teahouse at the head of a pass. The altitude was 2,300 metres, our highest point in Iran. There was a fierce wind blowing, rattling the leaves on the trees outside the teahouse and bringing a strong scent of autumn.

All the way across Iran, Iran Air had been providing us every morning with neatly packed airline lunch boxes. *En route* from somewhere to somewhere in the sky we would probably have yawned and discarded them, but now we seized them eagerly. Investigation of the contents was one of the day's high points. Today, however, I had forgotten to pick our boxes up from the pile at the start line and Phil was not well pleased. I left the car and ran into the teahouse to see if I could find him a replacement meal.

It was a revelation. There was a glass counter and blue-painted tables and metal chairs, like a Greek kafenion. Greg was sitting happily at the marshal's desk with a glass of tea in front of him. I bought great papery sheets of the local delicious unleavened bread, a dish of fresh honey in the comb, and a double handful of dusty, intensely sweet tomatoes. Lunch fit for a king, I thought. Intending to run the fifty metres to the car to fetch Phil, I set the food down on a table and asked the navigator ahead of me in the line to keep an eye on it in case a gust of wind lifted the sheets of bread and blew them away like kites.

'Why should I?' he snapped.

I thought he was joking. 'Because you are my friend,' I countered.

'But my time is before yours. Why should I stay to guard your things?'

I swallowed my smile. 'Never mind, then. Just let it blow away.' I ran to the car and back. When I reached Greg with my road book for stamping he scratched his prickles sympathetically.

'What was all that about?'

'Dunno.'

There was ample time allowed for the next section so we sat outside under the tree to eat and drink mugs of strong black tea. Phil wasn't over-enchanted by my lunch provisions, being more of an enthusiast for sausage, egg and chips, but Howard and Chris loafed by and helped to finish up the food. They always loafed everywhere, with an air of baffled and faintly aloof amusement, and yet still managed to be riding high in 7th place.

After we moved on, Phil saw that I was upset by the meaningless dispute with the other navigator. Tiny events assumed disproportionate significance in this isolated bubble of endless forward momentum and I sat with my head turned away, snuffling a bit. At length he pulled in to the side and switched off the engine.

'It's an easy road. Why don't you drive for a while?'

By way of comfort he was offering me the best solace he could come up with, a second chance to drive the Amazon. It was a sweet gesture. Sort of.

'No thanks.'

'Go on. Just for 10 ks,' he cajoled.

I wanted to accept, but I didn't want to drive. In fact, worse than not wanting to, I didn't think I could even get it into first and pulling away from a standstill without a series of hops and a shaming stall. I doubted I'd even have the confidence to pilot my own sleek and easy car down to Sainsbury's once we got home. If we ever got home.

'No thanks.'

'Well, all right. If you're sure you don't want to.' His relief was plain to see.

We covered the uneventful distance to Tabriz. Apart from an unfurling menu of sudden new anxieties about the car, the only thing we had to worry about was the stone-throwing. In the worst places we had to negotiate a hail of rocks, which was unpleasant enough for us but must have been terrifying for the crews in open cars. Most of the perpetrators were sad-looking undernourished children, not thugs at all. Phil developed a technique of driving threateningly straight at them and sending them scattering through the scrubby roadside bushes, skinny bare legs and arms flailing as they raced away. Once we caught up with the father of one of these children, although the boy himself escaped.

'We are guests in your country, and you throw stones at us?' I wondered.

'Sorry,' the man said, the word contradicting his demeanour which suggested *infidel, and a woman to compound the offence*. It was yet another face of Iran, the obverse of the official courtesy and smooth welcome extended to the rally as a whole.

As we approached Tabriz we met the first heavy traffic for days. Private cars with two or three youngish men in them drew level with us for a good look, and then set out to prove by accelerating, cutting in, undertaking and hooting, that they could drive faster and more daringly than us. We thought even more eagerly of tomorrow, and the border.

The hotel in Tabriz offered secure parking, and Phil rolled up his sleeves at once. The list of worries now included the front wheel bearing, a leak from the diff, another leak from the gearbox, a wobble in the steering, a leaking and possibly holed rear fuel tank, and a cracked distributor cap. Dan needed to change his worn front brake pads but he had lost his spares, along with the tent, back in Tibet. Phil gave him ours, which may have compensated in part for our deficiency in team spirit in the middle of the journey, wherever it had been. When I tried to think back on the way we had come and remember what had happened where, it felt like looking down a long, convoluted tunnel toothed with rocks and pierced with shafts of sunshine. I noticed that I was already beginning to think of it in the past tense.

Phil was hungry, and therefore irritable. I went inside to see what I could do.

The Water Wars were at their height. The Bentley boys had discovered that plastic sanitary bags made the best bombs, but supplies were running low. Jon Turner intercepted Melissa who was crossing the lobby and steered her to the reception desk, one arm protectively around her shoulders.

'My wife is having a *very heavy* period,' he explained to

the clerk. 'Could she please have two dozen sanitary bags?'

The wars showed signs of escalating even further. John Vipond had made the mistake of looking up when his name was called from a balcony overhead. He caught a bucketful of water full in the face.

One of our guides explained that there would be no food in the hotel until dinner, but he found me a little toothless old man and assured me that my new friend would take me out to buy whatever I needed. It was a religious festival, and the shops were already closing. But my guide seemed to know everyone in town and he tapped on the door of a closed café and persuaded the owner to let us in. I ordered chicken salad sandwiches by pointing to the first English-language item on the plastic menu and holding up three fingers. When they arrived, amazingly, they were huge, juicy subs, loaded with meat and mayo. On the way back to the hotel, we passed a street vendor with a brazier and a big vat of what looked like maroon plush croquet balls. I pointed and raised my eyebrows, and Mr Toothless grinned an expanse of gum and helped me organise the right show of rials to buy one. The object was hot and sticky and I bit into it with care. It was a braised beetroot in thick sweet and sour sauce, and utterly delicious.

My friend wouldn't take any money for his time, or even a pack of Marlboro. He patted my arm, just as if I were an equal instead of a woman, and waved goodbye. With the American-style sandwiches in my hand I realised we were getting close to the wicked and wonderful west again. Tomorrow, *alcohol.*

The weary faced, overalled three-quarters of Team

Amazon was pleased with the subs and cold tins of Coke, but they were less interested in the beetroot even though I carved it into appetising slices with my penknife. In the end I ate the whole thing myself, and made a mental note that if I got up in the night I wasn't to assume in a panic that I was having another haemorrhage.

Phil handed me a brown plastic cup with four knobs on the top. It was the distributor cap, and it did indeed have a hairline crack in it. My next assignment was either to find somewhere to buy a replacement, or to mend the existing one. Nail varnish or Araldite were quoted as the best glues.

One of the Iranian Motor Federation members was just setting out for a motor spares outlet with a long shopping list, and he obligingly took our distributor cap with him. In the meantime I turned to a back-up quest for nail varnish. I thought Jennie Dorey might be the best bet, and went to look for her.

The Doreys had had their Morris Minor engine rebuilt, with a welded piston. They were back in the running from Tabriz, but sadly they were now near the bottom of the order along with the Packard, the Mark VII Jag, the Buick, two of the three Astons and David's Allard.

'What colour would you like?' Jennie beamed.

The new distributor cap arrived along with the soup at dinner. The replacement looked identical – same colour, same number of knobs – and I was very pleased with my arrangements. But Phil announced that it was minutely the wrong size. He had already glued the cracked one, having found some Araldite, which I thought was a pity. I liked the idea of rallying with Jennie Dorey's *Red Hot Red* holding us together.

We did have another spare cap, but it wouldn't function with our present ignition system. Phil glanced furtively over his shoulder as he explained this. Our electronic ignition was our one single *tiny* infringement of the rules, which barred non-standard modifications. To worry about this detail seemed to me to be an irrelevance, in view of the rumours which were gathering momentum about some of the other cars which had never been scrutineered before the start. The gossip centred on the front-running Willys jeep, and two American 1950 Ford Club Coupés which were whispered to be megabucks sports cars inside heritage shells. I had never seen under the bonnet of any of them, and even if I had done and they had had the innards of a Ferrari Testarossa bolted in there I wouldn't have known the difference, or cared particularly. But some people who were playing by the rules did care, very much.

I sighed. Another two hours in the car park in prospect.

We had plenty of company out there. Adam's clutch plate had finally sheared and he and Jon had the Bentley completely stripped out. Spiky-haired, oily and intent on their job, they both looked about fourteen years old. I peered inside and they showed me what they were doing, and the broken plate. I suddenly saw how strong and simple and logical the fine old car's workings were and for the very first time I felt a shiver of acquisitive, petrol-headed admiration. I stepped back quickly, knowing that the last thing on earth I needed was to develop a taste for vintage Bentleys.

*

In the morning the rally streamed eagerly towards the border, 276 kilometres away. We were as eager as anyone, but everyone was passing us. Dave Bull roared by with a merry toot on the horn, and the Dangerfields and the land crab and the Iranian Peykans.

Phil's face was a mask of gloom. He hated to be overtaken.

'What's up?'

'Don't know. The power's right down. Listen, she's missing all the time. Must be the crack in the distributor.'

We drove for 100 km in tense silence, dropping further and further behind.

Okay, I thought. Get ready for it. This is China all over again. We're going to break down, lose time, miss our gold medal.

I'd become blasé, taking for granted the car's imperturbability and Phil's sure touch with it, and now I was going to learn just how lucky I had been all the way from Tuotuoheyan.

'Shit. We'll have to stop. I'm going to try and buy another cap.'

We were passing through a grubby little town and the road was lined with tyre outlets and mechanical workshops. I rummaged for my purse, ready to go and buy one more knobby brown plastic cup. Phil hoisted the bonnet, and then he started to laugh.

'What's funny?'

'Come and see.'

I looked, and saw that one of the leads had worked loose. The car had been running all morning on three cylinders. We clapped hands, and leaped into our seats

again. The Amazon streaked forward like a foxhound
with her nose to the scent. We were back in our proper
position by the time we reached the border.

The queues for the emigration formalities were familiar now. I mooched along the line with paperwork and
passports in my hand. David Brister was doing the same
thing.

'Keith and I may be a pair of daft old buggers,' he
mused, 'but what is this thing about yellow cars?
Whenever you get someone cutting you up or jumping
the queue or mucking things up, it's always a *yellow* car.'

I agreed that proper consideration ought to be given
to the semiological significance of yellowness as associ-
ated with cars and crappy behaviour.

We passed out of Iran, and drew up in the Turkish
compound. Very slowly and very deliberately I took off my
veil and tore it in half. It made a satisfying rending noise.
Phil offered to go and change our rials for Turkish lira
with one of the hard men doing currency deals before the
barrier, so I gave him a thick wad representing about two
hundred and fifty dollars. Quite soon he came back again.

'Did a good deal,' he announced. 'Big notes. I've got
literally millions of lira here.'

I gave the money in his hand a suspicious glance.

'How many millions, exactly?'

'Um, one, two, three.'

'About twelve quid, then. He saw you coming.'

Phil was enraged. He was already jumping out of the
car. 'I'll go back and sort him out. That's him, look.'

The man had four days' growth and a leather jacket,
and plenty of mean-looking cohorts. I didn't think I

wanted to run around trying to enlist David and Keith and Richard Dangerfield to back Phil up in a fist-fight against a currency shark. I grabbed hold of his belt and hauled him back into the car.

'Don't even think about it. You'll get your hair in a mess. And your face, probably.'

He glared, and then we caught each other's eyes. It was always good when we made each other laugh, and we laughed now all the way across the border and out into Turkey.

We headed west past Mount Ararat. The mountain stood up like a great seamed tooth against a pink-tinged sky.

I felt unaccountably drowsy, maybe with the sensuous satisfaction of baring my head and arms in the sunshine, maybe with delayed relief after the morning's mechanical alarm. For the first time in our journey I fell fast asleep in the navigator's seat. Phil drove uncomplainingly, with the route notes on his lap, all the way up the long, steep climb to our day's destination. It was Palandoken, the Turkish ski-resort, near Erzurum. I woke up when we pulled into the car park in front of the single big hotel. There was a view of snowy summits in the distance and in the foreground green slopes and the familiar wiry apparatus of towbars and chairlifts. It was like any one-season ski-resort before the snow falls, bare and morose and scribbled over with machinery. But we didn't care much about the scenery.

Sarah Catt and Paul Brace were stamping road books in the lobby.

'The bar's thataway,' Paul pointed.

As we crossed the border we had gained an hour and a half. It was still only lunch-time . . .

The hotel was like ski-hotels everywhere. There were wooden floors, not yet dripping or echoing with the clump of ski-boots, and a vast, empty ski-room, and a wood-panelled kitschly decorated bar-restaurant that might equally have been in Mürren or Méribel. Thomas Noor, wonderful bonhomous Thomas whom not even Iran had managed to subdue, was already in place at a table with Maria and Melissa. He held up a bottle of red wine by the neck.

'Rosie! Have a drink!'

You bet.

The day tilted gently sideways into a warm bath of booze.

After a long lunch I can only remember a series of snapshots, although they must have been connected somehow.

Swimming in the hotel's cup-sized pool. Phil singing in the shower. Taking a siesta and somehow waking up raring to go again. An even longer dinner with florid speeches, sitting next to Adam and trying to explain to him what doing the rally had really *really* meant to me. Having a bit of trouble finding the *mot juste*, for some reason.

Then the wooden Bierkeller pretending it looked out on a snowy street in Kitzbühel. Where *were* we?

Yeah, Turkey somewhere. Doesn't matter. Never see anything anywhere, in any case. Lovely wine, though. Maybe one more glass.

Bar packed with people, roar of noise and laughter.

Werner Esch from the black Merc, number 54, and his beautiful daughter Sylvie. The Ashbys, father and son, from the, erm, Delage. Mick Flick and his partner Felix. The two sharp American girls from the media crew.

We were going to make it to Paris, all of us.

I kept feeling a goofy grin splitting my face. We were all friends, best friends. Wonderful. Seen and done so much together.

The young on their way down to the disco. Going to complete their social and sexual negotiations in a blur of beer and Turkish disco-pop.

I could go too. Hey, it was still *early*.

Bring the watch-face into focus.

Oh dear. Not early at all. In fact, hideously late. Too old for disco. Too old for anything except bed.

In the time it took to cross the bar and ride up in the lift, propositioned twice, separately, by two elderly gentlemen. Both with lovely, wonderful cars parked outside. Hmmm, why not?

Two thousand reasons, only.

Good to be asked though.

Head on pillow. Much, much too much red Buzbag wine in system.

Downstairs, distant roar of shouting and stamping and occasional breaking glass. Rally crews larging it. Thank God, not me.

Bad enough as it is . . .

Chapter Fourteen

It was just a little roadside café at the midday time control, with a terrace and a couple of tables with parasols, but it felt like heaven on earth. We had re-entered a comprehensible world.

I sat with my hangover, sipping Turkish coffee and watching Phil eat. I was having a small fantasy about restaurants. Specifically, I was imagining a little place on a harbour wall somewhere, maybe in Greece but more probably Italy. There would be that holiday smell of the sea and wild thyme and grilling fish just tainted with diesel oil from the fishing boats bobbing on the black water. There would be a white starched tablecloth and dignified place settings, a candle burning steadily within a glass mantle, and a luminous moon overhead. The restaurant would be laid-back but, of course, very *very* good.

Phil and I would be having dinner *à deux*. There would come a moment, maybe before or maybe after the peerless *tiramisu*, when he would lift his glass and touch it to mine. He would smile at me, his affectionate admiration tinged with tenderness.

'You have been the best partner anyone could have wished for. I will remember making this journey with you, sharing this great adventure, for the rest of my life.'

And I would smile modestly back at him, serene in my achievements and confident of my mature powers.

'Thank you,' I would murmur, 'you were the best, too. We have been a good team, haven't we?'

'How long have we got?'

Real Phil had finished his chicken and chips. I came back to earth, to a roadside café between Erzurum and Nevsehir, half-way through the longest day's driving of the whole rally. Cars were revving and chugging all down the endless road.

'What?'

'How *long*?'

I looked at my watch. 'Er . . . 17 minutes.'

'Right then. I'll go and check her over.'

The marshals summoned Adam and Jon over to the checkpoint, indicating that there might be a problem with their timings. As they leaned obediently over to check the details, *two* buckets full of water sloshed over them. John Vipond's revenge. The Bentley boys had been threatening Phil and me with a sanitary bag bomb filled with warm milk, but we stayed well out of range. Exploding milk would be too much to deal with on a Buzbag hangover.

The time control stamp clapped down on my book and I folded myself into the rally seat for the hundred thousandth time. We had driven 433 km today and there were another 306 to go.

The question of driving had come up again.

'Do you want to?' Phil asked, reasonably.

We reprised a conversation we had had before.

'Only if you are tired. You have to say, "I'm too tired to drive any more. Please will you take over?" Then I will, of course.'

'But I'd never *say* that.'

He couldn't admit a weakness. That took a certain strength.

It was a long, beautiful drive across Cappadocia. I sat and admired the scenery.

At last, we reached Nevsehir. Tired and stiff and desperate for a shower, I flung my door open. Too far, too hard.

Clang. The flange that held it in place popped out of the socket. And at the same time, with a despairing rattle of broken chain, the window glass slid down and disappeared within the door panel.

Fantasy Phil would have smiled forgivingly and maybe remarked fondly that I was so clever that it made up for my clumsiness.

Real Phil made a noise like a waste disposal unit swallowing cherry stones. Once, trying to overtake the driver we most hated who was deliberately balking us, he had muttered that he felt like ripping off his *head* and shitting down his *neck*. I knew that my neck was on the toilet seat right now. I took the road book and tramped into the hotel to hand it in. Of course, we were billeted in the dump down the road.

Nevsehir was only 9 kilometres from Goreme, a place of miraculous geological formations called fairy chimneys which were a big tourist attraction. The hotel was reportedly full because there were several busloads of Japanese there to admire the sight. I very much wanted to visit the chimneys too. Cellophane-wrapped miniature plaster replicas of them were being handed out to crews as they checked in, a gift from the local tourist authority.

The American driver in the line ahead of me accepted his gift with great enthusiasm.

'CHOCOLATE!' he cried.

'No, no. Is a replica of our local tourist site.'

'A tourist replica? I thought it was chocolate.'

'No, not chocolate. Is chimneys.'

'*Not* chocolate?'

Et cetera.

When I came back, Phil was still trying to lever the rogue flange back into place with a crowbar. I held the door at the wrong angle and the metal tongue obstinately refused to bend back into the slot. After several attempts he threw the crowbar on the ground and walked away.

Dan and JD sidled over. They coaxed the door into usable shape for me before Phil came back again. We drove a silent kilometre down the road to the bad hotel – which looked truly bad – only to discover that we weren't on the list there either. The nightly hotel hassle had swelled suddenly beyond mere irksomeness to rage-inducing proportions. I was very angry.

Back at the HQ hotel Sarah Catt discovered that the Turkish hostess was using the wrong list, and we did have a room there after all. Why not, I wondered furiously, make sure that the Turkish hostess had the right list in the first place? Then our 739 kilometres for the day need not have been pointlessly extended to 741.

It wasn't just me who was angry. The smaller tooth-brushless woman was having an apocalyptic tantrum at the desk. The scale of it was so impressive that it gained her a double room in the good hotel, which was sworn to be full to capacity.

With the hotel question finally solved I said hopefully, ingratiatingly, to Phil, 'It's only 9 ks out to the fairy chimneys. Look, here's a plaster model of them.'

I held it up enticingly but he failed to take the hint. He propped the bonnet open instead and stuck his head underneath. I went up to the hard-won room, ran a bath and lay in it with all the vodka miniatures from the mini-bar lined up in front of me. Afterwards, I called home.

Flora answered. 'Mum,' she sighed. 'You have been away *such* a long time.'

She reminded me that I had fastened a little silver chain around her neck before I left for the airport.

'I haven't taken it off since you went. The teachers at school keep telling me to, and I just say yes, and keep it on.'

'I'll be home soon. We'll have a good time in Paris.'

After we said goodnight and hung up the thought of the warm throat, and the silver chain and the significance she attached to it made me cry. I missed them all so much.

Last night, carousing and cherishing unsuitable propositions. Tonight, sobbing in a steamy bathroom. It was all

Rally Syndrome. I wouldn't be sorry when it released its hold.

Downstairs after dinner I met Dan, looking wry and empathetic He and JD had been out to Goreme while we were shuttling between hotels. He gave me a hug and I nearly cried again, just because he was being kind to me.

'This trip just makes me feel that I'm hopeless at everything. I can't even open the car door properly.'

He patted my shoulder. 'You are too eager to please. Just remember that you are the reason Phil's able to be here at all.'

'I really wanted to see the fairy chimneys.'

'You should have said, "If you're not coming, give me the keys".'

I should have done, but I never would, any more than Phil would have said that he was too tired to drive. That was the way we were, and the way we were was incontrovertibly different.

I went and sat as close as I could to Richard Curtis, who was looking particularly Caradoc-like again. He and Idris told me about Humpty Dumpty's adventures.

'Why is it called Humpty Dumpty?' I asked.

Jingers the mechanic had worked on restoring and preparing the Model B. They took it apart, Idris explained, and then put it all back together again.

It was an unforgettable day's driving across to Istanbul. I fed Pergolesi's *Stabat Mater* into the golden mouth of the tape machine, because that was what *I* felt like listening to.

We had almost as far to travel as the day before, but

even these long distances were much easier than the tedious and isolating business of crossing Pakistan and Iran. The weather was cool and settled, the sky was blue except for a few towering silver clouds, and the light was soft and clear. Before this I had only visited Istanbul and spent a couple of beach holidays on the Mediterranean coast, and I had no idea that this great, broad backbone of central Turkey was so beautiful. I could see the ribbon of road undulating in the far distance, perhaps as much as 20 kilometres ahead of us. The vast fields and folded hillsides were buff and cinnamon and pistachio green, with occasional rectangles of intense viridian. In the hollows of the land there were sprinklings of villages. The ochre-walled houses with red tiled roofs and shuttered windows looked almost Tuscan, but then the slender exclamation point of a minaret would deny the familiarity. There were stands of poplar trees with leaves turning gold, and low bushes at the roadside burnished mulberry red by the oblique sun.

The angle of the sun and the leaf colours and the smell in the air were autumnal, and this renewed evidence of the seasons' logic was intimate and natural and reassuring after the moonscapes we had driven through. I thought I had never seen anything so welcoming or so lovely. It made me construct a chain of scenes in my mind, reaching all the way back to China, and I knew that the biggest impression this wild trip had made was of the physical connectedness of the landscape and the peoples who seethed on its face. You skip across land masses in an aeroplane and there is no impression of the knuckle and shoulder and hip that mountain ranges and plains and valleys make as they fit together. Nor is there the sense of

ethnic precision married to global largesse with which
Chinese features meld into Mongolian, into Tibetan, into
Nepalese and Indian and Iranian and European. There
was a solidity and a munificence about the terrestrial
world that I had never absorbed before.

I remembered the thin and daunting yellow line on
the wall maps back at Brooklands. That line had thickened and flowered and burst into a million images.

From being a threatening place, the world – briefly, I
knew, and fancifully, and probably illogically, yet still it
did – seemed to have become fathomable and friendly,
because we had crossed nearly half of it.

The Amazon ate up the great spaces of Turkey and
those two days we spent driving the width of it were
amongst the most memorable of the trip.

There was one time control in the morning, at a fuel
station where we could also buy good coffee, and grapes
and sweet melons at the roadside – all the things we had
missed for weeks – and then the afternoon's control was
demoted to a passage check, without a time restriction, so
we pressed straight on towards Istanbul. The countryside
lost its yellow-gold splendour as we moved west on empty
motorways, around Ankara and down to the sprawl of
petrochemical plants and pollution edging the Sea of
Marmaris.

The traffic built up. We had been warned that the
Turks were mad motorists, but after the experiences of
the Indian subcontinent they seemed to drive like
Postman Pat by comparison. We came to the outskirts of
Istanbul and then, glinting in the distance, we saw the
Bosphorus Bridge. I had imagined breezing across it, the

scent of Europe strengthening in my nostrils all the way, but what we encountered in fact was a giant, exhaust-fuming traffic jam. We inched wearily forward in the gridlock of metal, cheek to cheek with the Rover belonging to a man called Jonathan Lux. His co-driver had had to fly home sick, and he now had Lord Montagu ensconced as his navigator. Judging by the set of their profiles, both of them were rather fed up.

The queue to cross the bridge seemed not to be moving. From having plenty of time to reach the control in the hotel on the European side, we began to worry that we would be late. The car started to overheat, and Phil turned on the heater to help it out. We grew hotter and thirstier as the minutes ticked past. Later we heard that a rally car had broken down on the bridge and then caught fire, thus holding up the traffic on two continents.

At last, we crept over the wide neck of water. Anticlimactically, we were back in Europe. We made it to the control just within our time.

On a rest day in Istanbul, with fantasy Phil at my side, there would have been a boat ride on the Bosphorus and lunch at one of the little floating restaurants, and then as the strong sunshine faded towards evening, a trip to the Blue Mosque. I had done all these things before and had no need to repeat them for myself, but I would have liked to share them with him.

Real Phil was as monofocal as ever. The car was booked in for a major service, and whilst most drivers would have been happy to hand over the keys for once, Phil wanted to be in on it.

Tony Barrett had made the arrangements from London, in his own quirky way. Instead of asking Volvo for an introduction to their local agent, he had gone to the Turkish owners of the greasy spoon café around the corner from the arches, where Phil and I had had so many of our starry-eyed pre-rally planning meetings. They had given him the name and address of a mechanic, and it was these details on a scrap of paper that I showed to the Turkish facilitator at the rally desk. The man made a phone call, and it was arranged that the café connection should come to the hotel to meet us and look at the Amazon An hour or so later he duly showed up, a good looking man with a shy smile who did not speak a word of English. Even so, he and Phil were immediately the best of friends, with a cheeky hotel bellboy acting as interpreter.

It was agreed that they would take the car off to the inspection pit and strengthen their pair bonding over the socket set. There was clearly no role for me in this scenario.

'I'll be back later,' Phil called over his shoulder. 'We'll go and look at the Blue Mosque.'

I wandered over to look at the rally notice board.

Idly, I read the order list. All the cars in the running ahead of us were serious contenders – the Willys jeep men, the Peykans, the Catts and the other rallyists. The two white Ford coupés were there, and Kurt Dichtl in his Silver Dawn, and Jon and Adam, the Dangerfields and sure and steady Murray Kayll, and Thomas and Maria. It would take a major upheaval to shake any of these out of position and now, according to RO, the competition was more or less over. If we could keep the car going we would reach Paris and win our gold medal, but Phil and I had resigned ourselves to climbing no higher than twenty-first place. Just cruelly short of our target.

I read the list again.

It put us in *twentieth* place.

Which name was missing from the familiar sequence ahead of us?

It took me two more minutes to work out that it was Chris and Howard. Inexplicably, they were now six places behind us. I was deeply pleased to be in the top twenty again at last, but that it should be at the expense of the Camaro boys took the shine off it somewhat.

For a solo celebration I called a taxi and went to the Istanbul shopping mall. It wasn't noticeably different from Brent Cross, and I spent a therapeutic hour at the Clinique counter as well as mumsily stocking up on fresh supplies of socks and underpants for real Phil. I was at the hotel in good time to go sightseeing, but a series of telephone messages from the garage kept putting the departure hour back and back. Phil was as happy as the dog with two choc-ices again, becoming meta-friends with half the mechanics in Turkey. They had changed the ignition, he told me. If there should be a snap scrutineering in an attempt to catch out some of the more blatant rule-breakers, we would have nothing to hide. Instead of visiting the sights I had tea with the Aan de Stegges and their Citroen mechanic. And at last, feeling for the first time since Palandoken that I could look at a real drink again, I went to the HQ hotel to see who I could find.

Colin was at the bar. We had one of those long,

inclusive talks that stuck out for me like isolated and precious signposts along the rally road. He told me that he and Melissa's father had been friends since boyhood. A series of tragedies had befallen Melissa's uncles, and a spiritualist told the family that the gods were angry with them. As soon as Melissa was born her parents went through the ceremony of handing the baby over to Colin, who was to divert the attention of the gods by becoming her father He had helped to look after her ever since, and he had taught her to ride a bicycle and scuba dive and taken her on camping trips.

'Her parents are not outdoor people,' he smiled, 'so I did that for her.'

I thought how lucky Melissa was to have him. In turn I told him about Charlie and Flora, and my own share of good luck.

When Phil finally came back it was too late for sightseeing, but we were in good time for dinner.

The organisers had advised us that the evening's programme would be a formal dinner in the HQ hotel followed by an interim prizegiving. We were all to attend, decently dressed. Accordingly the bad crowd went out to dinner elsewhere, dressed as we pleased. Colin and Melissa had arranged it, and after a taxi ride up and down the switchback hills of Istanbul's side streets we found ourselves in an elegant riverboat restaurant right under the great piers of the Bosphorus Bridge. Trev and Jingers were with us, and Chris and Howard, and Carolyn with her husband who had flown out to meet her – bringing with him a sharp navy-blue brass-buttoned blazer for Howard. Wearing it, Howard looked suddenly citified.

There were some women relatives of Melissa's too, and the presence of these new faces made a schizophrenic vibration for all of us between the time-warp of the rally and the reality of civilisation.

We sat around a big, white-clothed round table with the Bosphorus waters glinting alongside us – we were just tethered to the flank of Europe. Waiters in evening dress brought fish soup and pan-fried seabass and bottles of champagne, and it was like balancing on the lip of two different worlds. It was almost all over. Soon we would all be back in our metaphorical navy-blue blazers. Except for Phil, perhaps. I hoped that Phil would go on adventuring, and carrying the cargo of our deferred fantasies with him.

I sat between Howard and Trev. On the one side Howard and Carolyn and the others talked about money and sex and mobile phones, and we might have been at any dinner party in Chelsea or Gloucestershire, and on the other Trev chatted engagingly about crews and cars and bike racing, just as we had been doing all the way from China. It was a bit of a conversational balancing act, but I enjoyed it. Once in a while, I caught Phil's eye across the table.

'What happened yesterday?' I asked Chris, as soon as I had a chance. He was at his most Eeyorish.

'Time control,' he said lugubriously. 'Missed the stamp at the morning one. Thought it had been changed to a passage control, not the afternoon one.'

Just for this, they had incurred a 240-minute penalty and lost their gold medal.

'Haven't quite worked out who was to blame. We agreed on both of us.'

I thought this was democratic behaviour. Just to contemplate what would have happened if I had made a similar mistake made me shiver and reach quickly for my drink.

There had been some other disasters too. David and Andrew's land crab had broken down two days out of Istanbul. They put it on a truck, with directions that it was to be driven to Istanbul to meet them, and gloomily travelled onwards by bus. When I bumped into him at the hotel on the first night, Andrew was gloomier still. The car and the truck had both vanished.

David Arrigo and Willem Caruana had had endless setbacks in the Allard, but they had refused to give up. They had accompanied it on and off trucks and in and out of repair shops, they had slept at the roadside and in huts, and they finally caught up with the rally once more in Istanbul. They were ready to drive on into Greece.

The land crab and the truck did materialise in the end. David Wilks spent the Turkish rest day repairing his damaged engine, and was also ready to move on with the rest of the rally.

Sixty-six cars left Istanbul still in the main Challenge, and sixteen in the touring category.

I thought back to the prediction RO and the mechanics had made in China, that just twenty-nine cars would reach the Place de la Concorde.

All the organisers and officials were surprised by the powers of endurance of the cars and the tenacity of so many of the competitors. We would hear that this car or that one had blown its engine, holed a piston or suffered complete electrical failure, and was definitely out for

good. Then two days later it would reappear, restored and
still running, with its crew exhausted but triumphant. In
Istanbul I also saw Adèle Cohen, who with her husband
had entered in the Stutz that had had to pull out before
Lanzhou. Now she told me that they had been so determined not to miss the end of the rally that they had
driven one of their *other* vintage cars, this one a Bentley,
out to Istanbul and would be accompanying the field
onwards to Paris. RO had forbidden them to sport their
rally plates on the replacement car.

The gossip went that RO had only had five gold medals
made for presentation at the prizegiving. It seemed now
that he would need five times that many. Phil and I were
sure that one of them would be ours. And we were going
to hold on to our 20th place, come what may.

Europe seemed very small. And very beautiful.

We left Istanbul in the dark, at 6.30 in the morning,
and drove to the Greek border. We were subject to
European speed limits now, and to police who wouldn't
necessarily wave us past with a blind-eye salute. The pace
seemed much slower; it was as if we suddenly found ourselves on a motoring holiday after struggling so far.

Inside Greece we stopped for lunch at a roadside bar,
with JD and Dan and Melissa and Colin. There were scarlet geraniums in blue-painted tin cans ranged along the
top of the wall, and a table under a vine pergola and feta
salad to eat. It felt like an imposition to have to buckle
myself into the car seat again afterwards, to zero the trip
and open the route notes, instead of heading for the
beach. We drove onwards in convoy, around the curve of

the Aegean and through Kaválla to Thessaloníki, and even Phil was feeling mellow enough to accept the leisurely pace. Melissa was fast asleep in the navigator's seat of the Porsche with her headphones clamped over her ears. Colin found his way by following the Amazons. The stages were easy, no one lost any time.

At Thessaloníki we found a huge, rectangular summer-holiday hotel looking out over the harbour. It was one of those places where each room opened on to a little box of a balcony furnished with a white plastic table and two white plastic chairs. From our high balcony I leaned down to look at the cars lining up all over again, this time with the olive-green harbour water behind them. Gulls were dipping over the rubbish lapping against the sea wall, and the salt moisture in the air flattened and muffled the roar of engines turning over.

I could see Phil, running oily hands through his hair, and even at this distance I could tell he was doing the face thing.

'What's wrong?' I made myself ask when I went down to join him.

'It's the rear wheel bearing.'

'Show me?'

'I'm not going to take it apart now. But look, there's a lot of play. And this grumbling noise.'

He rolled the wheel and I laughed at first, remembering how Dan had told me that he had run out of words to describe the cacophony of different noises their car was emitting. A mere grumbling sound didn't seem to come very high up the scale.

'Have we got a spare?'

'One bearing, and a half-shaft. No bearing cap. And I've never replaced a bearing before. I know it's a big job.'

I wondered, very briefly, how it was that he and Mr Mechanic had managed to spend a whole expensive day at the garage yesterday, exchanging little presents and taking photographs of each other in front of the car, *without getting round to checking the wheel bearings.*

'Well. What shall we do?'

Phil looked unhappy. 'I think we'll have to run on tomorrow, and see how much worse it gets.'

It appeared that we didn't have any choice in the matter, as usual.

I knew that somewhere in Thessaloníki there would be the little fantasy restaurant. There was even the right scent in the air of salt and diesel fumes and fresh fish. But the boys were getting fidgety. England was playing Italy in the World Cup qualifier, and it was becoming essential to find a bar with a television tuned to the sports channel.

I left them to their pleasures and ate a solitary picnic in the hotel bedroom with a copy of *Elle* belonging to Melissa. I hadn't had a book to read since I had jettisoned them all to save weight, long, long ago in Golmud. The only one I held on to was a little Faber paperback of *The Waste Land*, and I had given that as a present to Melissa. I missed it in the desert. (*Come in under the shadow of this red rock. I will show you fear in a handful of dust.* Fear everywhere, but exhilaration also. That was the balancing act, to be able to set one successfully against the other – managing real life's Rally Syndrome.)

The last weeks were the longest time I had ever spent
without reading matter. On the walk to Everest I had
carried *Wives and Daughters* in my rucksack. In the real
world I was careful about never, ever running out of books
to choose from, and I dreaded a tube journey or a
doctor's waiting room without a novel to see me through.

When I was a little girl there weren't very many books
at home and only the glass-fronted cupboard in the big
room of my primary school, where the Everest book lived,
had stood between me and the dry canyons of fictionless
boredom. Books were a shelter rather than a resource in
those days and I read blindly and utterly indiscrimi-
nately – Enid Blyton, *Tarka the Otter*, *Angel Pavement* and
Reader's Digest. The County Library visited once a
month, with flaking hardbacks piled in big metal-cor-
nered wooden boxes that were fastened with a padlock on
a hasp, like the treasure chests they were. Later there was
the Travelling Library, a big van that stopped on the village square once a fortnight and offered library editions
of Ian Fleming and Hammond Innes and later still, at
boarding school, every book that we owned had to be
inspected and initialled as suitable by a member of staff.
Bad books – I was able to discriminate by then – were
accepted as readily as good ones. Suitable, I suppose, was
defined as containing no sex or swearing. By the same
token we were only allowed to have the Third Programme
on the radio on Sundays, and never any pop records with
vocals.

I was a scholarship girl, on a free place. When new
textbooks were handed out at the beginning of the year, I
could always tell which one was mine in the pile by the

missing jacket and shredded spine, just as the free uniform with which I was provided was always in the style that had recently been replaced by something more attractive. (Attractive being a relative term, of course.) This treatment, instead of teaching me humility and the unimportance of material goods, gave me a raging desire for designer clothes as well as a passion for the shine and scent of an unbroken hardback novel.

Yet on this trip I had hardly missed the tottering piles of books beside my bed. My mind was already over-stuffed with images and impressions, and mental as well as physical exhaustion dumbed and flattened me. But now, tonight, I longed for a book. Magazine journalese was thin and unnourishing. It was another indication that this disturbing adventure was coming to an end. In a week, exactly, we would be at the prizegiving Ball in Paris. I was counting the hours, but I was also trying to imagine how it would feel to be summarily cut off from all these people and their cars and concerns and vanities, which had become so familiar, as well as from the daily business of distances and minutes and mechanical stress.

A week to go, and 2,500 kilometres to cover. If the wheel bearings held out.

There had been some rumours that the next day, from Thessaloníki past Mount Olympus and over some of the old Acropolis Rally routes to the little seaside resort of Kamena Vourla, was going to be a tough one. The marshals had made amendments to the route notes, bringing forward time controls and shortening the time allowances, so it seemed that they were pushing us a little harder and hoping for a shake-up in the order. Phil was quietly worried about the bearings, but after checking them at the end of the first stage he announced that there seemed to be no significant deterioration.

We had a full hour to spare before our time came up, on a long slope of empty hillside. It was a windy, silvery morning with a cold bite in the air. Adam and Jon pulled in alongside us.

'There's a bar back down in the village. Come and have a coffee.'

We climbed up on the back of the Bentley and Adam accelerated away down the hill. Rally cars coming to meet us flashed their lights and hooted. Holding on tight, looking down over Jon's head as the wind forced laughter up out of my chest and peeled my eyes, I saw the plain old dials of the Jaeger instruments, and the dark-green leather curves of the seats. I wanted to stroke them. I was fond of the old Amazon, but it never stirred my admiration the way that this car did. That was something I had learned, which had seemed incomprehensible on the day at Brooklands – it was possible to fall in love with a car. Phil loved our Volvo, too. Technically it was mine, I suppose, because I had bought it and paid for it to be prepared and it was my name in the logbook and on the insurance papers, but it was Phil who had devoted so many months of his time and attention to it.

When we reached Paris, or London once again, I knew I couldn't just thank him for his contribution and ask for the keys.

I would have to give it to him: I wanted him to have it. Anyway, I couldn't even drive the bloody thing.

We reached the café and I lingered for a minute

outside, flirting with the Bentley and taking a picture to remember it by. The boys went inside, laughing at something, and when I followed them they were sitting at a table with a mirror behind it.

The sight of our reflections in the sooty glass stopped me short.

We had been driving and living and eating and drinking as a little group for so long and there had been scant opportunity for examining my appearance. I had *forgotten* I wasn't thirty, like them.

For a moment I was shocked, and embarrassed in case I had been guilty of some lapse of taste related to this oversight, and also envious. Why should I be – and look – so much older and tireder than they were, when there seemed so little difference between us?

But then.

I knew what I was going home to, and what it had taken to achieve it. Phil was a loner, Jon was single. Adam was married with a baby, but he was still at the beginning of everything. And because I had been away, and thought about home from an uncomfortable vantage point, I also knew how much I valued it – that old cliché of travel. The almost twenty years that I had ahead of Phil and the others hadn't been stolen from me, nor were they empty. They were prizes that we had won, and their past tense made them invulnerable to any of the fears that even I could conjure up.

The barman put a thimble cup of viscous Greek coffee in front of me. I looked at fantasy Phil blondly posing in his leather flying jacket, and saw the sexy nose of the Bentley beyond the door, and the yellow leaves dropping from a pergola, and it was a moment of serene happiness and perfect contentment.

Such moments are, by very definition, short-lived.

On the way out of the time control Phil leaned over and busily but mistakenly zeroed the upper trip for me. Which inconveniently left me without a running total of the distance travelled against which to check our position and the intermediate instructions.

'Why did you do that? It makes my job much harder.'

'I'm sorry.'

'The navigating *is* my job. Don't try to take that over as well as everything else.'

'I'm sorry, okay? I made a mistake.'

The onward journey was less than cordial. We were passing the flying monasteries at Meteora. They looked like illustrations in a book of fairy stories, castles set on a magic pinnacle, but yet again there was barely time to glance, let alone to consider.

The lunch-time control was at a place called Kalabáka. There was a hotel and a restaurant, but Phil had already spotted a garage across the road and pulled in there. He jacked the car to examine the rear axle once again, and Dave Bull came over to confer. Dave's Rover was suffering problems with the bearings too. The two of them agreed that they could only continue for the rest of the day, with constant checking for possible deterioration.

Most uncharacteristically, Phil hadn't eaten the mid-morning snack of a cold fried-egg sandwich that I made him every day from the hotel breakfast provisions. Usually he demanded it within half an hour of leaving the start.

'I feel sick,' he announced now.

Immediately I went to stock up on bottled water and
tissues and wet-wipes from the garage shop, secretly
pleased with the idea that he might, for a change, need
me to look after him.

'Tell me if you're going to be ill,' I said as he drove on.

He regarded me hollowly. 'Nah. I'll just open the door
and puke.'

He didn't even do that. An hour later he was asking me
what there was for him to eat.

It was a stirring afternoon, driving through the foothills
of Mount Olympus and negotiating a special gravelly off-
road stage that took us over tight bends through thick
conifer forests. At one point we rounded a sharp corner
and saw RO at the roadside watching us fly past.

'Fuck, missed him,' Phil said drolly. 'Shall we go back
and try again?'

It was fun but the time allowances were still generous,
and if they were easy for us they were also easy for everyone ahead of us. We weren't going to climb any higher up
the order on today's showing, although we heard later
that the Dutchmen Harm and Tonnie had managed to
crash their Amazon by skidding sideways into a bridge.
They were still running but they lost 76 minutes as a
result, slipping below Dan and JD in the list.

Team Amazon now represented the top two Volvos.

There was another time control in a gilded valley near
the site of the battle of Thermopylae. Wandering up the
dusty road, tired and dreamy with the extravagant
scenery, I found Thomas and Maria sitting at a table
under a tree with a fruiting vine scrambling through the
branches. Thomas beckoned me over.

'Have a drink, Rosie.'

There was a silver-gilt flask on the table, and four silver-gilt nesting cups. I took the cup he gave me and tasted. It was a large shot of vodka, in which a peeled quarter of a luscious ripe fig was marinating.

I told the Noors, with a smile hooked to my ears, 'I think that's the best drink I have ever had in my entire life.'

Thomas and Maria were so cool and Continental, just as Howard and Chris were cool in a rather different, ironic-Brit style. Real Phil and I, by contrast, were a deep-litter, oily, egg-sandwich shambles of suppurating uncool. I was reflecting mildly on this as I pottered onwards to the marshals.

The neat vodka hit the bottom of my empty stomach like a bite out of a hot chilli pepper. Motherly Betty and her partner were leaning against the bonnet of the Frontera with the chequered flag hanging loose beside them. Hmm, hanging loose, like me, I thought and beamed vaguely. I handed over my book with a cheery flourish.

'Car 82, due 15.24.'

Betty gave a little gasp, but it was too late. I raised my eyebrows at the rally clock on the Frontera bonnet. It showed 15.23 and fifty seconds and she was already writing 15.23 in my book, which gave me a one-minute penalty. And, since early arrival carried a double charge, my little interlude with the vodka had cost us two minutes. I went back to the car and owned up to Phil, reckoning that this cancelled out the fiddling with my Terratrip. He took the news rather frostily. It wasn't our best day together.

The road led onwards around the beaches of the western Aegean, and over hillsides policed with cypresses, through Lamía to Kamena Vourla and the night's stopping place. It was a pretty little town, with harbour restaurants already opening to catch the end-of-season business, and an empty hotel overlooking the rippled sea. The local rally club was out in force to greet us, with their classic and vintage cars all polished up. Inside in the deserted bar, RO stepped out in front of Phil and me.

'You were going well today.'

'We always are,' Phil answered as we passed by. It was the only remark RO addressed to us over the whole trip.

Phil and I took our glasses of ouzo outside and sat by the pool in the slanting light. There was a fringe of leaves floating on the chilly water, an overturned chair in the uncut grass, and lights reflected from the branched lamp standards on the terrace. Birds were coming to roost in the spruce and maple trees, and I could hear the throaty putter of a vintage car arriving to a polite round of clapping. In the bar, someone was picking out a tune on the piano. All these falling cadences were melancholically appropriate. We were almost there, it was almost over.

'I'm going to look at the bearings.'

'Of course.'

I finished off my drink on my own.

It was bad news. The day's special stages and slightly increased speed had wreaked more damage. After an inspection, Jingers' verdict was that one bearing was in bad shape, the other dreadful. They would both have to be replaced; the first problem was to find appropriate parts. Fortunately, I learned from the mechanically literate, bearings were universal rather than specific to Volvo. We consulted Theo Voukidis, who had the necessary local expertise. His suggestion was that we get up very early in the morning and take a taxi back to Lamia; tonight, being a Sunday, was no good.

It was getting dark now. We sat in the dust, the picture of disheartenment. If the bearings went altogether, before Phil could replace them, we'd be on a truck to Paris. To have come so far, and to lose our gold medal . . . To have come so far and not to make it at all . . .

Dan and JD had been working under their own car, but Dan came over to talk. He told us that both their rear shock mountings had started to crack again, but he couldn't face going out to have more welding done. Their speedometer cable had broken too, so they had no Terratrip or mileometer to navigate by.

'We'll have to follow you the rest of the way,' he said.

'Doesn't look like we'll be going much further,' I sighed.

Phil stood up, wiping his forehead with the back of his hand.

'I'm going to see if I can bodge it up with what we've got.'

He started stripping down the back axle. Brake fluid spurted out of a tube. The clamp light he was working under slipped and I tried to wedge it more securely.

'Will you see if you can find someone with some bearings grease?' he asked.

I trudged around the emptying car park. Carolyn and Chris and Howard and Melissa were all going out to dinner at a nice place on the harbour. I wanted to go with them, very badly. I wanted to go with Phil even more, but it was just dawning on me that the little place with the white cloths was never going to materialise. Most of all, I was profoundly tired of hovering in the dirt around jacked-up cars, fetching beers and finding spanners and feeling helpless and yet obliged to help.

Andrew Snelling gave me a murky tin of bearings grease. Werner Esch was just locking up his Mercedes for the night. I knew that Werner had a garage business at home in Luxembourg; he was knowledgeable about all kinds of cars.

I tried my luck. 'Werner, could you spare five minutes to look at the Amazon? I think Phil's out of his depth.'

Werner liked Phil, as everyone did. He came at once. Two minutes later he was in his shirtsleeves, underneath the rear axle.

I sat and watched. It was plainly a hideous job but it was a pleasure to see Werner working because he did it so deftly and surely. Dan and Phil were adept enough, but they still quite often did things on a trial and error basis.

The pitted bearing was lifted up for us to examine, and then filled with grease. I wrote down the Timkins numbers of the spares we would need to buy tomorrow, and our ally smoothly and unhesitatingly slotted the pieces of the axle together again. It was fascinating, in a slightly appalling way. Not only had I learned that you could fall in love with a car, I could also see that there was poetry in motor mechanics.

It was too late to go out to eat. The hotel dining room was our only option, where the food was bad and the service slow and grudging. None of this was Phil's fault, my ill-humour least of all, but I took it out on him. I went to bed angry, and got up in the morning in the same frame of mind.

'It was really good, the little place where we ate last night,' Carolyn told me as we waited for the morning start.

I brooded on the blurred, tempting glimpses of so many places, and the sights I had missed altogether because Phil had been obsessed with the car and because out of some sense of loyalty – misplaced – I had stayed to support him.

When I talked about this to Dan he said bluntly, 'I don't know why you didn't go out to smart dinners and sightseeing with Chris and Howard and Carolyn, instead of hanging around in all those car parks. Phil didn't want you there.'

That hurt.

We had to drive to the car ferry at Patras. It was another beautiful day, on a route that led us westwards through blue and sepia hills past Mount Parnassós. There were a couple of short stages, up and down hairpin bends, but nothing that caused any of us to lose time. It seemed that RO was right, the real competition had ended at Istanbul, but the challenge for us was now the heart-in-mouth business of whether the car would hold out. At every control, Phil jumped out to listen to the noise the rotating wheels made, and to check the amount of play. We communicated in terse half-sentences.

In the middle of the day, we were passing through an

exquisite little hill town. There was a square lined with
cafés and shaded with plane trees, and a view over tiled
roofs to the mountains. Phil looked sideways at me.

'Do you want to stop for a coffee?'

'Yes, please,' I smiled at him, at the same time disconcerted to be so easily mollified.

He drove on, past another half-dozen inviting little
places, and came to the outskirts of the town. In such a
lovely spot it would have been hard to find a drab corner,
although this came close. There was a fuel station, and a
little hotel next to it with a doorway opening on to the
street. Phil pulled into the garage forecourt and, discovering to his disappointment that it didn't have a drinks
vending machine, he went into the hotel and brought
out two cups of coffee. He put mine into my hand and
nodded to a white plastic chair beside the fuel pumps.

'I'm going to see if I can buy the spares,' he said, and
went.

After a little while JD and Dan came by and saw me sitting there. I told them the story of real Phil stopping for
coffee.

'It's a metaphor for the whole trip. In the heart of clas-
sical Greece, taking a break on a filling station forecourt.'

It was hard not to laugh, and after a minute I did so. It
was funny, and it was also such a neat illustration of the
space between us. I wanted a view and congenial company and a memory to store away, and Phil wanted a hot
drink, to fix the car, and no hassle. While I was still laughing I thought I had the answer to all those magazine
articles and pieces of pop polemic that ask what women
really want. What they want is exactly, completely

definable as what men don't want, although they try to pretend that they do. Partly.

We reached the ferry terminal at Patras via the motorway along the coast, switchbacking past a series of little bays and sunlit beaches. Once we were through the time control at the terminal gates we joined a mass of rally cars waiting to board the Ancona boat. Phil disappeared yet again in search of the elusive bearings and caps, and I was in charge of the Amazon. I was sitting on a low wall talking to David Brister when our words were briefly drowned by what we took to be the rumble and vibration of an exceptionally heavy passing truck. A while later we learned, via the satellite news on the television in the booking office, that it had been an *earthquake* with its epi-centre in Greece.

I looked over my shoulder. The ferry port was sunnily busy and unaffected, but Phil had been gone for a long time. I was anxious about him, even now.

The line of cars moved forward and I was left staring at the Volvo. The keys dangled in the ignition. I would probably have to negotiate a steep ramp and a series of manoeuvres directed by impatient Greek seamen in the tight, booming confines of the ship's bowels. I was supposed to be an adventurer, a round-the-world rally competitor, and I knew I couldn't drive this car on board that ship. My hands went sweaty and my mouth dried at the thought. I didn't even have the most basic motoring confidence left. I despised myself for this weakness, but it was a fact.

I ran to find Dan.

'Will you drive our car on board?'

'Of course.'

He raced it forward to a new queue configuration. There was still some more waiting to be done.

It was dark when Phil eventually returned, with the spares.

'Well done,' I said stiffly. I had been relieved to see him back safely, out of the earthquake's imagined rubble, but it didn't last.

'Thank you,' he responded equally stiffly.

He drove the car into the ship's hold, where it was locked up and placed out of bounds. It was going to be a 20-hour journey across the Adriatic to Ancona, Italy, and there was to be no work done on any of the cars whilst the ship was under way. The bearings would have to wait for attention until tomorrow night, in Rimini, if we could make it that far. We had a neat little cabin, one narrow bunk above and one below, no space to move around each other.

'Why did you have to ask Dan to drive the car for you?'

'How do you know about that?'

'He told me. Couldn't wait to tell me.'

'Why do you *think* I had to ask him?'

Within seconds we were having an argument, a proper, stand-up, door-slamming row, weighty with bitterness and resentment. Like any married couple on the downhill slope. Our parody marriage was breaking up fast, and unfortunately it was doing so in just the same ugly way as a real one.

After I slammed the door and found myself outside in the corridor it occurred to me that like a typical dysfunctional couple, Phil and I had clung together somewhat in the last few days. I couldn't immediately recall when I had last spent time with anyone in the group without him being there – it had probably only been a week ago, but quite short intervals in real time stretched into aeons by the rally clock. I felt awkward, going into the crowded bar, like a newly separated wife.

I had dinner with Carolyn, and David and Willem from the Allard. Later, in the distance at the far end of the saloon, I could see Phil drinking and talking with a group of the men. After dinner I went to bed and slept, and when I woke up in the morning he was still asleep in the bunk overhead. I went to breakfast and he appeared and sat elsewhere, and I plodded back to the cabin and lay on my bunk intending to have a clear think about how to negotiate the way out of this impasse and onwards to Paris.

The door opened and Phil sidled around it. We looked warily at one another.

'Come and lie down,' I said, and he did so. At least the rabbit-in-the-headlamps look had gone. We put our arms around each other and our heads together, and listened to the steady note of the ship's engines.

'Talk to me.'

'What about?'

'Anything you like. Last night.'

'I was talking to the guys in the bar. They were saying it can't be easy for me, being with you, the way you are.'

'Ah. And how is the way I am?' I was thinking hard. We had been travelling for a long, difficult time, but I couldn't recall that any of those people had seen anything but my public face. Unlike Phil, who had seen some faces – up the hairpins and at the roadside on the icy plateau and across the desert – that I hadn't even known I possessed.

'You seem very controlled and confident and dismissive. People – men – find you frightening.'

I digested this information. It is disconcerting to find that the external image is completely at odds with the view from inside. I knew it was a wrong assessment; I was often meaninglessly angry, much more with my awkward self than with the more amenable world, and I understood that my anger might give me an intimidating aspect. But it was rooted in weakness and bereavement and defensiveness, and it did not give rise to confidence or self-control, only the crack-glazed superficial veneer of them. I also knew that my lack of self esteem was innate. It was too late to eradicate it but I figured that acknowledging the problem went part of the way to compensating for it – something like the way that accepting that you have curly hair for better or for worse finally helps you to stop fiddling about with straightening lotions and hair dryers.

'I'm only just finding out that you aren't confident at all, even though you seem to have achieved everything anyone could want. It isn't just your driving you aren't sure of.'

I smiled with my face against his shoulder. It was very comfortable there after so many weeks of being fended off.

'You're right.'

'I thought we were different. But you are the same as me.'

'How is that?'

Very carefully at first, unpractised, Phil began to talk about himself.

The things he told me belong to him, but in his confiding he gave me the piece of himself that I had sought ever since we met. And I hadn't been able to reach for it before because I had made the blind-eyed mistake – a very big mistake, much bigger than the one his friends in the bar had made about me, because I was closer to him – of accepting the version of himself that he projected on the world.

Phil wasn't invulnerable or even impervious. He was just almost impregnably defended. Once or twice on the journey I had suspected it, but it had taken until now for us to read each other properly.

We had more or less unthinkingly embarked on an adventure together that meant we had to be capable, and to appear so to one another. Phil had tried to be infallible and I had overplayed my weaknesses so as, in a way, to diminish them. Without those responses, and the partial subterfuges that they involved, we would probably have understood each other quicker and much better.

But it didn't really matter, I thought. We had achieved a friendship now.

We lay for a long time and talked, while the sea churned blue-grey past the porthole. It was one of the best, for me, one of the happiest and the most valuable moments of the whole adventure. Real connections with another human being are the most elusive and the most satisfying achievements of life. That was another discovery I had had confirmed for me on this motorised odyssey.

In the end, naturally, Phil started to think about food. He turned my wrist to look at my watch – his was amongst the trail of possessions he had mislaid along the way.

'Time for lunch.'

He rolled off the bunk and fidgeted around the cabin.

'Or we could stay here, and I'll shag the arse off you . . .'

He was being ironic, of course.

To indicate as much he had chosen the most quintessentially Philistine of the wide variety of philistine expressions available to him. (I reviewed the other possibilities. *A good seeing-to* was probably near the top of the list.) He was also acknowledging what might be expected of him in the cosy situation in which we now found ourselves, and politely making a humorous nod towards it, as well as reinforcing his projected image as a man ready and able to deal with whatever bizarre emergency might crop up between the Great Wall and the Place de la Concorde.

He wasn't nearly as obtuse as he pretended to be, and he certainly wasn't insensitive.

For me, just briefly, fantasy Phil and real Phil slid together and almost coalesced. He had a blurred outline, rather like an imperfectly registered colour print, but it was near enough a complete picture to be tempting. He wasn't even wearing the sheikh's turban, and in that minute I still fancied him.

I said, 'Lunch, I think.'

For a full nanosecond afterwards I regretted the decision.

'Oh-*kay*,' he agreed, with apparent relief.

We went to lunch, laughing merrily.

Phil spent the afternoon playing backgammon with the Iranians, and I stared out of the saloon windows at the flat blue Adriatic.

We docked at Ancona in the early evening. On my way down to be reunited with the Amazon I passed the driver of the Bentley Continental having a huge altercation with a pair of stewards and the ship's purser outside an empty cabin.

'All gone, all my luggage, stolen,' the man was shouting. He waved at the bare interior. 'I want the thief caught. Maybe it's an Albanian stowaway.'

The Bentley boys had struck again.

Chapter Fifteen

It was a short dash up the motorway from the port of Ancona to Rimini. The car just about held out, although the grumbling of the bearings turned to an outright clamour.

There was a huge storm as we drove, with slabs of water driven up by truck tyres sluicing the windscreen, and pale tongues of lightning licking the dark sky. Summer was over. Rimini itself was huddled behind the rainwashed seafront, the network of deserted streets shiny under the deluge and patched with soaking fallen leaves.

It was a joy to be in Italy. The hotel was old, and plain, and dinner was waiting for us as soon as we arrived. It was as if I had requested my fantasy meal in advance. There was *antipasti* including rucola salad – how I had wished for rocket, back in Iran – and pasta with tuna and asparagus, and grilled swordfish, and tiny fruit tarts, and good red wine from the Veneto, and the best coffee I had ever tasted. We ate with JD and Dan and Colin, and the Doreys, and Pim Bentinck from the Railton Straight 8 and his two co-drivers. There was a lot of laughing and refilling of plates and waving for more wine. Phil and I gave the meal our full attention, in anticipation of the night to come.

It was 11 p.m. when we finally went out to address ourselves to the bearings.

Phil had persuaded the receptionist to find us a place in the underground car park, so at least he wouldn't have to work outside in the downpour. There was a steep ramp leading up to the street and a navy-blue square of rainy night sky at the top of it, and down in the hotel's bowels the car waiting for attention in the close beam of clamp lights, like a patient on the operating table.

At first Phil had plenty of company and the benefit of more advice than he could assimilate. Dan and JD joined in and Dave Bull came to watch; he had decided that he would leave his Rover's bearings as they were and trust to luck. Jonathan Lux's co-driver David Drew had rejoined the rally at Istanbul, and he came to offer his opinion as a mechanic. Jingers was eager to help too, but RO had warned all the official mechanics that they were not allowed to help out competitors except in roadside breakdowns or emergencies. It was funny to see Jingers sliding forwards to look at the axle as it was dismantled, and then skipping backwards with a furtive glance over his shoulder in case anyone should suspect he was involved in the work.

Time passed. Midnight came and went, and the crowd of advisers thinned considerably. The half-shafts were removed from the axle casing and the new bearings fitted on to the ends. Reassembly should have been a tedious but straightforward process, but it was not going smoothly. By 1 a.m. only Dan and JD were left of our original supporters, and then JD yawningly announced that he must go to bed or fall asleep where he stood.

Phil and Dan worked on and I sat on a spare tyre, remembering what Dan had said but still wanting at least to be there.

Michael Kunz, the navigator from the Triumph Vitesse that was two places and 20 minutes ahead of us, came unsteadily down the ramp to see what we were doing. He was beamingly, owlishly drunk.

'C'n I get you guys a *drink*?'

He fetched beers for Phil and Dan and a cup of chocolate for me that was more like a bowl of hot melted mousse.

'S'what's happnin?'

Phil and Dan weren't very communicative, but Mike didn't seem to mind. At length he drifted away again.

I put some sad cello music in the cassette player. The clamp lights threw highlights on Phil and Dan's frowning faces as they moved around the car, and cast elongated shadows over the concrete floor. The darkness seemed to thicken in the recesses of the car park. Sitting on my tyre in the chiaroscuro I thought it was like being in a picture by Rembrandt: *Portrait of Mechanics At Work* maybe. I didn't share this artistic insight with them.

They kept reassembling the axle and finding that it locked tight. The rear wheels would not turn, and so they would have to strip it down all over again and slide little plates of metal called shims in between the hub and the axle casing, to change the pressure of the half-shafts against the differential.

I watched this routine two or three times, and each time they put the wheels back on there was the same problem, or else there was too much play in the propshaft which was the opposite symptom.

It was now three in the morning. The rear end of the car was entirely dismantled, there was brake fluid and bearings grease everywhere. I resisted the impulse to whine to Phil, 'But what if you can't fix it in time for the start?'

I did ask him some trivial question, and he snapped back, unsurprisingly enough. They were both deeply weary. It was generous of Dan to have stayed up all this time.

I judged that it was the right moment to leave, and quietly slipped away to bed. There was some commotion and shouting and crashing going on downstairs in the lobby, but in the end everything went quiet.

I was still awake when Phil eventually came in.

'Fixed?' I asked when he lay down beside me.

'Fixed.'

It was 5.30, and there was a grey smudge of light over the sea. With a 7.45 alarm call to come, it seemed hardly worth going to sleep.

In the morning I heard the story. The problem was that they had taken the axle apart and begun reassembling it from the wrong side, so it had been a process of trial and error to put it back again with the shims as spacers against the differential gears. At last there had been a breakthrough of understanding, and we now had impeccable new wheel bearings.

'Well done.'

'Thank you.'
Beep.
Rimini to Maranello, 229 km.

Maranello was always referred to in conversation as 'legendary Maranello' although it was hardly a legend in my book, since I had never heard of it. It turned out to be – as it was also invariably described – 'the birthplace of Ferrari'.

The route to our lunch-time rendezvous with some red cars involved a morning of steep hill climbs through San Marino. Our Amazon went like a dream. The aftermath of the storm was a clear day with the sun drawing the mist off the vineyards and warming the stone campaniles on the hilltops. We negotiated precipitous hills, and twisting lanes between red and russet woodlands that occasionally opened up to give a view of the blue sea in the distance.

The distances were short and the navigating more demanding, particularly because the marshals had introduced an extra test – some secret passage controls that had to be carefully watched out for. Road book stamps had to be collected at these passage points as well as at the time controls.

It was a good day. Phil and I were cheerful, and happy to be together.

'We can't quarrel any more,' we insisted to each other. 'There isn't enough time left to make up again.'

After crossing the Rubicon river, like Caesar, we drove on towards Modena and Maranello. At a fuel stop we went into a bar for espressos, and I heard the story of last night's noisy outburst in the hotel lobby from the mouth of the protagonist himself.

He had been out to a bar, and had picked up a woman – a big, strapping one. They had returned to the hotel together to do some more drinking and the driver had happened to murmur to the night porter that he had met his prize in the such-and-such bar.

'Which bar did you say?' the porter asked.

A famous transvestite hangout, as it turned out.

Realising that his catch was a man, the driver tried to dismiss her but she wouldn't go without full payment, and fell on him. Somehow or other, either arriving late or departing early, RO was passing and was drawn into the thick of the fight. The police had to be called to break up the fray.

The time control was in the foyer of the Galleria Ferrari, a sharp new glass-and-steel museum and Ferrari-badged shopping opportunity. Most of the men were wandering between the cars in the exhibition in a state of glassy-eyed arousal. Most of the cars were either scarlet or custard-yellow (which made me glance around warningly for David Brister) and looked as if someone had sat on them. It was quite good fun to buy Ferrari T-shirts and Ferrari work overalls and Ferrari dressing-gowns and hats and pencils and postcards at the gallery shop, but the lunch afterwards was much better. It was a picnic in the little amphitheatre outside the gallery, and there was even a tiramisu to follow the prosciutto and salami and bread and cheese.

In the afternoon we travelled northwards, through flat-ter countryside towards Lake Garda. Every corner we turned brought a different and more perfect little scene of fading yellow walls and sun-blistered green shutters, grey old church and plane tree-shaded square, hollowed stone steps and balcony with scroll of ironwork. Italy was where all tired and jaded rally drivers should end up, I thought, to have their glazed eyes reopened and their senses refreshed.

Absorbed in all of this I let the route notes sag on my lap. I missed a left turn and we motored straight on, with the Dangerfields and one of the white Ford coupés following unthinkingly in our wake.

As we did a U-turn a half-kilometre up the road, I waved apologetically.

'Sharpen up!' Richard Dangerfield called. 'If we're going to follow you blindly you had better get it right.'

We wound through the chain of little towns and resorts along the shores of the Lake.

'Big windsurfing place, this. The wind funnels straight down from the Alps and rips across the water.'

Windsurfing was yet another of Phil's outdoor-boy enthusiasms. The water looked innocuous enough to me, a wide blue sheet swimming with the reflections of piled-up clouds.

We reached Gardone Riviera, our stopping place for the night. I handed in the road book yet one more time, another day without penalties. It was too easy now. The rally was ending as it had begun, in a procession.

We hauled our kitbags out of the back of the car and wandered into yet another hotel. We seemed to have been performing these rituals for an aeon of time, and the end of it was suddenly close enough to touch. We had a room with a window framed in bougainvillea, and a little wrought-iron balcony looking directly over the lake. Beyond a terrace with flowers in tubs there was a jetty, with a view to an island, and the mountains beyond. Inevitably a pair of swans slid across the water.

It was too picturesque – too easy, like being on a holiday, and I missed the dirt and the threat and the desert.

I sat on the balcony floor with my back against the wall and rested my chin on my knees. Phil had disappeared and I was glad of the solitude although I didn't use it to work out anything as significant as what all these people and places had meant to me. I just sat, and the sun went down on my left, and I let the impressions sift down through my head towards a settling place, like dry sand running through my fingers. The moon rose to the right of me and as the colours drained out of the view Dan appeared on the terrace below. He dropped off the end of the jetty and swam away, his narrow head drawing a vee of silver ripples in the navy-blue water. I listened to the wavelets slapping and gurgling under the planks of the jetty. I was tired, from the lack of sleep last night and the much deeper tiredness of a long time on the road. It was like having every sense sharpened to pin-bright, hallucinatory intensity.

From the open window of one of the rooms overhead there was a loud burst of laughter. It went off in my head like fireworks.

I collected it all up, testing the strength of recall. I was already afraid with the finish line in my mind's eye that I would forget too much of what had happened, that I hadn't properly contained it or fixed it in memory's glass.

*

In the bar before dinner, I went and sat next to Trev.

'Trev, do you think I'm frightening?'

His jaw dropped. 'You what?'

'I thought not.'

Phil and I took Dan and JD out to a celebratory dinner, to thank them for helping us to replace the wheel bearings and for being Team Amazon. It was a rather grand restaurant, in the lakeside villa that Mussolini had built for his mistress. At last, there was starched napery for me and phalanxes of impeccable waiters and sommeliers. No one blinked at real Phil's Ferrari T-shirt or JD's ripped jeans. The concierge at our hotel had telephoned ahead to advise them that we were long-distance drivers and couldn't be expected to summon up ties and jackets and a little black dress with a pearl choker. In fact most of the other diners were rally crews too, although all of them were better turned out than we were. Anton Aan de Stegge waved at me from across the room, the men from the pink Rolls-Royce continued their aloof dialogue. We moved everywhere, had moved for so long, in this perpetual continuum of people. How would it be when we were all dispersed again?

Dan and I discussed marriage, although not to each other.

'Can you recommend it?' he asked at last.

'Oh, unreservedly,' I told him.

I drank a lot. We all did. It seemed the best way to deal with the melancholia of endings, and the anticipation of imminent reunions. I had no idea how I was going to pick up the patterns of routine again. Nor, I suppose, did any of us who had made the journey.

The four of us walked back through the cypress groves and ruined villas beside the black lake. There was a thin mist rising off the water and a mysterious waft of piano music. It was like being in an Italian art movie. I kept expecting Monica Vitti to appear in a drift of white linen.

'You're very quiet this morning,' I said to Phil.

'Tired,' was all he would admit to.

'Tired enough to need me to drive?' I tested.

'We have had this conversation.'

So he carried on driving, and I prodded the distances out of the Terratrip. It was crossing-the-Alps day. The tiny scale of Europe was even more apparent. One minute we were in the green-gold country around the Italian Lakes, the next we were high in the Alps and crossing into Austria. The sky thickened with cloud and icy rain fell, on the edge of snow. We passed through St Anton and I craned to see the slopes where I had skied, and then we were climbing through long snow-tunnels over to St Christoph, and a time control. Sleet splattered across the windscreen before turning into proper snow, white-dusting the grey mountainsides. We were rolling up towards the Arlberg Pass when we saw the officials' Frontera at the side of the road. It was supposed to be one of the sneaky passage controls, but it wasn't quite sneaky enough because everyone had seen it. On the control, Greg motioned me to wind down my window and I was fool enough to do as he asked. Trev and Rick and Jingers leapt out of hiding and dumped armfuls of snow into the car, so I sat for the rest of the day in a melting snow-drift.

We shot through Lech and another time control at Schwarzack, and onwards to the German frontier.

One last stage to drive to Überlingen, 70 km away on the Bodensee – Lake Constance. Less than 48 hours to Paris.

We passed Dave Bull with his Rover jacked up at the roadside. Angela was standing looking perplexed and Helen's face peered out at us through the rear window.

'Bearings have finally gone,' Dave said miserably.

'What are you going to do?'

'Drive on, very slowly.'

There was nothing we could do to help him out. Not much further on we came to one of the Peykans, down on its offside axle at the roadside. We saw Mohsen Eijadi running away from his car and then, with a double-take once we had passed, we realised that he was chasing his rear wheel as it bowled away down the steep hill. One of the other Peykans was right behind us, so we drove on once more. When the order was published that night we saw that Mohsen had managed an impressive roadside repair, although the time he lost cost him a drop from third place into eighth.

We stopped for fuel as dusk fell, and fooled around in the garage shop buying chocolate and drinks and a present of a chamois leather for the Amazon.

'She deserves a present,' Phil said tenderly.

Almost as soon as we were moving again I looked at the trip reading and then at my watch.

'We'd better get a move on. *Bugger* it. Why did we waste all that time at the garage?'

It was soon dark, and it was raining, we had 50 km to

drive and 45 minutes to do it in, and the road ahead was an unbroken stretch of roadworks, traffic lights, and crawling queues of commuting Mercedes and BMWs.

'We're not going to make it,' I suddenly realised. 'Not in this traffic.'

All the way from Istanbul in twentieth place, and now we were going to blow it on the last day but one.

'Yes, we are going make it,' Phil snapped. He stamped his foot down and pulled out into the empty opposite lane. With his thumb on the horn he overtook a long line of traffic, and swung back to take the head of it just as the light turned green. This manoeuvre was greeted with a fusillade of angry hooting.

'Phil, for *fuck's sake* . . .'

'Watch this.'

This time he swung the wheel the other way. He churned up the grass verge and narrowly missed a shrub bed as he skidded past a couple of trucks and whirled back on to the road.

'Phil . . . *stop it.*'

He looked happier than he had done all day. Thumb on horn, foot hard down, yelling imprecations at the law-abiding German motorists as we raced past them. When I glanced round I saw that there was a ribbon of rally cars behind us, all of them doing exactly the same thing. Everyone was chasing their times. The wet night became a dazzle of flashing lights and sliding metal.

This lasted for 15 long minutes.

Then we saw a lone, bedraggled figure sheltering under an umbrella at the roadside. A little arm flagged us down. The face of Colin Francis, Clerk of the Course for Istanbul–Paris, appeared in Phil's window.

'This stage is cancelled,' he told us in his Welsh sing-song. 'Just make for Überlingen in your own time.'

Phil slumped back in his seat again. He lit a cigarette and blew a disparaging cloud of smoke.

'Time allowance too short for the distance and road conditions. Another cock-up.'

'You were enjoying yourself.'

'Too right I was.'

Later we learned that so many motorists and passers-by had telephoned the police to complain about the rally drivers that the police had insisted to the organisers that the stage be cancelled.

We drove on, through the murk, to Überlingen.

Some members of the Feit family were there to meet us. Each of the cars wore a fluttering black gauze ribbon in acknowledgement.

The last night but one. There was one more view from another bedroom window, another black lake with chains of light reflected in it.

Everyone wanted to cling together. All of our tight little group went out to dinner, and we sat in a noisy circle around a big table. Next to me Greg shook his spiky head and blinked wonderingly behind his specs.

'I have had the best time. Just the best time of my life.'

Back at the hotel, the Bulls were just arriving in the cab of a low-loader, with the Rover on the back.

They had driven on a short way after we passed them, and then there was a terrible bang and a grinding crash as the rear right-hand side of the car hit the road. They were on a downhill slope, without brakes now, and Dave managed to slow and finally stop the car by dragging the wheels against the kerb. When he got out, shakily, to inspect the damage he saw that the wheel, brake drum and half-shaft had broken off and disappeared, presumably down the ravine on the other side of the road. The end of the differential tube had nothing coming out of it except a plume of burning oil.

Once the car and the crew finally reached Überlingen, Dave began ringing round Europe, with David Drew's help, to try and locate the necessary parts to enable them to continue – a complete half-shaft, hub, brake drum and brake anchor plate. It was David Drew who finally tracked down what they needed.

In Vienna.

A Rover enthusiast called Michael Meyer-Harting didn't actually have the parts himself, but he knew that his friend Joseph Unger did. At two in the morning Michael woke Joseph and they went round to the garage together and dismantled a car, so the Bulls could make the last lap to Paris. The only problem remaining was how to convey the parts over the 650 kilometres between Vienna and Überlingen. The solution that finally presented itself was a light aircraft that flew between Vienna and Altenrheim, a little airport near the end of the Bodensee. The next flight would arrive at Altenrheim at four o'clock the following afternoon. If all went well Dave could transport the car to the airport on a truck and strip the axle down ready for the moment when the parts came off the plane. He could then fit them, and make the dash for the last stop at Reims. If he and the car could make it to the start line on the last morning and drive on to Paris, they would still win a silver medal.

It seemed that Phil and I had been lucky to escape with a mere all-nighter in the garage at Rimini.

Fittingly, I was having my last signpost conversation of the trip, as well as the first, with Chris Taylor. We were back in the bar at the hotel, but reluctant to go to bed. We shared another bottle of wine, and tried to unravel for each other what all the days and all the distance had really meant.

It was a bit late in the evening for anything intelligible to emerge.

Upstairs, real Phil was already in bed.

'Night,' he said when I came in, and slid into the familiar coma.

'Goodnight, Phil.'

I listened to his breathing. After a few minutes, I fell asleep too.

The last day's rallying. We had 565 km to travel, through the Black Forest and across the Rhine into Alsace, and from there on across to Reims. We left on our minute, 8.03 a.m. *Beep*. Just over 28 hours to the finish line.

It was a cold, sunny morning. Our road climbed steadily through vineyards and meadows and then entered the forest, where dense black conifers alternated with patches of broadleaf woodland. The leaves were changing colour in sheets of flame and gold, and blue-grey patches of snow lay between the trees. There were broken sheets and crusts of snow at the roadside too, and we began to pass little ski areas with a couple of lifts and a cluster of wooden huts.

When we left the trees behind we came out into a wide, white expanse of snow with a handful of buildings and a church with a slender green spire. We were at the day's first time control, at the top of the Kandelpasse. The light was blinding, striking diamonds out of the snowfield. The cars were pulled up at the roadside or tracking danger-ously into the snow, and the crews were out taking photographs and throwing snowballs. It was fun, but a big mistake to drive into the snow. Dan almost burned out his clutch trying to reach the road again, and I had to balance my weight on our rear bumper while Phil steered his way out. Maladroit to the last, I fell off on my head when the car bounced and slewed. I lay in the snow for a minute, dazed. Phil didn't look back.

He had been very subdued all morning. His entire attention had been fixed for so long on Paris, just on get-ting the two of us and the car safely to Paris, but now even monofocal Phil was obliged to look beyond that. He had given up his job with Exodus, he didn't have a home of his own to go back to. No wonder he was thoughtful.

'Do you want to drive?'

We were waiting at the time control. I looked at the black snake of road bisecting the banks of glittering snow, and the view across the distant valley into France.

'Yes.'

We changed places. Phil handed over the road book for stamping and zeroed the trip.

I didn't stall the car, or run into the back of the Noors in front of us. Everything felt startlingly loose and sloppy, the gears and the brakes and clutch and steering. The poor old Amazon was worn out, but I made it move forwards and then I was nudging it down the hairpin bends into the valley. It wasn't a test of personal adequacy after all – it was just driving.

'Not too fast on the bend. Brake now,' Phil said.

I looked straight ahead, watching the dapple of light and shade on the tarmac.

'Good. You're doing really well. How does it feel?'

'It feels okay.'

I drove us out of Germany and on to Riquewihr, in Alsace. It was a medieval wine village, enclosed within walls, pretty and over-restored and tourist-ridden. As a special dispensation the rally was allowed to pass through the fortress walls and up the narrow cobbled street to the time control, and then out again through the great portcullis at the top. Phil agreed that it was probably best if he negotiated this himself, so we resumed our accustomed positions before the entrance gate.

With Phil in the driver's seat we rolled onwards towards Reims, through open pastureland and vineyards and orchards.

'Three ks. Turn left at roundabout, signpost Bruyères.'

'Okay.'

We listened to our familiar music and exchanged information about the route, but otherwise we hardly spoke.

I felt tired and flat, and also sad, and I suppose Phil was feeling the same. We had come a long, long way.

Dan and JD were in front of us, and Melissa and Colin behind. Phil stuck his arm out of his window and made winding up gestures to Dan; faster, go faster. We had done all of this so often, and after tomorrow it would be finished.

There was another time control in a place called Wassy, and a final stretch of 123 km to Reims.

The city was busy and clogged with traffic, and there was a punitive one-way system that took us in a great loop because I missed a turn in the route notes. We were tired and stretched when we reached almost the last time control, TC number 95, at the Reims hotel. I handed over the book and it was stamped, due time 19.02, actual time 19.02, '90th anniversary PEKING to PARIS. SURVIVOR'.

The film crew who had been covering the event saw us and the director came and pushed his furry microphone into my face. The cameraman pressed up alongside. I had a brief flashback to the night at Quetta and the media lights shining into our eyes.

'Rosie, how do you feel?'

I muttered something about elated and triumphant and very relieved.

'And how has it been, travelling with Phil.'

I said that it had been wonderful, marvellous. He had been the best possible driver and companion. It was what I finally felt.

The furry mike shifted in Phil's direction.

'How about you, Phil? How do you feel about it? Were you a good partnership?'

'Yeah. I did some navigating today, you actually do have to concentrate quite hard.'

'And what are your plans after this adventure?'

He gave his camera smile, straight into the lens, and swept back his hair. 'More adventures,' he said, and went on to list what they might be. Afterwards the interviewer thanked us both, with a little lift of the eyebrows at me, and moved on to his next victim.

It was all in the heat of the moment, but it was entirely and maddeningly predictable. Phil hadn't thought to praise me in return or to thank me for playing my part in our enterprise. And it was just as infuriatingly predictable that I minded so much. Anger bubbled up in me all over again, but it had been a long day and it was the end of a long trip, and I said nothing. We went silently into the last hotel and up to the last bedroom. There was no view from here. There were elaborate drapes and nets but the window was blind.

Phil sidled away at once, not even stopping for a shower. I had mine, and changed my clothes, and then looked at my watch. It was dinner-time. I tried to override my feelings but I felt temporarily too prickly and hot with uncried tears to go downstairs. It was stupid to feel so hurt by a moment's thoughtlessness, and I longed to tell someone outside the claustrophobia of the rally, but Caradoc and the children and my best friends were already on their way to Paris to meet me. There was no one to talk to.

Instead I reminded myself about what I had learned on the road, about the differences between Phil's perception of me and my own, and the importance of not relying on other people to prop up my faltering sense of self-worth. Of course there would be no little harbour restaurant, and we would never drink to our joint achievement nor wrap it up for each other with the ribbon of mutual admiration. That was all sentiment, and fantasy Phil was exactly that. Real Phil was an adventurer, and adventurers are hard people. He had got what he wanted out of me.

I acknowledged all of this as coolly as I could. Then I applied a lot of lipstick and congratulated myself on having been a fine navigator and a tenacious travelling companion. And finally I went downstairs to the bar and ordered a bottle of Reims' finest.

Chapter Sixteen

Prince Borghese reached Paris via St Petersburg, Warsaw and Berlin on 10 August 1907, exactly two months after leaving Peking. His remaining rivals, the two de Dion Boutons and the Spyker, were a full twenty days behind him. It was raining as the triumphant Itala reached the finishing line outside the *Le Matin* newspaper office, just as it had been when the cars left Peking, but the bad weather didn't dampen the enthusiasm of the crowds or the warmth of their welcome. There were cordons of soldiers to hold back the press of people, and mounted patrols of the Republican Guard rode at the front and rear of the procession.

The Parisians waved their hats and umbrellas and handkerchiefs in the air, and their shouts of 'Vive Borghese' rolled and thundered ahead of the car with a noise like waves breaking. At last, the car came to a standstill at the entrance to the newspaper offices. For a long, confused moment Borghese and Barzini and Guizzardi, the chauffeur and mechanic, sat motionless, unable to comprehend that the incredible journey was over at last.

Barzini, the journalist, described the emotions of the Itala crew just before they reached their goal.

'The last few hours seem everlasting. They are hours of joy, but also of anguish – of a sudden, vague, inexpressible anguish, which makes us silent and gives us all the appearance of disappointed men.'[1]

This was the first time the journey had been completed since 1907. We had come by a different route from Borghese and his companions, and unlike the pioneers we had had maps as well as roads – of a sort – for most of the way, and satellite phones and laptop e-mails instead of the occasional telegraph offices. But there were similarities too, mostly in the ambivalence of our feelings as the end of it all came within reach.

Car 82 left Reims at 9.10 a.m. on 18 October, with only 160 km to travel. We were luckier than Borghese in yet another respect – it was a brilliantly sunny morning, with a pale-blue sky laced with vapour trails and all the trees in the Reims boulevards turning to October gold and amber.

Dave Bull and his wife and mother-in-law also crossed the morning line on their designated minute. Their Rover parts had arrived in Altenrheim airport at 5 p.m. the previous evening, where Dave was waiting with the car all prepared to receive them. By 5.35 p.m. they were ready to roll again, and they headed for Reims via Zürich, Basle, Colmar and Nancy. At 3.30 a.m. on the 18th they

[1] *Pekin to Paris: An Account of Prince Borghese's Journey Across Two Continents in a Motor-Car.* Luigi Barzini. E. Grant Richards, London, 1907.

were in the last hotel with all the rest of us, not much shorter of sleep than anyone else and definitely more sober. They deserved their silver medal.

As Adam and Jon pulled away from the Reims start line, a black bin-liner water bomb plummeted from a balcony of the hotel and exploded neatly and drenchingly between them.

It was an easy last drive, that morning, through slow weekend villages and lush farmland and past quiet war cemeteries.

I felt as sad as Barzini had done, and we were just as silent as the trio in the Itala ninety years before. The appearance of disappointment clung about us too: we had done everything we aimed for, we were coming in to Paris in 20th place overall and the gold medal was ours, but there was more than a simple sense of melancholy that everything was over. I hadn't driven my share of the distance, and Phil and I had in the end misunderstood each other. There wasn't time to bridge that chasm now – we would have to wait until we were back in England, in our separate lives, to see whether we had after all made a real friendship out of our journey or whether proximity and necessity had been the only glue that held us together.

I believed we would be friends in the end. We had quarrelled and made up enough times before, and we wouldn't ever again have to endure the pressure of driving and eating and sleeping and being afraid together. We could meet once in a while for a drink, and reminisce, and go our different ways.

I knew that everyone I cared most about in the world

was waiting in Paris for me, but I kept looking at the stream of rally cars all heading for the same point and remembering that they had been family and friends for weeks on end. Theo Voukidis' Chevy was immediately ahead of us, Mick Flick overtaking, the Triumph Vitesse just behind. I was going to feel bereft without them all even though I wanted more than anything to see my husband and children, and to be normal again, and no longer slave to the Terratrip or to Phil's exacting leadership.

The last kilometres flashed past in a blur of trying to remember the views and the impressions and trying to fix them in place with answers to all the questions I knew would be coming.

Why did you do it?

I only knew that I had wanted an adventure, as an antidote to anxiety like a dose of serum for snakebite – or rather Phil had offered me one and I had accepted it, blind. I owed him thanks for that.

What did you learn from it?

I had gained a few more pieces of personal insight, most of them uncomfortable. But I had survived.

And I had had an unforgettable journey, the thin yellow map line blossoming for every kilometre, painful or pleasurable, between the Agricultural Museum car park in Beijing and the Place de la Concorde. I believed that the real pleasures and satisfactions of what we had done would dawn slowly, in retrospect, in the months to come.

And did you and Phil – you know?

There had been times when I thought about it. I was fairly certain there had been times when he was thinking about it too.

But, fortunately enough, it happened that the times didn't coincide.

'Straight over at crossroads with traffic lights, one km.'

'Got you.'

We came to the last intermediate time control, close to the Paris *périphérique*. It was a chaos of cars and drivers, and no one seemed to know what to do or what order we were supposed to leave in. We set out again, on the very last leg.

'Take left lane, then underpass. Signpost Pantin.'

'Okay.'

There were no cavalrymen but there were Peking to Paris officials on street corners and traffic islands, wearing red caps and bibs, waving as we passed and pointing us onwards.

We came into Paris proper, and we had still barely spoken since leaving Reims. We were driving beside the river under the trees, past the tall lamps with branched arms and white globe lanterns. Notre-Dame was on our right and in the distance a glimpse of the Eiffel Tower.

'Do you want to drive across the finish line?' Phil asked.

'No, thank you.'

'Why not?'

'Because I haven't driven any of the rest of the way.'

'All the more reason.'

It was generous of him to offer up his moment of glory and maybe I should have accepted in the same spirit, but I didn't. We crossed the Seine in our accustomed places, and the Place de la Concorde lay ahead of us.

There were cheering crowds here, not quite requiring cordons of soldiers to control them but thick enough, and the channel for the cars to pass through grew narrower as people swarmed closer and patted the bonnet and roof of the car and called their congratulations in through the windows at us. I remembered Linhe, and the million Chinese who had come out to watch us go by.

In the amorphous crowd I suddenly saw my sister's face. She was running forwards with a bunch of flowers in her arms and at the sight of her my own face crumpled up.

We had reached home.

Behind Lindsay there were more familiar faces, and wide smiles and hands coming through the window to grab hold of mine. Phil's family was there too, and his girl-friend, and even Tony Barrett wearing a red jumper instead of his customary grey one and a leather hat plonked on his head like a saucepan.

'It's all over. End of story.' Phil said.

In the midst of the cheering and clapping and camera clicking I heard a sound like a sharp snap.

We were surrounded and taken up again by our real families and our proper lives. I looked around and saw the same thing happening to Theo Voukidis and the Rietbergens and the Bentley boys. The rally family broke off there and then and the shear was absolute. It was a bewildering sensation but at the last second I felt a swell of happiness and elation and profound relief. The last flutter of Rally Syndrome.

'Caradoc and Charlie and Flora are waiting ahead on the finish line. They want to see you cross it,' Nick and Jenny Evans told me.

We inched ahead in the slow procession of cars, drawing our supporters with us. Phil leaned across me and clicked off the Terratrip. The digits faded into blankness for the last time. No more *beep* in my ears or in my dreams.

I saw a tent, and the finish line, and then their three faces. Unable to wait any longer I jumped out of the Amazon, probably slamming the door too hard behind me, and ran to them. Edith was with them too, and my step-niece Angharad on her very first trip abroad. My father had stayed at home because he never liked to travel far from Caerwys.

When Caradoc put his arms around me I asked him stupidly, 'Will everything be all right now?'

'Of course it will,' he answered, knowing exactly what was needed. 'You're home.'

When I held them, my children seemed bigger and taller and more self-assured than when I had last seen them. They had even brought a group of their friends to see us arrive, the biggest tribute.

It was a precious moment.

The book was stamped for the last time. *13.31 p.m., TC 99, Paris party!*

We had made every single one of the 99 controls within our maximum permitted time allowance. Gold medal.

John Vipond patted me on the back. 'Well done, Rosie.'

Caradoc had brought two wreaths of laurel leaves and now he put one around Phil's neck and one around mine. We sat on the roof of the car to have our pictures taken, and I felt a slight impostor in my racing driver's winning laurels with a bottle of champagne.

Damon Hill I had turned out not to be. Not that it mattered now.

There was a big, formal dinner in the evening in a Paris hotel, followed by a prizegiving. There were too many people and too much noise and it was disorientating to see the rally faces separated out from their cars and set around with strangers who were their friends and families. It was even more bizarre to see how clean and shiny everyone looked. Melissa was a vision in a tiny John Galliano frock, and Phil had scrubbed up nicely in a dinner jacket. The new evening dress that I had had carefully fitted on me before I left now seemed to have enough folds of spare fabric in it to contain the Bentley as well as me. That didn't matter much either.

The best joke of the evening was David Tremain's. In a last spasm of laddishness he had given away his expensive ticket for the dinner at one of Carolyn's carefully placed tables of smart people, and gone out to get drunk. By some freak chance, the random recipient of the ticket was Tony Barrett.

Carolyn came across the room to me. Her eyes blazed with more furious brilliance than her diamonds.

'Who is that . . . *person?* He claims to have some connection with you.'

I looked. Still wearing the grubby red jumper, although he had at least taken off the saucepan hat, the Ancient Mariner was locked on to suave Anthony Buckingham from the disintegrated green DB5.

'Erm – our mechanic, actually.'

'Well. *Really.*'

I would have given quite a lot to have had a bugging device hidden in the floral arrangement on that table.

The podium at the prizegiving after dinner was loaded with silverware, and RO was up there waving his arms to orchestrate lights and music and looking as if he were directing a Nuremberg rally instead of just a car one. But I thought that he deserved the glory, by and large. It had been quite a feat of organisation.

Sixty-six cars finished the course in the main Challenge, with sixteen in the touring category. Phil and I were pleased with our achievement, although we didn't win any of the cups.

'If only Tony hadn't sited that coil on the heater,' he sighed.

'There's no point thinking of it like that.'

The overall winners of the 1997 Peking to Paris Motor Challenge were the characters in the Willys jeep. They had accrued just 17 minutes' time penalty over the 42 days of the competition. One of them made an incomprehensible speech that seemed to refer to the rumours about his vehicle not being quite 100 per cent original.

There were numerous other cups and trophies for the winners of different classes. Even the bad crowd was represented – Adam and Jon won the prize for the highest-placed vintage car, and a second award for being all-round good guys and champion practical jokers. The Leading Lady Driver prize went to Carolyn, who had steered the Land Rover into 14th place. (As I was the named entrant in our crew and therefore technically the driver, it was funny and ironic to see that I was her runner-up, in twentieth.) The all-women's crew prize was won by the toothbrushless pair, and something called the Richard Head award went to dashing David Arrigo.

At the end of it all, a series of film clips were projected on a huge screen. There was the Tuotuoheyan camp, and the Everest plateau, and the road to hell between Tibet and Nepal. I held on to Caradoc's arm, pleased beyond words to be where I was and not back there again. There was one sequence where the majestic Phantom V cruised through a river, with the cascades of a waterfall tumbling in front of it.

Watching it, I suddenly found that I had tears in my eyes.

Yes, I thought, that was what it was like.

I wanted to go home.

Caradoc arranged a wonderful Paris lunch the next day, to celebrate my birthday with all the people who had come to watch us finish the journey. Then we took the train and the tunnel back to London together.

I gave the keys, and the car, to Phil to keep. He drove his girlfriend back to England in it, and had all the damage and destruction put right, and then he sold it to another pair of rally drivers. The Volvo would go on doing what it had been prepared to do.

After the Place de la Concorde I never saw the old car again, and I was happy to let it go.

We had travelled a long way and done the best we could by each other. It had been ridiculous, but also in a way sublime.

To drive all that way, in those cars.

Peking to Paris – Classification at TC99 – Paris

Main Challenge

Num	Crew	Car	Cls	Total Penalty	Positions O/A	Cls
97	Surtees/Bayliss	Ford Willys Jeep MB	6	42d 0h17	1	1
23	Thomas/Zannis	Ford Club coupé	1	42d 0h21	2	1
50	Catt/Catt	Ford Cortina Mk I	3	42d 0h44	3	1
24	Jung/Vann	Ford Club coupé	1	42d 0h53	4	2
88	Crown/Bryson	Holden EH saloon	5	42d 0h55	5	1
52	Broderick/Broderick	Ford Anglia estate	3	42d 0h59	6	2
85	Javid/Heday	Peykan Hunter	3	42d 1h42	7	3
87	Eijadi/Khadem	Peykan Hunter	3	42d 2h 8	8	4
28	Dichtl/Dichtl	Rolls Royce Silver Dawn	2	42d 2h12	9	1
86	Kazerani/Razzaghi	Peykan Hunter	3	42d 2h15	10	5
77	Hardman/Dean	Aston Martin DB5	5	42d 2h18	11	2
78	Kayll/Kayll	Mercedes Benz 250 SE	4	42d 2h19	12	1
90	Dangerfield/Dangerfield	Holden HR	5	42d 2h30	13	3
98	Ward/Tremain	Land Rover Series IIA	6	42d 2h56	14	2
48	Tinzl/Tinzl	Peugeot 404	3	42d 3h26	15	6
21	Hartley/Turner	Bentley 4.5-litre Vdp	2	42d 3h30	16	2

44	Sackelariou/Snelling/O'Neill	Wolseley	4	42d 3h44	17	2
47	Thomason/Kunz	Triumph Vitesse	3	42d 3h59	18	7
80	Noor/Bouvier-Noor	Mercedes Benz 250 SEC	4	42d 4h 7	19	3
82	Thomas/Bowen	Volvo 122 Amazon	3	42d 4h18	20	8
13	Van der Laan/Graal	Citroen 2CV	1	42d 4h29	21	3
92	Meyer/Geiser	Mercedes Benz 280SE	4	42d 4h30	22	4
41	Richmond/Newman	Citroen 2CV	1	42d 4h42	23	4
74	Flick/Munnenthaler	Mercedes 220 SB	4	42d 5h17	24	5
69	Orteu/Davies	Volvo P122S Amazon	3	42d 5h27	25	9
26	Dalrymple/Dalrymple	Cadillac 62	2	42d 5h29	26	3
58	Voukidis/Vartholomaio	Chevrolet Bel Air	5	42d 5h55	27	4
71	De Witt/Haukes	Volvo 122 Amazon	3	42d 5h58	28	10
53	Selci/Campagnoli	Citroen 2CV	3	42d 6h16	29	11
57	Morris/Morris	Austin A90 Westminster	4	42d 6h35	30	6
17	Binnie/Thompson	Bentley 4.5	2	42d 6h55	31	4
51	Dodwell/Obert	Hillman Hunter	3	42d 6h57	32	12
55	Multon/Laughton	Austin A90 Westminster	4	42d 7h43	33	7
76	Minassian/Grogan	Peugeot 404 sedan	3	42d 8h17	34	13
20	Carr/Wyka	Ford V-8 convertible	1	42d 9h 3	35	5
19	Ciriminna/Ingoglia	Fiat 1100 Cabriolet	1	42d 10h18	36	6
91	Bellm/Taylor	Chevrolet Camaro	5	42d 10h22	37	5
73	Koppel/Kuhn	Triumph TR6	4	42d 10h24	38	8
62	Sternberg/Gillies	Volvo 122S Amazon	3	42d 10h35	39	14
49	Klokgieters-Lankes/Wheildon	MG YB	1	42d 12h20	40	7

Num	Crew	Car	Cls	Total Penalty	Positions O/A	Cls
99	Taylor/Davis/Pierce	Willys Jeep	6	42d 13h30	41	3
75	Rietbergen/van Overbeehe	Volvo PV 544	4	42d 15h53	42	9
54	Esch/Esch	Mercedes Benz 300 B	4	42d 15h55	43	10
68	Ong/Syn	Porsche 356 SC coupé	3	42d 15h59	44	15
10	Ashby/Ashby	Delage D8 dhc	1	42d 20h36	45	8
9	Idris Shah/Curtis	Ford Model B saloon	1	42d 21h 7	46	9
12	Dunkley/Dunkley	Bentley 3.5-litre	1	43d 2h 2	47	10
59	Bull/Riley/McGugan	Rover 3-litre P5	4	43d 3h16	48	11
8	Jessen/Jessen	Bentley 4.5-litre VdP	2	43d 4h14	49	5
14	Bv. Schoonheten/Hastedt/Ellison	Railton 8	2	43d 5h13	50	6
4	Acher/Young	Aston Martin Int.	1	43d 12h 7	51	11
67	Chiodi/Longo	Lancia Flavia coupé	3	44d 4h19	52	16
83	Wilks/Bedingham	Austin 1800 saloon	3	44d 5h 8	53	17
89	Aan de Stegge/Aan de Stegge	Citroen ID21	4	44d 6h52	54	12
65	Schneider/Jones	Packard Straight 8	5	44d 17h23	55	6
39	Brister/Barton	Rover 110 P4	4	44d 17h55	56	13
42	Matheson/Eve	Rolls Royce Phantom V	2	47d 16h15	57	7
7	Veen/Dean	Mercedes 630K sports	2	48d 2h38	58	8
81	Goldsmith/Laing	Aston Martin DB6	5	48d 17h15	59	7
27	Arrigo/Caruana	Allard M-type dhc	1	49d 8h53	60	12
64	Radcliffe/Webb	Jaguar Mark VII saloon	5	49d 11h34	61	8

No.	Crew	Car		Time	Pos.	
70	Janssen/Klarholz/Meier	Mercedes 220A	4	49d 13h45	62	14
16	Prior/El Accad	Railton Cobham Sln	2	50d 13h51	63	9
56	Cordrey/Phillips	Rover 100 P1	4	51d 9h51	64	15
25	Clark/Hughes	Buick 8 Special Sedanet	1	53d 12h 6	65	13
79	Buckingham/Mann	Aston Martin DB5	5	54d 10h58	66	9

Touring Category

No.	Crew	Car		Time	Pos.
93	Lux/Drew/Shaw	Rover 3.5 P5B coupé	7	42d 0h 1	1
36	Risser/Fortune/Wilson/Risser	Chevvy Bel-Air	7	42d 1h50	2
37	Wong/Wong/Wong/Wong	MGA sports	7	42d 2h 8	3
35	Schulze/Breuer/Schulze	Bentley Donington	7	42d 18h 1	4
40	Klabin/Dick II/Holzwarth	Land Rover IIa	7	43d 0h42	5
46	O'Neill/O'Neill-Tsicrycas	V.W. Cab.	7	44d 8h33	6
3	Rothlauf/Walter	Bugatti Type 40	7	45d 9h58	7
38	Tsicrycas/Karaoli/Lovric	Peugeot 403	7	47d 4h40	8
31	Stuttard/O'Sullivan/Anderson/Barr	R-Royce	7	47d 23h14	9
29	Hellers/Thill	Sunbeam Talbot 90	7	48d 10h48	10
45	Dorey/Dorey	Morris Minor	7	50d 2h26	11
32	Handlbauer/Handlbauer/Handlbauer	BMW 328	7	52d 2h30	12
63	Christiansen/Veys	R-Royce Silver Cloud	7	53d 0h52	13
34	Ainscough/Ainscough/Attwood	Chrysler 77	7	54d 0h 1	14
61	Noble/Noble	Bentley Continental	7	61d 23h 0	15
15	Saunders/Coote	Packard 903	7	63d 7h45	16
84	Moe/Granli	Morgan Plus 8 sports	5	Ret. Engine	

Num	Crew	Car	Cls	Total Penalty	Positions O/A Cls
5	Weissenbach/Huslisti	Rolls-Royce Ph I	2	Retired	
96	Challis/Jefferis	Land Rover Series I	6	Ret. Off Road	
66	Guliker/Guliker	Chevrolet pick-up	5	Retired	
2	Layher/Dick	La France Hooper sports	2	Ret. Illness	
22	Brooks/Brooks	Buick 59 Straight 8	1	Ret. Engine	
6	Cohen/Cohen	Stutz M Lancefield	2	Ret. Electrics	
1	Lord Montagu/Hill	Vauxhall Prince Henry	1	Ret. Overheating	
11	Kleptz/Kleptz	Marmon 34 Touring 4	2	Ret. Axle	
18	Noz/Noz	Ford Model A roadster	1	Ret. Engine	
33	Netto/Simoes/Machado/Netto	Ford Model B	7	Ret. Engine.	

Peking to Paris

Gold Medals

17	Binnie/Thompson	Bentley 4.5
21	Hartley/Turner	Bentley 4.5-litre VdP
23	Thomas/Zannis	Ford Club coupé
24	Jung/Vann	Ford Club coupé
26	Dalrymple/Dalrymple	Cadillac 62
28	Dichtl/Dichtl	Rolls-Royce Silver Dawn
41	Richmond/Newman	Citroen 2CV
44	Sackelariou/Snelling/O'Neill	Wolseley
47	Thomason/Kunz	Triumph Vitesse
48	Tinzl/Tinzl	Peugeot 404
50	Catt/Catt	Ford Cortina Mk I
51	Dodwell/Obert	Hillman Hunter
52	Broderick/Broderick	Ford Anglia Estate
53	Selci/Campagnoli	Citroen 2CV
69	Orteu/Davies	Volvo P122S Amazon
71	De Witt/Haukes	Volvo 122 Amazon
74	Flick/Mumenthaler	Mercedes 220 SB
77	Hardman/Dean	Aston Martin DB5
78	Kayll/Kayll	Mercedes Benz 250 SE
80	Noor/Bouvier-Noor	Mercedes Benz 250 SEC
82	Thomas/Bowen	Volvo 122 Amazon

85	Javid/Heday	Peykan Hunter
86	Kazerani/Razzaghi	Peykan Hunter
87	Eijadi/Khadem	Peykan Hunter
88	Crown/Bryson	Holden EH saloon
90	Dangerfield/Dangerfield	Holden HR
97	Surtees/Bayliss	Ford Willys Jeep MB
98	Ward/Tremain	Land Rover Series IIa

Silver Medals

4	Acher/Young	Aston Martin Int.
9	Idris Shah/Curtis	Ford Model 8 saloon
8	Jessen/Jessen	Bentley 4.5-litre VdP
10	Ashby/Ashby	Delage D8 dhc
12	Dunkley/Dunkley	Bentley 3.5-litre
14	Bv. Schoonheten/Hastedt/Ellison	Railton 8
19	Ciriminna/Ingoglia	Fiat 1100 Cabriolet
20	Carr/Wyka	Ford V-8 convertible
43	Van der Laan/Graal	Citroen 2CV
49	Klokgieters-Lankes/Wheildon	MG YB
54	Esch/Esch	Mercedes Benz 300 B
55	Multon/Laughton	Austin A90 Westminster
57	Morris/Morris	Austin A90 Westminster
58	Voukidis/Vartholomaio	Chevrolet Bel Air
59	Bull/Riley/McGugan	Rover 3-litre P5
62	Sternberg/Gillies	Volvo 122S Amazon
67	Chiodi/Longo	Lancia Flavia coupé
68	Ong/Syn	Porsche 356 SC coupé
73	Koppel/Kuhn	Triumph TR6
75	Rietbergen/van Overbeehe	Volvo PV 544
76	Minassian/Grogan	Peugeot 404 sedan
91	Bellm/Taylor	Chevrolet Camaro
92	Meyer/Geiser	Mercedes Benz 280SE
99	Taylor/Davis/Pierce	Willys Jeep

Bronze Medals

| 27 | Arrigo/Caruana | Allard M-type dhc |

25	Clark/Hughes	Buick 8 Special Sedanet
42	Matheson/Eve	Rolls-Royce Phantom V
7	Veen/Dean	Mercedes 630K sports
16	Prior/El Accad	Railton Cobham S1n
83	Wilks/Bedingham	Austin 1800 saloon
70	Janssen/Klarholz/Meier	Mercedes 220A
89	Aan de Stegge/Aan de Stegge	Citroen ID21
39	Brister/Barton	Rover 110P4
56	Cordrey/Phillips	Rover 100P4
65	Schneider/Jones	Packard Straight 8
81	Goldsmith/Laing	Aston Martin DB6
79	Buckingham/Mann	Aston Martin DB5
64	Radcliffe/Webb	Jaguar Mark VII saloon

Individual Touring Category – medals

93	Jonathon Lux	Rover 3.5 P5B coupé
36	Bud Risser	Chevy Bel-Air
37	Peng Yew Wong Senior	MGA sports
35	Arnold Schulze	Bentley Donington
40	John Dick Senior	Land Rover IIa
46	John O'Neill	VW Cabriolet
34	Bill Ainscough	Chrysler 77
63	Christiansen/Veys	Rolls-Royce Silver Cloud
29	Roby Hellers	Sunbeam Talbot 90
38	Tsicrycas	Peugeot 403
31	Roy O'Sullivan	Rolls-Royce
61	Noble/Noble	Bentley Continental
32	Herbert Handlbauer	BMW 328
15	Saunders/Coote	Packard 903
3	Rothlauf/Walter	Bugatti Type 40
45	Dorey/Dorey	Morris Minor

Warner Books now offers an exciting range of quality titles by both established and new authors. All of the books in this series are available from:

Little, Brown and Company (UK),
P.O. Box 11,
Falmouth,
Cornwall TR10 9EN.

Fax No: 01326 317444.
Telephone No: 01326 372400
E-mail: books@barni.avel.co.uk

Payments can be made as follows: cheque, postal order (payable to Little, Brown and Company) or by credit cards, Visa/Access. Do not send cash or currency. UK customers and B.F.P.O. please allow £1.00 for postage and packing for the first book, plus 50p for the second book, plus 30p for each additional book up to a maximum charge of £3.00 (7 books plus).

Overseas customers including Ireland, please allow £2.00 for the first book plus £1.00 for the second book, plus 50p for each additional book.

NAME (Block Letters) ....

....

ADDRESS ....

....

....

☐ I enclose my remittance for ....

☐ I wish to pay by Access/Visa Card

Number ☐☐☐☐☐☐☐☐☐☐☐☐☐☐☐☐☐☐

Card Expiry Date ☐☐☐☐